USA TODAY bestselling author **Heidi Rice** lives in London, England. She is married with two teenage sons—which gives her rather too much of an insight into the male psyche—and also works as a film journalist. She adores her job, which involves getting swept up in a world of high emotion, sensual excitement, funny and feisty women, sexy and tortured men and glamorous locations where laundry doesn't exist. Once she turns off her computer she often does chores—usually involving laundry!

Lorraine Hall is a part-time hermit and full-time writer. She was born with an old soul and her head in the clouds—which, it turns out, is the perfect combination for spending her days creating thunderous alpha heroes and the fierce, determined heroines who win their hearts. She lives in a potentially haunted house with her soulmate and a rumbustious band of hermits in training. When she's not writing romance, she's reading it.

UNEXPECTEDLY HIS

HEIDI RICE

LORRAINE HALL

MILLS & BOON

First published in Great Britain 2024
by Mills & Boon, an imprint of HarperCollins*Publishers* Ltd,
1 London Bridge Street, London, SE1 9GF

www.harpercollins.co.uk

HarperCollins*Publishers*, Macken House, 39/40 Mayor Street Upper,
Dublin 1, D01 C9W8, Ireland

This book contains FSC™ certified paper
and other controlled sources to ensure responsible forest management.

For more information visit www.harpercollins.co.uk/green.

Printed and Bound in the UK using 100% Renewable Electricity
at CPI Group (UK) Ltd, Croydon, CR0 4YY

AFTER-PARTY CONSEQUENCES

HEIDI RICE

MILLS & BOON

To Lucy and Nat!

I had so much fun working on our fabulous stories,
let's do it again soon.

PROLOGUE

Four years ago...

'HEY, MR LANDRY, what is it about British bad girls that makes them so hot, do you reckon…?'

Cade Landry stood in the Las Vegas event space, with the lights of the city's famous Strip glittering thirty-five storeys below them through the panoramic windows, nursing a glass of vintage bubbles which cost more than his first car, and scowled at the bad girl in question on the other side of the exclusive venue. She was dancing on a table, her slender figure moving in sensuous rhythm in a scrap of jewelled red satin which barely covered her butt.

'I don't know, Chad,' he shouted above the music from a world-famous DJ he'd paid to finish the evening with some fun after the formal event. Fun which was descending into a free-for-all thanks to the wild child and her posse. 'But whoever she is, she's leaving,' he added.

Exactly how old was she? Because she looked like an out-of-control kid who'd had one too many tequila slammers—and wasn't even legal to drink. He'd told security to get rid of them when they'd arrived ten minutes ago, but the guard looked as dazzled by her antics as the other guys around her.

'Don't you know who she is, Mr Landry?' Chad piped up again, his voice filling with awe. 'That's Charlotte Courtney.'

Damn.

He'd heard of Charlotte Courtney. Part-time model, full-time wild child, who'd hit the headlines hard a year ago when she'd chopped all her hair off and flounced out of a lucrative contract.

He dumped his glass on a passing tray and headed through the crowd, letting his temper build.

Yeah, Cade knew all about kids like Charlotte Courtney.

A poor little rich girl—who had never had to toe the line.

As a poor-boy-made-good from Louisiana, whose mom had kicked him into the system, age five, because feeding him had been too much trouble in between feeding her habit, he was the perfect person to teach her a lesson about how to behave herself. And not cause a ruckus in his place at his expense.

Which made the surge of protectiveness more than a little aggravating when a hand reached out from the crowd to slap her butt.

The girl swung round, her face a picture of outraged contempt, and kicked out at Mr Handsy. Cade could hear her giving the guy hell—in a British accent which was sharp enough to slice through flesh. The surge of protectiveness was joined by fury and an equally aggravating spurt of admiration for her.

He blocked another guy from getting too close as he reached the table, which had started to wobble.

'Take your hands off me, you creep,' Charlotte shouted at the man.

'How about I get you out of here, kid,' he bellowed to her above the music.

'Who are you?' she demanded. The flash of outrage in her eyes, though—which were a stunning, sparkling and surprisingly lucid emerald—had his admiration disappearing fast.

Who the hell did she think she was? Gate-crashing his event with a crew of hangers-on and behaving as if she owned the place?

'Cade Landry,' he shouted back. 'This is my place and my party. And as I didn't give you an invitation, I figure it's time you left.'

She scowled—obviously not liking his tone. So it caught him off guard when she shouted, 'Okay, thanks, Sir Galahad,' and took a flying leap off the table—and into his arms.

He staggered back, as no more than a hundred pounds of lithe female landed on top of him. He braced himself just in time to catch her, and stop them both from ending up on their butts. She looped her hands around his neck and wrapped her legs around his waist with impressive agility.

He inhaled a lungful of her scent—wild summer flowers and clean female sweat—for his pains. Her beautiful face—all high cheekbones and wide green eyes—broke into a grin.

'Well, don't just stand here, Galahad,' she demanded. 'Move. Before we end up as tomorrow's internet sensation.'

He didn't take orders from anyone any more, and especially not spoilt little rich girls. But Cade decided she had a point about the crowd as the cell phone lights blinked on around them.

Once he'd whisked her out of here, away from prying camera phones, he could give her a piece of his mind. He set off through the crowd, forced to do the chivalrous thing, when he wasn't a chivalrous guy, his anger building with each stride.

Eventually, they made it into the elevator lobby, the music pounding behind them. Another security guard stood by the door.

'Mr Landry, sir?' he said, taking in the sight of the girl in Cade's arms just as her fingernails brushed across his nape—sending a jolt of something he didn't like one bit rippling through his system.

'Get the rest of them out of here, too,' he snarled. 'And tell your colleague he's been canned,' he added.

The man nodded and rushed back into the venue as Cade dropped his cargo onto her feet.

'Don't you think you're being a bit of a spoil-sport, Sir Galahad?' she said breathlessly, the playful glint in her translucent green eyes—the emerald hue reminding him of the Hand Grenade cocktails he'd once served by the dozen on Bourbon Street during Mardi Gras—telling him she didn't have one single clue how close she was to getting a damn spanking.

He'd worked eighteen-hour days, seven days a week, for over a decade to stop people judging him for a past he couldn't change, and she'd nearly trashed it all in a single night with her antics.

He stabbed the elevator call button. 'Ya think?' he growled.

'Yes, I do think,' she remarked in that crisp accent, which had a smoky purr which only added to his irritation. 'You seem quite uptight.'

She brushed the short cap of honey-brown curls back from her face, and he noticed the smudge of glittery cosmetics that made her huge doe eyes look even bigger.

His gaze drifted down her figure. Her legs looked about a mile long thanks to the place mat–sized sparkly red dress and ankle-breaking heels. With the height boost from her footwear, her face was almost level with his, which, given that he was six-three, was a rarity. But despite her height, her body reminded him of a gazelle, slender and toned but also fragile. That she didn't have a bra on was something his body noted. And then discarded. His gaze snapped back to her face.

'Fair warning, kid,' he snarled. 'Next time you decide to shake your booty on a table, don't do it in my place.'

The flushed excitement on her face disappeared as her lips flattened, and her breasts rose and fell in a huff of outrage. Her stunning eyes narrowed, as if the Hand Grenade was about to detonate....

So little Miss Court Trouble wasn't used to being told no. *Tough.*

Cade Landry had no problem calling out reckless behaviour.

Surface beauty was just that, shallow and unearned. What mattered was a person's core. And from the things he'd seen so far, Charlotte Courtney was just like every other entitled rich kid who thought they were a grown-up but had no idea how to act like one.

Charley glared at the man sucking all the available oxygen out of the lobby area with his tall, dark, impossibly annoying handsomeness.

How typical... Charley Courtney's hunk in shining armour turns out to have a judgemental streak as broad as his mile-wide shoulders.

'I see, and how do you plan to stop me, *exactly*?' she demanded, calling him on his self-righteousness.

She knew about Southern men and their manners. She'd met a few after she'd been headhunted by a modelling agency at age sixteen—and ended up in the US working the catwalk while being hit on by a load of much older guys. Of course, Cade Landry hadn't actually hit on her. If anything, he had seemed surprisingly undazzled... But give him time.

'How about we kick off with having you arrested for underage drinking,' he replied, folding muscular forearms over his chest and making the seams of his tuxedo bulge... distractingly.

'How do you know I'm underage?' she demanded, determined to hold her own.

His gaze swept to her bottom with enough indifference to make all her nerve endings stand on edge. 'Don't make me laugh, kid.'

The way he said 'kid' in his Southern-fried accent couldn't

have sounded more condescending if he'd tried. The judgemental approach was new, she'd give him that, and somewhat unexpected. Men rarely tried to correct her behaviour these days... But even so...

'I'm not a kid,' she sputtered. 'I'm eighteen.' In fact, she'd turned eighteen that morning.

She'd only come out tonight with the guys from the photoshoot in Caesars Palace to escape the direct hit of her father's latest passive-aggressive text—one line informing her he would have no time to see her when she returned to London after her latest assignment. He hadn't mentioned her birthday. But then, it wouldn't be the first time he'd forgotten.

Maybe her celebration had got a little out of hand, but no one else had tried to stop her. How typical that this man had appeared from the crowd like an avenging angel only to turn out to be a pompous ass...

Why Mr High and Mighty and his bulging biceps were having an unfortunate effect on her libido, though, she had no idea.

She hated to have her behaviour examined and found wanting by people who knew not one single thing about her life. Plus she didn't even *like* sex, because she had discovered—when she'd lost her virginity to a photographer after her first catwalk show in New York—it was totally overrated.

'That's still a kid from where I'm standing...' he said, but then she saw the flicker of something behind the cool expression.

'You think I'm a child? *Really?*' she challenged him, desperate to believe she'd seen something more than disdain.

His gaze darkened—and the frown on his brow became a crater.

He really was stupidly handsome. Tall and muscular with a shock of unruly black hair, his deep tan suggesting he either spent a lot of time sunbathing or he lived outdoors. She doubted he was an idle man, though, because his physique—and the way he had caught her and carried her out without breaking a sweat—appeared to have been forged in fire, rather than an expensive gym. The small scar which bisected his eyebrow and another visible through the stubble on his jaw made it obvious he hadn't led a charmed life. But then, neither had she. The only difference was her scars weren't visible.

Just when she thought she'd finally got the upper hand, the sexual tension snapping between them impossible for even Mr High and Mighty to deny, he huffed out a rough laugh. And the frown disappeared.

His firm lips kicked up in a wry smile so sensual it had her heartbeat sinking into her abdomen.

'Don't you think you've played with enough fire tonight, Charlotte?' he said as he unfolded his arms and leaned past her to press the button on the lift panel.

He loomed over her, forcing her to look up. A novel experience, because at five-foot-eleven in her heels, she was rarely at this much of a height disadvantage.

How did he know her name?

But then, she knew how, and struggled not to wince. Didn't everyone, after her meltdown at Paris Fashion Week a year ago?

'My name's Charley. No one calls me Charlotte,' she declared, determined not to be overwhelmed by his woodsy cologne, or the mouth-watering close-up of his Adam's apple, displayed against the open collar of his shirt alongside the flickering flames of an elaborate tattoo.

What would he do if she kissed him there, where the pulse in his throat throbbed in unison with the one in her panties?

His cool blue eyes turned to a searing sapphire, which

made the pulsing awareness tense and melt at the same time. Surely he had to feel it too.

'I built this place, Charlotte,' he murmured. 'And I hosted the party you just tried to turn into a dumbass free-for-all…' He paused, clearly enjoying judging her—the hot, self-righteous jerk. 'With your childish behaviour.'

'*Childish*…?' she hissed, knowing she'd never been a child. Not really.

She yanked back her outrage when she spotted the sparkle of amusement in his eyes. Was he deliberately trying to wind her up? Because it was totally working.

His cheeks tensed. He was waging a battle not to laugh, something he was struggling to hide.

Adrenaline surged up her torso. Why she found the spark of connection so thrilling, she had no idea. It had been a long time since she'd been attracted to any guy. Or had the desire to flirt with one. But something about Cade Landry—and his determination to see her as a girl instead of a woman—called to her inner demons.

She wanted to taste those lips so badly. Wanted to make him admit he saw her and she mattered. What would it be like to have those sensual lips taking hers in a ruthless kiss? Exciting? Exhilarating? Validating?

The throbbing in her sex matched the rush of blood in her ears. She breathed in a lungful of his delicious scent—man and musk and pine woods. A sob of surrender slipped from her lips, inviting him in.

She lifted her arm and curled her fingers around his nape. 'Kiss me, Landry,' she whispered, the feeling of empowerment making her feel euphoric. 'You know you want to.'

But instead of covering her lips with his, he took her hand from around his neck and stepped back, the contempt in his eyes unmistakeable.

'Kiss you?' he murmured. The euphoria in her belly became sharp and jagged—the distaste in his tone something she'd heard before from her father. 'Why the hell would I want to kiss an off-the-rails kid with an attitude problem?'

The lift doors swished open behind her, the sound masked by the brutal thunder of her heartbeat.

'Now get out of my place, before I call the cops,' he finished, the disgust in his eyes searing her soul.

She stared, speechless with humiliation, as he turned and walked back into the event without a backward glance.

She rushed into the lift, suddenly desperate to get away from him—and the rejection echoing in her ears. She stabbed at the button, the hot, angry tears burning her eyeballs. She bit into her lip to stop them falling as the lift doors closed at last.

She hadn't cried since the day her mother had died, when she was eight years old. She certainly didn't intend to let a few harsh words from a staid, boring, self-righteous jerk with a superiority complex make her cry now.

But as the luminous glitter of the neon cityscape was revealed in the glass wall on the far side of the lift, Cade Landry's sharp words echoed over and over again in her head. Her stomach dropped like a stone, the stunning view of Las Vegas only making her feel smaller and more foolish and insignificant.

She wanted to hate Cade Landry for being as cruel and dismissive as her father. Why should she care if he didn't see her? Didn't want her? When other men did?

But as the scenic elevator tracked down the side of the building, and the miserable sinking sensation in her stomach bottomed out at her toes, instead of feeling righteous and fierce and independent, all she really felt was how she'd felt throughout her childhood. Vulnerable…and unlovable… and invisible…and hideously alone.

CHAPTER ONE

July 4, the present

CADE LANDRY WRAPPED a towel around his waist, ready to head into the sauna behind his squash buddies, Zane de-Marco and Adam Courtney. They met every couple of weeks to thrash out their frustrations on the court. But that wasn't the only reason he was here today.

Courtney had suggested a meet-up to discuss…*something*?

Being a cagey Brit, the guy hadn't specified what, but Cade could make an educated guess. He had his suspicions both deMarco and Courtney were involved in the recent spike in the share price of Helberg Holdings. Courtney probably wanted them both to give him a free run… But no way in hell was that happening.

Helberg was a heritage brand—old-school, traditional, with a legacy which went way back. The company also had a real estate portfolio to die for, which Cade knew Landry Construction could bring back to its former glory.

Now Reed Helberg was dead, the company and all its assets were up for grabs. Owning that name, that history, that legacy would prove Landry Construction had class, something money alone couldn't buy, and would finally allow Cade to reclaim a miserable memory from his childhood, which Helberg had incidentally been a part of.

No way was anyone taking Helberg away from him. Not even his squash buddies...

But as Cade went to shut his locker, his phone buzzed. A text from Dan Carmichael, the CEO of the PR consultancy he had hired to work on brand management for the planned Helberg buyout, appeared on screen.

He lifted the phone back out of his gym bag. And scowled.

Cade, we have a problem. Have you seen the puff piece in Blush about you and deMarco and Courtney? It's getting a lot of traction on social media. I'm not sure being called out as one of the #OneDateWonder billionaires is what we want for the brand atm.

OneDateWonder? What the...?
He clicked on the link Dan had added, because he had never heard of a magazine called *Blush*. He scoured the headline, then the piece itself—which was illustrated with a host of snapped shots of him and Adam and Zane at a string of events in the last couple of months with a lot of different dates. And cursed. Loudly.

His chest tightened and his blood pressure spiked, his fury matched by the frustrating sense of impotence, as he scanned the comments on social media which Dan had also flagged.

Apparently, he, deMarco, and Courtney were at the centre of a gathering viral storm, featuring a bunch of insulting hashtags—*#OneDateWonders, #billionaireblueeyedboysclub, #mancandysummer* and *#catchthemifyoucan* among them.

The internet debate, focussed exclusively on their sex lives, made all three of them look like jerks.

Could this derail what he wanted to achieve with Helberg?

Making Landry Construction respectable, aspirational, and the leading brand in high-class luxury properties was his life's work. But just when he was about to take the next step, the *final* step, some dumb magazine article had decided to turn his private life into a dirty joke.

He slung his cell in his gym bag and slammed the locker door.

He could take a joke as well as the next guy, but having his private life ridiculed reminded him way too forcefully of being mocked as the only kid in senior high who didn't have a prom date—because he couldn't afford a corsage, let alone tux hire. He wasn't that cast-off kid any more. He could buy whatever he wanted now. But he'd be damned if he'd let anyone laugh at him for clickbait.

He walked into the sauna and dropped onto the bench opposite Courtney. The view of the Manhattan skyline through the treated glass reminded him of how far he'd come since being shunted around a string of small towns in Louisiana— a the foster kid nobody had wanted to keep.

He cut off the pity party in his head as he picked up on the conversation between Zane and Adam. Didn't take long to figure out his hunch had been right about Courtney's motives for calling this meeting when the Brit added, 'I need you both to back off...'

'Helberg? Not happening...' Cade said bluntly.

'No can do,' Zane added, making Adam Courtney frown.

'It's a once in a lifetime opportunity, y'all,' Cade drawled.

He didn't let on he had personal skin in this game. Revealing how important it was to him to buy the company would make him look weak. And while he liked these guys well enough, they weren't *that* close. Plus, he knew they both had a killer instinct—from the way they played squash.

'Then we have a problem,' said Courtney with a gravity Cade had come to expect from the guy. After all, he'd inherited his family's business at twenty-eight.

He certainly had a lot more gravity than his kid sister,

Charlotte, Cade thought ruefully, recalling something he'd discovered a couple months back.

Adam Courtney was the older brother of the poor little rich girl he'd crossed swords with in Vegas four years back and had never been able to forget…completely.

The family connection had been a surprise. Cade would not have put the measured, well-spoken, close-lipped guy sweating manfully opposite him together with the wild child who'd been shaking her booty on a table. Cade had never spoken about that long-ago encounter with Courtney because he'd been trying to forget the girl's luminous green eyes, her fragile beauty, and her inappropriate come-on ever since.

So why the hell are you thinking about her now?

'Actually, we have problems. Plural,' Cade said. He needed to focus on that article and not his close encounter with Courtney's sister—which was ancient history.

'What the hell are you talking about?' Adam replied, with just enough frustration to rile Cade.

'Clearly you don't read *Blush*,' Cade growled.

'The women's magazine?' Adam looked nonplussed, clearly not as clueless as Cade about trashy celeb culture. 'You read that?'

'No, I don't read it,' Cade snarled…because…*really*? 'But my PR consultant does. He just texted me. Did y'all know we are the star players in their latest dumb article? "The Billionaire Bachelors Least Likely to Marry." Apparently, we three have been tagged the One Date Wonders… The guys with the longest odds, and they've already started a tally on how many dates we'll have racked up by Labor Day.'

'You're kidding?' Zane said, looking more amused than outraged. 'Who I date is no one's business but mine. And I'm not going to stop—I've no plans to settle down. Ever.'

'Neither do I,' Adam added, not sounding remotely amused.

Me either, Cade thought but didn't add.

'They're turning our sex lives into a joke—and getting a lot of traction,' Cade continued. 'And that's not the kind of media attention I want for my business. Do you?' he finished.

He hadn't worked his butt off his whole life to be taken seriously only to garner this kind of attention.

'Exactly how much traction are we talking about?' Zane asked, the smug grin gone.

'The hashtag One Date Wonders is the top trending topic in the US on most of the main apps today. That much,' Cade answered. 'And just about every American female online seems to have an opinion now about our sex lives... We're basically the red meat at the centre of a social media feeding frenzy.'

Adam winced. Zane looked thoughtful for once.

'My PR team are freaking out about it,' Cade continued. 'Personally, I don't give a damn what a bunch of clickbait junkies and their enablers think of my dating habits...' Except he did, kind of, or the article wouldn't have made him so mad. 'But no way in hell am I letting anyone make me look like a jerk who can't keep his junk in his pants.'

'We need to find a way to shut it down,' Courtney said.

Silence fell. But as the temperature in the sauna rose, so did the hackles on the back of Cade's neck...

Maybe deMarco and Courtney weren't *as* pissed about the hit to their reputations, but then, they'd never had to fight for respect the way Cade had. Courtney came by it naturally, being from old money in the UK, and deMarco was enough of a bad boy not to give a damn what anyone thought about him.

But Cade did give a damn. And somehow, the more he thought about it, the more furious and frustrated he became.

'What if we take ourselves off the market?' Zane offered,

with the reckless twinkle in his eyes Cade recognised from when he was about to make a killer shot on the squash court.

'Forget it,' Cade said. Was deMarco nuts? 'No way am I *actually* getting hitched to shut this down.'

'Absolutely not… It's out of the question,' Adam concurred.

At least two of them hadn't gone to the dark side.

'Did I say anything about getting hitched?' Zane said, as if they were both fools. 'This is a countdown, right? So how about we stop the clock before it even starts. All we have to do is date one woman—and one woman only—from now until Labor Day. Simple.'

'You're kidding. You actually want to pander to this garbage?' Cade said, a little astonished. Having his sex life ridiculed on social media was bad, but having to curtail it to suit some glossy rag's clickbait agenda was worse.

'Not particularly, but I'm betting you two are going to break long before I do,' Zane said, with that feral glint still in his eyes.

'I'll take that bet, because the last time I looked, you're a bigger serial dater than the both of us,' Cade replied wryly.

'You don't even know what the stake is,' Adam pointed out. As if they were actually going to bet on their sex lives…

'My Helberg shares,' Zane shot back, surprising the hell out of Cade, but also making his heartbeat slow—the way it did whenever he was about to close on a sweet property deal.

'Hold on a minute. You'd bet on Helberg?' Cade asked, sure he could not have heard that right. 'Are you serious?'

deMarco's feral grin answered the question before he did. 'Sure. Why not? It's Independence Day today,' Zane continued. 'What if we meet back here on Labor Day. Winner takes all accumulated shares and has an unimpeded run at Helberg.'

Cade frowned. *Damn*. Despite how uncomfortable it made

him feel letting the press dictate his sex life for the summer, the bet was mighty tempting. It provided a way for the three of them to square off over Helberg without driving the share price up any higher—while also nipping all the unwanted social media attention in the bud and minimising the hit to their reputations.

And best of all, Cade could totally win this bet.

Given deMarco's track record with dates, he was at least as much of a hound dog as Cade. Courtney was a dark horse who also had a lot more class than the two of them, but Cade would still take his chances.

Especially when Courtney hissed, 'Have you completely lost your mind?'

And it occurred to Cade that if Courtney was anywhere near as reckless as his kid sister, keeping it in his pants wasn't going to be any easier for him than his buddy Zane.

The arrogant thought had the picture of those stunning emerald eyes swirling through Cade's memory again... But now, instead of the fragile strung-out kid, he couldn't help wondering...

What *would* she be like now? Because he'd heard whispers she had cleaned up her act and stopped modelling a while back.

He cut off his curiosity, though, along with the strange surge of adrenaline.

Get a clue, Landry.

Charlotte Courtney might be four years older, but she was probably just as much of a handful. There was a reason why he preferred women who were sophisticated, mature and predictable. Something he suspected the former British bad girl would never be...

Zane hitched his shoulder in a confident shrug. 'This *Blush* business is an annoyance, right? But I'm more interested in sorting out which of us gets Helberg. This is a good

way to take you guys on and beat you once and for all. Two
birds, one stone.'

'It's nuts,' Cade had to admit. 'But it also makes sense.'

Could he do it, though? More than two months, dating
only one woman?

The prospect didn't fill him with joy. He liked sex. It was
one of the few recreational activities he allowed himself. And
he enjoyed the thrill of the chase even more...

'It's ridiculous.' Courtney did not sound happy.

Okay, so now Courtney sounded like he was protesting
way too much.

Cade rarely dated the same woman twice—because it
tended to give them ideas of the eligible bachelor variety—
but he could make an exception for a few months. There had
to be a woman who could hold his interest for more than a
couple of dates. And not every woman was looking for a
commitment. All he had to do was find the right one.

'You got a better idea?' Zane fired back. 'Because the
likelihood of us stepping out of each other's way just because you asked nicely is...*what*?'

Cade couldn't help it, he laughed. 'Afraid you'll lose,
Courtney?'

He found himself relishing the challenge of going up
against these two, already calculating the logistics of how
to win the bet.

He was headed to the Bay Area this afternoon, to check
out some of the properties in the Helberg portfolio on the
West Coast which were ripe for redevelopment—in the hope
of closing this deal soon. Why not scope out suitable dating options over the weekend at the same time? Seeing as
he was going to be based mostly on the West Coast for the
summer, it made sense to hook up with someone on that
side of the country.

Plus, he'd had an invite tonight to the lavish Fourth of

July bash tech billionaire and fellow Louisiana native Luke Broussard and his wife, Cassandra, hosted every year on the estate Landry Construction had built for them and their ever-expanding family in Marin County. Cade hadn't intended to go. With three children at the last count, the Broussards tended to invite a lot of families to their events and, as a rule, Cade didn't do families. But the evening bash was an adults-only affair—which had a reputation for being exclusive and private as well as fun and informal. The perfect place to start looking for a woman who was engaging enough to hold his attention until Labor Day in early September, but who was also as commitment-phobic as he was—without getting caught on camera before he had made a choice.

Thoughts of Charlotte Courtney popped up again, reminding him of a rumour he'd heard that she was a friend of Broussard's wife, Cassie, another aristocratic Brit and a successful entrepreneur. Hadn't Luke told him Cassie had bought a dress from her because the former wild child had started some kind of fashion brand?

He frowned. Why the heck had he even remembered that?

Okay, maybe he *was* a tiny bit more than just curious about how that kid had turned out, and whether or not she had *really* managed to turn her life around, but that was it. The last thing he needed for his summer date was someone volatile or reckless or confrontational—even if she was pretending to be a businesswoman now, instead of just a bratty kid.

'Not at all,' her brother, Adam, replied, with a tiny hint of superiority which probably came with all that stellar breeding, something his sister sure as hell hadn't inherited. 'Quite the opposite,' he added. 'So, just to clarify: we date one woman each, between now and Labor Day. Anyone caught dating more than one woman in that time relinquishes their claim on Helberg?'

'Right. I'm in,' deMarco concurred.

'You're on,' Cade replied, shoving the unhelpful thoughts of Adam's kid sister out of his head. He doubted she remembered him with much positivity either, given the expression on her face—angry and devastated at the same time—when he'd given it to her straight about her behaviour four years ago. So the smart move would be to give her a wide berth if she did happen to turn up at Luke's bash. And Cade prided himself on always making the smart move.

Adam stared at them both. Then a smile curved his lips. 'May the best man win,' he declared.

Cade nodded and smiled back—because he intended to do whatever it took to ensure the best man would be him.

CHAPTER TWO

That night

CHARLEY TOOK AN unsteady breath as she stepped out of the taxi onto the torchlit lawn of the staggering stone-and-glass mansion on the Tiburon Peninsula.

Built on an extensive piece of untouched land in Marin County, the Broussards' home had spectacular views. The lack of any nearby developments afforded the guests, as they walked to the dramatic arched entrance, a panoramic vista which included Angel Island, the Golden Gate and Bay Bridges, and San Francisco's towering skyline across the water.

Charley was no stranger to luxury living, or the parties of the rich and famous. After all, she'd once been one of their number, in her own backhanded fashion. But she'd learned the hard way to hate that life—the wild parties, the endless hotel rooms, the long workdays and even longer play nights which had eventually become a blur of overindulgence, anxiety, and exhaustion, sucking up all of her adolescence.

She lived frugally now, in a flat in London's up-and-coming East End bought from her earnings as a model—her new life funded by the trickle of revenue from the growing cache of exclusive clients she had managed to impress with her innovative and eclectic dress designs.

Her passion for fashion was one of the few upsides of her short-lived career as a teenage catwalk model, which had mostly just exposed the ugly grit behind the glamour of the industry. But after three years at fashion college in London, learning her craft as a bespoke designer, and an end-of-year show which had piqued the interest of Cassandra Broussard—enough for the tech billionaire's influential wife to become her first buyer—she was now set to finally make a success of her life...on her own terms.

So when Cassandra's email had dropped into her in-box, inviting her, oh-so-casually, to one of the most sought-after and exclusive social events of the summer on America's West Coast, she'd maxed out her credit card to buy an economy class ticket to San Francisco International—and spent every spare evening in the meantime sewing by hand the cocktail dress she was currently wearing—without a single hesitation.

All she needed to do now was model the design at the Broussards' party, without making it too obvious she was touting for business...

Cassandra had handed her a golden opportunity to show-case her signature design style with the exclusive Silicon Valley crowd who were Charley's dream clientele. Now, if she could just get a handle on the butterflies in her stomach, which had turned into dive-bombers on the flight across the Atlantic...

She brushed shaky palms down the bronze silk which stopped mid-thigh and tucked the matching purse under her arm, thinking momentarily about all the hours she had spent painstakingly sewing on the beading.

Look confident. And no one will know you're terrified of doing this sober!

The ankle boots she'd chosen to go with the dress—because, for a garden party, heels were definitely out—clicked on the stone path in time with her rampaging heartbeat. She took a deep breath and offered the uniformed security guard a bright smile along with the QR code on her phone.

The man nodded after checking her ID, then handed her over to a young woman in a tailored suit—who beamed at her.

'Miss Courtney, I'm Alex Burley, Mrs Broussard's assistant. Luke and Cassie are delighted you could join them tonight. Would you like me to give you a tour of the estate, or do you want to go straight through to the party? There's a lounge area by the pool, cocktails on the terrace, or the band, who have started a dance set in the garden.'

'Brilliant, Alex, thanks,' Charley said with a confidence she didn't feel, but had learned how to fake years ago.

She needed to locate Cassie and say thanks to her personally for the invite, and the opportunity. But the sound of the music coming from below the house—a joyous if unfamiliar mix of R&B and rock 'n' roll accompanied by some insane fiddles—was undeniably infectious.

'Actually, I'd love to check out the band,' she said, because she needed to loosen up before she started networking.

'Good choice.' Alex beamed some more, then led her around the house before excusing herself.

Charley walked down stone steps into the garden, enchanted by the informal surroundings—which had the vibe of a music festival rather than a posh society party.

Fairy lights adorned the arbour of trees and twinkled in the glimmer of twilight, framing the view across San Francisco Bay and making it magical as well as breathtaking. The fast-paced fiddles had been joined by an accordion on the stage, and the dulcet tones of a singer—whose throaty French patois seemed to sink into Charley's soul—had her heels tapping of their own accord.

But what enchanted Charley more was how unselfconscious everyone seemed. As if they were enjoying the chance to let off steam, rather than trying to be seen.

The throng of guests chatted and laughed, drinking more beer than champagne, while a huge hog roast was being served on the level above the stage. The dance floor had been laid out under the stars, and was packed with people young and old, some famous, most not, wearing everything from jeans and T-shirts to boho dresses and designer couture as they twirled and boogied in a couples' dance.

In the centre of the mêlée were Luke and Cassandra Broussard.

Charley's pulse kicked against her throat, and she felt weightless for a moment—which had to be her excitement at the stellar business opportunity tonight's event presented, and not the romantic sight of the Broussards dancing together in joyous unison, as if they were completely alone.

She didn't believe in love. Her own parents' marriage— from the little she could remember of it—had been a disaster. And her brother, Adam, had never managed to hold down a serious relationship as far as she knew.

But even so, Charley found herself spellbound.

Cassandra Broussard was a brilliant businesswoman who was warm and kind, and also impossibly serene and sophisticated. But tonight, wearing a summer dress which floated around her body as her husband launched her into a twirl, she looked incandescent. When she threw back her head and laughed at something her husband had whispered in her ear, Charley had the weirdest urge to believe what the Broussards shared was real and would last, when Charley had never had such a cheesy thought in her entire life.

Not even as a little girl.

Especially as a little girl. The vague memory of her mother's broken sobbing and her father's brutal criticisms soured the happy glow.

'Hello, Charlotte. Why aren't you on the dance floor?'

The low, husky voice at her earlobe had Charley swinging round to find a fierce blue gaze she recognised locked on her.

'Or better yet, on one of the tables,' he added, his Southern drawl edged with amusement.

Sensation streaked through her, burning away the last of the romantic glow.

'Cade Landry, what an unpleasant surprise,' she murmured, then wanted to kick herself when the rich sapphire of his irises twinkled like the damn fairy lights.

Fabulous! The man had caught her totally off guard, or she never would have admitted she remembered him or that brutal humiliation from four years ago.

She swallowed, trying to stifle the unwelcome sensations already making the hair on her neck tingle with awareness.

She'd been eighteen and seriously messed up back then, or she never would have thrown herself at him and exposed herself to his ridicule. She was twenty-two now and had left that miserable phase of her life behind—weirdly enough as a direct result of his brutal rejection, which had finally made her confront how far out of control her life had become and how vulnerable she had made herself to men like him. But she would rather die than admit to him that his cruel slap down had helped turn her life around. Because she doubted he'd care. Plus, she had stopped looking for approval in all the wrong places... Especially from overbearing billionaires like Cade Landry, who—from the amused, indulgent expression on his handsome face—still had an ego the size of Las Vegas and the rough-hewn, rugged muscles to match...

Rough-hewn...rugged...? What the heck?

What was she doing noticing the defined contours of his chest through the tight white T-shirt, and his long legs and lean waist displayed to perfection in worn jeans?

She didn't do needy and desperate any more. And she

didn't get turned on by anyone—however fit they might be—because in her limited experience, sex was about as much fun as a root canal.

So stop checking out his pecs, then.

'How about you dance with me and we test that theory?' he said, with an audacity she should have expected from a player like him.

She'd read all about Landry and her brother, Adam, and Adam's mate Zane deMarco, and their giddy dating shenanigans in an article on the plane…which would have been funny if it hadn't been illustrated with so many candid photos of the man in front of her with a host of different women on his arm. Beautiful, smart, stunning, sophisticated women…

Making her far too aware of how swiftly he'd slapped down her clumsy attempts to seduce him, once upon a time. Okay, she'd been off the rails and screwed-up, but he hadn't needed to be so cruel.

'What theory would that be?' she asked, annoyed by the adrenaline spike at the sparkle in his eyes.

'The theory that you and I can't be friends now, Charlotte,' he said.

'*Friends?* Really? You think we can be friends? Have you forgotten how you kicked me out of your place four years ago? Because—FYI—I haven't.' Good grief, did he really think she wanted to give him an opportunity to slap her down all over again? She might be a lot more resilient now, a lot more aware of her own worth, but she wasn't a masochist, or an idiot.

But then his gruff chuckle at her snarky response made her heartbeat accelerate. Disconcerting her.

'Sure, why not? Aren't you a woman now, Charlotte, instead of a kid?' he said, the provocative question entirely deliberate. Was he coming on to her?

She should be insulted, but she wasn't...*quite*. Which was even more disconcerting... But then, Cade Landry was an exceptionally hot guy—and unfortunately, he knew it.

'Actually, I was a woman back then,' she said, because she owed it to that wayward girl to defend her. 'You just didn't have the guts to handle me.'

His eyebrows launched up his forehead. And she congratulated herself on the direct hit. But then his lips curved, and his hot gaze roamed over her. Not with disdain this time, but with approval, which was a great deal more disturbing.

Her sex clenched and released, just as it had four years ago, a response she'd never felt for any other man.

Oh... Hell. Seriously?

'Sounds to me like you've held a grudge for four years because I wouldn't kiss you,' he said.

'Sounds to me like your ego is still the size of Pluto,' she shot straight back, refusing to confirm or deny. Maybe she had been devastated at the time—disproportionate to his actual crimes—because she'd been so vulnerable then, behind the bad girl pose. But he'd still been an overbearing humourless arse, so there was that.

'Touché, Charlotte,' he said, the teasing tone tempting now, rather than judgey. 'How about I say sorry for being so blunt last time we met...and we start over.'

It wasn't much of an apology, but somehow, it helped to ease her anxiety at seeing him again, and being reminded of that awful encounter in Vegas.

He held out his hand. 'Dance with me...' he asked again, the glow in those searing sapphire eyes hot enough to thaw the polar ice cap.

The urge to accept his invitation—simply to rewrite that chapter in her misspent youth, she told herself staunchly—had the anxiety downgrading even more...

But then the band dived into another fast-paced song.

The couples on the floor whirled around, their intricate steps a dance Charley had never seen before—and knew she couldn't pull off without making a fool of herself.

She'd once loved dancing, on tables especially, but sobriety had made her less of an extrovert. And she didn't want to end up on her backside wearing her signature dress. Especially not in front of Mr Ego-the-Size-of-Pluto.

'Of course, I would totally take you up on your generous offer,' she lied without a qualm. 'But I'm not sure I should help you get one up on my brother so soon in the One Date Wonder stakes.'

He winced. 'Is there anyone who has not read that damn article?'

She chuckled, surprised to have found a chink in his armour without even trying. 'You aren't flattered?'

She'd always assumed guys like him loved to flaunt their playboy image.

Her father had cheated on her mother with impunity and made no attempt to hide it. After her mother's death, his sordid sex life had even threatened to bring down the family business. But it had taken years for him to be held to account. Cade Landry, on the other hand, looked genuinely uncomfortable.

'Flattered? At having my dating history ridiculed for clickbait?' he scoffed. 'No. Would you be?'

'Of course not,' she replied. 'But the standards are different for women. Especially...' She raised her fingers to do air quotes. 'An "off the rails kid with an attitude problem".' She placed her hand on her hip. 'And, if I recall correctly, you judged me accordingly when you met me.'

'Charlotte, you were drunk, underage, and shaking your booty on a table at two a.m. when I met you. So you weren't doing a whole heck of a lot to challenge that assumption.'

'I wasn't drunk,' she said in her defence.

Because I remember every single detail of that encounter with far too much clarity.

'But getting back to you...' she continued, because Cade Landry did not need to know how often she'd thought about him. Or that his brutal dismissal of her charms back then had been the wake-up call she'd needed to stop making a spectacle of herself and confirming everyone's low expectations. The man's ego was enormous enough. 'You're not doing a whole heck of a lot to challenge that article by asking me to dance when you were photographed with Jenna Carmody two nights ago at the Met.'

She thought she had him bang to rights. But instead of looking chastened, his sensual smile returned—which only made him look more delicious. *The rat.*

'Have you been keeping tabs on me, Charlotte?' he asked, with the same arrogance she remembered. But why did his attitude towards her feel exhilarating now, rather than critical?

'I don't need to keep tabs on you...' she fired back. 'Your dating history is kind of hard to miss.'

'Fair point,' he murmured. Before she could congratulate herself, though, he added, 'Although Jenna and I aren't dating. She's in a long-term relationship, and she only came to the gala as my plus-one because her partner, Melanie, had the flu.'

'I'm pretty sure that still qualifies as a date,' Charley said, trying to maintain the argument, but oddly disarmed that he had bothered to explain the situation.

'Not in all the ways that count,' he said, his voice becoming a husky purr. His gaze took on that hot glow again, and his hand reappeared. 'This dance, on the other hand, has a lot more potential...'

The seductive tone was back with a vengeance. She couldn't deny the powerful urge to say yes any more. Forcing her to come clean.

'I'd love to accept…' She glanced at the dance floor, where the band had begun another high-tempo number. 'But I can't…'

'Why the heck not?'

'Because I've never danced like that. I don't even know what kind of music they're playing…even though I think it sounds fabulous.'

'It's Zydeco. Because Luke is a Cajun boy from the Bayou Teche.' The devastating smile became a devastating grin. 'You've really never danced the Cajun two-step?'

'Nope,' she said. 'There aren't a lot of Cajuns in Shoreditch,' she added, which was where she lived in East London.

'Then you've missed out.' He beckoned her again with those long, strong fingers. 'I can teach you to Zydeco. All you have to do is follow my lead…like a good girl.'

Four years ago, the provocative comment would have inflamed her rebellious nature, but now all it did was inflame her senses—the wicked glint in his eyes tempting her to share the joke rather than become the butt of it.

She suddenly had a vision of following Cade Landry's lead in other ways.

The man *was* a bona fide player, but he was currently unattached, and into her. And she'd once wanted him desperately. She'd never envisioned wanting him again—not after that brutal rejection—but the liquid pull in her abdomen was impossible to ignore as he waited for her to take the bait… or chicken out. Maybe dancing with him now could be a reward for making the changes to become, if not a good girl, then at least much more together now than she had been that night in Vegas.

In the interest of full disclosure, she added, 'I'm terrible at following anyone's lead. And I've always found good girls remarkably dull.'

He laughed, the rich sound making the heat in her abdomen throb. Then he captured her fingers, his warm skin rough against hers as he tugged her towards him.

'That sounds like a challenge I can't resist,' he said as he lifted her hand and buzzed a kiss across her palm.

The jolt of heat arrowed down. The intense gaze was something she recognised from long ago, but it wasn't cold this time. It was scorching her skin in the most delicious way possible.

'Okay. I'll dance with you.' She grinned, feeling daring for the first time in a long time. 'But be warned, you might lose a few of your toes.'

'I've always figured toes are like good girls...' he declared as he led her onto the moonlit dance floor. 'Overrated.'

'It's just an easy two-step, but with more of a booty sway...' Cade clasped Charlotte's left hand and placed his free hand on her waist to direct her movements. 'But let's not get too fancy right off.'

'Yes, let's definitely not do that!' she remarked, her face a picture of concentration as he showed her the forward and backward steps, and helped her to roll her hips in time with the music. 'I do not want to fall on my arse in this dress,' she added.

He laughed, the comment as infectious as the scent of her—sultry and fresh—on the night air. And the feel of her in his arms.

'And it's such a nice arse,' he offered, using the British word.

He'd been determined to avoid Charlotte Courtney if she showed up at Luke's party. He had important business tonight if he was going to secure a summer date to win the bet.

But the second he'd laid eyes on her, strolling into the garden wearing a wisp of a dress which hugged her slender curves, the rush of adrenaline had been followed by a heady shot of desire. And all the reasons why he shouldn't approach her and shouldn't pander to his curiosity about her had flown right out of his head and drifted away on the warm sea breeze.

After their ten-minute conversation, he'd made the welcome discovery the fragile, lawless girl had become a stunning, strong and forthright woman—her brittle edges replaced by a refreshing sass.

She moved with the same easy rhythm he remembered from when she'd danced on that table, but she seemed more circumspect now—which only charmed him more.

The band launched into an old Cajun classic, full of rhythm and swing—the fiddles joined by bass guitar and the whine of a harmonica. The dance floor was packed, and the slower tempo allowed him to hold her closer. But as the familiar musical lilts flowed through him, she tensed.

'Relax, Charlotte. Ain't nobody grading you, I swear.'

Her gaze, which had been locked on her feet, met his. He found himself drowning in that bright green gaze, her lips a feast he wanted to taste so badly his mouth watered. Ironic, given that when she'd offered them to him four years ago, he'd been appalled.

She grinned. 'Easy for you to say.' But she softened enough to brush against him in a sensuous rhythm, which could get awkward fast.

He lifted her arm and stepped back. 'Go for it,' he murmured, and she took the hint.

Her ripple of laughter as she spun round under his arm was almost as intoxicating as the breathless excitement on her face when she landed the turn and slapped her palm against his chest to regain her balance.

He launched her into another twirl.

'Enough!' she chuckled as she fell back into his arms.

Damn, but she was delicious, and a remarkably fast learner.

He imagined a host of other things he would love to teach her…

Whoa, boy. Don't go getting ahead of yourself.

He needed to find the perfect summer date, and Charlotte would always be an unknown quantity. Plus she was based in the UK, so however attracted he was right now, she wasn't likely to be the woman who could help him win Helberg. But who said he had to find his date tonight? Why not just enjoy himself—and satisfy his curiosity once and for all?

He clasped her waist, anchoring her hips, as the band dived into another tune. Their easy moves became more potent, more passionate, a dance of ecstasy and joy. The swift streak of heat and excitement felt familiar and yet entirely new as they moved to the beat—and she lost her inhibitions, becoming bolder and brighter and more dazzling.

When was the last time he'd danced the Zydeco? And taken the time to relax and enjoy himself with a woman who fascinated him? He picked up the pace, captivated when she followed his lead effortlessly, and added some booty shakes that had his senses reeling as fast at the fiddles.

The soft, silky dress and the firm, toned flesh beneath moved against his palm as they pressed closer, the dance floor filling, the heat rising.

Time faded as the night flew past in a haze of sensation.

By the time they'd danced for almost an hour, they were both breathing hard, covered in a light sweat in the muggy night. The press of the other bodies, the scent of burning pork and salt on the sea air was underlaid with the sultry perfume of flowers and female sweat.

She laughed up at him. 'This is so fun!' she said, her excitement clear and uninhibited. 'But I can't believe I haven't crippled you.'

'You're a natural,' he said, tugging her back towards him. Her palm flattened against his chest as the band's set moved into a slow dance. He settled his hand on her hip to hold her close. She didn't protest.

Her body pressed so intimately against his made the heat pound. Her eyes widened. Was she aware of the reaction he couldn't control? Her lips parted, reminding him of their meeting four years ago, except that this time, they were irresistible.

But as the last note died, and the band announced they were taking a break, she stepped away from him.

He knew they probably ought to cool off, him especially, but he heard himself ask, 'How about some hog roast?'

He waited patiently for her answer, while not feeling patient at all. Something had happened on the dance floor, something vivid and potent—and mutual. She'd captivated him, that much was obvious, but he needed time to think before he acted on this attraction. And considered all the angles. Even so, he knew he wasn't ready to let her go.

Her face glowed from their recent exertion, but her expression became wary.

'I should start networking,' she said with a candour he had not expected. 'To justify the exorbitant cost of my airfare.'

'Is this about your designer brand?'

'You know about that?' Her face flushed with pleasure, and he realised her business couldn't be the vanity project he'd assumed it was when Luke had mentioned it.

'Luke told me you made a dress for his wife, and she loved it.'

Her face glowed. 'Yes, I did. I'm so pleased he told you that. Cassandra Broussard has been wonderful. I'm sure she only invited me tonight because she knew how much it could boost my business...'

'How so?' he asked, genuinely intrigued.

He wished now he'd taken the time to check her out on the internet—something he'd avoided to convince himself he wasn't *that* interested in her.

'I'm modelling one of my own designs,' she said, giving him an impromptu twirl, and filling his senses with another lungful of her intoxicating scent. 'What do you think?'

'Stunning,' he said. Although he couldn't help thinking while the dress was pretty enough, the woman inside was the real stunner.

Her grin widened. 'You see, that's exactly the reaction I was hoping for. But I need to get myself in front of all the potential clients here—who would be mostly female—and wow them with this dress, so they want to commission me,' she added breathlessly. Then she chewed her lip. 'Although...' She glanced around as people filed past them, heading for the dining tables set up by the treeline or the terraces above. 'I really did not expect anything like this.'

'Like what?' he asked, enchanted by the flush on her cheeks and the fierce purpose in her eyes.

'Something fun and not at all formal. It feels a bit rude now to start touting for business, even incidentally...'

He captured her hand. 'How about we eat some burnt pig while you tell me who you want to target,' he said. 'I may not need a designer gown,' he added. 'But I know most of the women here. So I can introduce you around.'

'Is that a good idea?' she said, sounding doubtful. 'I want to sell bespoke haute couture by Trouble Maker, not piss off all your former lovers.'

'Hey.' He choked out a gruff laugh. 'First off, we're not dating...' *Yet.* 'Second, I don't sleep with every woman I date. And last but not least, I'm not so prolific that I know every woman in the Bay Area in a biblical sense. You shouldn't believe everything you read.'

'Duly noted.' She looked suitably chastened, but then she smiled. 'You really don't mind introducing me around?'

'Of course not. I'm happy to boost your business any way I can,' he said, surprising himself. Truth was, he wasn't usually a sociable guy, and he never networked at parties. But he was more than happy to help her out, if it meant having her by his side for the rest of the night and keeping that flush of pleasure on her face.

'Well…' She chewed her bottom lip some more. 'That's actually an offer I'm not sure I can afford to refuse…business-wise.'

'Then don't… But let's start with the offer of burnt pig,' he said.

'Absolutely,' she said. 'I'm starving.'

He chuckled at her enthusiastic response, her smoky voice arrowing straight into his groin.

'Cool.' He patted his belly, enjoying the way her gaze tracked down his torso. 'The dancing has made me ravenous, too.'

Although it occurred to him that roast pork wasn't going to satisfy the main reason he was ravenous right now—forcing him to reconsider his priorities again as he led her toward the barbecue pit.

CHAPTER THREE

'I GUESS THAT'S my cue to leave,' Charley murmured as the last of the red, white and blue fireworks died in the night sky.

'So soon?' Cade replied, his hand warm on her lower back as he pulled her against him to avoid the couples heading back into the garden.

'It's nearly midnight,' she said, basking in the focussed gaze she had been basking in all evening…the jolt of awareness getting harder and harder to ignore.

Who knew? Cade Landry really was Sir Galahad.

He'd shepherded her around for over two hours, introducing her to female entrepreneurs and businesspeople—as well as a number of wives and girlfriends of the male business people he knew—whose contact details she now had safely secured in her phone. The boost to her business from this evening's networking offensive would be invaluable, and Cade Landry had facilitated it. Even though she'd realised he wasn't much of a social animal. He didn't seem uncomfortable so much as aloof. And from the surprise on a lot of people's faces—including their hosts when Charley had eventually thanked Cassandra in person—she'd gathered he rarely showed at events like this one.

But she had to admit it wasn't her business initiatives she had been thinking of every time he rested his palm casually on her waist, or smiled that sensual smile full of masculine approval while telling people to check out her dress.

'Which makes it approximately eight in the morning UK time,' she finished, trying to focus on all the reasons why she needed to leave now.

She had a cheap motel booked near the marina which was calling her name. Even though she didn't feel remotely tired, because the giddy excitement of being the sole focus of Cade Landry's attention for the evening had become more than a little addictive.

But Cade hadn't made a move, and she wasn't entirely sure now if she had read his signals all wrong. Was he into her, or was he just being helpful to a fellow businessperson? Because apart from those small, incidental touches, he hadn't made any significant attempts to come on to her since they'd danced their hearts out.

She'd assumed he wanted her…but what did she really know about reading signals? Given that she'd always been so awful at sex? And she hadn't even had any since the first time she'd tried to kiss him…which had been a complete disaster.

'I appreciate everything you've done for me this evening,' she said, her excitement deflating. 'I wouldn't have had the guts to approach most of those people. It was very generous of you. You're actually a nice guy, Sir Galahad,' she teased, covering the flicker of inadequacy.

You don't need his approval, Charley.

His lips twisted in a wry smile. 'The one thing I'm not, Charlotte, is nice,' he said. 'But I made you a promise earlier in the evening, and I never break my word.'

'Okay,' she said, the tension almost as delicious as the sudden spurt of anticipation.

He ran his knuckle down the side of her face. The possessive touch had the endorphins she'd been keeping in check exploding through her system like the fireworks display they'd just witnessed.

'I'd like you to come home with me tonight,' he said, his gaze filling with the molten heat she'd noticed while they danced but had since assumed she must have imagined. The sensual smile made her insides clench. 'But if you're too jet-lagged, or you're just not that into me, I can escort you wherever you want to go.'

'That's…direct,' she whispered, trying desperately not to throw herself at him—something she could acknowledge now she had wanted to do, ever since he had guided her so sensually through the dance. And she'd let him.

That she hadn't read his intentions wrong was even more intoxicating. But something about the insistent pulsing in her sex felt too much like that out-of-control girl.

'Direct is how I roll,' he said. 'When I want something.' He hooked a tendril of hair behind her ear. The casual, oddly possessive gesture made the hunger flare and throb. 'And tonight I want to taste every inch of you and make you moan.' His voice dropped to a husky purr. 'But you need to be sure that's what you want, too.'

It was supposed to be a question. But it didn't sound like one, because her body was already desperate for his touch and had been ever since she'd turned in the garden hours ago to find him watching her…maybe even before that. Maybe even dating right back to that reckless girl who had looked for approval in sex and never found it.

He was the only man who had ever said no to her, she realised—which made his desire for her now all the more exciting. And validating.

'I want you, too' she admitted, because she'd never been coy.

'Thank God,' he said, the scorching heat in his gaze making her realise it had cost him to hold back. 'Then let's get the hell out of here.'

But when he clasped her fingers and strode from the terrace, heading through the house towards the front lawn, the swirl of anticipation in her gut tangled with familiar insecurities.

As they arrived at the valet station and a shiny black SUV appeared, she tugged her hand free.

The sound of the band starting the late-night set floated over the night air but did nothing to calm Charley's nerves. Her life had come full circle since their meeting in Vegas. But it had been years now—four years, to be precise—since she'd been intimate with anyone. And she'd never been any good at it.

'If you've changed your mind, I can take you home,' he said, more perceptive than she would have expected.

'I haven't changed my mind...' she managed around the growing ball of embarrassment wedged in her throat. 'I'm just...'

Good grief, how do you explain to a man who could probably make most women come at thirty paces that you have never had a satisfying sexual experience?

'I'm just not very good at one-night stands...so if you're expecting a sex goddess,' she babbled, 'you're going to be disappointed.'

Rather than looking appalled, Cade's gaze sharpened, and the heat in his eyes flared. The hot brick between her thighs started to pound.

'Just to be clear, Charlotte.' A confident smile curved his lips. 'No one's going to be grading you on your performance in my bed, either.'

'Good to know,' she mumbled.

Fabulous, Charley. Why not just tell him you're a terrible lay without telling him you're a terrible lay?

'And I happen to be a goal-oriented overachiever who always rises to a challenge,' he added. 'So we're good.'

A laugh burst out of her mouth, his comment so arrogant it somehow managed to be self-deprecating at the same time.

'And let's not forget an ego the size of Pluto,' she said, the knot of embarrassment in her throat releasing.

'Yup,' he said. 'Which, luckily for you, happens to be well-earned.'

She was still chuckling as she climbed into the passenger seat—and the hot, liquid rush of anticipation gushed into her panties.

It was a thirty-minute drive from the Broussards' place to Cade's condo in the Embarcadero. It might as well have taken ten years.

Cade kept his eyes on the road, inhaling Charlotte's intoxicating scent—which had been torturing him all evening—as he wound through the leafy suburbs of Marin County, passed over the Bay on San Francisco's iconic Golden Gate Bridge, then took the 101 through the Presidio, up and down the famous streets of Pacific Heights and Nob Hill and into the built-up areas of downtown. By the time he pulled into the parking garage behind the Ferry Building, the tension in his gut was on a knife edge…

The vintage R&B station he'd found on the radio had done nothing to chill the heat in his gut ever since Charlotte had climbed into his car.

Hell, ever since she'd agreed she wanted him, too. And then told him, with that wary candour, she was no sex goddess—which had to be code for *All the guys I've slept with have been selfish bastards.*

He hadn't lied. He loved a challenge. And he had always been goal-oriented, plus the chemistry between them was nothing short of explosive.

But the hunger which had gripped him ever since they'd danced together had only got worse over the last couple of hours. He had to get a handle on it before he got her naked if he was going to make good on his promise and show her a good time.

He switched off the ignition. Marvin Gaye's sweet soul voice dropped into a charged silence. The heat surged as Charlotte released a careful breath.

'San Francisco is a beautiful city,' she murmured. 'How long have you lived here?'

'I don't,' he said. 'I mostly live in Manhattan, but I keep the condo for when I'm working on the West Coast, because I hate staying in hotels.'

'So do I,' she said. 'It was one of the things I hated the most about modelling. Having my home in a suitcase, being constantly jet-lagged, ordering bar snacks off room service menus because I hadn't eaten all day and that was all I could get at stupid o'clock in the morning. Watching the light blinking on the smoke detector, unable to sleep...' The nervous rush of information cut off abruptly, and she sent him a self-deprecating smile. 'The soulless grind of luxury living has to be the epitome of first-world problems for the spoilt little rich kid I was then, right?'

Her defensiveness, though, told a different story. He'd dismissed her as a spoilt brat that night, just like everyone else, but he could see now it must have been tough getting thrust into that whirlwind when she was still a kid.

'Were you spoilt?' he asked. 'Or just young and unprepared?'

She let out a hollow laugh. 'Who knows.' She shrugged. 'But I'm glad that girl is long gone.' Leaning across the console, she cradled his cheek. 'Are you finally going to kiss me now, Landry?'

He chuckled, the moment of introspection dispelled on a wave of want. Placing his hand on her waist, he dragged her closer and whispered, 'You don't have to ask me again, Charlotte.'

He captured her lips at last. She tasted sultry and sweet. But when her mouth opened on a shocked sob, the kiss went from provocative to carnal in a heartbeat.

He feasted on her, cupping both cheeks, and threading his fingers into her hair to release the soft mass from the chignon which had started to collapse while they danced.

He angled her face, and she opened for him, allowing him to thrust deep and take more. But as she tried to get closer, the seat belt restrained her.

He lifted his head, traced his thumb over her flushed cheek. 'How about we take this upstairs. Making out in a car is overrated.'

'Good plan, Galahad.'

He jumped out and headed round the hood to meet her at the passenger door. But as she got out, he scooped her into his arms.

She laughed. 'Nice catch.'

She placed eager kisses across his jaw, his chin, his cheek as he marched to the elevator and stabbed the call button with his elbow. The doors opened immediately, but it seemed to take another eternity of torture to finally arrive at his penthouse.

She was still wrapped around him as he walked into the foyer and through into the main living area. The glass walls of the corner penthouse gave him a staggering view of the Bay Bridge and the sprinkle of Oakland's nightlights in the distance, but it wasn't the view which made his breath hitch when he set her on her feet.

She choked out a stuttered sob as he dragged his hands up her thighs under the short mini dress to fill his palms with her soft, responsive and—*what the hell?*—naked butt.

A thong! Lord, help me.

'Were you wearing this the whole time we were dancing?' he accused her, the knife edge becoming painful.

She nodded. 'I love thongs. They're so comfortable.'

He groaned. 'You could have flashed the whole party every time I sent you into a spin…'

'And your point would be…?' She chuckled, giving him a tantalising glimpse of the reckless kid who had once danced on a table.

He laughed too. So the reckless kid wasn't dead and gone—but her bad girl energy was so much more intoxicating now.

Her fingernails rasped across his nape—and sensation arrowed into his groin.

'I think I should punish you,' he murmured, holding her hips. 'For risking getting us both arrested.'

'I agree,' she teased with a throaty purr.

He was still chuckling as he buried his face in her neck to lick the pummelling pulse in her collarbone, while massaging her bare butt and riding his thumb under the string. She shifted, cradling the ridge of his erection against her belly.

He sucked in the musty aroma of her arousal, but then she stiffened.

He pulled back, and saw both giddy need and wary tension in her lust-blown pupils. Small white teeth dug into her bottom lip, making him aware of the reddened skin around her mouth, and on her neck, where he'd given her beard burn.

Slow down, man.

'Hey, are you still with me?' he asked, resting his hand on her neck to stroke the delicate skin with his thumb.

'Yes, yes, of course,' she said too swiftly, as if she was trying to convince herself as well as him. 'I want this,' she added, but she sounded less sure than she had when they'd been devouring each other in the elevator.

He forced himself to loosen his hold a little.

'There's no rush, Charlotte. We can take as long as you need. Tell me where you like to be touched?' he asked, determined to take this at her pace.

She blinked, her eyes dark with arousal, but also wary. Emotion tugged hard under his breastbone.

'Honestly, I'm not sure,' she said. 'No one's ever asked me that before.'

The forthright response was both adorable and kind of sad. He'd bet good money she had lost her virginity long before she'd met him four years ago, but the puzzled frown on her face made her seem like an artless girl—learning about her own desire for the first time.

Right about now, he wanted to murder every guy who had taken from her and given so little back. But the weight of responsibility was also a novel feeling. Could he be the one to show her she had always deserved so much more?

Aware of her nipples standing out like bullet points against the bronze silk, he thumbed one rigid peak. She jolted, her eyes widening.

'How do you like to touch yourself?' he asked, his throat raw as he continued to caress her lazily, not wanting to lose the connection, but careful not to push. 'Can you show me?'

Her pale skin darkened. 'I like what you're doing right now...' she managed. 'But I think it would feel even better if I was naked.'

He let out a strained laugh, the bold comment crucifying him a little.

'Then let's remedy that,' he said.

Gripping the hem of her dress, he drew it gently over her head and threw it away. She quivered, her small, firm breasts barely disguised by red lace.

He found the back hook of her bra, released it. She sighed as he took off the lace. He skimmed his thumb over one ruched nipple. Her vicious shudder rippled through his over-wrought body.

Damn, but she was gorgeous. And so responsive…

Lifting the quivering flesh, he dragged his tongue over the swollen peak. She moaned as he drew the hard tip into his mouth and began to suck gently.

She grasped his head and arched her back, instinctively pushing herself into his mouth. Her panting breaths encouraged him as he learned what she liked the most, tormenting and torturing her until the hard peaks elongated even more.

Her musty scent filled his nostrils—sweet and spicy. But he took his time, determined to draw out her pleasure and contain his own—even as her eager, artless responses battered his self-control.

At last, he could wait no longer, cupping her sex, delving beneath the satin shield of her thong. She gasped, so ready and tender each stroke made her buck against his fingers.

He circled the stiff nub, grazing over and around it as he gauged her responses. The pants became sobs, her chest heaving beneath his mouth as he continued to tease her breasts.

'Oh… That's…' She strained against him, her head falling back against the glass wall, the lights of the bay sparkling in her glossy hair.

He lifted his head, blew across her damp nipples, reddened now from his attention, and continued to work her clitoris with his thumb. He pressed one finger, then two inside her—his breathing becoming ragged at the realisation of how tight and wet she was. For him.

'Relax, Charlotte, and let it take you…' he coaxed, focussing his caresses on the slick heart of her at last.

She jerked, bucked against him, her hands grasping fistfuls of his shirt as she shuddered through the climax—the tortured sounds she made part pleasure, part pain.

Her body sank against the glass as the orgasm ebbed. He withdrew his hand, rested it on her hip. And waited for her eyes to open.

The green gaze locked on his, her expression dazed. Something pure and strong cinched tight around his ribs.

She seemed fragile and strangely vulnerable in that moment—her hair a soft, tangled mess, her breasts reddened from his lips, her sultry fragrance filling the room, and her face unable to hide her astonishment. As if the bad girl had been stripped away to reveal the needy, neglected girl beneath.

'How…how did you do that?' she asked, perplexed. 'I've never… Well…'

The swell of affection and pride—because he had given her something precious—made his lungs tighten. How could she be so bold, jaded even…and yet also so unsure?

She was much more complex and fascinating than he could have imagined.

'It's not hard to pay attention…' he said, then pressed his palm to her flushed skin. 'How do you feel about another round?'

The chance to explore all those facets, unravel more of the puzzle she represented, excited him beyond bearing.

It occurred to him he'd become impossibly jaded about sex too, because her unguarded response to each touch, each caress, was somehow more erotic than the most practised seductress.

A grin split her features. 'Much more enthusiastic now.'

Gripping his shoulders, she leapt into his arms—the reckless girl returning. He caught her with a huff, his hands gravitating to her backside.

'But I want you naked too, Galahad.'

'No problem,' he said, enjoying her demanding tone.

He strode into the master suite and dropped her on the bed, then ripped open his shirt.

Her eyes flared with excitement as she watched him strip. 'What's the tattoo on your shoulder?' she asked.

He paused as her avid gaze roamed over the ink he'd got at seventeen to celebrate flipping his first house—a broken-down two-storey Arcadian in Breaux Bridge, Louisiana, which he'd gutted and remodelled over one endless, back-breaking summer.

'A phoenix,' he said, embarrassed by the dumb decision now, made when he'd been drunk with excitement about the big fat profit burning a hole in his wallet. 'Kind of a cliché, but it seemed appropriate at the time,' he added, because he'd come to despise that ink in some ways, and the naive kid who had thought he'd be accepted, just because he had money to invest.

'It's cool,' she said as she kicked off the ankle boots she still wore. 'And very hot!'

He smiled. Maybe that decision hadn't been so dumb after all?

He ripped open his pants, shoved them down. But as his erection bounced free, thick and long and impossibly hard, surprise flared across her features.

'That's impressive,' she said, the bold tone husky with desire, but also unsure again.

He'd had compliments before about his physique—he was a man who women had always liked the look of, even when he'd been broke—but something about the stunned yearning in her gaze when it rose to his, the captivating mix of awareness and shock, had him feeling like a real knight in shining armour for the first time in his life.

A knight who planned to show Charlotte Courtney exactly what she had been missing.

Cade Landry is actually a sex god!

Excitement vibrated in Charley's gut as she devoured the

sight of Cade's heavily muscled body—in all its naked glory. The small scars, the flamboyant tattoo in faded red and gold of the mythical bird flaming across his left pec and shoulder, the defined lines of his hip flexors, the washboard abs, and the sunburnt bronze of his skin which paled at his groin, framing the massive erection that jutted out from the nest of dark hair.

She swallowed around the new blockage in her throat. And stared.

But as he fished a condom out of the bedside dresser and rolled it onto the mammoth erection with casual efficiency, it occurred to her he was a lot more experienced at pleasuring women than she was at pleasuring a man.

And she'd never had any satisfaction at all from penetrative sex.

The truth was, all her sexual encounters up to now had been furtive and rushed, crude and unmemorable…

She forced herself not to tense up, tried to concentrate on the epic orgasm she'd just had—which had been as surprising as it had been exhilarating.

Cade had taken his own sweet time and devoted himself to her pleasure first and foremost. Which just went to show, the few guys she'd slept with before him had been incredibly selfish, dating right back to the forty-something photographer who had slammed into her in a studio bathroom when she was sixteen and convinced her it was her fault she hadn't enjoyed it.

She wanted to believe she'd just turned a corner—with Cade Landry's expert help. But as he climbed onto the bed and gripped her ankle to tug her towards him—fierce possession in his eyes—her breath hitched. She did not want this to be another encounter she ended up regretting.

She pressed a hand to his chest. 'Wait.'

'Problem?' he asked, his hands stroking her hips in a way which made her heart thunder against her ribs.

'Not specifically...' she said, far too aware of the thrusting flesh brushing against her thigh. Being in that state had to be uncomfortable, but in her experience, men found it a lot harder to slow down once they got it inside you.

'I just... I don't want this to be over too soon.' She gripped the hot length as carefully as she could. 'So how about I take care of you?'

He jolted as she stroked the turgid flesh, but then he pressed a kiss to her cheek and grasped her wrist to remove her hand from the powerful erection.

'I'm in no rush, Charlotte,' he said, the amusement in his voice belied by the intensity in his expression. 'Let's make this all about you. Because believe me, I'm already being taken care of...'

'You *are*?' she asked. But she felt gauche and insecure when he chuckled.

'Do you have any idea how captivating you are?' he countered without answering her inane question. Before she could come up with a coherent answer, he murmured, 'How about I show you...'

It wasn't a question, as he held her firmly in place to nuzzle her neck, then proceeded to kiss his way—with infuriating patience—down her torso.

He worshipped her with his mouth, his tongue, his teeth. His lazy focus made her aware of each sweet, sensitive spot he discovered. The maddeningly slow caresses turned her collarbone, her breasts, her nipples, her belly into one enormous erogenous zone. Her back bowed as he awakened every nerve ending—building a new maelstrom of need. She grasped handfuls of the sheet as he finally blew across the soaked satin of her thong.

She gasped, desperate, devastated as he traced the edge with his tongue.

'Please…take it off…' she begged, the thin swatch of fabric a frustrating barrier.

'Why yes, Mizz Charlotte,' he teased, the husky edge in his voice vibrating against her skin before he eased the thong off.

She lay hesitant, expectant, the mix of brutal pleasure and vicious anticipation making her desperation increase, as he parted her swollen folds and lathed his tongue across the needy flesh.

She lurched off the bed, her fingers fisting in the luxury linen sheets again, her eyes screwed shut.

'Easy, Charlotte, hold on to it this time,' he murmured, the tone arrogant but full of a confidence which only made her feel more alive, more needy, and more secure. And very happy to let him lead. 'We've got all night.'

She parted her thighs, brushed the silky waves of his hair she could reach with her fingertips to urge him on, as he went to work, devouring her with his tongue, but retreating every time she edged too close to another glorious release.

Pleasure swelled and twisted—taut, tight, painful—building her desperation.

The wave barrelled towards her just as he rose above her, his broad shoulders cutting out the night.

Clasping her hips, spreading her wide, he surged deep in one powerful, all-consuming thrust. The thick erection stretched her unbearably, but her body was so slick, so ready, he impaled her with ease.

She sobbed, shocked by how the thick intrusion made the climax intensify. He established an undulating, unstoppable rhythm and forced her to follow, reminding her of the dance. She clung to him again, trusting him to show her the way.

She dug her heels into the mattress, her knees gripping

his hips, and rode the brutal wave, which rose to crest again as he pounded into her, the pleasure so much, too much… much more than enough.

She cried out, her voice hoarse, as she dived into the hot vat of stunning sensation.

'Look at me,' he growled, his tone raw.

Her eyelids flew open, and she found him watching her with that fierce intensity—but he was lost now too in the maddening pleasure… His movements became jerky and frantic. His gruff shout of completion pierced the thick fog of afterglow.

Triumph filled her—sweet, visceral, overwhelming— as he collapsed on top of her, following her head first into the abyss…

CHAPTER FOUR

WELL... HELL...

Cade eased out of Charlotte's body and flopped onto his back on the bed—exhausted, drained, and still tingling with the power of his orgasm.

She moved beside him, her breathing as uneven and unsteady as his.

He managed to turn his head and caught her staring back at him. Her lust-blown pupils and the flushed glow on her skin both a validation and a warning.

Had she felt it too? The intensity of their connection? Because he'd never experienced anything like it before. And he'd slept with a lot of women—maybe not as many as his reputation on social media suggested, but enough to know that had been spectacular. And he was not a guy given to hyperbole.

A smile edged her lips, her expression more open than he had ever seen it, making her seem artless—and impossibly young.

'Thank you, Sir Galahad,' she said, her gaze unguarded. 'Finally I know what all the fuss is about.'

He forced out a gruff laugh.

'You're welcome, Mizz Charlotte,' he said, trying to lift the weight pressing on his chest.

They'd been waiting to explore their chemistry for hours. And he didn't do deferred gratification, if he could help it...

Plus it had been a month since he'd had any sex at all. And a whole lot longer since he'd slept with a woman as captivating as Charlotte Courtney.

But what they had shared was still only sex. Ultimately, this hookup was no different to all the others. It couldn't be.

She yawned and let out a throaty sigh, which had the heat in his groin pulsing.

Seriously? How could he want her again so soon after that mind-blowing orgasm?

But then she dragged herself off the bed and began rooting around for her clothes.

He propped himself up on his elbow. 'What are you doing? It's two in the morning.'

She glanced over her shoulder, having slipped on the thong, flashing him a delicious view of her rear end.

'Heading back to my motel before I drop into a coma,' she said. 'I haven't slept for close to twenty-four hours now, and I'm out of practice doing all-nighters.'

Surprise was followed by disappointment. He wasn't ready for her to leave. Another first.

'Come back to bed,' he said, grabbing his shorts and tugging them on to cross the room. He lifted the silk dress out of her hands before she could slip it over her head. 'Sleep here.'

'Won't that get weird?' she asked with her usual directness. 'Tomorrow morning?'

He brushed her hair back to hook the unruly curls behind her ear, captivated all over again, and he wasn't even sure why. She wasn't wrong. He wasn't a snuggler—once sex was done, he preferred to sleep alone—and mornings after could be just plain awkward, if his latest hookup had expectations of anything more substantial. But somehow, with Charlotte, he doubted that would be a problem.

And weirdly, her reluctance only made him more determined to get her to stay.

'Why would it be weird?' he asked to delay her.

She shrugged. 'Walk of shame-wise? You really have to ask?'

'I'm not ashamed of what just happened,' he countered. 'Are you?'

'No, of course not,' she said, but a hot rush of colour suffused her features.

He pressed a kiss to her forehead, feeling strangely protective of her. As a kid she'd been left to fend for herself in a very adult world. No wonder she was wary of being caught leaving his place. After the *Blush* piece—and the viral storm still raging online—he knew what it felt like now to be objectified by social media's keyboard warriors.

'How about I help you to leave incognito tomorrow?' he said. 'The people hounding me on social media aren't aware I'm in San Francisco yet.' Or he certainly hoped they weren't.

He'd like to see her again, but he could take his time if no one found out what had happened tonight. Luke's party was famous for its privacy. And they hadn't been seen anywhere public. So they were both good.

But why not make Charlotte his summer date after all? They'd have to figure out some stuff—logistics-wise—because she lived in London. And her brother might pitch a fit—but it would be worth the extra effort. One thing was for damn sure, he didn't see himself getting bored with her soon.

She looked at him for the longest time, the flush on her pearly skin intensifying. His insides clenched. The desire for her to stay overnight and be here in the morning was unprecedented. And did not have one damn thing to do with the bet, if he were being honest.

Then her face broke into a huge yawn.

'Come on.' He took her hand, drew her toward the bed. Throwing back the sheet, he guided her in, then climbed in to drag her body against his. Spooning for the first time in his life.

His body responded accordingly.

She shifted against him. 'FYI, I'm far too shattered to do anything about that...'

He smiled against her hair, his arm tightening around her waist. 'Ignore it. It'll go down eventually.'

Although it took a while, because listening to her breathing deepen was impossibly arousing, too.

He stared out into the San Francisco night, his body pounding with need, and wondered when and how he had become so enchanted by her.

But as he drifted into sleep himself, finally letting the hunger go, he persuaded himself his desire to keep Charlotte for longer than he'd originally planned was all about finding a way to win the bet...while also having an entertaining and enjoyable summer.

No big deal.

CHAPTER FIVE

CHARLEY'S EYES FLUTTERED open to find her nose pushed into firm tanned flesh which smelled of salt and pine woods and man.

Mmm... Delicious.

But then full consciousness returned.

Cade Landry!

She was wrapped around the man she had spent one incredible night with at Cassandra Broussard's party. But the awareness making all her pulse points pound was soon joined by a wave of panic.

She shifted away from him, her disorientated senses becoming aware not just of all the places her body felt different—well-used, a little sore—but also that the night had meant more to her than it should.

Why else was she still in his bed? She had never spent the whole night with a guy.

She could remember the stunning orgasms, him coaxing her to stay, the promise to help her leave this morning in secret—and her insistence staying was a bad idea. So why had she succumbed?

Jet lag? Maybe. Exhaustion? Possibly.

But even as she tried to convince herself there were lots of practical reasons for her to fall asleep in Cade's bed, the panic in her chest became a ticking bomb.

Stop analysing your stupidity and get out of here—now.

Galvanised, she edged off the bed. He lay, still fast asleep, taking up most of the available space. She stared at him for one precious moment. Weren't guys supposed to look boyish and less threatening and overpowering while asleep?

Trust Cade Landry to be the opposite. His hard, handsome face—the stubble on his jaw almost a beard now—was even more devastating. Serious and hot, and totally intimidating.

The ticking time bomb pushed into her throat as she recalled how careful, how intent he had been on her pleasure, her response to him.

No man had ever made love to her with such focus.

Not made love...had sex.

He'd said himself it was no big deal. All he'd had to do was pay attention. She'd obviously just picked the wrong guys to get intimate with before Cade.

No biggie.

He frowned in his sleep, shifting. And she jerked back.

She scrambled off the bed, her heart now pressed against her larynx.

She gathered her discarded clothing and slipped each piece on—from her signature dress, now hopelessly crushed, to the tangled thong.

As she yanked on her ankle boots, she became brutally aware of the discomfort between her thighs, the tenderness in her sex. She needed a shower. But she wasn't about to risk waking him, the ticking bomb threatening to explode.

Her flight home was booked for three o'clock. She had enough time to catch a cab back to her motel in Marin County, grab a shower and her luggage, then head to the airport.

She paused while scooping up the purse she'd dropped in the living room.

The penthouse's panoramic view of the Bay Bridge and the heritage building in front of them—ornate and dazzling in the sunlight—had the breath she'd been holding clogging her lungs.

The memory of the approval in Cade's eyes all through the evening and during their night together—as he'd played her body like a virtuoso, and she'd enjoyed every minute of it—filled her with a fierce yearning which only made her feel more exposed. And frankly idiotic.

Orgasms were one thing. Even breathtaking, life-altering, mind-blowing ones. But the fact Cade had been the man to deliver them—a man who in a weird way had changed the course of her life four years ago—felt significant. But she refused to be one of those women who confused great sex and electrifying chemistry with something more.

She turned from the magnificent view and spotted a note-pad on the coffee table.

She jotted down a quick note. Then screwed it up and stuffed it in her purse. It took two more attempts before she got the right mix of friendly and flippant.

As she walked through the parking area ten minutes later, she refused to acknowledge the regret making her chest ache.

She was not that needy, messed-up girl any more.

This wasn't a walk of shame. She didn't care if her make-up was smudged, her dress wrinkled and her scent more than a little musty. She was one hundred percent responsible for her actions last night. And she'd had a good time. An illuminating time.

But she would shove this memory away in a box marked 'Your First Booty Call to Remember' and then forget about Cade, finally, because she'd come full circle from the reckless girl he'd met four years ago.

And she had no doubt at all, Cade Landry would be grateful when he woke up to discover she had taken the initiative—and left before things could get awkward.

Thanks for an epic night, Sir Galahad! If I ever get the chance to dance the Zydeco again, I'll think of you. C

Cade stared at the note—which he'd found propped on the coffee table after spending ten minutes searching the apartment for his overnight guest.

Her sultry perfume had woken him from vivid erotic dreams—in which she was the star player, his groin hard and throbbing. And now *this*...

She'd run out on him.

He scratched his stomach, still groggy and strung out after the deepest sleep he'd had in months, and read the note again.

The blip in his heartbeat, though, refused to subside. But as he scanned the note a third time, looking for any kind of hidden meaning, any hint she planned to get in touch with him again, anger tangled with the hollow ache in his gut.

She hadn't even left a cell number. This was the female equivalent of *wham, bam, thank you, ma'am.*

He'd been given the kiss-off before—back in high school, when the rich, pretty, popular girls had been happy to use him for kicks but had never wanted to date him in public—and it had stopped bothering him a long time ago.

So why did Charlotte Courtney's kiss-off note bug him so much now?

Perhaps because he thought he'd left that easily used kid behind after he'd made his first million. Perhaps because these days, he was always the one to disengage first. Maybe even because he'd decided late last night that Charlotte would be the perfect summer date to see off deMarco and her brother when it came to the Helberg bet?

But as he screwed up the note and lobbed it into the trash, determined to forget it, and her—Charlotte's breezy, brazen, couldn't-give-a-damn-about-you note still bugged him. Big-time.

What the hell had he expected? Yeah, it had been a memorable night, one of the best he'd had in a while. But that was as much to do with the fact he'd been working his nuts off for months, preparing the groundwork to bring Helberg and its assets into the Landry brand, as it did with Charlotte.

As for making her his summer date? He could always find someone else…

They hadn't arrived at the Broussards' together, and the press had been long gone by the time they'd left. No one knew about last-night's hook up, so his options were still open.

It was all good. Or at least it ought to be…

But after showering and changing, he gave in to the urge to contact his cleaning crew, to ensure they put fresh linens on the bed so he wouldn't be able to smell Charlotte when he returned that evening. Which was more than a bit obsessive—because they didn't need reminding to change his sheets.

As he headed out for a series of meetings with his architects—to discuss plans for one of Helberg's old hotels in the Presidio—he couldn't shake the hollow ache in his chest. Or the constant blip in his heart rate…

While he spent the day discussing the cost and scope of the renovation work needed, thoughts of Charlotte—so captivating, so fierce, so forthright and alive as she discovered the joys of Zydeco and sex—kept intruding and making him lose the thread of the conversation.

By the time he got back to the apartment that night, he was exhausted and still preoccupied with every damn detail of what had happened between them—which wasn't like him at all.

He'd never had trouble moving on before, even back in high school.

But he couldn't shift the unpleasant thought that something had slipped through his fingers, something he wanted and couldn't have. Something he hadn't even known he wanted until he'd met Charlotte Courtney again—and danced with her in the moonlight.

He wasn't that reject kid any more who allowed other people to call the shots or let himself be hurt because people thought they were better than him.

So why had he let Charlotte's crummy kiss-off note make him feel like that again?

Damn her.

CHAPTER SIX

One week later

'HI, CHARLEY. I'VE asked our photographer, Rapinda, to send you some shots from our Fourth of July event.' Cassandra Broussard's voice was warm and friendly on the other end of the transatlantic phone line. 'The ones of you in your dress are terrific, definitely something to use on your social media channels.'

'Wow, really? Thank you so much, Cassie.' Charley beamed as she took in the view from the new space she was hoping to rent for Trouble Maker Designs, overlooking Shoreditch High Street. The elevated overground train line and the market stalls below gave the space a funky urban setting which was perfect for her brand. The bright, airy offices of an old printing warehouse also gave her the space she needed to hire some seamstresses. Working out of her front room wasn't going to cut it any more. 'I've had four commissions already from the connections I made at your party. I really can't thank you enough.'

Her new best friend gave an easy laugh. 'My pleasure, Charley. We don't usually issue photos from the event to the media, but Luke agreed the shots of you and Cade Landry were too good to waste. You guys look fabulous together.'

'Right. Thanks,' Charley said, her excitement downgrading at the mention of the man she hadn't been able to stop thinking about for over a week. 'It was fun,' she added.

Too much fun, really. Because she hadn't been able to stop second-guessing her decision to run out on Cade ever since.

If only she could start sleeping again, without dreaming about his hands, his lips, his tongue inciting her senses, the wry sensual smile curving his lips, or the tattoo on his chest tensing as he came with a throaty roar...

Heat exploded across her collarbone.

Yes, if only...

'Okay, well, my work here is done,' Cassie said, thankfully not asking any awkward questions about Cade.

As soon as the call ended, Charley checked her in-box and found a link to a file-sharing site. After pressing Download, ten photos flashed onto her phone.

As she examined each one, her heartbeat slowed, and heat burned her cheeks.

Rapinda Patel was clearly another of Cassie's protégés, because her work was exquisite, the shots vibrant and yet so fresh and real, capturing her and Cade in sharp focus on the dance floor—amidst a blur of colour.

Her bronze silk minidress looked incredible—sultry and sophisticated, but also fun and flirty. It made a statement about the Trouble Maker brand which Charley couldn't have replicated even if she'd paid a fortune for studio shots... But it was the two of them together—Cade's striking handsomeness, the strength of his body, the rugged appreciation in his expression and the fierce joy on her face as he launched her into a twirl—which made the biggest impression, adding raw sex appeal and dreamy romance to the compositions.

She let out a slow breath. She had to use them.

Surely he wouldn't care? It was a tiny bit dodgy to use his image without his consent. But contacting him was out of the question... He might think she hadn't moved on the way he had, and hearing that low, sexy Southern accent again would not help with her sleep deprivation.

She swallowed down the foolish yearning making her chest ache...just a little.

You made the right choice, Charley. Time to concentrate on your business now, instead of a one-night stand that didn't mean anything...

Decision made, she framed her three favourite shots, opened all the Trouble Maker accounts on the different apps she used, wrote a quick caption, and launched the stunning shots onto the internet before she could start the second-guessing game again.

Confidence and excitement—and a strange breathless-ness—washed away the prickle of unease as likes started popping up seconds later.

Cassie Broussard had given her the shots to use. And what would be the point of going to the most exclusive event of the summer season in the US if she couldn't take the best advantage of it?

Anyway, she needed the confidence boost, because she had to ring her brother Adam now...and beg him to release fifty thousand pounds from the trust fund her mother had left her that he still controlled. She'd made a point of never dipping into it before. Partly because she wanted to succeed on her own terms, but mostly because she had got the hump when she'd asked Adam for some start-up funding after graduating from fashion college and he had insisted she write a business plan. If that wasn't code for 'I don't trust you to make smart, career-focussed decisions and not muck this up', she did not know what was. She'd decided to use her own savings from her catwalk days to get started.

But she couldn't possibly handle all the commissions she already had on her own. So she was going to have to suck up her pride and persuade Adam she was a good investment. Maybe she didn't have a business plan which would impress him—she wasn't the CEO of a Fortune 500 company, after all—but she knew what she wanted, she knew the fashion business, and she had verifiable proof now her designs were good enough to attract the clientele she needed to turn Trouble Maker into a success.

End of.

Even so, her palms were sweating as she switched off the whirlwind of notifications on her phone and dialled Adam's private number. It was six in the morning Manhattan time, but Adam always woke up before dawn because he was a total workaholic—when he wasn't being a One Date Wonder.

As expected, her brother picked up on the second ring—sounding alert and aloof and as if he had shaved and showered and probably taken a five-mile run already.

'Charley, is there a problem?' he said without a hello.

She sighed. 'No! Why do you always assume there's a problem that you need to fix when I call you?'

'Because there usually is,' he said far too patiently. 'I distinctly recall getting a call at five a.m. when you had to be bailed out of a cell in Barcelona for swearing at a police officer.'

'That was years ago. And I didn't swear at him. It was a translation problem.'

'Or the time you ran away from St Jude's and wanted train fare to get to London.'

'That is actually ancient history.'

'The point is, Charley, you never phone me unless there's a problem. I always phone you.'

'Okay, fair point.' She bit down on the urge to point out she had been the one to phone once, begging to come back home after their father had sent her off to boarding school. But Adam hadn't been interested in talking about those messy things called emotions at the time. And now she was positive he only rang her out of a sense of duty and to check she wasn't still making a mess of her life. But she had to ask him a favour, so buttoning her resentment was necessary.

All part of being a grown-up businesswoman and not a screwed-up wild child.

'So why *are* you calling?' he asked bluntly. Adam didn't really do small talk any more than Cade Landry.

Then a thought occurred to her, a way of easing into the conversation about trust funds and business initiatives.

'I thought you'd like to know I was at tech billionaire Luke Broussard's Fourth of July bash in Marin County last weekend. The photos I just posted of me wearing one of my designs are already going viral, which is going to be invaluable publicity for Trouble Maker. *Free* publicity. *Organic* publicity. Plus, I picked up four new commissions while I was there. So I've decided to expand my operation...'

'Let me take a look,' he cut in, using the authoritative tone he always used when they spoke about her business— as if he was the only person in the world who knew how to run one efficiently.

'I posted them on all the Trouble Maker accounts,' she murmured, although the silence suggested he wasn't listening while he loaded them onto his phone.

A prickle of unease worked its way up her neck and then slithered down her spine as she imagined her brother examining the shots of her and Cade Landry dancing together... Surely he wouldn't be able to tell they'd done a lot more than just dance?

'Is that Cade Landry?' he asked, the interest in his tone surprising her. Adam never asked about her social life. Usually because it would mean talking about his own.

'Yes, I... Do you know him?' Heat scalded her cheeks.

'We play squash occasionally,' he murmured, obviously

still examining the photos of them dancing in minute detail. 'How do *you* know him?'

Terrific. Why hadn't she guessed her brother would know the man she'd had a torrid one-night stand with? Of course he would. Her luck was just that good.

She was still struggling to come up with an answer—which didn't sound like a lie—when Adam added, 'Because you seem extremely...close.'

'Stop looking at Cade and me and look at the dress!' she replied, exasperated and desperate to deflect the conversation before she spontaneously combusted from embarrassment. 'The point is those photos have already got a lot of views and...'

'Damn it, Charley, please tell me you didn't sleep with the guy.' The frustrated comment came so out of left field—because she and Adam *never* talked about anything *that* personal—the knee-jerk response was out of her mouth before she could consider how much it revealed.

'And that would be your business, why, exactly?'

He swore on the other end of the line. 'He's a player and a loner and is not good relationship material...'

'I'm not that naive, Adam,' she said, oddly intrigued by Adam's insight into Cade Landry's character. She'd guessed Cade was a loner at the party, but why did it suddenly seem significant?

'He's also in the market to acquire Helberg Holdings,' Adam continued.

'So what?' She knew Adam was after Helberg because their father had sold their mother's much-loved jewellery business, Montague's, to Reed Helberg for a single dollar out of spite. Although she'd never quite figured out why Adam was so hung up about buying it back again. Their mother had died fourteen years ago. But then, Charley had never presumed to understand her brother's motives for doing anything. She suspected it had something to do with the focussed and controlled and extremely dull person he'd become after their mother's suicide. But then Adam had been much closer to their mother than Charley had, probably because he'd had a chance to know her before her mental health had been so fragile and she'd become disconnected from reality.

But what did any of that have to do with her and Cade?

'So, I made a bet with him and Zane,' he said, sounding almost hesitant—not like him at all. 'Which you're now mixed up in.'

'What bet?'

The long-suffering sigh was new, too. When was the last time Adam had struggled to talk down to her, or explain in a patronising way what she needed to do next...?

'It was thought to be a good way to decide who should have Helberg without driving up the share price.'

'Adam, would you please get to the point. What bet did you make with Cade, and how could it possibly involve me?' Because that made no sense whatsoever... Adam had no idea she and Cade had ever met before their night together a week ago.

'We only date one woman for the duration of the summer, until Labor Day.'

What the...?

'Are you serious?' she murmured.

But before she could even acknowledge exactly how crass their bet was, between three grown men for goodness' sake, Adam replied.

'Unfortunately, yes, I wouldn't joke about anything that involves Montague's. I suspect he hit on you to provoke me.'

Her blood went cold, the humiliation she'd felt once before in connection with Cade Landry dowsing her like a bucket of ice water...

She hadn't just slept with Cade. She'd had the best sex

of her life with him. And she thought they'd connected on some emotional level. He'd made her feel seen, feel cherished, feel important—and all the time he'd only picked her to have a go at her brother? And to win a bet?

The bastard.

'How did you get those photos?' Adam asked. 'The party was over a week ago.'

'Why is that significant?' she said, her chest still imploding with mortification.

'He hasn't been seen dating anyone yet in public. But now those pictures are going viral, he's going to have to stick with you. Unless I'm overreacting and he *didn't* intend for you to be the one woman.'

Adam's reasoning didn't make her feel any better. In fact, it made her feel much worse. Cade had slept with her and then decided, *what*? That she wasn't someone he wanted to date for the whole summer? No wonder he'd offered to usher her out of the building incognito the next morning.

The absolute bastard.

And she'd now messed with his plan by publishing those photos.

Well, good.

Now he wouldn't be able to date anyone else for the rest of the summer. She hoped he died of sexual frustration. She let the anger in to fill up the empty space inside her—the empty space she remembered only too well.

Because it had always been there. Every time her mother looked right through her as a little girl. Or every time her father refused to be moved by her grief, or her unhappiness, or the reckless bad behaviour she'd resorted to as a teenager to get his attention. Or every time Adam had been condescending or patronising as a way not to engage with who she was as a person.

What a fool she'd been to think for a moment the night

she and Cade had shared, the connection they'd made, had been real.

'Fine, well,' she said, feeling broken again, in a way she hadn't in four years. 'That makes me feel so much better. *Not.*'

'I'll fix it,' said Adam, as if this was somehow his problem, when she knew it was all hers.

'No, *I'll* fix it,' she replied.

'I'm sorry. I did not mean for you to get caught in the middle of all this,' Adam began.

'I need you to release fifty thousand pounds from my trust fund.' She sliced neatly into his mea culpa, desperate to change the subject before the last of her confidence got flushed down the toilet. 'I can send you the contract for the space I'm planning to rent and the projections for the equipment and staff I need to hire to get my new commissions out...'

Perhaps there could be an upside to how devastated and humiliated she felt right now? The grinding pain in her stomach a reminder never to trust rich, entitled men who danced like gods and knew how to make you beg.

'That's why I was *actually* calling you...' she finished.

Not to have a debate about my recent dating history, which has made me feel like crap.

'I'll speak to the bank and have them release the funds,' Adam said without an argument—which meant he had to be feeling really guilty.

Unfortunately, though, it wasn't Adam she wanted to punch in the gut.

'Send over your projections,' he said, morphing into CEO mode, which was his default. 'I'll check them over and...'

'Thanks Adam, will do,' she said and disconnected the call. Before he could say more.

She needed to breathe, to ease the grinding pain in her stomach.

But as the pain twisted and tightened into hard, greasy knots, the idea of the new warehouse space she would now have the money to rent didn't fill her with the joy it had twenty minutes ago.

Had Cade Landry soured that, too?

She hated that he'd got to her. That she had liked him. That it had been more to her than sex, even though she'd spent a week trying to convince herself otherwise.

She considered deleting the photos of them together on the internet, because they were horribly tarnished now, too. Not a bright, beautiful moment of romance and possibilities and raw vivid sexuality, but a testament to what a fool she'd been to believe, for even a second, he'd seen more in her than just an easy conquest.

But as the likes and reposts and notifications continued to mount during the day, she began to relish the opportunity to get the word out about her business. When she started getting calls from journalists, she fielded the ones about her 'exciting new romance' with Cade by neither confirming or denying they were an item, stoking the media storm deliberately.

Why should she have any qualms about using the so-called 'Latest It Couple Romance' between the One Date Wonder Billionaire and the Former British Wild Child Turned Fashion Sensation to publicise Trouble Maker—when he'd had no qualms about using her?

A text arrived a few hours later from a withheld number. It simply said,

Charlotte, we need to talk...

She blocked the number, then booked the three-week buying trip to Italy which she had been planning for months to source fabrics for her designs. She could work on the designs for her new commissions from a base in Lake Como—the heart of Italian silk manufacture—while also visiting factories she'd short-listed in Tuscany and Puglia for the best wool and cotton producers.

Completely coincidentally, it would keep her out of London until the celebrity gossip mill had run its course.

Of course, her absence would also make it impossible for Cade Landry to contact her, which was just as well, because she never intended to see or speak to that rat bastard ever again.

CHAPTER SEVEN

Three weeks later

As the Landry chopper settled onto the lawn of the lavish belle époque villa hotel on the banks of Lake Como, Cade could feel the fury and frustration he had been holding in check for weeks start to choke him.

The hotel's staff rushed to meet him. Not surprising, given Landry Construction had spent a small fortune booking out every single room. Alongside the staff was the detective he'd hired—when Charlotte Courtney had hurled him into the middle of a social media tornado, then blocked his calls and disappeared.

As soon as the detective had contacted his PA with her whereabouts, he'd taken the company jet to Italy—more than ready to give her one hell of a nasty surprise.

'Clear to disembark,' the pilot announced.

After ripping off his headphones, Cade strode from the big black bird to be greeted by the young female investigator.

'Where is she?' he shouted above the thunder from slowing the blades.

'I can take you to her, *signor*. She is at a silk factory fifteen minutes' drive from this location.'

'No.' The last thing he needed was for them to get caught in public having a catfight.

Because he had no doubt Charlotte was not going to agree

to what had to happen next without an argument. Her out-spoken behaviour had captivated him in San Francisco. All it did now was infuriate him.

The prickle of awareness at the thought of seeing her again—and forcing her to return to the US with him—called him a liar. He dismissed it, because his libido and their combustible chemistry were not the driving force behind this situation any more.

The woman was a reckless, impulsive nightmare. But she'd left him with no choice. They were going to have to be a couple for the rest of the summer if he was going to win Helberg—a direct result of her decision to post those damn photos without asking him first.

The helicopter lifted into the sky and disappeared across the lake.

The approaching twilight gave the water a golden glow. The four-storey Italianate villa nestled into terraced botanical gardens which now housed a five-star hotel and spa couldn't have looked more romantic.

Cade frowned. *How damned ironic.*

But the estate was also situated at the end of a private road. After spending a day moving the guests out at his request, the management had been more than willing to accommodate his meeting with Charlotte in complete privacy.

There would be no photographers, no press, and no members of the public to interrupt them—or witness any temper tantrums—while he explained to her in words of one syllable the consequences of her actions.

She'd got her pound of flesh—using his image to push her business. Now she was going to have to deal with the fall-out—just like he'd been dealing with it for three solid weeks.

'She's going to be here tonight?' he asked as they headed across the manicured lawn. 'And she doesn't know I'll be here?'

The detective nodded. 'Yes, her driver and the *agriturismo* where she has been staying have been generously compensated for their cooperation.'

Cade nodded. It had been a major operation—and cost a small fortune—but no way was he giving her the chance to run out on him again.

The hotel manager arrived to greet them both as Cade and the detective walked into the hotel's grandiose foyer.

'We have *la terrazza privata* ready for your evening meal, Signor Landry, as soon as your guest arrives,' the hotel's executive manager said with a confident smile. 'It is *bellissima* in the sunset, perfect for *un appuntamento romantico*.'

A romantic date, my ass.

Cade's Italian didn't have to be fluent for him to guess even the middle-aged Italian hotel boss had probably heard of the media furore surrounding his 'romance' with Charlotte—which had only started to calm down in the last week.

Great.

The inconvenient prickle of awareness became a definite hum as he headed up to the penthouse suite and showered off the twelve-hour flight.

The fury and frustration which had been driving him for weeks—every time he got doorstepped by another celebrity hack, every time his team hit another dead end while trying to locate Charlotte, every time he relived the moment when he had woken up alone in his Embarcadero apartment and found her damn kiss-off note—finally began to ease. In its place, anticipation and something which felt a lot like exhilaration surged. As the sun sank towards the lake, he imagined the not so *romantico* date he had planned for this evening's entertainment, once he finally had Charlotte back where he wanted her.

'*Carlo, dov'é questo*?' Charley asked the local driver she'd hired as the cab wound down the poplar-flanked driveway of an extremely expensive lakeside estate.

Carlo had told her—from what she could gather with her rusty Italian—that Signor Chiesa, the farmer she'd been staying with for two weeks, had arranged alternative accommodation for her tonight because of a broken *something* at his farm. But this couldn't be right? It looked way outside her budget.

'*Non posso pagare,*' she added, trying to explain she couldn't pay for this place.

'*Si, si, é tutto pagato,*' Carlo replied.

It was all paid for... *Really?*

Her eyes widened as the cab drove out of the trees and a magnificent villa appeared, situated in palatial gardens on the edge of the lake. The historic structure's ornate plasterwork and lavish design were a testament to a bygone era of nineteenth-century grandeur. It looked more like a royal palace than a hotel, despite the discreet sign announcing it as La Bella Grande Villa Hotel.

Charley was still staring at the luxurious building as she stepped out of the car.

She asked again—in her broken Italian—if Carlo was sure this was the right place.

But he simply smiled and nodded, then handed her the precious case full of samples she'd spent the day collecting before firing off some fatherly advice about getting a good night's rest. She was still standing there, dwarfed by the magnificent hotel, as she watched Carlo and his cab disappear back down the driveway.

She took a deep, steadying breath. The stunning Italianate villa's plasterwork was bathed in an amber glow from the sunset.

Well...if Carlo says it's the right place, it must be.

She didn't know how Signor Chiesa had managed to find her a place this classy for her last night in Italy at no extra cost. It seemed pretty deserted. Perhaps they didn't have that many bookings?

She tightened her fingers on the handle of her briefcase and yawned, her frown lifting—and a weary smile forming. Why not enjoy it? After all, she'd earned a bit of extra luxury.

The last three weeks had been incredible. And utterly exhausting.

After several days in Venice negotiating with a family-run supplier who had been making luxury velvet since the seventeen hundreds, she'd headed to Tuscany and Puglia to source the most incredible wool and cotton blends. And for the last two weeks, she'd travelled throughout Lombardy, finishing at the silk weavers today—where she had commissioned some unique embroidered silks at a very reasonable price.

Of course, in the back of her mind the whole time had been the social media storm she'd caused in the US. Italy was far enough removed from the whole debacle she hadn't been dragged into it. But in a weird way, that had actually made her start to feel a little guilty—once her knee-jerk fury with Cade and his stupid bet had faded.

He'd been a total jerk. But she had been a bit of one, too.

She'd deleted the photos last week, but the damage had already been done. Not correcting the journalists she'd spoken to before leaving London about the state of their relationship, or rather non-relationship—just to annoy him—had also been a tad immature. She'd seen a huge increase in traffic to her website, so she didn't feel *that* bad. But now her buying trip was over, she would need to extricate herself from their fake relationship.

She walked up the steps into an enormous marble entrance hall—which was also surprisingly quiet. Where *were* the other guests? Was the place even open?

Who cares, frankly?

Tonight she needed a warm bath and then a long night's sleep in the lap of luxury.

Her energy levels had been on zero for days—a low-grade nausea making it hard for her to focus. And even though she'd loved the little *agriturismo* farm she'd used as her base in Lombardy, it would be quite nice not to have to make small talk in Italian over dinner with Signor Chiesa and his wife.

She rang the silver-plated bell on the mahogany reception desk nestled next to a lavish sweeping staircase. A young, smartly dressed woman appeared, wearing a tag which said *Alessia, Reception*, accompanied by a bellboy in full livery.

Wow, this place is seriously plush.

Charley struggled to control her grin. She was going to have to send Signor Chiesa a thank-you message for arranging this.

'Signora Courtney, Aldo will take your items to your room,' the efficient young woman said in perfect English as the bellboy bowed and took Charley's briefcase, then disappeared. 'We have already put the rest of your luggage in the Como Suite.'

She had a whole suite in this beautiful place? Seriously? Charley felt the weariness ease a little more.

But before she could thank the manager, the woman was already leading her through a huge—and completely deserted—dining salon.

'Let me show you to the lakeside *terrazza*,' she announced. 'Where we have your evening meal waiting.'

'But I didn't order anything,' Charley said hastily, a little less pleased as she calculated the cost of a meal in a place like this.

The woman glanced over her shoulder and smiled. 'The meal is included in your accommodation, Signora Courtney.' And, because she was clearly a mind-reader, added, 'There is no extra to pay.'

'Oh, okay, *grazie*,' she said, not wanting to seem ungrateful—even though she wasn't sure she wanted a meal. She'd been queasy all day and had hardly eaten. But maybe the lack of food was precisely why she felt so depleted? And the menu here was bound to be amazing. Perhaps it would tempt her appetite out of hiding?

Charley followed the woman past the empty dining tables. They walked through a pair of elegantly appointed glass doors. The view was even more breathtaking on the wide terrace which wrapped around the building, the red-and-orange glow of the sunset casting a redolent light over Lake Como and the centuries-old poplar trees, the water lapping gently against a private dock.

Charley sighed. The relaxed, perfectly appointed elegance of La Bella Grande was straight out of a luxury tourist brochure. The super-efficient receptionist led her to a single table, draped in white linen and laid with fine china and crystal stemware...for two people.

Charley frowned again as Alessia excused herself.

How odd. Was another one of the hotel's guests going to join her?

Her exhausted brain was still trying to process the table setting when she heard footsteps. A tall figure appeared, silhouetted in the dying sunshine, at the far end of the terrace and strode towards her. She blinked.

Was she hallucinating? Because he moved just like...

Then the light from the dining room illuminated dramatic features—and a deep husky voice sent shock waves through her fatigued body.

'Hello, Charlotte. About damn time you showed up.'

CHAPTER EIGHT

CADE LANDRY? In Lake Como? What the...?

'What are you doing in Italy?' Charley finally managed to ask, her head starting to ache.

And why do you look so gorgeous? she thought, annoyed with her physical response to him. Still.

The catastrophic frown on his face gave her the answer before he replied.

'I'm here to see you,' he said. 'Didn't you hear we're the new It Couple everyone back home is talking about?' His tone was low and husky, reminding her too forcefully of their one night together, but there was carefully leashed fury beneath—and the ruthless bite of disapproval. 'I've been taking the heat for three weeks for those photos. Now I've finally found you, I set up this meeting in private so we can get a few things straight.'

He sounded angry—*really* angry. And while she could sort of sympathise on one level—perhaps it had been a bit cowardly to throw him to the wolves, then high-tail it to Italy—his self-righteous tone, and the judgemental frown, had her own anger at the hurt he'd caused returning full force. Not to mention that he'd just completely ruined her surprise luxury lakeside break.

He must have been the one to pay for all this. It had never been a lucky coincidence, a heaven-sent reward for all her hard work over the past three weeks. It had simply been a billionaire's trick to trap her so he could tell her off again, like he had four years ago.

Well, this time she wasn't going to run off with her tail between her legs.

'I get it. So *you're* the injured party now, are you?' she hurled the accusation back at him. 'When you were the one who chose to sleep with me on a bet?'

His scarred eyebrow launched up his forehead. *'What?'*

'You heard me. The asinine bet you made with my brother and his friend. I know all about it. Adam told me. The only-dating-one-woman-for-the-summer thing. That's why you're here, isn't it? Because you're stuck with me now so you can win some stupid property deal. But tell me, when did you decide it wasn't going to be me? That you would just use me and then discard me? While we were having the best sex of my life or before that? While you were deliberately seducing me with your dance skills?'

And why did you decide it couldn't be me? That I wasn't good enough?

The pathetic question echoed in her head, but she cut it off.

He'd made her feel cherished, and then he'd trashed it all. And hurt her, when she'd convinced herself long ago she couldn't be hurt. It would be funny if it didn't make her feel so exposed. How could she have fallen into the age-old trap of mistaking great sex for actual emotional engagement?

'And as if that isn't bad enough,' she carried on, because he seemed to have been struck dumb by her offensive, 'you bribed Carlo and Signor Chiesa to do your bidding. Of all the sneaky...'

'Wait a damn minute,' he roared, cutting off her outrage in full swing. '*You* ran out on *me*, not the other way around. And the bet had nothing to do with why I asked you to dance. Or why I slept with you. I wanted you and you wanted me and we were so damn good together I haven't been able to forget you. And believe me, I've tried.'

She took some solace from his angry acknowledgement their lovemaking had been special for him, as well, but then he spoilt that, too.

'But you're damn straight we're stuck together now for the rest of the summer—because acquiring Helberg is important to me and my business. And I'll be damned if I'll apologise for paying off whoever I had to, to get you here. Do you think I want to be in Italy, hiring out a whole hotel, just so I can talk with you in private because you were too immature to answer a single one of my texts or calls before blocking me? *Newsflash*, I don't. Any more than I wanted to be asked intrusive questions about my sex life by every celebrity hack from here to California… Questions you encouraged by making out like we were a couple in all the interviews and free publicity you got off the back of those photos.'

'I never said we were dating!' she managed in her defence, but the trickle of guilt at his outrage was starting to play footsie with the nausea in her stomach.

'You didn't deny it, though, did you?' he snarled. 'So here we damn well are.'

His angry words were still echoing across the lake— her own fury starting to choke her—when a young waiter cleared his throat loudly, making them both aware of his presence.

'*Signor, signorina*, would you like your antipasti now?' the poor boy asked, the two loaded plates in his hands trembling.

The nausea bounced into Charley's throat at the scent of roasted garlic. 'No,' she said.

At the exact same time, Cade commanded, 'Serve us, then leave.'

The waiter did Cade's bidding and shot off.

'Sit down,' Cade said, the low-grade fury suggesting he was holding on to his temper by a thread.

'I'm not eating with you,' she replied.

'Sit. Down. Now,' he demanded through gritted teeth before grabbing one of the chairs and smacking it down on the terrace. 'Or so help me, I will pick you up and put your butt in that chair myself.'

She glared at him. 'Go on then, manhandle me. All that makes you is a bully who is bigger than I am. As well as a sneak.'

She was not scared of his temper. The last thing she needed was to have a tussle with him, because she would probably lose, but she also knew he wouldn't hurt her. So she was more than ready to take her chances. And fight dirty if she had to.

He glared right back at her, the muscles she remembered admiring straining under the white shirt he wore with suit trousers. He thrust his fingers through his hair, dragging the thick waves back from his face, his movements stiff with anger. The charged silence seemed to snap between them, their standoff creating a force field of righteous fury and bruised egos.

But then he swung away and shouted a profanity into the night air. When he turned back, his features had relaxed a fraction. Enough for her to see the frustration in his face.

'Sit down, Charlotte,' he said again, but this time his tone was more resigned than furious. 'I won't touch you.'

It was enough of a climb-down to let her keep her pride.

Grudgingly she perched her bottom on the chair he'd pulled out. But once she was seated, she was grateful for the support, because her knees had begun to shake.

She'd never been afraid of confrontation. Had always

been ready to speak her mind. But maybe she'd been a bit too ready.

He lifted an expensive bottle of wine out of the ice bucket next to the table.

'You want a drink?' he asked.

She shook her head. This answer, at least, was easy.

He poured himself a generous glass, then took a gulp. She had the sense, though, he wasn't really tasting it.

'I don't bully women,' he said as he placed the glass on the starched linen tablecloth. 'And I refuse to feel bad for doing what I had to do to get you here. But my temper got out of hand, and for that I apologise.'

'Fine.' She nodded. 'Then I guess I can apologise for posting those photos without asking you first.'

'Okay. Apology accepted.' It wasn't exactly a truce, but it was close enough. Until he added, 'But now we need to talk about the consequences.'

'What consequences?'

'Don't play dumb, Charlotte,' he said, the edge back. 'I'm not about to forfeit Helberg. So you're gonna have to accompany me to the States tomorrow morning. And date me, in public at least, until Labor Day.'

She stared. Not really believing he could actually be serious. Unfortunately, though, he looked deadly serious.

'But that's...'

Ridiculous? Extreme? An over-reach of epic proportions?

She was so astounded at the steely determination in his expression she was speechless, for one whole second. 'I refuse to do it. I don't want to date you, in public or in private. We don't even like each other.'

'We like each other well enough,' he said implacably, as if he hadn't just yelled a profanity across Lake Como for most of Lombardy to hear.

'I see. Do you shout like that at all your girlfriends, then?'

'Nope, but I've never dated a woman before who's as contrary as you are,' he announced. Strangely, although frustration still tightened his tone, she could also see approval in his expression.

That would be the same approval which had derailed her common sense once before. The answering pulse of awareness in her belly, right alongside the nausea, only disturbed her more.

What was wrong with her? Cade Landry was a domineering alpha jerk. He was only here because he needed her to win a stupid bet—and he'd used underhanded methods to put her at his mercy. How could she possibly still be attracted to him?

'It won't work,' she said. 'Apart from the fact I have more important things to do than being your stunt date for the summer—such as setting up my workshop in London and working on my new commissions,' she added forcefully, to make it clear her business was just as important as his. 'We'd end up killing each…'

'Would those be the new commissions I helped you secure at the Broussards' *fais*?' he cut in, slicing through her indignation and making guilt flare in her queasy stomach.

'I don't see how that's relevant…?' she managed, determined to believe it wasn't.

So *what* if he'd helped introduce her around at the party? He'd only done it because he wanted to get into her knickers. And the quality of her work spoke for itself.

'Uh-huh…' He placed his elbow on the table and leant forward, which made her uncomfortably aware of the way his tailored shirt stretched across his pecs. 'Well, how about this for relevance? If you don't accompany me and pose as my loving girlfriend for the next five weeks, until Labor Day, I'll sue you for invasion of privacy, and using my name and image without my permission to garner free publicity for your business.'

She stiffened, shocked by the steely threat, and the flicker of challenge in the sapphire blue eyes. Was he getting off on this?

'You wouldn't dare!' she snapped. He was bluffing. He had to be. 'And anyway, it would be completely counterproductive... If you sued me, it would torpedo your chances of winning that bet.'

'Try me,' he murmured. 'But fair warning, Charlotte. You don't want to underestimate how ruthless a guy who grew up in the child welfare system in St Martin Parish, Louisiana—being bumped from one place to another like a piece of trash—can be. Or how dirty I'm prepared to fight to get what I want.'

She tensed, shocked by the ruthless tone and the brittle cynicism in his eyes.

But then her heart wedged in her throat as she noticed the muscle ticking in his jaw, and the scar which cut through the day-old stubble on his chin—and she digested what he had revealed about his past without intending to.

She'd been vaguely aware of the stories about his background. That he had grown up in foster care and come from nothing to build the Landry empire. It was all part of the self-made man myth which he had helped to promote. But there had been a raw note in his voice when he talked about the boy who had felt like trash, which was very different from the man she had met in San Francisco and all those years ago in Las Vegas. The charismatic, arrogant, supremely confident man who hadn't appeared to have a single chink in his armour.

And the strangest thought occurred to her.

Had she hurt him? By running out on him that morning? She tried to bury the sentimental thought. She couldn't drop down that rabbit hole again, of believing they had shared more than an intense physical connection. But she couldn't seem to stop herself. It occurred to her his presence here, his decision to fly to Italy and buy out a whole hotel just to trap her into having a private dinner with him, and his determination to make her date him—rather than just dating no one for the rest of the summer to keep to the one date rule—didn't make a lot of sense.

She cut off the wayward thought because it wasn't helping with her nausea, especially when he picked up his fork and began to eat the antipasti, apparently waiting for her to capitulate. He ate calmly and methodically as if he didn't have a care in the world—and hadn't just threatened her with legal action to bend her to his will.

Think on that, Charley, before you start getting choked up about his difficult childhood.

Whatever Cade Landry had been through as a boy, he certainly wasn't vulnerable any more.

'Even if I wanted to, I can't spend the next five weeks in the US,' she said, trying for pragmatic, because having a pissing contest with someone as ruthless as he was not likely to end well for her. 'I've signed contracts, so my clients could sue me, too, if I don't deliver. And I'm about to start hiring seamstresses to help with the work who will be based in London.'

To her surprise, the muscle in his jaw relaxed.

'I have an event I want you to attend with me in Manhattan tomorrow night. But after that, I'll be based on the West Coast. You can't stay in London if we're gonna make this fly, but I can have my people organise suitable workspace in San Francisco and have anything you need shipped out to the West Coast so you can relocate your business there for the summer. You can hire whoever you want for the duration. All expenses paid, including their salaries.'

The offer was surprisingly generous and, annoyingly, more than a little tempting.

Adam had released the fifty thousand pounds from her trust fund, but money was still going to be tight until she saw the turnover from her new commissions. The salaries for the two seamstresses were also a big expense, because she wanted to hire the best.

But she wasn't ready to surrender yet…especially as she wasn't sure where the little leap in her belly—which felt too much like exhilaration—was coming from.

But then another problem occurred to her.

'Wait a minute. Are you expecting me to move in with you?' she asked, appalled.

Having to act as his loving girlfriend in public would be tough enough, but she was still stupidly attracted to Cade—probably for the simple reason he was the only man who had ever given her an orgasm. While she did not plan to beat herself up too much about the arousal pulsing insistently between her thighs, as she watched him eat in the sunset, she also did not want to tempt fate any more than was absolutely necessary.

He lowered his fork, but the instant denial she had been hoping for didn't come. Instead, his lips curved in the sensual smile which always made her blood pressure rise.

'I don't have a problem with exploring our chemistry some more. It's just sex after all. A basic physical urge which we happen to be very good at. You said yourself it was the best sex of your life.'

'Right,' she muttered, the telltale blush—which only he had ever been able to trigger—firing into her cheeks.

Why on earth had she blurted *that* out? Talk about giving the man ammunition.

'I'm not going to deny, it was damn good for me too,' he continued, not helping to diminish the blush one bit. 'But it wouldn't be part of the deal, no. You can live wherever you want—and I'll fund all your living expenses, just as long as you're close enough that I can call on you to accompany me to any and all events I choose to attend, some of which may be at short notice.'

'Okay, well, thanks for clarifying that,' she murmured grumpily.

So basically, she would be totally at his beck and call then. *Terrific.*

He chuckled, which made her feel even more exposed, and transparent. And wary.

It's just sex.

That's what he'd said. And he was right. So why couldn't she stop her heart beating too fast at the prospect of fake dating him?

He tore off a chunk of bread and used it to wipe the olive oil off his plate. 'Eat your supper and think about it,' he said far too easily. 'We can figure out all the details tomorrow before we fly out.'

She tensed at the definitive statement.

'I haven't said I'll go with you yet,' she protested, even though she wasn't sure she had much of a choice.

No doubt he was more than ruthless enough to follow through on his threat to sue. And in some ways, she couldn't blame him. She *had* created a media storm, however unintentionally. And while she was still super aggrieved at the thought of that stupid bet, this negotiation had at least established one thing.

Theirs was not and had never been an emotional connection.

Plus, if she was being entirely practical, the chance to have him pay for everything for a whole five weeks would be great for her business. She could work on the commissions and get the revenue from them into the bank to invest with her fifty thousand pounds when she returned to the UK. And dating him would give her loads more free publicity, because she intended to wear her own designs at every event he suggested.

Perhaps there was a way to turn this disaster into a professional opportunity?

'I'm also not that hungry,' she admitted.

His eyes narrowed, studying her with an intensity she found unsettling. 'You look washed out, Charlotte. Are you unwell?'

It was the last thing she had expected him to say. But even so, the silly flicker of emotion at the gruff concern in his voice shocked her.

'I'm fine...' she said, although she didn't feel fine. Not only was she exhausted and still feeling sick, her emotions were all over the place—especially where Cade Landry was concerned. Which could not be good. 'It's just...it's been a long three weeks. And I'd like to go to bed now—in the very expensive luxury suite you paid for so sneakily,' she added, unable to miss the opportunity for a final dig. 'To consider your proposal.'

He nodded, not reacting to the jab. But when she stood up, he stood, too.

He walked around the table and snagged her hand before she could make the speedy exit she'd planned. Rough calluses rasped against her palm and had a predictable effect on the pulsing in her sex. But before she could find the energy to tug her hand free, he had lifted her fingers to his lips and brushed a kiss across her knuckles.

The gesture was chivalrous, and strangely compelling, but not nearly as compelling as his husky tone when he added, 'I intend to make this work, Charlotte, for both of us. Get some sleep.' His lips curved in that tempting smile she remembered far too well. 'And enjoy the suite, which you'll be glad to hear cost me a fortune. We leave at ten tomorrow morning. We can discuss everything you need and make all the necessary arrangements on the flight to the US.'

She could have said no and argued with him some more—but the arrogant assumption that she had capitulated already was tempered by his concerned expression. And the warmth of his touch.

She hadn't signed the lease yet for her new workspace in Shoreditch. She'd have to juggle a lot of stuff, but she could set things in motion on the plane tomorrow with his help. And she definitely planned to take full advantage of his financial support while posing as his stunt girlfriend. Not to mention tonight's suite. Knowing his sneakiness had cost him a fortune would be some consolation at least.

She gave a weary sigh and nodded. 'Fine, I'll come to the US, but I want my own place.'

'Sure.' His sensual smile made the pulse in her belly pound harder, though, the challenging expression unmistakeable.

She dragged her hand free but had to bunch her fingers into a fist to neutralise the buzz on her knuckles which was now playing havoc with the pulse in her sex.

As she trudged up to her room, she wanted to be furious with him—and with herself—for being forced into this position… She thought of Adam and his stake in the bet. She didn't want to make her brother lose Montague's, the jewellery company owned by Helberg, but frankly he was on his own for entering into such an idiotic agreement with Cade and Zane in the first place. Plus, she'd never quite understood why buying back their mother's old jewellery company meant so much to him. Their mum had taken no interest in it herself at the time of her death, as far as Charley could remember.

As she sank into a hot bath in the enormous clawfoot tub

in front of a marble terrace which looked out over the lake, it occurred to her she wasn't angry with Cade any more, because all she really felt was hopelessly confused. And even a little scared, thanks to the flicker of anticipation in her stomach alongside the nausea.

Because that flicker reminded her of the girl who couldn't resist taking stupid risks simply to make herself feel valued—which she had always ended up regretting.

What she needed to remember was that Cade Landry was a dangerous man, because he had the power to make her *want* to do those impulsive, reckless things again, no matter what the consequences...

CHAPTER NINE

SOMETHING'S WRONG.

Cade frowned as Charlotte slept in the leather seat opposite him in the Landry jet.

Why did she still look so exhausted? And why did he feel uncomfortable about the fact she hadn't put up more of a fight this morning? Wasn't having her at his mercy exactly what he'd flown out to Lake Como to achieve?

But he couldn't shake the uneasiness in his gut as he observed the slow rise and fall of her breathing.

He'd been braced for an argument when she'd appeared for breakfast at the hotel. So he'd made sure he was well ahead of her—by setting up a team to relocate her business to San Francisco for the rest of the summer and getting his EA to handle any issues with her visa status. But there had been no fuss, no more angry words. Instead she'd spent breakfast discussing options for her workspace and accommodations with his property management team on the West Coast while picking at her food.

From the fascinating conversation he'd listened in to with interest, he'd discovered she was a smart, erudite businesswoman who knew what she wanted but could also be flexible and take expert advice when needed. Both qualities Cade considered invaluable when making a startup like hers a success.

She'd appeared worn-out last night, once he'd taken the

time to really look at her. And while she'd finished what needed to be done this morning once they had boarded the Landry jet in Milan—settling on a space hire in the Embarcadero and a condo in the same building as his—she'd barely touched her lunch before dropping back to sleep.

He'd driven himself to exhaustion too, once—especially during the early days—pulling eighteen-and twenty-hour shifts, fuelled on coffee and adrenaline and ambition for weeks on end. He knew what it looked like when the inevitable crash came. So why was he so upset at the thought of Charlotte burning herself out?

Her welfare wasn't his concern.

But as she shifted on the seat—struggling to find a comfortable position—he undid his belt. Touching her probably wasn't smart. He'd learned that yesterday evening when her stunned reaction to his knuckle buzz had left him hard and aching. But he needed her well-rested by the time they hit New York. Being photographed at the party tonight would establish her as his summer date—and hopefully give the media what they wanted so they would leave him the hell alone. Plus, he hoped to run into Zane deMarco—who had some explaining to do about the candid shots of him getting up close and personal with a Helberg employee at a pretzel stand while he had already racked up at least one other date for the summer so far.

He unclipped Charlotte's belt and scooped her into his arms.

Her eyes opened just as he got a lungful of her scent. The streak of sensation hitting his groin wasn't helped by the sight of her wide green eyes and her heavy sigh.

'What are you doing?' she murmured, still groggy.

'Taking you to the bedroom in back,' he said. 'I want you awake when we get to New York.'

She blinked, but instead of protesting, she looped an arm

around his neck, tucked her head against his collarbone, and yawned. Her warm breath brushed his neck, sending the sensations in his gut into free fall.

'Thanks, Sir Galahad,' she mumbled.

After placing her on the bed, he eased off her sneakers and tucked the quilt over her, the arrow in his gut becoming sharp and insistent.

The constriction in his ribs tightened as she turned away from him and curled onto her side, fast asleep again.

Just sex. And chemistry.

He headed back to his seat, determined to work for the rest of the flight. But he couldn't shake the disturbing thought that his motives for chasing Charlotte all the way to Italy, and blackmailing her into returning to the US with him, might be about more than just the bet he had to win...

'How are you feeling, Charlotte?'

Charley forced a strained smile at the low question from the man sitting opposite her in the chauffeur-driven car—who looked typically devastating in a designer suit—as they cut through the snarl of evening traffic in Manhattan's Meatpacking District.

'Fabulous. Bring it on,' she said, trying to sound confident and bold, despite the knots in her stomach.

At least the low-grade nausea of the last few days had faded after her catatonic-like sleep on his plane. She'd had a solid six hours to add to the ten hours in Italy the night before. She still didn't feel entirely herself, but she felt better than she had when she'd agreed to this charade—give or take the odd heart bump and the hot pulse in her abdomen every time she was near her fake date.

Although this arrangement didn't feel particularly fake any more.

Especially after she had woken up on the plane to find him carrying her to bed with that watchful expression on his face.

He had been staring at her the same way ever since his car had picked her up at the stylist's ten minutes ago—as if he were assessing her well-being.

'We don't have to stay long. I've booked you a suite at the hotel the event is at for tonight,' he added. 'Then we fly to the West Coast tomorrow.'

'Thanks,' she managed.

She hadn't seen him since they'd landed at JFK four hours ago. After disembarking, she'd been whisked off to a private beauty therapist's—where she had been primped to within an inch of her life—and then the stylist's, where a selection of her designs had been waiting for her.

'And thanks for getting my wardrobe shipped over in time for tonight,' she added.

'It was part of our deal,' he said simply.

True, so why did it feel like more?

Cade Landry was a take-charge, demanding guy who got things done—and his competence was as sexy as the way he filled out a tuxedo. But why did this situation suddenly feel so overwhelming?

He'd thought of everything in preparation to present her as his date at this event—and establish their status as a couple.

It's about the bet, Charley. Remember that.

She smoothed her palms down her gown. The sky-blue tulle and chiffon creation was a prototype she had been working on for months. The exposure it would get Trouble Maker at a statement party like this one was going to be invaluable.

Surely that was why she was nervous? After all, she had once revelled in showing off for the media—back in her bad old days. The nerves couldn't have anything to do with the scent of his woodsy, spicy cologne, which brought back a host of other disturbing memories.

The car pulled to the kerb in front of a huge brutalist building which towered over this entrance to the High Line, the camera flashes visible through the tinted windows.

He stepped out of the car and leaned back in—blocking her from the chaos outside—to offer her his arm.

'Let's do this, Charlotte,' he murmured, the low Southern accent rippling over her skin as his eyes deepened with encouragement, and that disturbing approval.

Her unruly heartbeat and the knots in her stomach went haywire.

'Sure thing, Sir Galahad,' she quipped back, trying to even her breathing as she climbed out. He shielded her from the cameras, and the shouts of the photographers and celebrity journalists. But as the muscles in his forearm tensed beneath her fingers, her sex clenched in unison.

When was she going to stop feeling so attuned to this man?

They ran the gauntlet together with his arm around her the whole way. As if she were special to him, when she knew she wasn't. They were ushered into one of the private lifts, alone.

She let out a relieved breath. 'Well, that was hideous.'

'It should keep them happy for a while,' he murmured, still watching her with eagle-sharp eyes.

'I'm just hoping they got a good shot of my dress, and they remember to mention Trouble Maker,' she managed.

How did he do that? Suck all the oxygen out of the lift? Because he'd done the exact same thing four years ago in that lobby in Vegas... And why would she rather suffocate than step away from him?

A smile curved his lips, as if he knew the war she was waging with herself.

Good grief, was she still so transparent?

'I'll have my press people make sure they mention the dress,' he said. His gaze travelled over her figure, sparking a predictable endorphin rush. 'It's striking,' he murmured. 'But not as striking as the woman wearing it.'

'Are you trying to flatter me into submission now?' she asked, aiming for flippant, but getting breathless instead.

'Is it working?'

'It doesn't need to,' she said as the air continued to clog in her lungs. 'You've already got me exactly where you want me.'

'Not quite.' He touched her cheek with his thumb, then skimmed it down the side of her face.

She shivered instinctively, the naked need in his eyes shocking her. But still, she couldn't step away from the flame.

'I want you back in my bed, Charlotte.' He trailed his thumb across her lips, and they trembled. 'And I think you want to be there, too.'

His hand settled on her neck, that dangerous thumb stroking the giddy pulse in her collarbone.

She should tell him to take a hike. It's what they'd agreed to. But how could she? When they both knew he was right. And she'd never been a good liar.

The lift bell pinged, and a breath gushed out of her lungs. *Saved by the bell, literally.*

The doors opened onto a lavish lobby area, accented in vintage mahogany and butter-soft leather. The staggering view across the Hudson River to Jersey City looked impossibly enchanting despite the throb of sound and fury coming from the DJ manning the decks in the party space beyond. The view, though, was nowhere near as heart-stopping as the glint of purpose in his eyes.

Could he see her need? Feel the pulsing ache which had been driving her nuts since he'd appeared in Lake Como? *Probably!*

'Showtime,' he murmured.

But as he took her arm and led her into the party, it wasn't the strobe lighting, or the wall of noise, or the press of bodies making her heart pound.

It was the giddy pulse of arousal—and something more—every time he introduced her as his, every time his palm settled possessively on her back or her hip or her waist, every time he leaned close to shout something witty or provocative above the throbbing beat of the music—and everything his words kept echoing in her head, a tantalising promise, impossible to deny.

I want you back in my bed, Charlotte. And I think you want to be there, too.

I'm out of the bet. I don't want it. You and Adam carry on without me.

Zane deMarco was out of the running for Helberg.

Cade knew he should feel elated as he watched the guy disappear after the pretty brunette from Helberg's HQ—who was not the date who had arrived at the event on deMarco's arm. This development was better than anything Cade had hoped for when he'd cornered Zane on the balcony outside while Charlotte was in the restroom. But the stunned look on Zane's face when the Helberg woman had stormed through the crowd towards him, looking ready to murder the corporate raider, had soured the moment somehow.

What was going on between deMarco and the Helberg chick? And why did Cade feel unsettled about the way whatever it was had made Zane throw in the towel so easily?

Stepping back into the party, he spotted Charlotte coming out of the restroom. Something deep and visceral tugged hard in his gut. And he headed through the crowd of dancers towards her, determined to forget about the damn bet for the rest of the night.

She'd done her part this evening without an argument.

Acted like they were a couple for the cameras and then danced with him—her slender body gyrating in his arms, effortlessly seductive, while also being frustratingly just out of reach.

Everything was working out just how he wanted it. So why did he feel so on edge?

Her gaze locked with his as he reached her, and he saw something fierce and yet guarded in her eyes. Something which sharpened the arrow of need in his gut. And suddenly he knew why.

He'd been by her side all evening, inhaling her intoxicating scent and feeling her shiver of response every time he touched her—those casual, intimate touches between couples that were supposed to be for show, but hadn't been, ever since he had cornered her in the elevator.

He grasped her hand. 'We're done here.'

Her eyebrows shot up. 'Excuse me?' she said, as if she didn't know exactly where tonight had always been heading.

'We're leaving,' he added, tugging her through the crowd.

The elevator in the entrance area had too many people to catch it, so he slammed his palm against the emergency exit and took the stairwell.

'Cade, what on earth…' she cried, her fingers tugging against his hold as he took the stairs to the penthouse level. 'Where are you taking me?'

'To your suite,' he said and tightened his grip.

His EA had given him a key card for her room, which he was supposed to pass to her once they were through at the event. That had been the plan, anyway, to escort her to the suite, then head to his place on Fifth and meet her at the airport tomorrow for their flight to San Francisco.

To hell with that.

They needed to establish some ground rules for the next month, or this arrangement was going to be unworkable.

And ground rule number one was to stop pretending this was just about the bet. Because it was also about the sex.

The memory of her in his bed was still giving him hell—pheromones-wise—but worse was the memory of the morning after, when he'd woken up to find her note.

That he was still hung up about that note made it clear they had unfinished business. Business they could only finish by dealing with the sexual tension which had been building between them all night.

He pressed the key card against the door to the High Line Suite and marched inside. The darkness through the room's glass walls glittered with the lights from the Jersey shore and the boats on the Hudson. The spectacular view didn't register, though, as he swung around to press Charlotte against the wall and cup her flushed cheeks.

'Tell me you don't want this, too,' he demanded, 'and I'll back off.' But he'd be damned if he was going to avoid stating the obvious any longer.

She stared at him, her lips pursing into a tight line, but her beautiful eyes had dilated almost to black.

'I suppose you think the caveman approach is a turn-on,' she said, but beneath the sharp tone was the husky note he recognised.

'Are you telling me it isn't?' he challenged her, brushing the ridge of his growing erection against her belly.

She didn't push him away. Their showdown bristled with energy, but unlike the one in Lake Como, this time it was heady desire, not anger, which sizzled and sparked between them.

He kissed her neck, captured the pulse thundering in her collarbone, and began to feast on the sweet, sultry taste of her skin.

She swore, then let out a shuddering sigh. And grasped his head to draw him closer.

The last of his control snapped like a high-tension wire, his hands cupping her butt, finding firm, naked flesh beneath the dress.

Another thong, bless the Lord.

She relaxed into the kiss, lifting her leg to hook it around his hip, notching the erection in his pants against the tender spot between her thighs.

He rubbed her through their clothing, feeling the ripples of her response, revelling in the delicious musk of her arousal.

She gasped, her head thudding back against the wall, undulating her hips to locate the perfect contact, to demand more.

'We need to be naked...' she managed.

He lifted his head, his mind fraying, her bold request reflected in the shocked arousal in her gaze—which was as vivid and desperate as his own.

'Yeah,' he guttered out. But as he fumbled to find her zipper, frantic to feast on her again, she shifted back and batted his urgent hands away.

'Let me. I don't want you to rip it.'

He laughed, the indignation on her face releasing some of the tension in his gut.

But as she stripped off the floaty blue fabric and wriggled it past her hips, leaving her in nothing but her bra and thong, the tension cinched tight again.

He cradled one breast, brushed his thumb across the rouged tip visible through the lace.

Damn, had her breasts got fuller, or was that his overactive imagination? Because she looked magnificent. She'd always been beautiful, but her figure seemed lusher and even more mouth-watering than it had their first night.

She jolted against him, the soft sob enough to turbocharge his own arousal.

He lifted her breast from its lacy prison and captured

the stiff peak in his mouth. He suckled hard as her nipple hardened against his tongue. She thrust her fingers into his hair, her body shuddering violently, her response nothing short of electric.

'That's so good…' she cried.

He delved beneath the satin thong with urgent fingers to find her hot and wet and ready.

She bucked as he worked the swollen nub, his lips still devouring her breast.

He thrust one finger into the tight sheaf, but seconds later, she sobbed as her orgasm pulsed around him.

As she came down, he drew back and licked her dew off his fingers. The throbbing need in his groin was unbearable. She looked spent, dishevelled, her bra half off, her panties soaked with her release. He could smell her, that sultry, flowery scent, as her eyes opened. She looked dazed. Her climax so much faster than before.

'Again?' he asked, his need so strong now he wasn't sure he could stay sane much longer.

She nodded.

He fumbled to find the condom in his wallet, shrugged off his jacket, then ripped open the fly of his suit pants.

She stared at the thick erection, watching him with heavy-lidded eyes as he rolled on the protection with clumsy fingers.

'Turn around, Charlotte,' he demanded.

For once she didn't argue, bracing her hands on the wall, presenting him with the flushed flesh of her butt. The pain in his groin became immense. He needed to be inside her now.

He captured her breasts from behind, holding her steady as he plunged deep. Her swollen flesh was exquisitely tight, but so slick he lodged himself to the hilt in one powerful thrust. He dropped one hand to find her clitoris and pressed his thumb against it, desperate to make her shatter again before he did.

He established a punishing rhythm. The slap of flesh against flesh echoed around the quiet room alongside her sobs and his grunts. The pleasure built at the base of his spine, the pressure becoming exquisite pain, as he slammed into her and she pressed back to take more of him…to take it all.

He shouted as her sex clenched, her climax triggering his own brutal orgasm. The pleasure crested at last, the orgasm exploding through his nerve endings as everything he was, everything he wanted, became a blur of brutal need. And desperate release.

Charley pressed her forehead against the wall, with Cade's big body holding her up while also leaning heavily against her back.

His hand twitched, still cupping her breast. She flinched, aware of how sensitive her breasts had been, and how quickly she had shot to orgasm. Twice.

'You, okay?' he murmured into her hair, his voice as rough as she felt.

'I think so…' she said, not entirely sure.

When had she ever felt so raw? And so sated?

She hadn't intended to have sex with him again, but when he'd grasped her hand twenty minutes ago, the purpose in his gaze like a brand on her too-sensitive skin, and marched her down to the suite—after several hours of dancing—she hadn't been able to resist. Or object. Because she'd wanted him with the same urgency.

He shifted behind her, then drew out of her body.

Her tight flesh released the huge erection with difficulty, making her flinch again.

He grasped her hips, turning her to face him. She folded

her arms over her chest and the remnants of her underwear, feeling exposed as he adjusted his own clothing.

She couldn't stop shivering. The sex, the need, had been so basic, so elemental, she hadn't given a single thought to the repercussions of what she was doing. Or the fact that the tourists on the evening cruises below could have watched everything.

'Hey?' he said, cradling her cheek, already fully clothed again, unlike her. 'You sure you're okay? That was kind of intense.'

She nodded, then forced a smile. 'I certainly hope no one on those boats has binoculars, or we just gave them quite a show.'

He let out a rough chuckle. 'I certainly hope the glass is treated, or I'm gonna sue!'

But as their laughter died, the awkwardness returned. She should ask him to leave, to create some space and distance between them. But she couldn't shift the knot in her throat, or the wave of emotion which suddenly threatened to level the last of her common sense.

She looked away from those piercing blue eyes which seemed to see so much more than she wanted them to. 'I need to take a shower.'

'Want me to join you?' he asked.

She laughed. The man was nothing if not persistent.

'Given what just happened, I'm not sure that's a good idea,' she said, but as she went to walk away, desperate to maintain what was left of her dignity—her mind racing with all the implications of what they'd just done—he snagged her wrist.

'I hope you know, Charlotte. There's no way of putting this genie back in its bottle. And I sure as hell don't want to, do you?'

She should tell him she did, because that was the safest

course. She had committed to spending five weeks on his arm. Sleeping with him would only confuse things more. But the knot in her throat swelled, cutting off the denial, and forcing her to blurt out the truth.

'I honestly don't know,' she managed.

He tipped his head to one side, studying her for what felt like an eternity. Then he dropped his forehead to hers, his hands resting on her bare hips, making her more aware of her nakedness. 'How about we both take a shower—'

'I don't think...'

'Separately,' he interrupted her interruption before the panic could take hold. 'This place has two bathrooms,' he added, ever practical. 'But then I'd like to stay the night.'

The possessive demand made her heartbeat jump in her chest, Still she couldn't find the will to tell him no. To establish any boundaries. And not just because she felt washed out, both emotionally and physically. But also because she wanted to be held, the way he had held her once before. She'd run out on him then. And maybe that was why this need had come back to bite them both on the arse.

Perhaps it really was just a case of getting this desire— and the yearning for his approval, which had to be a holdover from her childhood—out of her system once and for all.

She nodded. 'Okay.'

She spent a good twenty minutes scrubbing the scent of him off her over-sensitised body in the shower. But after pulling on an old T-shirt, she found him lying in the huge double bed, waiting for her. With his dark hair damp and slicked back from that extraordinary face, and his chest bare—the phoenix tattoo flaring over one broad shoulder— her heart thundered against her ribs again.

Why did he have to look so irresistible? It wasn't fair.

He lifted the sheet, beckoned her into the bed. 'Don't

panic, Charlotte. I don't plan to ravish you again…tonight. I just want to make sure you're okay.'

She was pretty sure letting him care for her would only make things more dangerous. But she felt too tired to argue, or deny the pulse of longing, the swell of emotion making the knot in her throat start to ache.

Where was the harm in letting him watch over her for one night? When she felt so raw and on edge… She could establish that all-important distance after she'd regained her strength, and her sense of purpose, tomorrow.

No man had ever claimed her so comprehensively. Maybe she should give herself a break for feeling needy right now.

She climbed into the bed, rested her head on his shoulder as he tucked her against his side, and let the steady thuds of his heartbeat under her ear lull her into deep, dreamless sleep.

CHAPTER TEN

WHEN CHARLEY WOKE the next morning, groggy and sore, it took her a moment to figure out where she was as the stream of sunlight illuminated the room's luxurious furniture and stunning view. Then she became aware of Cade's arm wrapped around her waist.

She could feel his breath, slow and steady on her nape, feel his warmth against her back, cocooning her. But the moment of calm, the feeling of security, was quickly obliterated by the twist of nausea in her belly.

She flung back the sheet as the twist sharpened and threatened to surge.

She raced across the thick carpeting, vaguely aware of Cade's voice—husky with sleep—asking what was wrong behind her. She reached the bathroom just in time to flip up the toilet seat and heave.

Her tender stomach felt as if it were turning inside out as she lost everything she had eaten the night before. She didn't hear him come into the bathroom until his hand stroked her hair back from her face.

Finally the endless retching stopped, and she collapsed onto the bathroom's marble tiles, shaking.

She was vaguely aware of the sound of running water. He handed her a dampened flannel.

'All through?' he asked, his voice grave.

She nodded despite the achy exhaustion and the still

jumpy sensation in her belly as she wiped her face. 'It must have been something I ate,' she said weakly.

This should be excruciatingly embarrassing, but she felt too awful to care.

He handed her a toothbrush. As soon as the peppermint scent of the paste he'd added hit her senses, her stomach rebelled again.

She grasped the bowl, leaning over with a moan to retch some more. But mercifully there was nothing left to come up.

She felt fragile and pathetically grateful for his presence as he helped her off the floor and guided her back to the bed when she had finally finished vomiting.

'I'm calling a doctor,' he said, his phone in his hand.

'Don't be silly. It's just a stomach bug.'

He ignored her, but she felt too rubbish to argue further as she listened to him contacting one of his assistants and ordering them to have the nearest medic sent to the suite.

Embarrassment scorched her cheeks when he finished the call.

'Get some rest,' he said. 'The doctor will be here soon.'

She lifted her aching head and turned over to stare at him. He sat in the chair opposite, having donned his shirt as well as his trousers.

'This is silly,' she said. 'I'm sure I'll be fine now. I've been needing to do that for days.'

His forehead furrowed. 'What do you mean? For days?'

'I've been a bit queasy for a while, that's all. And tired. It must be a bug that's going round.'

'So not something you ate?' he said, his eyes narrowing.

'Well, no, maybe not.'

'Exactly how long have you been feeling nauseous?' Why did he sound so annoyed?

Her tired mind tried to grasp his mood, but she couldn't seem to grasp much of anything at all. 'Only a week or so.'

'A *week*?' He cursed. 'Why didn't you tell me before I dragged you to the party last night?' he added, confusing her more. It was impossible to tell from his expression whether he was angry with her now, or himself.

'Would it have made a difference?' she asked.

'Of course. I'm not a monster, Charlotte,' he said, getting increasingly aggrieved by the second, which only fascinated her more. 'I wouldn't have made you spend all evening on your feet. And I sure as hell would never have touched you if I'd known you were sick. You should have told me.'

'I didn't feel sick last night though. I think that was fairly obvious.'

He paced across the room, looking more agitated than she had ever seen him.

This was new. But while her stomach still felt super-delicate—and the heat in her cheeks at the thought of vomiting in front of him wasn't exactly abating either—his agitation was somehow reassuring.

In fact, she almost enjoyed it when the knock sounded on the door and he shot across the room to answer it.

Who knew? The way to make Cade Landry lose his cool, and that cast-iron control, was to puke your guts up in front of him.

He stood beside the bed, tapping his bare foot on the carpet, hovering over her as the nice Dr Ramirez introduced himself, then started to ask a lot of questions.

The doctor took her blood pressure, checked her pupils, then asked her more questions. But as Cade got more agitated, she found herself relaxing. The nausea had finally faded. And it was almost sweet to have Cade so concerned. About her.

When she was a child, she'd always felt like a burden whenever she was sick. She knew the staff had been paid to look after her because her mother was too fragile to spend any time with her and her father was always working—or banging his latest bit on the side—and her older brother was away at boarding school.

How strange to have that yearning for someone care to enough about her to look the way Cade looked now—agitated and worried—finally fulfilled in these circumstances.

But then her own composure took a major hit.

'Is there any chance you could be pregnant, Ms Courtney?' the doctor asked.

'No… What? *No!*' she sputtered, refusing to look at Cade.

'I see. When did you have your last period?'

Her mind slammed into a wall of sheer panic as she tried to remember the date. She hadn't had one in a while. But her menstrual cycle had always been erratic. 'I… I'm not sure. I'd have to check my phone.'

She was forced to look at Cade when he scooped up her purse and handed it to her. To her astonishment, his agitation had disappeared. But then, she couldn't gauge his reaction to the doctor's line of questioning because his expression had gone completely blank.

It took her forever to locate her phone, switch it on and open her calendar app. But as she scrolled through the weeks—looking for the red *P* she always stuck into the app to keep track of her cycle—panic started to claw at her throat.

By the time she finally located the *P*, then counted the weeks in between, her fingers were trembling. She lifted her head.

The doctor had a kindly, encouraging smile on his face. Cade, though, who stood behind him, was staring at her with an intensity she recognised, his stance rigid.

She wasn't pregnant. That would be nuts. He'd worn a condom that night. And they'd only done it the once.

'Charlotte, how long?' Cade prompted, his voice controlled, but with an edge which suggested he was holding on to his composure by his fingertips.

'Um…well, it's been a little over seven weeks… But really that's not unusual. I have a very irregular cycle,' she rushed to clarify, her cheeks burning now, because talking about her menstrual cycle with this man felt more intimate than having him inside her.

Which was almost as ludicrous as the notion she might be carrying his child.

This isn't happening. It can't be. It's too absurd.

But even as she tried desperately to convince herself the doctor had to be mistaken, all the ways in which her body had changed—the things she had dismissed as the emotional and physical stress of kick-starting her business and the fallout from her night with Cade in San Francisco—suddenly coalesced in her head into a burning pile of incontrovertible proof.

Her sore, heavy, oversensitive breasts. The queasiness which had begun over a week ago. The fact she'd had her last period three weeks before she'd slept with Cade that first night. Yes, her cycle was erratic, but not *that* erratic.

She pressed her hand to her stomach.

'And did you have sexual relations during that time?' the doctor asked gently, oblivious to Charley's shock and that strange feeling of horrified awe which was now pressing down on her chest.

Charley's gaze met Cade's. 'Um…yes, once,' she murmured. 'About four and a half weeks ago. But we used protection.'

'What kind of protection?' the doctor asked.

'A condom.' Cade's deep voice cut through the feeling of unreality. 'Which I was too distracted to check afterwards.'

The doctor nodded—still so calm, as if Charley's life wasn't going into free fall.

'Condoms are usually very reliable, Mr Landry.' He turned to address Cade. 'But I would still advise a pregnancy test. The symptoms Ms Courtney has described to me are very common in the first trimester.'

'How do we do that?' Cade asked, taking charge, because Charley had totally lost the power of speech now—her emotions pitching on a stormy sea of questions without answers.

Could I have made a baby? With Cade Landry? What if I have a life? Growing inside me? How do I even feel about that?

'You can get an over-the-counter test—they're very accurate—or I could arrange a blood test this morning at my office on West Twenty-Fifth Street...'

'We'll take the blood test,' Cade said with his usual pragmatism.

Charley should have been annoyed—this was her body he was talking about—but she couldn't seem to feel much of anything at the moment.

As the next hour passed, she sank deeper into the fog.

Cade accompanied her to the private medical facility in Chelsea. She had to sign a ton of forms, the nurse drew a vial of blood, and five minutes later they were led into Dr Ramirez's office. The clean white space looked out over the Hudson River, the scent of expensive leather and potpourri doing nothing to cover the scent of the man beside her.

She could have objected to Cade being there, but it seemed pointless.

The realisation they would always share this moment made her pulse race when Dr Ramirez appeared. And cut straight to the chase.

'Your blood test is conclusive, Ms Courtney. Given the date of your last menstruation, that would make you just over seven weeks pregnant.'

With Cade Landry's child.

The blood rushed out of her head to pound in her heart. Cade asked a string of pragmatic, surprisingly measured questions. But she couldn't hear them...because all she could hear were the clear, unequivocal thoughts in her head. Thoughts she never would have expected in these circumstances, but were there nonetheless.

How this happened, why it happened—or how impossible this situation is—doesn't matter. All I know is that this is my child. As well as Cade's. And I want to have it.

But how did that even work? When she had never considered becoming a mother until this precise moment...and had no confidence whatsoever she would be a good one?

Cade sat across from Charlotte in the limo as they headed out of the Midtown tunnel en route to JFK.

He'd made an executive decision to fly straight to San Francisco—and told his assistant to arrange to have Charlotte's luggage collected from the hotel on the High Line. They needed time to regroup and take stock without having to deal with any press attention.

Charlotte hadn't objected. But then, she hadn't said much of anything at all.

She was staring out the window of the car now, but he doubted she was seeing the buildings of downtown Brooklyn. She looked shell-shocked. He knew the feeling.

A baby. A child. *His* child.

He had no idea how to process the news they'd just been dealt by the doctor. And he had no doubt at all she was struggling to process it too, given that her hands were clasped so tightly in her lap the knuckles had whitened.

It felt as if they had entered an alternative reality. And there was no way to get back to normality ever again. The one thing he could process, though, was a fierce sense of protectiveness—towards both Charlotte and the child.

Weird on one level. Because he had never thought of becoming a father. But not that weird on another. Hadn't he spent his whole life building a legacy he could be proud of? Why had it never occurred to him until now that it would mean nothing if he had no one to pass his business on to?

But as he watched Charlotte—trying to gauge her reaction—he knew this wasn't a child yet. It wasn't even a baby. It was simply a pregnancy. And for him to feel so protective already—to be envisioning Charlotte's slender body heavy with his baby—was premature. What if she didn't wish to keep his child?

He cleared his throat. Her head jerked round and her gaze met his, her expression that of someone who had been woken from a trance.

'How does your stomach feel?' he asked. The doctor had given him a ton of advice about the morning sickness because he'd quizzed the guy while Charlotte had sat beside him in silence.

She placed a hand on her stomach, her throat contracting as she swallowed. 'Okay, I guess.'

It bothered him that he couldn't gauge her reaction, because all he could see was shock.

One of his greatest assets in business was his ability to read people and act accordingly to get what he wanted. Not being able to figure out how she felt about the pregnancy was a problem, forcing him to break cover.

'How do *you* feel? About having this baby?'

She stared. Her bottom lip started to tremble. She bit into it.

'I want to have it,' she said at last. The relief he felt was palpable. Then she added, 'But I'm also absolutely terrified.'

He could see her fear was genuine, and wondered where it came from. But before he could ask her about it, she said, 'And you? How do *you* feel?'

'Shocked,' he admitted. 'But also kind of thrilled.'

Her eyes widened, her pale skin flushing. Clearly she hadn't expected that answer.

'Really? You *want* to become a dad?' she said, sounding incredulous. 'I thought you'd try and pressure me into having a termination.'

He should have been insulted...but he let the knee-jerk reaction go. Because she was right about one thing. He hadn't actually thought of becoming a *dad*, per se.

The baby, *his* baby, represented a legacy to him first and foremost—a part of himself which was even now growing inside her womb. Strictly speaking it wasn't the thought of becoming a father, but rather that fierce sense of possession and vindication—at the thought of Charlotte not only having his child but also nurturing it, the way his mother had never nurtured him—which thrilled him.

But before he started examining his own reaction, he wanted to examine hers. Their current situation wasn't ideal. If they were going to negotiate this bombshell, they would need to work together. So it might be good to find out, when she had decided he was a total jerk?

'Why would you think I'd do something like that?' he asked.

'Because...' She huffed. 'Well, you're *you*.'

He coughed out a laugh, not sure whether to be insulted now or amused.

'Are you trying to say you think I'm a selfish bastard without *saying* I'm a selfish bastard?'

It was supposed to be a joke, but when she studied him, he wasn't sure he wanted to hear her answer.

'I don't know you well enough to know if you're a complete bastard,' she said. 'But I do think you're deeply cynical. And arrogant. And that you make sure you always get what you want—no matter the collateral damage. Which reminds me, rather unfortunately, of my father...' Before he could ask her about the man, she carried on. 'Then again, you held my hair while I was puking this morning—and took care of me when I didn't expect you to, which makes you not quite as much of a bastard as he was.'

'Gee, thanks,' he said, well and truly damned by her faint praise. What had she expected? That he would ignore her, or worse, be squeamish about a little vomit? 'Your old man sounds like a real peach,' he added.

'You have no idea,' she said. 'How about yours? Did you know him?'

'Nope,' he said, then added, before he could think better of it, 'I doubt my mother knew who he was either.'

'I'm sorry to hear that,' she said, sympathy shadowing her eyes.

'Why?' he asked, determined to deflect her pity. 'It doesn't sound like you got much out of knowing your old man.'

'True,' she said. 'But I'm not sure it's a good thing that neither of us has first-hand knowledge of what a dad is supposed to do.'

'I guess not,' he said, glad the flicker of pity had disappeared.

'I appreciate your directness about the pregnancy,' she continued, but the sadness and confusion still lurked in her eyes. 'I've got to admit, you're not the sort of man I would *ever* have expected to be thrilled about an accidental pregnancy. Especially with a woman like me.'

'Exactly what kind of woman do you think you are?' he asked, wanting to make this about her again instead of him.

'It's not what kind of woman *I* think I am. It's what kind of woman *you* think I am.'

'Uh-huh. Enlighten me,' he said, both annoyed and oddly intrigued by her candour.

'Reckless, impulsive, immature, entitled,' she said, her

tone flat and pragmatic. But he could see the hurt in her eyes, hear the defensiveness—and the echo of the fragile girl he'd first met. 'Basically, not the kind of woman you'd want to be the mother of your child,' she continued. 'If you'd had a choice.'

'You're right, you are reckless and impulsive,' he said, because he'd be damned if he'd sugar-coat his opinion of her. After all, she certainly hadn't sugar-coated her opinion of him. 'But entitled and immature?' he continued, determined to prove that while he might be arrogant and cynical, he wasn't as dumb as she thought he was. 'I may have seen that when we first met. I don't see it any more.'

'Perhaps you better tell me what you *do* see now…' she said, but then she turned away to stare back out the car window. And he realised she was braced to hear the worst—which made him consider his words carefully. He wanted to be honest, but he also had no desire to hurt that girl again.

'I think you're passionate, smart, brutally honest and hard-working, and someone who is not afraid of adversity. All of which make you a lot better suited to being a mom than my own mother…'

Her head swung back, and he saw her surprise, but then compassion darkened her eyes.

Why the hell had he mentioned his mom?

'So, tell me, if you want to have this baby, what are you so terrified of?' he said before she could start feeling sorry for him again.

Charley stiffened at the direct question. And the probing look in Cade's eyes.

She wished she hadn't told him about her fear, because the last thing she needed to do right now was discuss all her insecurities. Frankly, she was already freaking out enough—

not least about the thought of having a link to this man for the rest of her life.

A man who scared her on a lot of levels, and not because he reminded her of her father…but because, in many ways, he didn't.

Cade was certainly ruthless and arrogant. He was also forthright, and complex. His admission he was thrilled about this pregnancy had astonished her. It had also elated her on a visceral level.

But she knew she couldn't risk getting too invested in the way he had taken care of her this morning. Or allow his forthright defence of her character and her ability to be a good mother mean too much. All of which was no easy feat when her emotions were all over the place.

Gee, thanks, pregnancy hormones!

She placed her hand on her belly, rubbed the spot where their baby was the size of a prawn and admitted to herself she was also terrified of having to do something so important—something she wasn't convinced she would have any aptitude for—entirely alone.

What a mess…

'I just… I don't want to make a mistake,' she managed, because Cade was still watching her, waiting for a coherent answer…not that she had one to give him. 'I don't want to have this baby only to screw up its life, because I have absolutely no clue what I'm doing.'

He nodded, but the intense emotion which crossed his features had her heart bounding into her throat again.

'Does anyone know what the hell they're doing?' he said. 'Before they have kids?'

'I suppose not,' she said.

'Then I guess we'll just have to figure it out,' he said.

She nodded, feeling the emotion sting the backs of her eyes.

She blinked furiously, determined not to get sentimental about the *we* in that sentence.

But she couldn't help wondering about the tiny insight he'd given her into his relationship with his own mother. Was that why he was so driven? And why he refused to shy away from this responsibility? While she was glad he seemed willing to do this with her, she was fairly sure their mostly terrible—or non-existent—relationships with their own parents were not going to make parenthood easy for either of them.

'If we're *both* gonna prepare for this new reality, though...' he interrupted her chaotic thoughts with typical pragmatism, his gaze dropping to her belly '...we have a lot of stuff to discuss.'

The massive understatement made her smile. 'Ya think?'

He let out a rough chuckle. And the anxiety in her stomach finally began to ease. A little. But as the car took the exit to the airport, she felt the exhaustion she'd been trying to suppress all morning envelop her again.

'Would it be okay if we put that conversation on hold? I'm shattered,' she managed. It made her feel like a wimp, but she needed some downtime before she agreed to anything.

Cade Landry was a forceful and demanding guy who she knew wouldn't think twice about making decisions for her and their baby if she gave him too much leeway.

He frowned, not too pleased with her request. 'Of course,' he said at last. 'By the way, I've arranged a thorough checkup first thing tomorrow morning with the West Coast's top ob-gyn, who happens to be based in Pacific Heights.'

Oh, did you, now?

She clamped down on her annoyance at his high-handedness. He was being conscientious. Not controlling. *Much.*

'Do you know if the West Coast's top ob-gyn is a woman?' she asked.

His frown deepened, as if he didn't have a clue why that would be relevant. Because...*men*!

'Yeah, I think so.'

'Great, well, I'll see her then. Thanks.'

They arrived at the hangar, where the Landry jet was waiting for them. She could hear him making the final arrangements with an assistant, but tuned out the conversation as she headed to the bedroom at the back of the plane.

He didn't join her.

She was glad he'd taken the hint. Because as she strapped herself into the bedroom's seat for take-off, the exhaustion seeped into her soul, the emotionally charged conversation in the car—as well as the demands of her pregnancy—taking their toll.

As the jet lifted into the early afternoon sunlight, and the plane banked over Manhattan, her heart rose into her throat. But as the jet levelled off, her heart remained jammed under her larynx.

It was less than five hours since she had woken up in Cade's arms. She could still feel the pulse of awareness in her core, where he had taken her last night with such urgency, such passion...and she had enjoyed every second of it.

But since then, her whole life—*both* their lives—had been turned on their heads. She pressed her palms to her stomach. And while she already felt a connection with the new life inside her, she also felt completely and utterly overwhelmed.

CHAPTER ELEVEN

'I SHOULD GO downstairs and start unpacking,' Charley managed as she stared at San Francisco's bustling waterfront—the historic splendour of the old Ferry Building and the majesty of the Bay Bridge stretching towards Oakland.

Cade's penthouse apartment towered over the city's financial district and the Embarcadero and was even more magnificent in the daylight. But it also looked just how she remembered it—luxurious, expertly designed, more than a little impersonal and almost as intimidating as the man himself.

Funny to think she'd run out of here about a month ago now, sure she would never see Cade again, and here she was looking at the same spectacular view with the baby they'd made together that night growing inside her.

Okay, stop thinking about the prawn for two seconds, or you'll freak out again.

'Your luggage is here,' he said. 'I told them to put the downstairs condo back on the rental market.'

She swung round. 'Um…when exactly did I agree to move in with you?' she managed, annoyed by the he-who-shall-be-obeyed tone she was becoming far too familiar with.

She'd had a solid sleep on the plane. While she still felt off-kilter, she wasn't the fragile, over-emotional pushover she had been when they'd boarded his jet.

From the way he frowned—as if he couldn't quite believe she would contradict him—she knew it was way past time she started standing her ground. She might be pregnant with his baby, but that did not make her his property.

'When you spent a good ten minutes throwing up this morning,' he replied flatly.

Her cheeks burned. Trust him to bring that up. 'How is that relevant?'

Before she could follow up with all the reasons why it *so* wasn't, he had crossed the room and placed his palm on her cheek.

'Calm down, Charlotte,' he said softly, the concerned tone as disturbing as the sudden urge to lean into his hand. 'I don't want you on your own if you're sick again. That's all.'

She pulled away from his touch. But she couldn't deny the wave of emotion threatening to sweep away her perfectly valid objections to his high-handed behaviour. 'I still don't think I should move in with you,' she managed, far too aware of the needy feeling pressing down on her chest. 'This isn't even a real relationship,' she added. 'I'm just here as your stunt date for the summer.'

He tucked his hand into his pocket, but his gaze remained fixed on her. 'I think we've gone beyond that now, don't you?'

She stepped back, the tantalising aroma of woodsy cologne and soap playing havoc with her resolve now, too.

Surely this was just another example of her wacky hormones? Or was it the biology of pregnancy which seemed to make her body obsessed with the father of her child?

'I don't want to sleep with you again,' she said, although even she could hear the hesitation.

Could he see the yearning? Sense the arousal which was making her sex ache?

But he didn't call her out on the lie. 'The apartment has several guest rooms. Take your pick.'

'I… I still don't think it's a good idea.'

She would be living with him even if they weren't sleeping together. Wasn't that too intimate? What if she got suckered into thinking they were a real couple?

But then he disarmed her again. 'I want to be close by if you need me,' he said, a muscle ticking in his jaw.

'It's just morning sickness, Cade. It's perfectly normal. Most pregnant women get it,' she said, far too aware of the hole forming in her belly.

She recognised that hole, and the urge to fill it, which had made her do stupid things once.

She didn't want to be that reckless girl again, looking for approval from a guy like Cade—who she had discovered today had the unique ability to seize on her weakness and exploit it.

'I still want to keep an eye on you,' he said, the placid, persuasive tone contradicted by the fierce determination in his eyes. 'And FYI, I don't give a damn about other women. The only woman I give a damn about is you. Because you're the only one having my kid.'

She drew in a careful breath. The curt statement struck at the heart of her insecurities…but also made her aware of something important.

This is about his baby. It's not about you.

She took a moment to control the wayward emotions which were way too close to the surface. Again.

What if this feeling of vulnerability, this urge to accept the support he was offering, was nothing to do with that needy, unloved girl—and everything to do with the strange situation they found themselves in? If that were the case, would it be so terrible to let him carry some of the burden? To let go of a little of her independence? As long as he understood that accepting his support did not mean he could dictate her life?

'I'm pregnant, Cade. I'm not an invalid,' she said. 'I still plan to set up a workshop while I'm here to work on my commissions. My business is important to me. Especially as I'm going to be a single parent in eight months' time.'

His gaze darkened. 'You won't need to support yourself. I've asked my legal team to draw up a financial agreement which will ensure my child will never want for anything. I also intend to compensate you generously for your role as its mother. I would never abandon that responsibility.'

She sighed, her panic and confusion downgrading considerably in the face of his rigid expression—and the shadow in his eyes. She'd triggered something she hadn't intended to, but she was glad she had.

From the little he had let slip about his past, she knew Cade had some trust issues. She understood what that was like—because she had several trust issues of her own.

Living with him scared her on a lot of levels. She couldn't allow herself to need his care or his attention too much. But maybe she should do the mature thing and start dealing with how scared that made her feel before she tried to deal with his insecurities too.

'I don't want your money, Cade,' she began.

'Well, tough,' he interrupted her. 'Because there is no way in hell I'm not supporting my own child.'

She put up her palm. '*Whoa...* That's not what I said. I said *I* don't want your money. We can certainly agree on a financial arrangement between us as parents for the upkeep of our baby. When it's born.' She placed her palm on her stomach and waited for the stupid wave of emotion to level out. It was good he was so determined to support this baby. His protective instincts and sense of responsibility didn't have to be a bad thing, as long as they established some boundaries—such as that *her* life and autonomy, and their baby's well-being, were two separate issues.

'But it's not a baby yet. It's barely an embryo,' she continued. 'My financial independence is important to me. I love my business. I want to make a success of Trouble Maker. You said you'd give my business your financial support while I'm here—as a trade-off for posing as your date. And I plan to hold you to that. But that's the only financial support I want from you.'

She could see the enormity of the mountain she had to climb though when his frown deepened.

Good grief, what on earth had he expected her to do while she was here? Sit around and twiddle her thumbs while he took charge of everything? Simply because she was pregnant?

She wanted to be angry with him, but had she created this rod for her own back by being so flaky over the last twelve hours?

Lesson to self: no more wimping out around Cade, no matter how crap you feel.

The thought was strangely motivating. She was bound to be tired from time to time—but she could remedy that by sleeping as much and as often as she needed to.

She had no idea how long the nausea was supposed to last—or what other symptoms she might be dealing with in future, other than a hyperactive libido every time she was within ten feet of her child's father. Because she had completely zoned out when Dr Ramirez had given them both the lowdown on the first trimester of pregnancy that morning.

No wonder Cade thought she couldn't hold up her end of this when she'd allowed him to take the lead on everything so far. Well, that ended now.

'I don't want you working if you're sick,' he said, his voice tight with irritation.

Well, that's not your decision.

It was what she wanted to say, but she swallowed the provocative reply.

He had to be struggling, too, with the enormity of what they were dealing with. Not just logistically, but also emotionally. But she suspected from his closed expression and what she knew of him already that he would rather cut off his tongue than admit it.

Cade was a guy who she doubted ever admitted a weakness. And who always wanted to be in charge, hence his desire to wrap her in cotton wool, rather than treat her as an equal... But what if that was a lay-over from his childhood, too, a way to avoid dealing with any messy emotions?

Well, he'd have to deal with them eventually. And her. And living in his apartment with him would give her ample opportunity to find out a lot more about his fears and insecurities too.

Until then, though, she could cut him some slack. Up to a point.

'How about we compromise. I can live here with you...' She puffed out a breath. 'In the guest room,' she added hastily, when his eyes darkened with something which only made her more aware of the heat pulsing insistently in her abdomen. 'But I continue to work on my commissions during the day, and I set up my workspace in the Embarcadero as planned.'

His piercing blue eyes narrowed. She could see he didn't want to give an inch.

'Or...' she continued, determined to make him see reason. 'I get a flight back to the UK tomorrow morning...' *Two can play the carrot and stick game.* 'And we forget all about the stunt dating. And you lose the Helberg bet. Your choice.'

His frown became catastrophic. She wondered if she'd pushed him too far. But she refused to back down. Surely he couldn't still carry out his threat of suing her over those photos? Not when he was so adamant about protecting the mother of his child? So she had him, and he knew it, but it might take him a while to figure it out...

Luckily, she was more than willing to wait.

* * *

Cade was so furious he felt as if steam was about to explode out of his ears. But far worse was the heat in his groin. And that unsteady, unsettled feeling in his gut.

The same damn feeling he'd always had when he'd been yanked out of one home to be dumped in another. He had always hated the loss of control, more than the not knowing where he would wind up next. Some of the foster homes had been great, some just okay, some not even that, but in each new place he'd learned to add another layer of I-don't-give-a-damn until it hadn't mattered to him any more how good or bad the homes were, because he knew he would survive regardless. And he had promised himself that as soon as he was old enough, he would get out of the system—and finally be able to live his life on his own terms.

But as he glared at Charlotte, it occurred to him that having a baby with her was going to mean losing some of that precious control…unless he could find a way to make her play ball.

The fact that winning the bet, even acquiring Helberg, didn't mean as much to him as keeping her and the baby safe only made the whole situation more infuriating. He couldn't afford to care *too* much, because he didn't trust her not to use that weakness against him.

He couldn't deny, though, as she stood in front of him, her arms folded, her stance stubborn and determined, that being bested by her was also kind of…well, hot.

How had she managed to turn the tables on him so neatly? Because no one did that. Not any more…

Then again, everything about her was a turn-on.

Of course, he wasn't about to tell her that, because she had too much power already.

He wasn't sure how she had sneaked under his guard. But this fierce need would pass, once they'd finally got the chemical reaction they shared out of their systems. So the no sex rule was a problem. Then again, no way would they be able to keep their hands off each other for a whole five weeks while they were living in the same apartment.

'You're damn sneaky, too, when you want to be,' he said, unable to keep the admiration out of his voice.

He hated to be beaten, *ever*. But who would have guessed this poor little rich girl would have the backbone of a Trojan and the tactical smarts of a five-star general…or that he would find the challenge she represented not just infuriating, but also compelling?

She sent him a quick grin, full of relief and no small amount of triumph. The pleasure she derived from her victory turned her green eyes to a rich emerald.

'I'm going to take that as a compliment,' she said.

He hadn't intended it as one. But even so, he found himself smiling back.

'Do we have a deal?' she asked.

'I guess,' he said, forced to concede she had won this round. *Mostly*.

But as she walked by him, he yanked his hand out of his pants pocket. 'How about we shake on it?'

Her gaze darted to his. But she took his hand—because she was way too overconfident.

Big mistake.

He felt her tremble of reaction as his fingers closed around hers and his thumb caressed the rabbiting pulse in her wrist.

She yanked her hand free—sent him a quelling look, telling him she knew exactly what he had been up to with that wrist stroke. Then marched off to check out the guest rooms.

But his smile spread as he watched her go.

Yeah, you can run again, sugar, but you can't hide—not from me and sure as heck not from this chemistry. Not for long anyhow.

CHAPTER TWELVE

One week later

'CADE, YOU'RE HERE!' Charley stared at the man standing with his back to her in the huge open-plan kitchen area of the equally massive penthouse apartment they had been sharing for seven days. The man she had been managing to avoid for all seven of those days by getting back before him each evening from the workshop she was establishing a block away, and heading straight to her bedroom—because she was way too exhausted to socialise. Or eat a meal with him.

Dressed in a simple white T-shirt—which stretched distractingly over broad shoulders, a muscular back and a lean waist and dropped just shy of his equally impressive butt showcased in faded jeans—he looked relaxed and at home... The casual clothing reminded her uncomfortably of the jeans and tee combo he had looked so delicious in at the Broussards' party.

So delicious, they'd ended up creating a baby.

He turned slowly, and she spotted the meat mallet in his hand.

'Are you cooking?' she asked, stunned.

It was barely six, and the man was a workaholic. She hadn't even realised he knew where the kitchen was, because the steel-and-marble space had remained spotless and unused—despite the groceries he'd had his assistant stock the fridge with the day after they arrived.

That would be the day when they had had their last proper conversation. Or rather their last disagreement. Because he had wanted to accompany her to the ob-gyn appointment that morning, and she had point-blank refused.

He had been annoyed, but to her surprise, he'd backed off without much of a protest. And she'd hardly seen or spoken to him since, because he left before she woke each morning and didn't return until nightfall.

Truth be told, she had been beyond grateful to be left to her own devices for the past week. Her life—and their relationship—were confusing enough without dealing with the simmering sexual tension which was always there when she was in the same room with Cade.

He had texted her each day, usually a curt line to ask her if there had been any nausea. But luckily that one episode in New York seemed to be the worst of her morning sickness over with, after her new ob-gyn, Dr Chen, had given her lots of tips on how to avoid a recurrence—as well as a ton of different vitamins to take.

Apart from ensuring his 'people' were on hand to help her with setting up her workspace—and dealing with the insane amount of paperwork necessary to hire the two brilliant seamstresses she had found—Cade had made no demands on her socially, as per their fake dating agreement. Nor had he insisted on spending any time with her in the evenings—after checking in on her when he arrived back from his office.

But as he put the mallet down on the chopping board, and she saw the two thick steaks lined up on the counter next to an enormous array of fresh salad ingredients, she realised her reprieve was over.

'I wanted to catch you tonight before you hid out in the bedroom,' he said.

'Hid out? What is that supposed to mean?' she protested. 'I've been tired. It's hard work setting up a business and being pregnant...' she added, but before she could get up to full steam, he lifted his hand.

'Let me rephrase. Before you crashed out in the *guest* room.'

The emphasis on *guest* seemed significant, but she didn't get the chance to question what he meant by the inference before he ploughed on, cutting her outrage off at the knees. 'I've done some reading on what's best to eat during pregnancy...'

He had?

She couldn't quite hide her surprise. Or the press of something wrapping around her ribs. She'd been making the effort to eat regularly and often, as per the doctor's orders, but she hadn't had the time or inclination to cook for herself.

'Apparently bland and packed with vitamins and protein is a good call—so I figured steak, a baked potato and a side salad would work.'

'You're going to cook a meal for me?' It was a silly question, as he'd just said as much, but even so she felt the wall of emotion hit her unawares.

'Yes.'

'Oh,' she said, blinking as ridiculous tears stung her eyes.

It was just the pregnancy hormones making her overemotional. She'd already established that. She brushed the moisture away with her fist, but then he tilted his head to one side, scrutinising her in that way he had which made her feel seen.

And the wave of emotion crested again.

'Hey, now...' He walked around the counter, clearly as

disturbed by her over-the-top reaction as she was. 'My cooking isn't that bad, I swear.'

She found herself laughing and crying at the same time.

He brushed her tears away with his thumbs, his gaze unguarded for the first time. But the fierce concern only made her feel more vulnerable. And more scared.

'It's just the pregnancy hormones,' she murmured, stepping away from his gentle touch and wiping her eyes—feeling desperately exposed and pathetically needy.

'Uh-huh,' he said, but she could see the question in his eyes.

'They hit me unawares sometimes,' she added. 'And make me overreact to anything even remotely triggering. Sorry.' That had to be it. She'd persuaded herself over the past week that her initial panic about relying on Cade too much didn't apply. This wasn't about who she'd been, but who she was now. And as she'd started to come to terms with the reality of the pregnancy, she had become more convinced that it made sense to lean on him, at least where the baby was concerned. So why did this feel like too much?

'There's no need to apologise,' he said, but then he added, 'Why would you be triggered by me cooking for you?'

She sighed. She didn't want to answer. Because it felt too personal. And if she told him the truth, too revealing.

But she could see she'd been a coward in the past week. She *had* been hiding out in her room, avoiding him. One of the reasons why she'd decided to stay here was to get to know him better, to deal with a few of his insecurities too, and discover what kind of a father he would be.

But didn't that require conversation? Time spent together, talking openly?

There were so many things she wanted to know about him—about his past, his childhood, the things which kept him up at night, which drove him so relentlessly, even the reason why acquiring Helberg seemed so important to him. But if she wanted him to reveal his secrets, his vulnerabilities—then she had to be willing to do the same.

'I guess because no one has ever cooked a meal for me before—well, not like this,' she offered.

'I see,' he said. He didn't seem all that surprised—maybe no one had ever cooked a meal for him either. But the thought made her consider how tough his childhood must have been in comparison to hers, and she found herself backtracking.

'Which is, of course, nonsense, now I think about it. Even though he ignored me, my father paid a small fortune to the staff when I was little to make sure I was well cared for while my mother was alive. Then I went to a string of expensive boarding schools—with a host of catering options. And the last thing you want when you're a catwalk model is to have someone cook you a meal before a show...' She began babbling, because his scrutiny had only become more intense. 'Just in case you gain a couple of millimetres on your hips and can't get into the designs assigned to you. So apparently, the pregnancy hormones are making me feel sorry for myself for no reason.'

He frowned. 'I'm not sure having someone paid to care for your needs or being forced to starve yourself counts as no reason,' he murmured. Then he threw her completely by asking, 'What happened to your mother?'

'She died when I was eight,' she said.

'That's tough,' he said, his gaze darkening with sympathy.

'Not particularly. We were never close. She spent most of my childhood living at the family estate in Northumberland while I lived with my father in London. And she was so unhappy. She just wasn't ever really *there* even when she was, if you know what I mean... So when she took her own life, I didn't feel the loss. Not the way Adam did.'

'But you were just a little kid. Even when your mama

isn't around, it still hurts when they're gone,' he said, his gaze filled with a compassion she knew must come from his own experiences.

She seized on the small insight. 'When did you lose your mother?'

His gaze became instantly shuttered before he gave a harsh laugh, devoid of humour. 'I didn't lose her. She lost me.'

'How do you mean?' she asked.

His expression went carefully blank. 'She left me in a department store in Baton Rouge when I was five years old. Told me to hide out and she'd come back to get me. So I did, until the nightwatchman found me the next morning and called the cops.' He shrugged, but the movement lacked his usual grace. 'And that's how I got kicked into the system.'

Charlotte touched his hand, her heart racing—the lack of emotion in his voice and his blank expression only making his story sadder. It wasn't hard to see where Cade's trust issues came from now. 'Cade, I'm so sorry. That's dreadful.'

'Not really. She was a junkie. I was better off without her.'

'Even so, no child should have no one,' she said, the emotion threatening to overwhelm her again. No matter how unseen she'd sometimes felt as a child, however much of a burden she'd been made to feel, she had never been alone. Some of the staff and teachers paid to care for her had been kind and nurturing, and she had always had Adam. However dysfunctional their relationship had been at times, he had always been there for her in a crisis.

'I wasn't alone. I had myself,' he said as he skimmed his thumb under her eye. 'Please don't start crying again.'

She laughed and sniffed back the tears, stupidly relieved all of a sudden. She'd been so terrified of relying on him too much, but surely sharing the burden together could be mutual? It didn't have to leave her overexposed. If he was exposed too.

Before she could probe further, though, he lifted her bag off her shoulder and slung an arm around her waist to direct her towards the kitchen's breakfast counter. 'Take a load off while I finish supper.'

He'd changed the conversation deliberately. Clearly, getting him to talk about his past was going to be a work in progress, but she felt deeply moved by what he'd shared. And once she'd climbed up on the stool and managed to tamp down on the inevitable buzz of awareness from that proprietary touch, watching him cook her dinner was captivating too.

She gave herself permission to enjoy the moment and not overthink it.

He worked quickly and efficiently, slicing the salad ingredients with the speed and skill of a chef.

'Where did you learn to chop so fast?' she asked.

He glanced up. 'I worked as a short-order cook in a diner while doing my MBA at Yale,' he said. 'I had a couple of scholarships to cover tuition, but I was already investing the money I'd earned flipping houses into building a property portfolio, so working the breakfast and the late shifts in between the classes and assignments kept me afloat.'

'When did you sleep?' she asked, astonished. Surely the workload at Yale's renowned business school would have been enormous enough? 'And socialise?'

'I didn't do either, much.' He sent her a wry smile as he fired up the griddle. 'You don't need all that much sleep in your early twenties. And I've always been a loner, with a passionate aversion to small talk,' he added by way of explanation while pulling two jacket potatoes covered in tin foil from the oven.

'Have you always worked this hard then?' she asked, fascinated.

The man wasn't so much a workaholic as a work machine... But his drive and ambition—and almost preternatural focus on getting what he wanted—suddenly seemed as hot as the scent of his woodsy cologne, and the sight of his biceps bulging beneath the short sleeves of his T-shirt as he hammered out the steaks.

She shifted on the stool. *Fabulous.* Even watching him cook aroused her.

'I guess.' He shrugged as he set the steaks on the hot griddle. 'It's not difficult to motivate yourself, though, when you love what you do.'

Plus, hard work was the only way to make your mark if you came from nothing, the way he had. It was a sobering thought.

She loved what she did too, now. And she'd worked extremely hard to get her business operational. The challenges she'd faced in the last few days as she interviewed seamstresses, organised for Landry Construction to employ them to comply with her visa status, and began work on her newest commissions had been frustrating and time-consuming but also exhilarating. What she had achieved already with Trouble Maker meant so much more to her than being able to look elegant prancing down a catwalk without falling on her bum!

But she'd never had the sustained focus he had, and she'd never been reliant on herself alone to survive and prosper. She could see that more clearly now.

'How do you like your steak?' he asked, breaking her out of her revelry and making her aware of her stomach grumbling from the delicious scent of sizzling meat.

'Medium rare is good,' she said.

She watched him as he finished off the meal—splitting the potatoes, adding generous amounts of butter and sour cream and chives, tossing the salad in a dressing he rustled up from scratch, and flipping the steaks. By the time he'd finished, she felt oddly humbled and stupidly emotional again. And hopelessly turned on.

Cade Landry might be arrogant, and overwhelming, and cynical, and tightly controlled when it came to his emotions as well as his work ethic—but all those things also made him exciting and fascinating...and really hot.

'Dig in,' he said as he placed the loaded plates on the breakfast bar and climbed onto the stool across from her.

She didn't have to be asked twice. She cut into the perfectly cooked steak, put it in her mouth and let the meaty juices dissolve on her tongue.

'Delicious,' she moaned.

'Yeah,' he said, his gaze roaming over her in a way that made her skin tingle.

The sweet spot between her thighs—which only he had ever found—rejoiced right alongside her taste-buds. She stiffened, acknowledging the danger. Apparently, Cade Landry's culinary skills were as seductive as all his other skills....

They ate in silence. She polished off most of the enormous steak and made inroads into the potato and crisp salad. But once he had cleared his plate, she was forced to admit defeat.

'You done?' he asked.

'Yes, thanks, it was very good,' she said as he scooped up the plates, cleaned the remnants of her meal into the waste disposal and loaded the dinnerware into a state-of-the-art dishwasher.

'So, I think I'll head to bed,' she said, trying to lessen the sexual tension threatening to devour her almost as efficiently as he had demolished his steak.

Because watching the man do domestic chores was stupidly sexy, too. Who knew?

The confidences they'd shared about their pasts, their childhoods—and the fact they had both, in different ways, been abandoned by their mothers—threatened a level of intimacy which she needed to process before she did anything daft.

This still wasn't a real relationship. She had to remember that. He'd only offered her more than the other women he'd dated because she carried his child. An accidental conception didn't make them a couple.

But as she got off the stool to head to her bedroom, the delicious steak she had devoured now sitting like a brick in her stomach—her emotions churning right under it—he strode around the kitchen counter and snagged her arm.

'Wait up, Charlotte.' He tugged her around to face him. 'Don't run out on me again,' he said, and she heard the tension. 'This doesn't have to be a stunt relationship, not when we both want each other so much.'

He rested a hand on her hip.

She could move away from him, tell him she didn't want him with the same urgency, the same need. But how could she? When her sex was already aching to be filled. The need to protect herself from any romantic delusions, though, was still paramount.

'I'm not sure that's smart,' she said.

'Why not?' he asked as emotion swirled in his eyes.

Because I'm still a little scared I could end up needing you too much.

She pushed the terrifying thought away this time. One thing she'd always been was a realist. Even as a little girl. He wasn't offering love, and she didn't want it. Because that would leave her more vulnerable, and she was vulnerable enough already.

'I'm scared of becoming a burden or a responsibility,' she said.

And wanting something I can't have.

That was how she'd always felt as a child. Because of the

mother who had been too sick to acknowledge her, the father who had never cared about anyone but himself. And the big brother who had treated her for so much of their lives as a duty to be managed.

Cade swore softly, still holding his hand on her hip his body vibrating now with the same frustration she felt.

'That's not how I see you, Charlotte. You're witty and vibrant and infuriating and sexy as hell. I don't want to take your independence away from you... But I've gotta tell you, living here with you, knowing my kid is growing inside you and being unable to touch you, is driving me nuts.'

She lifted her head and looked into his eyes. She saw the need and the passion which matched her own. And felt herself melting.

'You can touch me, Cade. I *want* you to touch me. As long as we're clear that's all this is. Nothing more than an itch we both enjoy scratching.'

He cradled her cheek, and she saw the flash of triumph—the aching desire. And felt oddly hollow inside.

But she knew she had to stand firm.

She had been broken before, in so many ways. Whatever happened, she had to prevent herself from being broken again—but she could do that as long as they set out clear parameters for this relationship.

'Understood,' he said, his hand stroking her neck, his thumb toying with the thundering pulse in her collarbone. 'But I want you in my bed, not the damn guest room.'

She nodded. She could give him that—it was the practical, grown-up solution.

Giving in to this raw, insistent need was dangerous. She understood that. But physical intimacy was only that, and as long as she understood this, surely it didn't have to derail her emotionally...

'Yes, okay.'

Before she had got the words out, he boosted her into his arms.

She wrapped her legs around his waist and pressed her mouth to those hard, sensual lips as he carried her into the bedroom they had shared once before... The bedroom where their baby had been created. But as she bared her body to him, she promised herself she would never bare her soul.

CHAPTER THIRTEEN

Two weeks later

CADE GROANED, clinging to his sanity, the pleasure threatening to burst through his veins like wildfire as he thrust heavily into Charlotte, barely aware of the power shower thundering down on them both.

Not yet. Not yet. Hold on.

His mind blurred, his knees trembling, his fingers digging into her hips as he held them both upright with the last of his strength, adjusting his thrusts to stroke the spot inside her he knew would take her over.

Her body tightened on his, her sob of surrender triggering his own orgasm as he crashed over at last. He groaned, the climax intensifying as he sank his face into her wet hair, drowning in brutal sensation. *Again.*

How could their chemistry still be so damn strong? So damn frantic? When they'd been making love like rabbits for two weeks straight. Every morning, every evening and any stolen moment in between...

He stood, letting the vicious afterglow wash over him, only vaguely aware of the water jets still pummelling his back. Until she shifted, reviving from the titanic orgasm first.

'We should get out of here before we dissolve,' she murmured.

He let out a rough chuckle. And how could she still captivate him? When he'd been living with her for three weeks?

Shouldn't he be bored by now? Eager to consider other living arrangements?

She was over the morning sickness, hadn't had an episode since that first one in New York. She didn't need him to watch over her so closely.

But not only couldn't he keep his hands off her in the bedroom—and everywhere else in the apartment, even the damn kitchen counter yesterday evening—he had become addicted to her company, too.

They ate together each evening now, and although her attempts to pry more details out of him about his past had started to become problematic, he'd deflected them by exploiting their voracious appetite for one another whenever she got too close. It was bad enough she knew the truth about his mother. He didn't want her to know any more.

Luckily, their lovemaking gave him an easy out from the probing queries, the questions he had no intention of answering…and in the last few days, she'd stopped asking them.

But that wasn't the only cause for concern.

He found it next to impossible now not to return from work early—or surprise her at her workspace in the Ferry Building so he could escort her back to the apartment in the evenings—because he enjoyed spending time with her so much. He loved hearing about the latest news on her commissions, checking out the designs she was working on—not that he knew a damn thing about haute couture. Her enthusiasm was captivating, and he was proud of what she'd achieved in such a short space of time.

'Water off,' he demanded, grateful for the voice-activated controls. Then lifted her from him.

She left the cubicle, and he took the opportunity to check

out the subtle changes caused by her pregnancy before she had wrapped a towel around her naked body.

Her breasts had become fuller and more sensitive, and although he couldn't see a bump yet, her waist had thickened slightly. Although that could be the food he'd been feeding her every chance he got. Charlotte had a voracious appetite for his cooking too, and he loved to watch her eat.

But what he enjoyed more was the surprise on her face when he made the effort for her.

Kind of weird, because he'd never been a nurturer, but he couldn't seem to shake the feeling of connection. Their upbringings couldn't have been more different—but in many ways they'd survived the same loss. When she'd talked about losing her mama too, the vulnerability on her face had stirred something inside him he couldn't explain.

However wealthy her folks had been, she had grown up without their emotional support. But while he'd built a wall around himself so he didn't need the validation of anyone but himself, he sensed she had never done that.

It made him ashamed for having once dismissed her as spoilt and entitled when she'd been the opposite. But her open, generous nature also made him wary. Was he becoming too dependent on her company? That kinetic connection? The spectacular chemistry? Should he be weaning himself off her before her pregnancy became more pronounced? He couldn't afford to get suckered into needing anyone. He'd been there as a kid, and it had nearly destroyed him.

He strolled out of the shower, feeling the familiar throb of awareness when her gaze skimmed over him. Colour heightened her cheeks as she looked away again.

'I should probably head to the other bathroom to get ready for tonight,' she said, all business. 'What's the dress code again?'

'Smart casual, I guess,' he said, trying to remember what

event it was and why he had accepted the invitation—when all he wanted to do right now was have her again.

He hooked a towel around his waist, but when she headed past him, he grabbed her hand. 'We don't have to go if you're tired.'

She blushed, then smiled—the dazzling smile which always made his heartbeat slow.

'Hmm…' she said, stroking her chin like a professor discovering the meaning of life. 'Is that a Landry euphemism for "Why don't I jump you again so I can tire you out even more?"'

He tugged her into his arms, enjoying the way she always challenged him, the hunger increasing. 'You got me,' he murmured.

'Not gonna happen, Galahad,' she said, dancing free, still smiling provocatively. She took a few more steps back as she wrapped the towel tighter. 'This is another great opportunity to show off one of my creations, which I am not about to throw away because you are completely insatiable. So have a cold shower and I'll see you in the lobby in twenty looking fabulous.'

He swore under his breath, really wishing he hadn't accepted the invite. He didn't want to share her for the rest of the evening with anyone.

He forced himself to ignore the thought.

The plan—such as it was—had never been to keep her forever. It was time he started getting a handle on this obsession.

But as she walked away, the yearning gripped his chest regardless. And it occurred to him it was going to be a lot harder than he had ever thought it would be to let her go. Eventually.

She turned at the door.

'Changed your mind?' he quipped.

'Nope,' she said despite the flush of arousal. 'I forgot to tell you. My first sonogram is next week. Dr Chen has scheduled it for the Friday before Labor Day. I thought...' She hesitated, panic stabbed under his breastbone.

'Is there a problem?' Was there something she wasn't telling him? 'With the baby?'

'Oh, no, not at all,' she said. Relief made him feel lightheaded as she continued. 'I just thought you might like to put it in your diary...so you can come, too.'

He opened his mouth ready to say he'd be there. He wanted to see the life growing inside her. He'd thought about it often, especially late at night, when she was sleeping and the thoughts he couldn't control bombarded him.

Would his child—*their* child—be a boy or a girl? Would it have her charisma? His drive? What would they call it?

But right alongside those thoughts had been the yearning which he recognised from long ago. The desire to belong, to be a part of a family, to have someone care for him, the way his own mother never had. The yearning which had never been fulfilled. And could destroy him if he gave in to it again.

With that yearning came the memory of fear and panic, the scent of floor cleaner and the gentle voice of the guard asking, *Where are your folks, boy?*

He swallowed the knee-jerk answer and took a mental step back.

'You sure that's smart?' he asked, trying to think of a viable excuse not to go. 'We don't want to get photographed going into an obstetric clinic together. Because that would reignite the press attention we don't want.'

'I see your point,' Charley said carefully. Even though she didn't.

It had taken her days to mention the appointment to him.

Because she wanted so desperately for him to come. But she had been waiting for an opportunity to mention it, and it hadn't materialized.

Cade never willingly spoke about the baby.

She'd tried to convince herself that was normal. That men probably didn't really connect with their baby until it felt more tangible to them, more real.

And he seemed invested in the pregnancy itself—insisting on cooking nutritious and delicious meals for her. And always asking her how she was feeling. She'd noticed the careful way he caressed her breasts when they made love, aware of how sensitive they had become. And she loved the possessive way he rested his palm on her belly, where their baby grew, when he thought she was asleep.

So many times she had wanted to turn over and ask him what he was feeling, what he was thinking. But she'd held back, scared to risk breaking cover. All her old insecurities told her she might not get the answer she wanted, so it was better not to ask.

They had time, lots of time to deal with the reality of becoming parents before the baby arrived. They'd only been together for three weeks, and they weren't a couple in the traditional sense.

But despite all those careful qualifications, her determination not to let his reticence bother her, she could feel the chill running through her at his blank expression now.

For a moment there, she'd seen the flicker of excitement in the deep blue of his irises. And hope had blossomed like a flower in her chest. Why had she been such a coward about telling him? Why had she avoided talking about the baby, too?

But the excitement had disappeared so swiftly, she wasn't sure if she had imagined it.

She didn't want to be needy, to seem insecure. Things

were good between them. Things were great. In many ways they'd become friends as well as lovers in the last few weeks.

She loved it when he touched her. Adored indulging the raw passion. But she found his attention even more intoxicating. She looked forward now to the conversations they shared each evening. He'd shown genuine interest in her business—and had offered her some invaluable advice, while also escorting her to numerous events which would give her creations exposure.

But she couldn't contain her dismay at his reasoning now. The press attention which had forced them together in the first place had died down a lot in the last month. Ever since they'd appeared at the High Line event together, the media had lost interest and moved on to the next big celebrity scandal... After all, Cade Landry wasn't a one date wonder any more, and she wasn't a wild child. Now they had shacked up together.

'The media could just as easily photograph me going to the clinic on my own. And put two and two together,' she said, deciding to press. She didn't want him being prevented from this seminal moment in their baby's life because of something which was unlikely to happen. 'But anyway, the only time we've been photographed recently is at public events. I don't think we're much of a story any more.'

'I guess,' he said, but she could still see the reluctance in his eyes.

Maybe she was making a big deal about nothing? Whether he came to the scan or not didn't have to mean anything. Perhaps his reluctance to attend the appointment really was just about logistics.

And anyhow, why did it matter how involved he wanted to be at this point? They were still months and months away from the birth. They hadn't even spoken yet about where she would be living when that happened. In theory, she would be back in the UK. But that was another conversation she'd avoided.

'How about you let me think about it,' he said carefully. 'I've got to be in Manhattan on Labor Day itself. And I may have to head to the East Coast a couple days ahead of schedule.'

'No problem.' She forced herself to smile. The jaunty I'm-all-right-Jack smile she'd perfected as a child whenever her mother looked right through her as if she wasn't there. 'I'll see you in twenty, then,' she said, and fled.

But as she retreated to the guest room—where she kept the array of designs for the public appearances they made—and put together a suitable outfit, she didn't feel her usual excitement about showing off her work. And when they arrived at the exclusive garden party in the Presidio, and her hand rested on Cade's forearm as he led her into the event, she felt the bitter pang of loneliness she remembered from so much of her childhood, even though he was right beside her.

CHAPTER FOURTEEN

One week later

'CADE, YOU MADE IT!'

'Yeah, I managed to get out of the meeting early.' Cade strolled into the obstetrician's waiting area. Guilt twisted in his gut, though, at the pleasure—and relief—in Charlotte's expression.

He hadn't intended to come. He'd lined up a ton of excuses over the past week—ever since she'd mentioned the sonogram. Valid, reasonable excuses as to why he couldn't make it.

He needed to start easing himself out of this relationship. He was getting too attached. The pregnancy, and the need to protect and support his child, were getting all mixed up in his head with his feelings for the baby's mother. And his inability to stop wanting her...all the damn time.

But as he had sat in on the internet call with the zoning commissioner and his architects on a development in Monterey that afternoon, all he'd been able to think about was Charlotte having to navigate this milestone on her own—the way she'd probably had to navigate so many others alone, just like he had. As the meeting had dragged on, his attention kept straying to the clock in the corner of his screen—and the guilt had twisted into tighter and tighter knots. Until he hadn't been able to bear it any longer. And he'd cut off the debate about permits and zoning applications, shot out of the office, jumped in the nearest cab and shouted at the driver to fight through downtown traffic to get here. Just in time.

But as he sat beside her and she grasped his hand, the look on her face so bright and happy to see him there, he felt like a fraud.

'Thanks for coming, Cade. I'm so nervous,' she said.

'You are?' he asked, surprised. He knew she'd wanted him to attend the scan, but she hadn't seemed worried. 'Why?'

'I think they check for any defects, as well as all the obvious things, like if it has the beginnings of a penis,' she said, her grin spreading over her whole face as her fingers tightened on his. 'Will you want to know if they can make an educated guess?'

'A guess about what?' he asked, not able to follow the thread of the conversation, the guilt increasing.

Why was he here? When he already knew he couldn't be a part of this baby's life, not in any tangible sense. Because it would mean being a part of her life too.

'The sex, of course!' she said, just as a woman in a white coat appeared.

'Dr Chen is ready for you, Ms Courtney.' The older woman sent Cade a welcoming smile. 'And, Mr Landry. We're so glad you could make it, too.' The nurse led them through the corridors of the state-of-the-art facility, but wouldn't stop talking. 'This is always such an important moment in a parent's journey, and it's always wonderful to have both parents here to witness it.'

Parents?

The word added weight to the guilty brick in his gut.

How could he be a parent when this child could never be more than an abstract concept to a guy like him? He'd never known his own father—had guessed the guy was probably one of the other junkies in the drug dens his mother frequented, according to the social worker's report he'd unearthed, before he'd stopped looking.

Charlotte let go of his hand to get ready for the sonogram in an adjoining room. He was introduced to Dr Chen as they waited in the examination room. She asked him if he had any questions, but he could feel the panic starting to strangle him. So he shook his head and didn't ask the questions he'd thought about often in the past couple of weeks—while trying not to think about them.

Charlotte reappeared wearing a simple green gown. Her conversation with Dr Chen—detailing her current health—floated in the room around Cade as she lay down on a long couch. He rubbed clammy palms down his pants legs, aware his hands were starting to sweat. The hum of the machine opposite them powered up as the screen began to glow with an eerie blue light.

The chemical scent of the gel the doctor put on the wand she held, and the sight of Charlotte's nervous smile as Chen pressed the wand to her bare belly, only intensified the chaotic swirl of emotions pushing at the edges of Cade's consciousness.

A fast-throbbing beat—like the ticking of an overactive clock—cut through the noise in Cade's head, and a picture formed on the screen.

'There we are,' the doctor announced with a smile in her voice. 'Junior has a nice strong heartbeat, you'll be glad to know.'

Charlotte's sharp intake of breath dragged Cade out of his trance.

'Oh, wow!' Her gaze connected with his.

The sheen of raw emotion was unguarded, and so beautiful and brave and unafraid in that moment, his own pulse accelerated to match the giddy ticking of the amplified heartbeat.

Cade forced his gaze to the screen as the doctor pointed

out the spine, the head, the legs and arms, already forming. The skull looked enormous to him, the body curled in on itself. No wonder they called it the foetal position. The screen became filled with lines and dots as the doctor took what she said were essential measurements. Charlotte asked questions, most of which he couldn't make out because of the blood thundering in his ears.

He couldn't stop staring at the life they'd made together. Because of a busted condom. The life that hadn't really been real to him until this moment—except as an opportunity to put his mark on the future. And on Charlotte.

What an arrogant jerk he'd been. To think he could manage his feelings towards this tiny human being the same way he managed his businesses.

Awe swept through him, stronger even than the afterglow when he made love to Charlotte. But right behind it was the fear. And the loneliness which made the weight on his chest crush his ribs. And suddenly he was back in that department store—waking up to find himself in the dark. Alone.

'Cade, do you want to know the sex?' Charlotte's excited question pierced through the old nightmare.

'Huh?' he managed, trying to drag himself back to the present.

'Dr Chen says the baby's sex is clear enough for her to make a good guess, if we want to know. Although it's not going to be one hundred percent at this point.'

But wouldn't knowing the sex just make this *more* real?

'Whatever you want to do is good with me,' he said, struggling to cover the panic with nonchalance.

'Okay.' A frown creased Charlotte's forehead. 'Well, I've never been very patient.' She turned to the doctor. 'I'd love to know. Are we talking penis or no penis?'

The doctor laughed and then pressed the wand back into Charlotte's abdomen. She pointed at the screen. 'You see that small nub? I think we're talking the beginnings of a penis, Charley.'

A boy? He was having a son?

The rest of the appointment passed by in a daze as he attempted to keep the wave of panic at bay. He could imagine the child clearly now. But it only made the fear and insecurity worse. Because he could also see himself as a boy, his earliest memories becoming more vivid, leaping out of the place where he'd kept them locked down for so long. The scent of trash and urine, the shouts which made him cower, the darkness closing in, the nightwatchman's torch searing his eyes and dragging him from sleep into a new terrifying reality. He'd been so defenceless then. How could he protect a child when he had never even been able to protect himself?

He managed to calm his breathing, get his giddy heart rate under control as he waited for Charlotte outside the sonogram suite.

When she appeared, she looked radiant. The short summer dress she wore clung to her body, accentuating her increasingly bountiful breasts. The shot of need was familiar, but with it was something else, something he'd noticed more and more in the past few weeks—something deep and visceral and raw. And almost as terrifying as seeing his baby for the first time.

Longing.

'So, it looks like the baby is going to have a penis,' Charlotte said as she tucked her arm through his. Her voice was light, her expression full of the joy he had seen in the suite. 'How do you feel about that? Did you have a preference?'

'No,' he managed, still feeling as if he were walking through a fog.

'Is the right answer…' she said, but her eyes had lost some of their happy glow as he escorted her to his car in the parking garage below the building.

They drove through the downtown streets, his anxiety increasing as the silence he couldn't fill stretched between them.

A part of him wanted to take her back to the penthouse, to sink into her, to make her sigh and moan and shudder in his arms—so he could make this simple again.

But it had never been simple. Not with her. And that wasn't just because of the baby. It was about so much more. His emotions weren't his own. He'd lost control long before they'd made this baby. He had to get it back or he would never be able to find his safe space again. And forget about that little boy hiding in a corner and waiting for someone to find him, to want him, when no one ever had.

'Cade, what's wrong?' Charley murmured as they walked into his penthouse.

She'd absorbed his silence in the car and tried to figure it out. But she had known something was very wrong ever since she'd come out of the dressing area at the clinic to find him waiting for her, his face ashen.

She'd been overjoyed to see him when he'd turned up for the appointment, having resigned herself to his no-show. And she'd been so happy and excited during the scan itself, especially once the doctor had declared the baby healthy. She hadn't really been aware of Cade's reaction—because she'd been so absorbed in the emotional hit of seeing the life they had created. But she was aware of it now, because it was impossible to ignore. He had looked stricken when she had found him in the waiting area. And now, it seemed as if he wasn't even here.

'I need to head to the airport,' he said.

'What?' she said, shocked by the abrupt statement and the cool tone.

'I have to be in Manhattan for Labor Day,' he replied. 'And I've got a lot to settle before then.'

'I know, but...'

Before she could say more, he had left her to walk into their bedroom.

She raced after him. 'Really, you have to go this evening?' she asked, hating the tremble of anxiety, confused now as well as shocked.

'Yeah.' He grabbed a bag from inside the dresser, began dumping clothes into it.

'Cade, is this about the sonogram? What's wrong? What happened to you in there?' she asked again, suddenly determined to face this situation head-on.

She'd thought they'd made a breakthrough this afternoon. That he was finally willing to engage with the reality of the baby instead of just the pregnancy. But why had she let him get away with his disengagement for so long? He'd wanted this baby, too. Weren't they supposed to be in this together? What was really going on here? Something about this felt hideously familiar, reminding her of all the times she'd begged her mother to see her, to respond to her, and she never had. Or tried to get her father's attention, only to be informed her feelings, her needs, really weren't important in the grand scheme of things.

He headed to the bathroom and reappeared with his hands full of his toiletries. He dumped them in the bag too, then zipped it up.

'Cade, stop!' She pressed shaking fingers over his. 'Look at me.' He lifted his head, his gaze finally meeting hers. 'What is going on? You have to tell me. You're starting to scare me...'

'Charlotte, I'm sorry,' he said, his voice so grave it only scared her more. But then he cradled her cheek, and what she saw in his eyes calmed the panic, at least a little.

Yearning. Need. Connection.

But when she leant into his palm, he dragged it away.

'You must have known,' he said, 'that this was only ever meant to be temporary.'

She heard it then, the finality, the dismissal. It cut her like a knife. And made her realise she had somehow convinced herself that this was more. That this was better. That this *could* be something. When it had always been nothing. For him, anyway.

There were so many things she could say as he slung the bag onto his shoulder.

What about the baby they shared? What about the emotions inside her which had blossomed and bloomed and grown over the past weeks every time he looked at her with such longing, such passion? Maybe even before that? Maybe right back to that night across the bay when she'd danced with him and felt truly seen for the first time in her life.

How could she have misinterpreted all of that so completely?

She felt her heart tearing and shattering, though, unable to voice any of it as he rested his hand on her abdomen and pressed a kiss to her forehead.

Tears scoured her eyes as she saw the sadness in his face. *It doesn't have to be this way. Don't leave me. Why can't you love me? Why can't I be enough?*

The terror returned as the questions reverberated inside her, but she couldn't get them past the huge lump in her throat. And as he stepped back, she made herself believe she didn't want to ask the questions, because she had always known the answers, and all she had left now was her pride.

'My legal team will be in touch about the financial arrangements for the baby,' he said. 'Stay here as long as you want. The place is yours. Landry Construction will continue to pay your business expenses and all your other costs for as long as you need.'

She didn't reply. She stood stoic and unbending as she watched him leave her.

But when the lift doors closed behind him, she walked to the window, and the tears came. They streamed down her face as the choking sobs queued up in her throat.

She rested her hand on her belly, where Cade had touched her for the last time.

Stroking the place where their baby grew.

Not theirs. *Hers*.

'You're not his any more,' she whispered, out loud to the empty apartment. 'You're mine. He doesn't want you, but I do.'

But even as she said the words, she knew a part of this baby would always be his, just like the foolish part of her heart which she'd opened to him—after convincing herself she wouldn't. After knowing she shouldn't.

The part of her heart he'd discarded all too easily.

CHAPTER FIFTEEN

Labor Day

Helberg is yours. I concede the bet. Give my best to Charley.

CADE STARED AT the text which had just appeared on his phone from Adam Courtney as he stood in the locker room of the club. He swiped sweat off his brow—caused by the hour he'd just spent on the treadmill—attempting to keep his focus on business. And not Charlotte.

In preparation for his meeting in ten minutes with her brother to declare the winner of the bet—which now wasn't happening.

Courtney had thrown in the towel, just like Zane a month ago. Cade had won the bet.

He should be contacting his finance team, setting the wheels in motion to snap up the rest of the Helberg shares. No other viable buyers had appeared since the three of them had made the bet on the Fourth of July. He was clear to finish the takeover.

Helberg was his.

But instead of the elation he should be feeling, he felt hollow. Empty. And more alone than he'd felt even as a kid when he'd had no one.

He sat down heavily on one of the locker room benches.

He could hear a couple of the other guys who were there on a vacation day, talking about Cornell's college football team and their chances for the new season, the showers running, a nineties rap anthem playing on the speakers.

But all he could really hear was Charlotte and the last words she'd said to him—hopelessness and confusion in her voice.

What is going on? You have to tell me. You're starting to scare me.

So he'd told her. Not the whole truth, but enough of the truth so she would know he couldn't be a parent. He couldn't even be a partner to her.

And it seemed like she'd got the message, because she hadn't contacted him in the days since.

Give my best to Charley.

The offhand comment in Courtney's text seared his brain. Dating Charlotte had won him Helberg. Weird, it hadn't even occurred to him until this moment that she had given him this victory.

Give it up, man. This is what you wanted, what you worked for. All these years. You can't go back and change who you are, who you've become for her...or for the baby.

He forced himself to switch the phone on and texted his EA. His fingers shaking.

Tell finance to finish the Helberg buyout.

But as he switched the phone off and headed into the showers, the sense of triumph, the validation he should have been feeling, never came. And the hollow ache in his gut became a black hole.

Four days later

Charley stared up at the stunning Art Deco tower which housed the Courtney Collection as the cab she'd taken from the airport sped back into the afternoon traffic. Twenty-five storeys of luxury, elegance, and class, with her brother Adam's penthouse offices at the top.

Funny to think she'd never visited him here. Just another example of what a coward she'd always been. The truth was, she really didn't want to be here now. She felt so fragile and wounded and pathetic, and it wasn't as if she and Adam had ever had a particularly close relationship.

But in amongst all the heartache and recriminations she'd been heaping on herself over the past week—as she wound up her workshop in San Francisco, said goodbye to Rachel and Lanisha, her brilliant seamstresses, and worked out the logistics of her relocation back to East London—she'd realised she owed her brother an apology.

According to the reports of Landry Construction's historic takeover of Helberg Holdings—which had been all over the business news for two days—Cade had won the bet. Which meant he now owned Montague's, the jewellery company Adam had been so desperate to buy back.

She had arranged a twelve-hour stop-over in New York en route to the UK to say she was sorry to her brother.

As she introduced herself to the receptionist in the extravagant lobby area—where a towering wall of glass separated the refined elegance of the interior from the manic energy of Madison Avenue during the lunch hour—it occurred to her that her brother might not even be here.

Her hopes were dashed, though, when the perfectly made-up receptionist contacted his PA and directed her to a bank of lifts, stating Adam would see her straight away.

Her heart plummeted along with her stomach as the lift

climbed up the building. The scrape of tears which she refused to shed—because she'd shed more than enough of them already—made her throat feel raw.

Her mind started to wander to yet more devastating what-ifs as she was directed into the private penthouse office's double-height space by a friendly woman called Maggie who had met her at the lift on the floor below. Here too, the glass added so much light her eyes stung. She'd spent a good twenty minutes doing her make up on the flight from San Francisco, though, so hopefully Adam wouldn't notice the results of her week-long crying jag.

But what if she owed him more than an apology? Would he expect an explanation for why she'd dated Cade Landry for over a month—and then been dropped like a stone?

She covered her belly.

Should she tell him about the baby? She wasn't really showing yet, but they were siblings after all. And he was going to become an uncle…of the son of the man who had robbed him of Montague's.

She was swallowing rapidly, trying to get a handle on the latest wave of panic and misery—when her brother appeared on the mezzanine level and jogged down the steps to meet her.

'Charley? This is a surprise?' he said, but he didn't sound angry with her, weirdly. 'I certainly hope you didn't bring that bastard Landry with you.'

She jolted slightly before she noticed he was smiling, his expression relaxed. The joke only made her feel smaller and more insignificant, though. And hopeless.

She blinked rapidly, trying to hold back more self-indulgent tears. But as he got closer, his eyes narrowed, and he frowned.

'Charley, what's wrong?' he said with a perceptiveness which threw her back in time, to a memory from long ago.

A memory she realised she'd forgotten until this moment. Of standing and staring hopelessly at the broken earth of her mother's grave while shivering uncontrollably in the cold March wind. Until Adam had taken her hand and squeezed her chilled fingers. And made the shuddering stop.

He was looking at her now the same way—with concern, with understanding, with support.

The choking weight rose up her chest, and a sob lurched out of her mouth. The stinging tears scoured her throat, and the mask of competence and capability she'd been faking desperately for days collapsed…

She started shaking, not aware of what he was saying as he wrapped his arm around her shoulders. He held her close as the misery poured out of her and onto his clean white shirt. The flood of pain, of humiliation, was nothing though compared to the deep sense of loss.

But how can you lose something you never had?

His soothing words were gruff, but gentle and surprisingly not at all judgemental. At last, the raging storm of grief passed, and she became aware of the comforting scent of laundry detergent which clung to him. And the weight of his arm on her shoulder as he sat beside her.

How had they ended up on the couch? She didn't even know.

He handed her a tissue from the dispenser on the coffee table. 'Okay?'

She nodded, swiping her eyes. 'I'm sorry…' she managed, embarrassed. As well as heartsore. She'd spent the last year trying to persuade Adam she was a competent business-woman, and now she'd trashed that, too.

'Don't apologise,' he said, but then he surprised her even more when he asked, gently, 'Can you tell me what the problem is?'

She nodded again. But she couldn't look at him. 'Cade left me.'

She heard him curse under his breath, a very un-Adam-like expletive.

'And I'm going to have his baby.'

His hand tensed on her shoulder. 'Wait a minute. Landry got you pregnant, then dumped you?' He swore again, sounding furious.

She blinked. How odd. The show of emotion was so un-Adam-like, that and the fact he didn't look exasperated with her.

'To be fair, the getting pregnant bit was a joint enterprise,' she replied.

He shot off the couch and stormed across the thick carpeting, his rigid strides making his agitation clear. She hadn't intended to tell him about the baby, because she didn't think she could cope with a lecture. But all he did was continue to curse about Cade.

'You don't blame me?' she said, still astonished by his reaction as he marched back towards her.

'Blame you for what?'

'For getting pregnant with your business rival?'

His frown became a scowl. 'Do you want the baby?'

She nodded.

'Then blame has nothing to do with it,' he said without hesitation. 'But Landry has responsibilities, to you *and* to his child.' He thrust his fingers through his hair, making it stick up in haphazard spikes. 'I can't believe it...' he said, sitting heavily on the couch next to her. 'I'm going to be an uncle.'

She found herself smiling. It felt good, even though it hurt.

She sniffed. Then blew her nose loudly on the tissue. 'I didn't actually come here to tell you about the baby. It's not due for months,' she said. It felt important to have his support, especially as it was so unexpected, but it didn't really change anything.

'I'm going to kill him,' her brother said, apropos to nothing.

'Adam, really.' She laid her hand on one of the fists clenched in his lap. 'It's okay. He's been very generous. He's insisting on supporting the baby financially.' She'd heard from his team the day after he'd walked out. But somehow his generosity only made the whole thing so much worse. Because she couldn't hate him the way she wanted to be able to hate him.

'That's not the point, Charley,' her brother said, flipping his hand over to grip her fingers—reminding her of the eighteen-year-old who had anchored her once before, when he had been in so much pain himself. 'The point is he hurt you. He made you cry.'

She clasped his hand, fighting off more tears. 'Please don't be nice now, or you'll make me start crying again. And neither of us wants that.' She tried to smile. 'You know what's good about all this, though?'

He simply looked at her blankly.

'It's nice to have my big brother in my corner,' she said.

He folded her back into his arms. 'Of course I'm in your corner. Where the hell else would I be?'

She sighed against his damp shirt. 'I don't know...but let's face it, I haven't always been very lovable,' she said. 'Which is probably why Cade didn't want me either.'

She'd had to face that truth so many times over the last few days as she struggled to make sense of Cade's abrupt departure.

What an idiot she'd been—building up some ridiculous fantasy they could become a family while busy pretending all her flaws didn't exist. Convenient, but not reality. Why would she assume Cade would want her for the long haul when no one else ever had?

She had thought they'd made a connection, but what did she really know about honest, open relationships, seeing as she'd never had one of those either?

'Please tell me he didn't say that to you?' Adam demanded, looking even more furious.

She shook her head. 'Honestly? He didn't really give me an explanation. He told me he wanted this baby. And somehow I made a silly mistake and got that confused with him wanting me too. But while I was falling in love…he wasn't.'

Adam dragged her back, his hands gripping her shoulders as he stared into her face. 'Why the hell would he tell you he wanted the baby if he *didn't* want you too?' he said. 'It doesn't sound like you made a mistake. It sounds like he deliberately misled you. And who the hell wouldn't want you?'

She could feel the tears welling again at his forthright defence of her. If she didn't feel so broken right now, she would have been able to appreciate it more. Then the other things he'd said registered… 'But why would he mislead me about wanting the baby?'

'The bet,' he said, then cursed again.

The bet? She felt sick. The nausea she hadn't felt in weeks dropped into her stomach like a stone.

Was that possible? That Cade had been lying to her about the baby? Simply to ensure she would stay with him for those extra weeks? Could he have done something so manipulative?

'I can't believe he would be that cruel,' she said, desperate not to think it of him. But she'd been wrong about so much else. Why not this too? 'Do you really think he would lie about that?' she asked, feeling more insecure now, and vulnerable.

'Honestly, Charley, I don't know him *that* well,' he said,

but she could see the sympathy in his eyes and the under-standing. Why did that only make her stomach hurt worse? 'But I do know he's pretty ruthless in business, and he re-ally wanted Helberg.'

'But so did you,' Charley said, still trying to clarify, to reject Adam's accusations. Cade had never told her why owning Helberg was so important to him, but could it re-ally have been *that* important?

'Yeah, I did, because I wanted Montague's for personal reasons which I now know were pretty misguided.'

'What reasons?' she asked. Was it possible that Cade had had really compelling reasons too? Personal reasons? But even if he did, how could that absolve him? And why was she still making excuses for him?

Adam interrupted her panicked justifications. 'I wanted to get it back because I thought I was to blame for Mum's suicide.'

'What?' Charley's heart lurched in her chest at the flash of pain in his expression. 'But...*why* would you think that?'

He sat back down next to her and took her hands in his. 'That's not the point, Charley. The point is I don't think that any more. Ella made me realise her suicide wasn't my fault. Any more than it was *your* fault that both our parents ig-nored you growing up.'

'Okay,' she said, surprised at his intuition...but also strangely empowered by the bold statement. He was right. A part of her *had* always believed it was her fault. And she supposed she had internalised that hurt, that feeling of re-jection. But how did Adam know? Then again, Adam did seem different today. Not just more relaxed and a lot less guarded, but also surprisingly emotionally astute. 'Who's Ella?' she asked, wondering if this woman she had never heard of had something to do with it.

Flags of colour appeared on his cheeks. 'It's a long story...

and I'd like you to meet her. *Soon*,' he said forcefully. But before she could get over her shock—was her commitment-phobic brother actually in love?—he squeezed her fingers and added, 'I think we should focus on Cade first. And how exactly we're going to make him pay for this…'

'There is no *we*, Adam.' She tugged her hands out of her brother's grip. And stood up. Her legs were still shaky, her insides twisted into hard, greasy knots. But Adam's support had finally made her realise something important. They had both been failed by their parents. And she'd carried that sub-conscious belief—that she needed to earn approval and attention, because she didn't deserve it—ever since she was a child. Did that explain why she'd been such a coward this past week, too…? Dissolving into tears and recriminations and blaming herself for Cade's desertion, without ever really wondering why he'd left?

She had let him walk. She hadn't fought. She hadn't even asked for an explanation. Because deep down she'd blamed herself, still believing that she was essentially unlovable. But if he had done what Adam suspected him of doing—said he wanted this baby just to win a bet…she wanted to know so she could start the long slow process of getting over him. Because if he had, he had never been the man she had fallen in love with—not even close. And the only way to do that was to suck up her pride—and her pain—and confront him. Before she lost her nerve.

'This is my life, and I plan to sort it out,' she added, because Adam was still looking at her with sympathy in his eyes. 'On my own.'

She'd been so scared she wouldn't be good enough to be a mother. Scared she couldn't handle it alone. Terrified of coming to rely on Cade. So that when she had fallen in love and he hadn't loved her back, she'd convinced herself—just like she had as a little girl—that it was her fault, her mistake somehow. But she could see now, whatever Cade's motives, she hadn't been wrong to fall for him. She had simply been wrong not to ensure he deserved her love.

To her surprise, instead of arguing with her or doubting her ability to go it alone, Adam simply nodded. 'Okay, Charley,' he said. 'I hope you give him hell,' he finished with a solidarity he had never shown her before.

Whoever you are, Ella, I love you already.

'Don't worry, I will,' she said, feeling stronger now than she had.

As she left Adam's office and called a cab to take her to Landry Construction's offices uptown, she realised that whatever Cade's motives turned out to be, she would be okay.

The bottom had dropped out of her world. But she wasn't the one running away. Not this time. That would be Cade.

And not only did she deserve answers from him about why he was running, she also deserved to be loved. And no one was going to convince her otherwise...

Not any more.

CHAPTER SIXTEEN

'MR LANDRY? Miss Courtney is here to see you.'

Cade's gaze rose from his laptop, propelled by the surge of emotion at the mention of Charlotte's name.

'Charlotte's here?' he managed, before the woman herself—the woman who had haunted every one of his dreams and all his nightmares for a week, the woman who he'd had to stop himself returning to a hundred times—marched into the space behind his executive assistant, Grady.

'Yes, Mr Landry…' The young man glanced round, only to be mowed down by Charlotte. 'I'm sorry, Miss…'

'Thank you so much, Grady,' she cut the poor kid's protests off at the knees.

Cade stood and came out from behind his desk.

The emotion turned to pride and a powerful sense of relief. The stunned sadness of a week ago was gone. The sadness he'd caused and hadn't been able to forgive himself for.

'Please, Miss…' Grady began.

'It's okay, Grady,' he said, finally managing to find his voice around the tight, painful feeling in his throat. 'Leave us alone and hold all my calls.'

He hadn't meant to hurt her. But he knew he had. It was just one of the things that had tortured him—the guilt as well as the longing.

Grady left the room and closed the door behind him.

Charlotte stopped beside the drawing table, where he had

been working late all this week so he wouldn't have to go back to his apartment alone and think about her.

'It's good to see you, Charlotte,' he said. And meant it.

He didn't know why she was here, and he really didn't care. Because he felt like a starving man eating for the first time in days as he devoured the sight of her in tailored pants and a fitted blouse, her silky hair rioting around her face.

She sucked in a breath, her expression a vivid combination of anger and determination.

'I need to know the truth...' she said carefully, but he could see the swirl of sadness in her eyes, alongside the storm of outrage. 'Did you tell me you wanted this baby when we found out I was pregnant simply to keep me with you until Labor Day? To win Helberg?'

'What...?' The accusation came so far out of left field, he couldn't make any sense of it.

'I deserve to know...' she said, her voice rising, her face rigid now with hurt. 'Because Adam believes you did, and the way you left... I need to know exactly how much you used me and the baby to win the bet. So I can start to forgive myself for falling in love with you.'

Falling in love with you...

The words made the ache in his throat sink into his heart.

He stared at her, desperately trying to figure out what to say. Part of him knew he should tell her she was right. That he'd never really wanted this baby, that he'd used the pregnancy the same way he'd used her. Wouldn't it be better for all of them? It would be the final nail in the coffin of this relationship. The relationship he'd been so terrified of nurturing or even acknowledging a week ago, when they'd seen the baby for the first time.

But somehow the words which would set him free, which would set them both free, wouldn't come out of his mouth.

Because he had missed her, so much, and he still wanted her, and he couldn't bear to lie to her again.

So he continued to stand there dumbly, absorbing the sight of her, unable to say anything at all.

She stepped forward, the sound of her pumps somehow deafening on the office carpeting. The sheen of moisture in her eyes twinkled in the afternoon light pouring through the windows…and everything inside him became harsh and jagged. The intense longing to touch her again, to hold her, to never let her go was like a kudzu vine wrapping around his heart and squeezing hard enough to make his breathing stop.

'I didn't set out to hurt you…' he said at last, which was at least the truth. But how could he have known she would come to mean so much?

'You coward…' she hissed, the single tear running down her cheek like an arrow to his heart. 'You can't admit it even now, can you? Why did you say you wanted the baby? When you didn't? How could you use the pregnancy just to win a bet?'

He should let her believe it, but the pain in her voice broke him.

'Because I didn't. The bet had nothing to do with my feelings for the baby…'

Or you.

She walked forward, lifting her fists, and pushing them against his chest. 'You're lying. I know you're lying.' Her sobs wrenched at his heart. 'Or why would you leave as soon as you won?'

'It wasn't about the bet…' He grasped her fists and tugged her into his arms, no longer able to stop himself from holding her. 'Not even in Italy.'

He felt the anger drain out of her until all that was left was the hurt.

She looked up at him, her ravaged face somehow so brave. 'Then why did you leave me?'

He cupped her cheeks, brushed the last of her tears away with his thumbs. The brutal agony washed through him all over again. That terrible feeling of never being good enough, strong enough, to matter.

But he'd mattered to her. And he'd thrown it away.

'I'm not sure I can explain it,' he said, so glad to have her in his arms again he was scared even now to tell her what a coward he'd been.

She shook her head, then dragged herself back, out of his embrace. He felt the loss like a blow to the chest. She was trembling, the pain in her eyes unvarnished, but despite the hurt he could also see her strength, which only made him love and respect her more.

'That's not good enough, Cade. You made me believe it was my fault, but worse than that, when Adam mentioned the bet...' She drew in a ragged breath. 'I realised I didn't know you well enough to tell if it were true. Because you always kept so much hidden.' She swung away from him and walked to the glass wall, which looked down on the city he'd conquered. Achievements which meant nothing without her. 'And that made me blame myself. Made me think it was my fault somehow...'

'Damn it, Charlotte.' He walked towards her, grasped her shoulders from behind, and pressed his face into her hair, unable to stop touching her, needing to hold her again. 'You have to believe me,' he said, inhaling the scent which had become a drug over the past weeks. 'I didn't walk away because of the bet.'

She turned to face him, dislodging his hands. And wrapped her arms around her waist to ward him off. 'Still not good enough, Cade. You have to tell me why you left.'

He sighed and drew back. And turned to stare out at the view, not able to look at her when he told her the truth.

They were so far above the manic energy of Manhattan. He should have been safe here, in the ivory tower he'd built to protect himself from ever needing anyone again.

But she'd breached it, just like she'd breached his heart.

'Because I was terrified of my feelings for you,' he murmured. 'Seeing the baby felt so real, but what was worse was knowing that eventually I would let him down. And you down. I had to leave you first, before you decided to leave me, like she did.'

Charley stood shaking, the emotion coursing through her almost more than she could bear. But then slowly, Cade's words registered. The fear behind them, but also the simplicity of feeling, the strength of his longing. Like hers.

But she didn't want to give in too easily. To be that needy girl again who had internalised all the hurt, the longing, the loneliness of her childhood. Now more than ever, she needed to be strong. She wasn't going to give him a free pass. If he loved her, *really* loved her, he had to prove it to her. She deserved that.

'But then why did you still close the deal?' she asked, her voice thick with tears. 'If you wanted to be with me? If you were simply scared of your feelings for me...' She let out a heavy sigh. 'Which I get, because frankly, I was pretty terrified of my feelings for you,' she added. He finally turned to look at her again, the shame in his expression giving her the strength she needed to say the rest of it. 'Why did you still claim Helberg?'

He dropped his head, shoved his hands into the pockets of his trousers, his stance so tense she could see what it was costing him to find words for feelings she doubted he had ever confronted before.

He lifted his head at last, his blue eyes dark with the emotion he'd refused to let her see…until now.

'I thought if I claimed Helberg,' he said, his words measured, but the tone brittle with self-loathing, 'I could get back the feeling of being safe again. Of being invulnerable.' He shook his head. 'But it didn't make any difference. Even though I've been working to acquire the damn brand for…' He sighed and looked down at his feet again. 'A long time.'

'Why?' she asked, because she wanted all the answers to questions she'd never felt able to ask him before. '*Why* was Helberg so important to you?'

He raised his head, the scar on his eyebrow levelling as he frowned. But just when she thought he wasn't going to tell her, he let out a rough, guttural, hopeless sigh.

'It's pretty dumb,' he said.

'Not to me it isn't.' She wouldn't let him off the hook.

He looked away, but when he began to talk, she knew the monotone of his voice masked a deep emotion she doubted he had ever revealed to anyone before now.

'The department store…in Baton Rouge,' he said, but then his voice trailed off.

'The place where your mother abandoned you?' she prompted.

His gaze met hers. And he nodded. 'It was Helberg's flagship store in the South. She used to take me there when she wasn't too strung out. She knew I liked to play in the toy department. And the staff were kind. They'd let us stay for hours and never threw us out.' He hitched his shoulder, the gesture somehow both wary and ashamed. 'I loved that place so much. It was clean, and everything was perfect. It's the only good memory I have of her. She wasn't much of a mama, but she was so young and messed up. I think, deep down, I figured if I could own Helberg, restore the brand, bring it back to its former glory, I could prove she had loved me once, too.'

She stood trembling. The picture he'd painted was so sad and so vulnerable. And she realised however much he had tried to leave that boy behind, that abandoned child had always been there inside him. Scared to love. Terrified to ask for more. In case it made him that vulnerable again.

No wonder he had been frightened of the love building between them, too.

She walked to him, banded her arms around his waist and pressed her cheek to the rigid muscles of his chest. 'Oh, Cade, you idiot.'

He wrapped her in his arms, the deep sigh making his muscles relax. 'Can you forgive me for being such a dumbass?'

He shifted back, framed her face in his palms, then pressed his forehead to hers. 'If you'll give me another chance, I swear I can make it up to you,' he vowed. 'Every damn day. I love you, Charlotte, so damn much. I'm gonna sell Helberg. It never meant what I thought it did anyway.'

The hope blossomed inside her, stronger this time. And so much more sure.

'I don't want you to do that, Cade. Especially if Helberg is your only real connection to your mother.'

He gave her a weak smile, but she could see the same fierce hope reflected in his eyes.

'Don't you get it, Charlotte? I don't need Helberg now.' He boosted her into his arms, the smile becoming a grin as she stroked his hair, his cheeks, the rough stubble on his chin, letting him know they were good. They were okay again. That she had already forgiven him. 'Not if I've got you. And our baby.'

She chuckled, elated, as he captured her face and began

to kiss her as if his life depended on sealing their connection, exploiting it. And glorying in it.

And as he showed her how much he loved her, she knew exactly how he felt.

Because her life depended on it, too.

EPILOGUE

One year later

'DO THEY FUSS like that a lot?'

Cade smiled at the question from Zane deMarco as he stood in the bright, airy kitchen of his new home—a historic brownstone with a big yard and ten bedrooms he'd bought seven months ago—and tried to soothe his fretful son. Luke Adam Landry was not happy at having been detached from his mama's breast five minutes ago—despite being fast asleep—and he was letting Cade and Zane and his uncle Adam know all about it.

'Only at three in the morning, usually,' Cade joked.

Zane's eyebrows lifted, but he looked more fascinated than horrified when he said, 'Seriously?'

Yeah, seriously, and at two and five and any time in between.

'Not always,' he said, deciding to give Zane a break.

Their small party had found out at the neighbourhood chapel only an hour ago, while they were baptising Luke, and Zane and Adam had been sworn in as his godfathers, that Zane and his partner, Skylar, were expecting. Seemed it had been a surprise for both of them, but a happy surprise, and Cade didn't want to scare the guy too much. Especially as all the trials and tribulations of parenthood in the past three months had been far outweighed, in Cade's humble opinion, by the incredible upside of meeting his son. And watching Charlotte blossom into the role of motherhood. She was magnificent, and he could not have loved her more if he had tried.

'He's just a little mad with me at the moment for interrupting his quality time with his mama,' he said easily—and just like his mama, Luke was more than ready to let anyone and everyone know his mind, Cade thought, his chest swelling with pride. 'And for letting the preacher dunk him in water. I'm not sure he's gonna forgive me for that for a while,' he added, remembering the indignant yelling in church which had nearly deafened them all.

Adam gave his new nephew a pat on the back. 'Good boy, Luke. You tell your daddy when he's out of order, and I'll back you up.'

All three of them laughed, but as Luke finally quietened, nestling against Cade's chest and dropping back to sleep with his whole fist shoved into his mouth, Cade remembered something he and Charlotte had agreed to that morning. 'By the way, Courtney, I have a baptismal gift for you.'

Adam's expression sobered. 'A gift? For me? But I'm not the one getting christened,' he said.

Trust the guy to be so damn literal.

But Cade only smiled. He liked Adam Courtney, a lot. All three of them had become much more than just squash buddies over the past year.

Although he found it hilarious now to think of them sat in their club sauna—the club they rarely had time to go to now—making that dumb bet to decide who would own Helberg Holdings, only to all end up winning something much more precious instead.

He liked Zane and Adam's partners too—Skylar and

Ella—who he and Charlotte socialised with now whenever all six of them were in the city.

'Charlotte and I would like to give you Montague's,' he said, cutting straight to the chase.

The work to rebuild the Helberg brand in the past year ever since the buyout had kept him busy—while he waited for Charlotte to pop and they'd both got to know their new son. But he had decided to offload Montague's and a few of the other assets. He'd wanted to gift the company to Charlotte, when he'd found out the connection to her mother, but she had insisted he give it to her brother instead. And he hadn't had a problem with that.

'Thanks,' Adam said easily. 'But I don't need it.'

'I'd really like you to take it, man,' Cade countered. 'Both Charlotte and I owe you—and Ella—big time for supporting us this past year.'

And helping give Charlotte the courage to realise our break-up was all my fault, not hers, he almost added, but didn't. Because as much as he liked and admired his new brother-in-law, and considered him a good friend, they were still guys.

'And she wants you to have it. She's far too busy with Trouble Maker…' His chest swelled again at the thought of how Charlotte had developed her business over the past year, mostly while pregnant. 'And with this little fella…' He kissed his son's downy curls, breathing in the sweet scent he adored of sour milk and baby shampoo. 'So she doesn't have the time to give Montague's the attention it needs.'

Adam looked non-plussed. 'Okay, how about I think about it?'

'You do that,' Cade nodded, realising how important it was to him to pay his dues to Adam Courtney… Because the man was part of Cade's family now too.

'Glad you two got that settled,' Zane cut in, the reckless

twinkle in his eye something Cade remembered from a certain sauna meeting on last year's Independence Day. 'Now where the hell is my gift? Because I've got my eye on some prime realty in SoHo that belongs to Landry Construction.'

'Go to hell,' Cade joked back, and they all laughed.

Four hours later...

'He's finally back to sleep. I swear he is almost as much of a handful as you are.'

'That's my boy!' Charley grinned at Cade in the bathroom mirror and popped her toothbrush onto its stand, unable to disguise her happiness at his exasperation...and the mouth-watering sight of his naked chest, the phoenix tattoo she adored highlighting his impressive pecs.

It was only ten o'clock, but they'd had a very full day, getting their son formally baptised and then enjoying some quality time with Adam and Ella and Zane and Skylar. She was more than ready for bed now. Especially when Cade wrapped his arms around her waist from behind and pulled her against him.

'I think I should punish you for encouraging him to defy me,' he murmured into her hair, his hands rising to cup and caress her breasts through the silk negligée she had worn specifically to get this reaction.

Excitement swirled alongside the joy as she felt the ridge growing in his pyjama pants to press against her bottom. They'd finally restarted their love life a month ago, and to her utter joy, it was as vital and exciting as ever...although they had to snatch their chances when they could now, because Cade wasn't wrong—Luke was somewhat demanding.

Although she wouldn't have had it any other way.

She lifted her arm to curl her hand around his neck, her

mind floating on the delicious wave of arousal and all the happy memories.

So much had happened in the past year, all of it full-on and chaotic and challenging and exhausting.

They'd got married in a small ceremony in Baton Rouge just before Christmas, to coincide with the opening of the new Landry Helberg Department Store—with Adam giving her away and Ella, who Charley already considered a sister, as her maid of honour. She'd also expanded the Trouble Maker brand into a fashion line, and recently moved to new premises in the brownstone next door—which Cade had purchased for her as a wedding present, and then gutted and rehabbed into an amazing shop and workspace. She'd had to take a back seat on her business, though, once Luke was born, but taking the time to nurture and enjoy her son had been more than worth it. The fear she'd once had of being a mother had been well and truly conquered by the rush of pure, unadulterated love she felt for their baby the minute he had been placed in her arms, protesting about the ten hours of labour he had just endured.

What had surprised her much more, though, was how willing Cade had been to reduce his workload too. And spend as much time as he could being a hands-on dad.

'Mmm…' she purred as Cade's questing fingers lifted her negligée to find her wet and ready for him. 'I think maybe we need to take my punishment into the bedroom,' she said, making him chuckle.

She swung round and leapt into his arms. And he caught her. Of course.

She shouldn't be surprised, she realised as she peppered kisses over his handsome face, that Cade had become such a hands-on dad. Because he had been as good as his word over the past year in every respect. More than ready to prove how much both she and now Luke meant to him.

'Do your worst, Mr Landry!' she announced as he marched into their bedroom.

'Count on it, Mrs Landry,' he said, then threw her on the bed…and proceeded to punish her in the most delicious way possible.

* * * * *

Did you fall head over heels for
After-Party Consequences*?*

Then you're sure to adore the other
installments in the Billion-Dollar Bet *trilogy:*
Billion-Dollar Dating Game *by Natalie Anderson*
Boss with Benefits *by Lucy King*

And don't miss these other Heidi Rice stories!

Stolen for His Desert Throne
Redeemed by My Forbidden Housekeeper
Undoing His Innocent Enemy
Hidden Heir with His Housekeeper
Revenge in Paradise

Available now!

PRINCESS BRIDE SWAP

LORRAINE HALL

MILLS & BOON

For anyone struggling to know their worth.

CHAPTER ONE

PRINCESS BEAUGONIA FREJA CAJA ISABELLA RENDALL sat
sandwiched between her parents in the back of a sleek car
that was winding through the curving roads of Divio, a
small principality nestled in the southern Alps.

Her new home.

She supposed she was nervous, in a way, but she was
also filled with purpose. She knew every step forward—no
matter how far out of her depth, no matter how challenging—was in aid to her twin sister.

She owed Zia everything up to this point, and now she
would return the favor.

She supposed a lifetime married to some crown prince
she'd never once met was quite the sword to fall on, but
Beaugonia had seen no other choice. Zia was *pregnant*,
and in love with the father of her children—whether either
of them wanted to admit it or not. Beaugonia may not be
an expert on love herself, but she'd certainly read her fair
share of books on the topic.

And certainly her sister couldn't be expected to marry
the crown prince of Divio in her state, even if Lyon Traverso would have married her already pregnant with another man's twins.

Unlikely.

Which also meant Zia couldn't be expected to continue on her life as heir to Lille.

Beau could have left it at that. Her father was a king and had the power to choose whatever heirs he liked—that was why Zia was heir in the first place, despite the fact Beau was three minutes older. But Beau had never been the ideal princess.

Maybe that, in part, was why she'd concocted this plan. Not only did it take the heat off Zia, but it ruined her father's plans. He couldn't *choose* an heir if she'd set herself up as one he couldn't hide.

Beau had reached out to Lyon herself. Even before Zia had been reunited with the father of her babies. The moment she'd learned of Zia's pregnancy, Beau had begun laying the groundwork, and Zia's upcoming wedding to Cristhian Sterling only pushed her plans into high gear.

Underneath her father's nose, Beau had gotten the agreements *herself.* So when she'd presented her father with her upcoming marriage to the crown prince, her need to be his heir in order to accomplish it, he had not had a choice.

He could embarrass them all and break off her agreement with Lyon, refuse to name her as heir. Or he could accept what she'd done. And she'd known, based on the way her father had treated her for the entirety of her life, he'd never choose embarrassment.

He'd berated her for what she'd accomplished once she'd informed him. If they'd been at home and he'd discovered what she'd done, instead of at Cristhian's estate out of the scope of King Rendall's power in Lille, he likely would have done a lot more than hurl insults at her.

But Beau didn't see the point in worrying over things that *hadn't* happened. She had plenty of worries in the present.

Like marrying a man she'd never met aside from emails and a spare few phone calls.

The car wound its way up to a staid, *ancient*-looking castle, majestic mountains soaring in the distance. The sun was just starting to set behind it, creating the kind of breathtaking scene that might ease the struggle of whatever she'd gotten herself into if she got to look out a window and see that every morning.

Neither parent had said anything on the flight from Cristhian's to Divio, not on this drive from the airport to the castle, and that didn't change as they were helped out of the car and led toward the castle entrance.

But as the doors opened, and they were ushered into a soaring room of archways and stained glass, full of stone and carpets and history you could practically see in the shadowy corners, her father finally spoke.

"We will go along with this farce, Beaugonia," he said in that icy, furious tone he wielded so well. Not loud enough other people might hear, not hot fury that might show to anyone around them. Just pure, cutting ice only she, and her mother, would hear or feel. "But you will not come crying to me when it is a disaster of your own making. If you embarrass me, I will end you."

Beau wanted to laugh. Cry to him? When had she ever? She'd cut out her own eyeballs first.

So she said nothing to him. She just waited as they'd been instructed.

The prince appeared at the curve in the staircase. She had never met Lyon Traverso, but she knew this was him from pictures. An older woman followed behind him. His mother, the countess, Beaugonia believed.

He *was* handsome. Even aside from pictures, Zia had always confirmed that. In the flesh, it seemed less a fact to accept and file away and more an actual...*entity*.

He seemed so *tall* gliding down the staircase in his dark, bespoke suit. His dark hair ruthlessly styled, and every moment as precise as a very sharp blade. The whole *state* of him seemed to back up the oxygen in her lungs. Such a strange response to one man.

Of course, so much about this man determined what her future would be like, so she supposed this feeling of being rooted to the spot was simply…anxiety. That's why it felt like carbonation in her chest.

He approached them, greeting Father and Mother first before he turned to her. His dark eyes took her in, and though she was usually very good at reading people from just a look, she had no idea what the expression on his face meant. Or hid.

And still, this was her fate. A fate she'd concocted for herself. Maybe they wouldn't love each other, but they had an understanding. A mutual agreement that Beau had negotiated herself. Perhaps it wasn't better than love, but it was certainly better than whatever her parents had.

She smiled at Lyon, willing herself to play a part she'd never been any good at playing. *Sweet, accommodating princess.* "It is a pleasure to meet you, Your Royal Highness." She offered her best approximation of a curtsey.

He bowed in return. "And you. Allow me to introduce my mother. Countess Ludovica Traverso." He gestured to the woman still standing behind him. She greeted them all with a regal politeness.

Her expression was easy enough to read. Distrust written into every sideways look.

"The wedding will be held in the chapel at nine," Lyon offered. "My staff is at your service, of course, so you may ready yourself in whatever ways you need."

"I'm still not understanding this *private* royal wedding situation we find ourselves in," the king blustered, as he was likely to bluster until the end of time.

The prince did not so much as even blink. Beau wasn't

sure he moved, exactly, but he gave the impression of being very *tall*, as though he were looking down at her father from a great distance.

She very much wanted to learn that trick.

"With the change in brides, we find ourselves in a delicate situation. I thought that was clear?" Lyon posed this as a kind of question.

The kind of question no one dared answer.

Father cleared his throat. Mother looked away. The countess studied Beau's dress as though she were cataloging any wrinkle.

"We will reconvene then. Marco?" He gestured a staff member over.

And that was it. Beau was led away from her one and only meeting with the man she would marry in just a few short hours.

She felt the tickle of panic at the back of her throat but breathed through it. They both knew what they were getting themselves into, and that was all that mattered.

"She's pretty."

Crown Prince Lyon Traverso's mother said this as if it were some kind of *shock*. He glanced at the countess. "And?"

"You know as well as I do that the Rendalls keep her as far out of the public eye as they can. I expected…" Mother trailed off, likely because she knew whatever she'd been thinking was not appropriate to say, even just between the two of them.

And the truth was, Princess Beaugonia Rendall *was* pretty. Not quite in the way her sister was. Princess Zia had been taller and more…effortlessly regal, it seemed to Lyon. Though he'd thought less of her looks and more about how she'd suited his purposes.

But Beaugonia had made a case that *she* would suit his purposes instead now that Zia was...well, it wasn't clear *what* had happened there, but Lyon had heard rumors.

And as much as he needed heirs, they needed to be legitimate and his own. So a wife who understood that, agreed to that, was far more important than her appearance. As long as she understood her place, everything else was immaterial.

Beaugonia seemed to know her place.

But, he could admit because his mother had brought it up, Beaugonia *was* pretty. Softer, smaller than her sister, and she held herself with a strange...reserve was the only word Lyon could come up with. A reserve that didn't match the cutting quality to her eyes—an intriguing array of shades coming to some sort of hazel conclusion.

In the privacy of his own mind, he could admit that he *was* a bit surprised as his mother had been. Maybe, without fully thinking about it, he'd expected exactly what his mother was getting at. A reason that the princess had been hidden away and Zia had been trotted out as the true royal.

"I do hope you know what you're doing," Mother said, moving about the room, the anxiety all but radiating off of her.

When was it not? Their position was precarious. Because he was not the son of a crown prince, or even the grandson of one.

Which came down the maternal side of things, and the kingdom of Divio had *concerns* about what that would mean for their young leader, shoved into the princehood—the highest royal step here in the principality of Divio—after a series of unfortunate events.

But Lyon was ready. He knew how to be a leader, and he knew his family belonged on the throne, regardless of the whispers. His grandmother had raised him to believe that this would be his fate—because she had known her brothers and their progeny would not last long.

She had always said they'd been train wrecks from day one. Selfish, careless and ruled by wants over any sort of duty.

She had been right. After his cousin's fiasco, there had been a vote to get rid of the monarchy altogether. It had not won, but it had been *close*. Any hint of scandal, and Lyon had no doubt Parliament would hold another one.

So all the training Grandmother had put him through had paid off thus far. He'd spent the past year, almost, trying to earn the trust of his country, with not a whiff of a demand for another vote.

Beau was the next step. A wife. Children—enough that there would be no question, no future concerns of who the next leader would be. Tradition. Respectability. Everything a citizen could want from their royal family.

Not one *whiff* of the scandal the other princes had loved to traffic in.

"She knows what's expected of her," Lyon said to his mother. To assure her. To assure himself. He'd had much longer to determine Zia's appropriateness, but what was one sister compared to the other? Zia had known her role, and so Beaugonia did too. He had spent the past few months ensuring it.

Maybe he hadn't met her in person as he might have liked, but he had made every other effort to ensure her offer was in good faith, and would not come back to haunt him. He had not found even a *hint* of scandal with Beaugonia, the little-known Rendall.

She was perfect. He'd make certain of it.

"We can still put this off, Lyon. Make certain she's the right answer. It took us months to decide Princess Zia was the correct choice. You've switched over to her sister in a matter of days."

Which wasn't true. He'd been exchanging correspondence with Beaugonia for months. But he'd kept that from his mother, and he didn't think it would assuage her fears any to let her know now.

Lyon turned to her and smiled. "I have it all under control. I will not disappoint, Mother."

She studied him, her dark eyes impossible to read. But she smiled in return. "Your grandmother would be very proud of you, Lyon. You were her greatest hope."

Yes. Grandmother had always told him that. He'd tried to carry that weight, but it tended to fit around his throat like a hand…squeezing. So much so that as a teen his mother had taken him to a therapist for his anxiety and he'd been put on medication.

His own failing, he knew, but his grandmother had never known, and he'd kept his anxieties under control thanks to those things ever since.

Lyon desperately wanted to loosen his tie right now, but he knew what his mother would say about that. She would worry even more than she already did that he was not in control of things. Particularly his own anxieties.

So he focused on keeping his breathing easy, his smile relaxed. He would make his mother proud, his grandmother proud—the way no man in her family ever had. It was his sworn duty.

His grandmother's brothers had taken the role of crown prince with more and more disastrous results. Their children hadn't fared much better. Divio had not seen a royal last more than two years in a generation.

Lyon would change that. And Beaugonia would be an essential part of it. She would be acceptable, she would know her place, and she would provide him with heirs, because this is what he'd decided.

And Crown Prince Lyon Traverso always accomplished what he decided.

CHAPTER TWO

BEAUGONIA COULD ONLY stare at herself in the full-length mirror. She looked like an entirely different person in this beautifully elegant white gown. A whole team of people she didn't know had swept in and done her hair and makeup. They had placed a glittering necklace of royal jewels on her neck. Her mother had provided a Rendall tiara.

Beaugonia was used to nice things, being a princess and all, but Zia usually got the full glamour treatment. Beau didn't go to parties or events. She wasn't seated at dinners. Her *faults*, as her father liked to call them, had meant she'd been hidden away for most of her life.

So she felt a bit like she was playing dress-up. Like this was all make-believe.

She wished Zia was here, though Zia didn't know what Beau was doing yet, by design. Zia would try to…stop this, no doubt. But she had Cristhian and the twin babies she was growing to worry about.

Still, it would've been nice to have *someone* on her side with her. Beau felt surrounded by enemies. Which was an exaggeration of course. People had to care about her to be her enemy. None of Lyon's staff thought much of her beyond their job. She was little more than a doll to them.

Her mother watched with shiny eyes and clasped hands like this was all a joy. And Beau wanted that to warm her, but she knew she was only in this strange position because her mother had never stood up for her. Or Zia.

Mother had never been an *active* enemy, but she had always been a passive one.

Father was somewhere, no doubt grousing about how she'd pulled one over on him, but he could hardly ruin anything without making their own kingdom look badly. So while he was an enemy, per usual, he was a neutered one.

That brought Beau some joy. That and the fact that tomorrow they would leave, and she would not really have to deal with them much anymore. She would have her own life. Her own kingdom.

No more locked rooms. No more being hidden away. She would finally be…*someone*.

"You look beautiful," her mother said, with tears in her eyes.

Beaugonia managed a smile at her mother. A woman who meant well but had no backbone. No…fight. She had let her daughters be bullied and threatened and manipulated their entire lives.

Beaugonia loved her mother, but she could not respect her, or lean on her, or trust her.

Beau was alone.

You have been on your own these past few months and you have done very well, she reassured herself.

She even gave her reflection a little nod in the mirror. She might miss Zia, but she was doing all of this for her sister.

And that alone would get her through.

Beau knew better than to worry about panic. A panic attack would come or it wouldn't, but worrying about *if* she would have one would only exacerbate the problem.

Things had come too far to be derailed by the attacks that had gotten her labeled *weak*, *an embarrassment*, *defective* and so on. This was a new life.

She had faith that she could keep her panic attacks hidden from Lyon. Particularly in a castle the size of this one. Divio wasn't known for wanting to hear from a *princess*, what with all their outdated ideas about male heirs and so on. Besides, once they had said heirs, Beau wouldn't need to spend much time with Lyon at all. She could just focus on being a mother.

A future that filled her with hope and joy. Maybe she hadn't thought much of being one before Zia had fallen pregnant, but now she thought… She wanted the chance to be everything her mother had never been. She wanted the chance to love, as fully and unreservedly as she loved her sister.

It wouldn't be her husband, but it could be her children.

"We will move to the chapel, Your Highness."

Beau smiled at the staff person and allowed a whole passel of people to lead her out of the room she'd been getting ready in and through long, wide hallways. Ancient hallways. How many women had walked down these halls in a fancy white dress to marry a man they didn't even know?

Probably quite a few. She wasn't unique. She was taking her place in the rich, bizarre tapestry of royalty. It was kind of like joining a club. And since she'd never been able to join much of anything, this felt like a positive spin on things.

She was brought to a halt in front of giant, dark wooded doors while a staff member whisked Mother off. So Beau was left with only the stern woman who seemed to be running tonight's event.

They waited there for ticking moments while Beau felt her heart beat faster and faster. What were they waiting for? What was she doing?

And just about the time she thought she might blurt out some ridiculous excuse to turn and *run*, the woman stepped forward and pulled open the chapel door. She gestured Beau inside.

And there was nothing to do but step forward, into the chapel.

It was a huge rook. Soaring ceilings, colorful stained glass. Much more ornate than the chapel back home which had a cozy, sturdy quality to it. This felt…delicate. Elegant. She could picture generations of Divio citizens and their pride in such a feat of architecture and art.

She almost smiled. Though she preferred sturdy and cozy, there was something genuinely uplifting about the way humans in all their faults and frailties could somehow put together something that looked like this.

A nudge had her remembering herself. She wasn't meant to stand here and gaze at the stained glass adoringly. She was meant to walk forward. She was meant to marry the prince.

There were few audience members as she walked down the long aisle, trying to remind herself to be graceful and calm instead of her usual efficient march.

The countess sat on one side in the front pew, her father on the other. A few staff members standing in the shadows, except the one currently ushering Mother to her seat next to Father.

And then in the center there was Lyon. He stood with perfect posture in a dark suit, looking like… She could not articulate it, but she suddenly understood the novels she loved to read about reformed pirates.

He was perfectly polished, looked every inch a prince in his bespoke suit and crisp edges, but something in his eyes felt…wild. Which was ridiculous and likely her imagination. Nothing Zia had ever said and no correspondence she'd had with the prince herself pointed to anything other than a very contained, careful, determined man.

She moved closer, meeting his gaze and feeling…something she could not quite define. She had not expected… whatever this was. Because it went beyond nerves—she knew exactly what nervousness and being out of place felt like. This was bigger, deeper. Less about her and the world around her and more about something…internal.

Perhaps it was simply that he looked *at* her. Not with the hate her father did, or the complicated push and pull of worry and disappointment her mother did. Certainly not with Zia's fervent loyalty and overdone protective instincts.

No, he looked at her as if she were a riddle to be solved. Which wasn't romantic in any way, and she didn't expect romance, she just didn't know why the effect of it all on her was one of…anticipation.

Maybe it was just new. She'd been stuck in the same old place, being the same old person for so long. Maybe this was a fresh start.

Marrying a stranger.

Condemning herself to the unknown.

Saving Zia and her babies.

If nothing else, for the rest of her life, she'd be proud of herself for that. She would stand tall in *that*. Besides, what was trading one jail for another? She'd get to be a mother in this one. She'd get to have some kind of role instead of being hidden away.

So yes. No doubts. No regrets. Only *I do.*

Lyon watched Beaugonia's approach. She looked lovely in white, her dark hair swept back. The dress was a bit much, but she walked under the weight of it with an elegance he had perhaps not expected of the Rendall twin who'd always been hidden.

There was a determination to the set of her shoulders as she approached, but there was something in the way her gaze darted about the large room that gave a slight air of… inner timidity, underneath all that outer strength.

This was good, he assured himself. It would endear her to the public. Confidence was important, grit to a certain extent, but the hint of something softer under all she had to be as crown princess was…intriguing. Would be intriguing, to the citizens she needed to win over.

When she finally reached him after the long walk down the aisle with soft strains of music playing, she expelled a careful breath, then turned to face him.

He'd expected to see nerves on her but was gratified by the grim kind of battle light in her hazel eyes. She knew what this was, and that was all that mattered.

The minister began with his greetings. Lyon only listened with half an ear, studying his bride-to-be. She studied him right back.

It was an odd situation. Even odder than his original arranged marriage. Perhaps because he'd gone out of his way to choose Zia, and he'd had ample time to ensure she, and her family and her kingdom would suit.

The woman before him had searched *him* out. Had left the king out of all their plans. Had been…determined. Even now, her determination to see this through was clear. Quite the turn of events from her sister who had been…wary if reluctantly willing.

Still, the identity of the sister did not matter. He would give Beaugonia all the same things he'd been determined to give Zia. A good life. A strong partnership. Children. Perhaps there would not be love or the freedom to do whatever she pleased, but Lyon was certain stability was better than all of that.

He was given the cue to agree to enter into marriage and offered a solemn "I do." A few words later, and Beaugonia was doing the same.

"You may kiss your bride," the minister intoned.

Her gaze flickered for just a moment at that. There were certainly some aspects of this arrangement that needed to be discussed that he had not felt comfortable putting in the emails and phone calls that had occurred in the past two days solidifying their arrangement.

But a kiss to seal the wedding ceremony was necessary and accepted, and while he and his mother might know this was a business arrangement, while Beaugonia herself might know, he wanted the whole of Divio to buy into the potential for a love story.

In other words, he wanted the photo op. So he dipped his head. He paused for a moment, waiting for her eyes to lose that wide-eyed *trapped* look about them. But they didn't. So he leaned closer, until there was just a breath between their mouths.

"Breathe, *tesoruccia*," he murmured. Low enough only she could hear. "It is only the brush of lips."

Her breath shuddered out, and this…did something to him. He did not know how to characterize it. A strange… *sensation*. Effervescent and light. When for as long as he could remember his life had been about carrying the weight of what needed to be done.

He wasn't sure he liked it, but that same responsibility demanded he not draw this out any longer. So he touched his mouth to hers. And, as he'd promised, it was only the slight brush of lips.

Nothing more.

No matter how it felt like *more*. How it opened up interesting possibilities of what *more* would need to entail eventually.

He straightened, trying to not let the wariness inside of him show on his face. Because there was…*something* there.

Attraction, simple as that, he supposed.

He had not expected any hint of chemistry with whomever his bride turned out to be. That wasn't the point. He wasn't sure he *liked* it, but he supposed as long as it was under his control, it might be useful.

"Welcome to your new kingdom, *mi principessa*," he offered.

She sucked in a deep breath, then nodded. "Thank you, *mio marito*," she returned, with decent enough pronunciation of his native tongue, all in all. She had clearly practiced, which was a nice gesture. One he appreciated.

Because the newly minted Princess Beaugonia Traverso was going to be everything he needed. There were no other options.

CHAPTER THREE

BEAU SAT THROUGH a tasty if uncomfortable post-ceremony dinner. Her father had gotten uncharacteristically drunk in public, and Mother had been forced to pretend he'd fallen ill and get help to usher him away.

His angry gaze had been focused directly on her, and she supposed she would have to count herself lucky that Lyon had wanted this ceremony and dinner to be small and private before they announced their marriage to his people tomorrow morning.

Once the king was out of the room, her entire body relaxed involuntarily. Father was gone. It was unlikely he'd stay around after his behavior this evening. He'd likely be totally gone by sunup.

She was free now. Of the king and everything he'd threatened her with for so long. She wanted to simply sag and cry in relief, but that feeling was tempered by a kernel of worry.

Because the idea of *freedom* begged the question she'd been avoiding. If Lyon knew about her shortcomings, would he have his own threats against her?

Well, it didn't do to dwell on it. The only thing she could think about was having children. *That* seemed to be Lyon's only concern really, and that would protect her.

She hoped. She'd make certain it did. Maybe she had no great examples of what good mothering should look like, but as she'd told Zia only a few days ago, they had an example of what it *shouldn't* look like, so that should be enough.

Besides, Zia was only weeks away from becoming a mother herself. She would learn the ropes and help Beau when it was her turn. They would be partners in this voyage into motherhood, as they'd been in everything else growing up.

Once Zia forgave her for stepping in and marrying Lyon, taking over as heir.

The dinner wrapped up. They were given congratulations by the staff and Lyon's mother. The countess said very little, but Beau didn't miss the way the woman studied her with suspicion.

Then Lyon was leading Beau out of the ballroom, his large hand on the small of her back, while her white skirts swished around. Feeling a bit like shackles at the moment. The idea made her want to laugh out loud, but she swallowed it down.

Up staircases, down hallways. Lyon said nothing, just led her, and she had no choice but to go along. Because he was her *husband* now. Because she thought she knew what she was doing.

More hysterical laughter wanted to break free. Who did she think she was, charging in to rescue Zia? To one-up her father? She should have stayed locked in a room, huddled in a corner. Maybe she belonged in one of those asylums her father always threatened her with.

Eventually, Lyon stopped at a grand door and opened it. He gestured her inside. Into what was clearly *his* suite. From this grand sitting room, she could see into a bedroom. Everything very elegant and well-appointed. But very…*masculine*. Not a floral or pastel in sight.

She hadn't let herself think too much about this. A wedding night. Maybe she'd been in denial enough to think he'd show her to her own room. With her own bed. With a staff to help her out of this dress. That the idea of *making heirs* might be introduced…later.

Instead, it was just the two of them. They were alone here and she did not know what he expected of her. She stood in the middle of the sitting room in this rather cumbersome wedding gown and wondered just what she thought she'd been doing.

"I realize immediately sharing a room might not be the easiest or most comfortable thing," Lyon offered. He *looked* perfectly at ease. Perfectly…in control. Like he knew exactly what he was doing. While her heart clattered around in her chest, thinking about the way he'd kissed her in the chapel.

Breathe, tesoruccia.

She needed to look up what *tesoruccia* meant.

"Unfortunately, for the optics of everything I'm trying to sell, it's important to act out the facade that we are… more traditionally married," he continued. "It's best if our union seems as genuine as it possibly can be, even inside the castle, so there's no question."

"Even though your country thinks you were engaged to my sister?"

"I was engaged to your sister."

"You had a business arrangement with my father. That is not quite the same. Do they even know that engagement was broken?"

He frowned a bit at that, and she knew she should have kept it to herself, but…well, it was hard not to correct people when they were flat-out wrong. One of her many flaws, she knew. One she'd promised herself to improve on in order to make sure this worked.

"No, but I am quite certain the previous engagement will work in our favor. The story will be that I sought a political marriage, but then I met you and fell in love. We hid the truth from the press until we could make certain…all parties were satisfied."

She supposed that might work. The positive to her mysterious status as the hidden away Rendall was that, really, anyone could believe anything about her. There was no way to prove anything about her was false.

Perhaps *she* might wonder why someone like Lyon— gorgeous and powerful and clearly very self-possessed— might be swept away from his princess fiancée by the likes of *her* lesser princess self, but she supposed that was up to his palace aides to conjure up for the press.

"We do not need to have this conversation while you are uncomfortable," he said, gesturing at her heavy dress. "Your things have been unpacked, plus a few items added for the responsibilities of the next few days. Please consider this space yours as much as mine."

She looked around and tried to imagine treating this space as *hers*. She wasn't sure that was going to be possible, but she also knew getting out of this dress wasn't going to be possible. And there was no staff hovering around to help her. Unless he called someone, and she had a feeling that wasn't in the cards.

For the *optics*.

She cleared her throat. "I cannot undo the buttons on the back of my dress on my own."

He had no facial reaction to that, but he did pause a moment. "Ah." He paused again, then moved forward, gesturing her to follow. "Come."

She followed him into the bedchamber and then into a huge en suite that led to another door, behind which was an entire closet and dressing area nearly as big as the bedroom itself. She peered around the room. She could see one side was clearly his, and one side was…hers.

She thought that this might be the strangest reality check of all time. Her own clothes hung in neat rows directly across from *his clothes*.

"Allow me," Lyon said, holding out his hands.

It took her a few quiet moments to understand he meant that she should turn around so he could unbutton her dress. Which was fine. Maybe the sleeveless nature of the dress meant she wasn't wearing any undergarments up top, but… but…she would just hold the dress up once he unbuttoned it.

She wasn't getting out of it any other way. Besides, whatever this was, she would grin and bear it. That had been the deal she'd made.

Gingerly, she moved so she was closer to him, with her back within his reach. At first, she didn't feel much, just the gentle tug of the dress moving. But as more and more buttons came undone, she began to feel…*him*.

It was such a strange sensation. No matter how often she'd been helped to dress or undress, it had never been a *man* back there. A tall, warm wall of *presence*. One whose fingers occasionally brushed the exposed skin of her back as he moved down the delicate row of buttons.

She held her breath, knowing if she released it some strange sound would come out of her that would no doubt be embarrassing in some way.

"All done," he said, sounding somewhat stiff. But when she turned to face him, his expression was arranged in a bland kind of smile. Even if his dark eyes seemed to…*glint*.

"Thank you," she managed to offer.

He nodded. "You're welcome."

She nearly barked out a laugh. He was her *husband*. This man. She was his wife. Standing in his closet, holding the sagging dress to her chest so it didn't fall. It was all so surreal. She didn't even feel *panic*. How could she? It felt like it couldn't even be real.

"I'll leave you to change." With that, he exited the closet and the en suite bathroom. So that she stood, still grasping her heavy wedding dress, completely at a loss.

What should she change into? Pajamas of some kind? What would be appropriate pajamas for sharing a room with her husband? For *optics*.

Or was he expecting something different? Something more? He'd made very clear the entire purpose of this marriage was for *heirs*. Multiple. Beau might be innocent, but she knew how heirs were made. And she read enough romance novels to know the nuts and bolts of *that*.

She really thought she'd been prepared for this, but the reality of Lyon somehow made it that much more…

She didn't even know how to finish the sentence. That's how little the reality of him matched up to her preparations.

She stared at the clothes in the closet. Some she recognized as hers her staff back at the Lille castle had packed up. Some items were clearly for her, but not her own.

Optics or no, this was going to be their own private bedchamber. She should wear something comfortable to bed. And if he didn't like it…well…

She closed her eyes and breathed out, using all those well-worn techniques to keep panic at bay. Sometimes they worked. Sometimes they didn't. But she was alone, so she wouldn't start adding to the panic by worrying if an attack was coming.

She just counted and breathed until she felt like she was strong enough to make a decision. She'd gone into this knowing she couldn't be herself. She had to be some… made-up version that would suit Lyon. Playing pretend in a way she'd never done before, because it was her turn to take a bullet for Zia.

Zia had protected Beau her entire life. She had stepped in between her and Father whenever she could. Zia had bent over backward to do the things an heir was expected to do, to keep the king from enacting threats against Beau. Beau *knew* Zia was the entire reason Father had never stooped so low as to put her in an asylum. That and how hard it would have been to keep a secret from the press and citizens of his beloved country.

But there was no way to be perfect here right off the bat. She didn't know Lyon well enough. She would have to accept that there was a learning curve and be open and ready for any changes Lyon might want made.

If he didn't like the pajamas she chose, she would march right back in and change. If he told her to do anything differently, she would. And if that started to grate, she would just remember the look of shock on her father's face when she'd told him she'd arranged to take Zia's place in marrying Lyon.

That all the papers were drawn up.

And he would have to announce her as heir.

That memory would keep her going for *decades*.

So, she picked out a pair of comfy leggings from her own clothes and a silk nightshirt. It was hardly lingerie, but there was a kind of sophistication to it that was elegant and could lend itself to anything hands-off…or hands-on.

Filled with determination—or at least she'd fake it till she made it—she returned to the bedroom. To find him unbuttoning his own shirt. His tie was already off, hanging over the back of a chair that sat nestled into a corner by the big window.

He really was beautiful. She knew she hadn't met a lot of men in her life, but he was so tall. His hair had an interesting wave to it, though he kept it short. Underneath the crisp white shirt of his wedding suit, a broad expanse of tan skin, well-muscled and impressive.

Did he work out? He must. No one just *looked* like that, surely, even a handsome prince.

He looked up, and she didn't miss the quick survey of her outfit, though she couldn't read his reaction to it. He straightened, and for a few moments they simply stood in silence regarding each other.

"Now that we have some privacy," he finally began. "We should discuss the more…delicate matters of our relationship."

"You mean sex."

He made a strangled noise. The kind of noise she often brought out in people, but she'd found being forthright and frank often helped quell her anxiety. Just say it. Just deal with the consequences rather than worry about what they might be.

She might have to work on curbing that impulse now, but for this moment, she needed it to keep her steady.

"Yes, I suppose I do," Lyon agreed.

But then he didn't say anything. He stood by the window, shirt unbuttoned. She stood by the en suite door in her pajamas.

He cleared his throat. Which should have seemed like a gesture of *some* kind of nerves, but he stood there looking so…*princely* and handsome and fully in control of himself, she didn't think he'd ever been nervous a day in his life.

"While heirs are my primary concern," he began, like this was a well-planned speech. Maybe it was. "And will need to be…secured sooner rather than later, we do not need to jump into such matters right away. We can get to know each other a bit first. Ease into things."

Beau carefully exhaled. That was actually quite…kind, all in all. She had not thought him cruel—their arrangements had now been a few months in the making. His correspondence had always been polite, his propositions always fair. So it wasn't that kindness *should* be a surprise.

Simply she was not used to it.

He moved then, taking a few steps toward her. Again, her breath backed up in her lungs. There was just *something* about him that drew out these new, overwhelming physical responses in her.

"Just because we have a very careful arrangement does not mean that it can't be mutually enjoyable. It does not have to be a...chore."

She blinked once. Trying to work through that. *Enjoyable.* She felt her cheeks heat, despite trying to be very *sophisticated* about the whole thing.

"I hear tell that I am not a hideous beast," he said in a soft, humored voice.

It was about the first sense that under all his duty, all his plans, all they'd agreed, that Lyon *might* have a personality. A hint of humor. And ego. Which she didn't mind. She'd much prefer a man who was sure of himself. She'd found men riddled with insecurity who had any kind of power tended to wield it in ugly ways.

"What about me?" she asked him. Because it was true, *he* was gorgeous. *She* might enjoy...things with him. But her...

He gave her a sweeping kind of glance that had a strange fissure of nerves dancing along her skin. "I can see that you are not a hideous beast, *tesoruccia*," he said, his voice... darker, it seemed.

Her body certainly found him convincing, if the heat in her cheeks was anything to go by. But her mind... "You think I'm pretty?"

"Yes."

"Prettier than Zia?"

He raised an eyebrow. "Is it a competition?"

Always. Not because she wanted any competition. Nor

did Zia. It was just…how they were seen. Two halves of one whole, but constantly determining which half was better. "No, but that answers the question easy enough."

"Speaking of your sister—"

He wanted answers, and Beau had some, but it felt wrong to offer them to Lyon. Not before Zia decided on her own fate. "I'd rather not. Not just yet."

He frowned a little, but he didn't press the issue.

"I haven't…" She gestured helplessly at what would be their marital bed. "Obviously. I have been…very sheltered."

"We will take it one step at a time."

"Step?"

"We shared a kiss just this evening. Consider that step one, and enough for our first night as husband and wife." He reached out, took her hand. He rubbed a thumb across her knuckles, then squeezed gently, reassuringly.

His hand was large, warm. It was the strangest sensation, because it sent a wave of nervy excitement through her. That anticipation she so liked to read about.

But there was also a…kindness. One of the few times in her life someone had reached out and offered physical reassurance.

"I think our arrangement will be quite…successful, Beaugonia."

She so wanted that to be true. Needed it. So, she corrected him. "Beau."

"Scusami?"

"My friends call me Beau."

His smile was warm, sweet almost. She knew she shouldn't hope for more out of this arrangement, let all those fictionalized versions of happily-ever-afters give her *ideas*. She was still who she'd always been. A little too direct, plagued by uncontrollable and unpredictable panic attacks, selfish and so on and so forth.

No handsome prince was going to sweep her off her feet.

But maybe…she would hope for a *successful* arranged marriage. Maybe she would allow herself to dream of an arrangement that was kind. And a physical relationship that could be more *enjoyable* than chore.

As long as she kept her true self under wraps, she was certain she could do it.

CHAPTER FOUR

LYON HAD NOT accounted for *wanting* his wife. It was a strange and disconcerting turn of events. He was a careful planner, and while all his life there'd been a certain level of flexibility required of him, he usually considered *every* angle before jumping into something.

It had become apparent, as Beau had walked down the aisle toward him, that he had not considered every angle. Because he'd been struck with the strangest feeling that his world had begun right in that moment.

Which he'd quickly flicked away, a pointless thought no doubt brought upon by the stress of the past few months. First, the knowledge Zia would not be marrying him, and then Beaugonia's alternative plan.

He had been *relieved* to have a plan, a way out of the folly he'd made for himself. It had never once over the months of dealing with Beaugonia occurred to him that Zia's hidden sister might be…interesting. *Or* beautiful.

He had always had to be careful when it came to women. He'd known, even before he'd been crowned prince, that being ruler was the end goal, and there could be no whispers about him that might hurt that eventuality.

He had watched the more wild and reckless members of his mother's family nearly destroy everything, all for a bit of fun here or there. He'd never understood them.

He had always found it easy to create short, respectable relationships with women, always knowing that he was looking for the perfect princess—above reproach. And when he had not found it, made sure he ended such situations with tact and kindness.

Any errant thoughts about needs, wants, or desires were to be ignored, cut off, shut away.

But now, he wasn't quite certain he understood himself. Or at least his reaction to Beaugonia. Prim and direct at turns. Shy, but not…hiding. The hazel of her eyes was a mysterious blend of colors that seemed to change in the light, with her feelings, or the color she was wearing.

Not that he couldn't *handle* this unexpected reaction, because of course he could. It was just *new*, and thus a little…concerning. He would need to reassess. Go about this entire thing a little differently perhaps.

Because they *would* need to broach the physical requirements of creating an heir, regardless of how he felt about her. He would need to make certain that he was in charge of this unexpected situation of being far more intrigued by her than he wanted to be.

Luckily, she also wasn't *immune* to him. He'd seen the way she'd watched him, particularly when she'd returned to the room when he'd been unbuttoning his stifling shirt and trying to *breathe* past all that…new uncertainty combined with the old anxieties of never quite living up to the expectation held for him.

It was a *positive*, he assured himself as he lay in bed next to her in the dark. Plenty of room between them in his very large bed. Her even breathing filling the room.

He hadn't been lying about his hope that the arrangement would be pleasing. If there was *some* chemistry, the necessities of their arrangement could be enjoyable.

As long as it wasn't *complicated*. As long as it wasn't…he

shoved that thought away, but *complicated* lingered, keeping him up all night. He stared at the ceiling, hard and beyond irritated with himself for not being fully prepared for a beautiful, interesting person to now be his lawfully wedded bride.

He needed a new plan. They had hashed out a very clear agreement, but he needed to make certain the realities of their situation didn't undermine said agreement.

He didn't think ground rules were the way to go with her. There was a little spark of something in her—not rebellion, that wouldn't do. Just a very assured sense of self that exuded from her every action, every word.

The woman who had approached him via email a few months ago with news his engagement to Zia would not go through had a very clear determination of how her life would go. It was what had first intrigued him about her offer. The only reason he'd held out on agreeing for so long was because she had refused to meet prior to the wedding.

But she'd systematically and carefully outlined her plan, and he had no choice but to accept the fact that it matched up perfectly with his own. That she offered him more than Zia had, because neither of them would have to pretend.

Except, he had a terrible feeling he was going to have to pretend now, because she was not the icy hermit he'd been expecting.

But he was a married man now. His plan to ensure the crown stayed stable was moving as it should. His internal thoughts and unexpected feelings wouldn't change that.

He wouldn't allow it.

He would simply get to know his new bride. Engage in that which producing heirs required. And ensure whatever odd sensations plagued him, he was always in control of them rather than the other way around.

As the sun rose, glowing between the gap in the drapes,

Lyon carefully slid out of bed and went to the bathroom to shower and try to clear his mind.

It was good, really. To face a challenge that made him sharper and sounder of mind. If things got too easy, he might get complacent and that would never do. His entire rule would no doubt be an exercise in fighting to regain all the control his great-uncles, uncles and cousin had pissed away for the past decades.

Until all that was left was him. Until the entire future of Divio rested on his shoulders. He dressed, though he kept his tie loose for the moment. He told himself he was full of all that determination that had grown shaky after the ceremony.

Until he returned to the bedroom.

She was sitting up in the bed, her cheeks a little flushed from sleep and her dark hair tousled as if he'd had his hands in it last night, just as he'd desired.

She yawned and stretched, looking perfectly…

Well, it wouldn't do to look too hard.

"Good morning," he offered, moving stiffly toward the window. He pulled the curtains back to a bright, snowy day below. He tried to imagine all that *cold* encasing him. "Today I will give you a tour of the castle, answer any questions you have. The announcement and pictures from last night will go out soon, and we'll host a dinner this evening. Then afterward we will film a short video that will go out to news outlets."

"Sounds perfect. I'll just go get ready."

He did not dare look at her even as he heard the rustle of sheets and the soft landing of footfall. He kept his gaze on the window, on the mountains, on all that *ice*.

When she returned, he allowed himself to look at her. She wore slacks with enough swishy fabric not to give much away about the shape of her legs. The dark green sweater she wore was a little more formfitting, but only a little. She looked elegant but cozy. Perfect for the morning ahead.

Because she *was* perfect. "Let us take a little tour on our way down to breakfast," he said, and then began to lead her out of his suite.

It was better in the daylight, he decided. Other things to focus on. *Movement.* Certainly not darkness and listening to her breathe and shift in her sleep. Not hours stretching out in front of him where he couldn't help but think of the way she'd looked when she'd just woken up.

He told her what every door was as they passed. Some he let her peek her head into, some they merely walked by.

"You can of course request to make any changes to our rooms you'd like. It will have to go through Mr. Filini, the head castle master, and myself, but as long as it's reasonable, there should be no problems."

"I doubt very much I'll have any changes."

He didn't know why that settled in him as an annoyance. He shouldn't want a wife who wanted frivolous changes when his entire *goal* was to make certain everyone in Divio looked at him and thought *stability.* Strength. Certainty.

He came to the last door before the staircase and held it open, gesturing her inside.

Her eyes lit up. Admittedly, the reaction he'd been hoping for. She moved forward, reaching out to touch the spines of a row of books. For a moment, she looked around at the shelves and shelves of books—old ones, new ones. Some ancient and passed down from generation to generation, some his own additions.

"It's the most beautiful room I've ever seen," she finally said, breaking the silence. She beamed at him and a warmth of satisfaction settled in his chest.

Perhaps there were some complicated reactions he hadn't

anticipated, but a woman who was bowled over by a library was certainly not a bad choice.

"You may of course make any additions you'd like. Your personal assistant will order any book for you."

"But you already have so many."

"No one can have too many books. And no collection should be so rigid so as not to allow entertainment that many users might enjoy."

"My father did not agree," she said, perusing the books. "The books *I* wanted to read, I often had to sneak read digitally through my phone. Which was fine enough, but I always wanted something…" She trailed off, then shrugged, gesturing at the room around them.

Lyon was no fan of King Rendall. The man was a supercilious braggart who used force more than intellect to impose his will on others. Lyon could admit to himself that part of Beau's proposition had been intriguing simply for getting around the king while still uniting Divio with Lille. And he felt that satisfaction again, because a man who imposed limits on reading was no leader.

"Did you always get around your father?"

"Not always," she said, a kind of carefulness about her. She did not meet his gaze. She focused on the books. "But when I could. When Zia and I could. But that makes it sound all bad, and it is not that. He simply cared more about his country than he ever did his children."

Lyon frowned. She did not say it in a censuring way, but he felt slightly…judged all the same. After all, he knew she did not hold her father in high regard, and neither did he.

But Lyon's priority was his kingdom, and he had made that clear. He had to offer his country stability for once, and with that priority came children who would fill their role as heirs. He had never really thought of them as more than that.

But they would be people. Like him. Like Beau.

He didn't like how…complicated that made the future feel. Because the future was simple. They would be the crown prince and princess of Divio and raise children to take their place, and bring Lille into the fold on the death of the current king.

But thought of *heirs* brought him back to the one clear answer he had not gotten from her. The one that left his mother still having trepidation about their arrangement.

Whatever the reason she had not been the heir did not matter. The deal was done. They were married. He would not *let* it matter.

But it was best if he knew before he introduced her to the kingdom of Divio as their princess.

"You're the older twin. You should have been the heir. Is that not correct?"

She shook her head, as though not at all surprised by the change in topic. "That is not how Lille has worked for some time. It was always going to be my father's decision which of his children he wanted as heir. Zia was…better suited. From a young age."

"Why?" He had not asked her this outright, though they had both danced around the subject in their correspondence as they'd worked out the details of their agreement. In the end, Lyon had accepted what she offered was more important than whatever she might be hiding.

He could only hope his instincts had not led him astray.

"When I was very little, before I even fully remember, I found crowds very…scary. I would do all right if I could hide behind Zia, or if I was simply speaking with someone one-on-one, but crowds terrified me. Understandable, I think, but not the best reaction for a princess. Zia, on the other hand, always knew what to say, how to smile and act, even as a toddler. I struggled with this until I was much older. But by that time, I was already defined by my behavior as a child." She didn't look at him as she delivered any of this information. She focused on the books. Then she pulled one off the shelf.

"May I take this one to our room?" she asked, clearly wanting to change the subject.

He shouldn't let her change the topic, as it felt like there were details she was leaving out, but it was still her first day as his wife. He could be kind and patient. "They are your books as much as mine, Beau. You may do what you like."

Her smile was pretty, a little shy. But it dimmed a little when he reached for the book she held. With clear reluctance, she relinquished it to him.

He studied the cover, then flipped it over to the back. "A romance?"

"My favorite. Don't worry. It's not an indictment on my hopes for the future or a romantic nature of myself."

He found himself puzzled, both that she felt the need to preface her statement with *don't worry* and... "Why do you enjoy them then if there's no romantic nature involved?"

She looked at the book in her hand. "As much as I enjoy a good love story, the thing that has always struck me about these types of books is that the main character always finds people who understand them and make them feel...seen. Not just a romantic partner. But friends or family. It's... nice. I like to read about things that make me feel good."

Seen. An interesting way of looking at it, he supposed. He, on the other hand, did not wish to be seen at all. But if she did... Well, he would make a point of it.

"Why don't you pick out a book for me to read. Something that would allow us to have a conversation. A book that would help me get to know you."

She looked at him for a moment as if he'd suggested she take off all her clothes and run through the castle naked. Then she looked around. "I think it will take me a while to decide what book that should be and determine if you have it."

Lyon nodded. "Well, if we do not, we'll have it ordered." He glanced at his watch. "We should make our way to breakfast." He moved to lead her out of the library, but she put her hand on his arm to stop him.

"But wait. What book would I read to understand you?"

He liked it better that she said *understand*, rather than *seen*. Understand he could do. He took a turn about the library. The options were endless. He'd always been a reader, and so many different books had helped shape him into who he was. But he supposed at the center of even his interest in reading was the man he wanted to be. He slid an old tome off a shelf and handed it to her.

She took it, studied the cover, then wrinkled her nose. "A family biography."

"Perhaps a bit dry, I grant you, but that is who I am. Who I hope to be. An extension of the legacy built in these pages. A legacy you are now a part of."

She took a long, careful inhale. "I suppose I hadn't thought of it that way."

"You will be the mother of the future crown prince or princess."

She didn't look up from the book, so he couldn't quite read her expression, but when she finally met his gaze, she smiled. "I think I shall quite like to belong to something."

And he wasn't quite sure why his chest felt…oddly constricted. But he smiled back, and led her to breakfast, ignoring the unknown feeling lurking there.

CHAPTER FIVE

THEY ATE BREAKFAST together and then Lyon gave Beau an extensive tour of the grounds. She kept waiting for him to foist her off on staff. To disappear somewhere, as he had when she'd first arrived last night. But he stayed by her side. She supposed it was so that everyone believed in their marriage as something more than an uncomfortable business arrangement. She could play along.

Happily, she did not feel the least bit panicked though everything was a bit overwhelming. But he had a very calming presence when they were out in the castle. He explained everything. Assuaged every anxiety about settling into a brand-new place without her even having to ask.

When it was time to get ready for the dinner, he introduced her to the team that would help her get ready. By name and position, so she knew exactly who to ask for anything.

The only thing she did not get a say in was the gown she was to wear. When she voiced some concerns about the strapless nature of it, she was assured that everything would be secured quite well.

No one *said* she didn't have a say, but it was clear she was not allowed to *refuse*. She would have been annoyed by that, but she was being poked and prodded and practically sewn into the beautiful dress and she didn't know how to access her anger with all that going on.

She was tired and a little achy and wondering how Zia had done this for years upon years. All this…physical rigmarole to look a certain way for a group of strangers. Events upon events where she had to smile and compliment and act the perfect princess.

All to protect Beau. Because even though Zia had been better at *being* the heir, she hadn't *wanted* it. Two silly, spoiled princesses she supposed, who wanted to be human beings more than some kind of emotionless figurehead.

But Zia had been blackmailed, essentially. Always working to protect Beau from whatever threats their father had leveled at her. And Beau had let Zia take the fall again and again.

Which was why she was here. Taking the final fall. And it wasn't so bad. She'd made her choices, and Lyon was… Well, she couldn't say he was *nothing* like Father, because she knew his kingdom mattered more to him than anything—if she hadn't gathered it from their correspondence, she would have fully understood it when he'd handed her that family biography. Family. Legacy. Tradition.

Yes, she was well versed in how rulers viewed all those things as paramount.

But at least Lyon offered some kindness along the way. Her father had never done that for her or her sister.

The door opened and Lyon stepped in, dressed crisply in a tux, his hair in perfect place. He looked every inch the handsome prince he was meant to be.

One of the women who'd done her makeup helped Beau up out of the chair.

"You look beautiful," Lyon said.

It was a rote compliment, but somehow Lyon delivered it with a note of gravity that made it feel *real*. She had never once felt *beautiful*. Never tried to feel that. She'd always considered it Zia's domain.

Lyon's eyes on her made a compliment she'd never craved suddenly feel...wonderful. And made her think about another night sharing his bedroom. Sharing his *bed*. What *steps* awaited her there.

Which was not at all what she should be thinking about.

"It's as if the tiara was made for her, don't you think, Your Highness?"

Lyon's gaze didn't move from Beau, but he nodded at the hairstylist. "It does indeed."

She didn't *feel* that way at all, but the fact Lyon's gaze stayed on her with such...intensity made her want it to be true. It made her want to stand a little taller and ensure all his compliments could be believed.

It was a very strange feeling, to want to impress someone. From a very young age she'd known that there would never be any impressing her parents, so she'd stopped trying. She hadn't worried overmuch what anyone thought of her because she had known her role. No role at all.

Now she had one.

Lyon took her hand, lifted it to his mouth and brushed a kiss over her knuckles. She wondered if she would ever know how to react to that in a way that didn't make her feel totally off-kilter. Like someone else. Someone who was not unwanted and hidden away.

"The announcement went well and will ensure that we have quite a few attendees at dinner tonight," Lyon said, leading her toward the door. "You will be introduced to some members of parliament. Some members of my extended family. After, we shall sit down and film our short video introducing you and our plans for the future."

"And just what are our plans for the future?"

"A responsible, trustworthy and charitable monarchy that will work with parliament rather than against it and usher Divio into an age of stability they have not seen for decades. A partnership with Lille, that will eventually lead to a union of our countries once you inherit the throne."

She hadn't been consulted in any of that, but then again, she had no actual stake in Divio except for that eventually she would be mother of the heir to the monarchy.

A legacy you are now a part of.

Lyon had said that. Not for an audience, but as if he'd actually meant it. "Will I be expected to speak?"

"My aides have prepared a few remarks for you, yes. After dinner, we will spend some time preparing before we film. It's not live, so you will have ample tries to get it right."

Beau tried not to let that worry her. If someone else had prepared the remarks, she could no doubt deliver them. In fact, that seemed preferable to a dinner meeting people. Having to come up with conversation in a crowd. That seemed far more the kind of recipe for panic.

But she knew the castle now, and she just assured herself if she started to feel the telltale signs—numb feelings in her limbs, tunnel vision, shortness of breath—she would excuse herself and go to the bathroom. Then she would hide.

Worst-case scenario, she'd claim food poisoning.

"You will be introduced to quite a few people this evening, so don't feel bad if you can't keep them all straight. We'll work on making certain you spend time with the people you should know."

"I have an excellent memory for names and faces. It usually only takes one meeting for me to remember people." Her memory had always been excellent. She learned things quite easily, and then they stuck with her whether she wanted them to or not. Her father hadn't cared for her ability to recall things that he'd rather she forgot. Or maybe he hadn't cared for her insistence and inability to let something wrong go.

She was going to have to work on that.

"Quite an asset," Lyon said, patting her arm.

When she glanced up at him, he was smiling. Like he meant it. She felt a strange sweep of…pride move through her. Like earning a compliment from him was exciting.

This was all so…strange. She'd known it would be, but so far it hadn't been strange in the ways she'd been *expecting*.

But Lyon led her downstairs and through a back hallway that would take them to the entrance to the ballroom where they'd be announced. Lyon's mother and a few staff members waited there.

One of them hurried over and said something in low tones to Lyon. Who nodded, but let Beau's arm go.

"I'll be right back." He left her standing there with the countess. Whose expression was…cool, at best.

Her gaze swept over Beau's dress. "You clean up quite nicely, Your Highness."

It didn't really feel like a compliment, considering she'd been "cleaned up" in her wedding dress last night. But Beau smiled all the same. "Thank you. Lyon's staff is superb. I'd certainly be lost if they weren't doing the work to…ah… *clean me up*."

"I suppose, but could I make one little suggestion?" She leaned forward as if it was some great secret, whatever she wanted to impart.

Beau fought the impulse to lean away. She forced her smile to stay in place. "Of course."

"Perhaps next time you could wear a color more fitting of the royal family," the countess said in little more than a whisper.

Beau looked down at the navy blue. More fitting? She opened her mouth to ask what the countess meant, but Lyon had returned and took her arm and began leading her to the entrance to the ballroom.

Beau looked back at the countess, with the stray thought that perhaps she'd just misunderstood what the countess had said. What she meant.

But the look on the woman's face was clear. It reminded Beau of the evil stepmother in *Cinderella*. Which was so overdramatic she shook her head at herself. There was nothing evil about the countess. Perhaps she'd be a difficult mother-in-law, a judgmental one, but Beau could weather it.

It couldn't be worse than her father.

As long as she doesn't find out.

Beau forced that thought away and focused on the room in front of her. People milled about, then stilled as the announcement came over the sound system.

"May we present Crown Prince Lyon Traverso, and your new crown princess, Beaugonia Traverso?"

Lyon led her forward, when she would have stayed stuck in place. Because while the crowd wasn't *huge*, all eyes had turned toward them. And the countess's comment about her dress color was rattling around in her brain even though it made no sense.

She felt a little tickle at the back of her throat. Anxiety, but not panic. She could handle the anxiety. She'd researched all sorts of ways to deal with the overwhelm of social situations. The panic attacks came out of nowhere. There was little to no warning and often no direct cause.

Lyon took her around the room and introduced her to people. She made certain she looked each person in the eye, smiled and remembered every name and face. Because she could handle that. She was *good* at that.

No matter what color her dress was.

These types of dinners had always felt interminable, but Lyon found himself so fascinated watching Beau that time passed quickly.

She hadn't been lying about a good memory. She seemed to remember everyone by name *and* face. She smiled. She charmed.

Or at least she charmed *him*.

Though he'd known everything would work out with her, or he wouldn't have consented to this marriage. He refused to accept anything but exactly what he wanted, but he felt off-kilter by the fact she seemed…utterly perfect. He'd been expecting a challenge. Hard work. Success, yes, but not without bumps in the road.

He tried to remind himself it was early yet, but the entire dinner went absolutely perfectly. While there were still plenty of parliament members who talked down to him, who did their little political poking, hoping to find a weak spot, he could see on each of their faces they were intrigued by Beau.

He had no doubt the citizens would relish this royal marriage. Some would remain skeptical of his worth for a while longer yet, and understandably so, but once the children started coming, every year he would prove he was here to stay.

They said goodbye to the remaining guests, and Beau said goodbye to everyone by name, impressing each of them, he could tell. Where usually at the end of these types of dinners he felt tired, with a headache drumming at his temples, and his collar all but choking him, tonight he felt… energized.

When his mother came over to them, he beamed at her. "I think we shall count that down as quite the success."

"Don't go counting your chickens just yet," Mother warned, though with a smile. "This is only the very first step."

"But a very good first step. Now, Beau and I must go record our message to the country."

"Beau. How…cute."

But Lyon wasn't paying much attention to his mother. He was focused on the next steps. If the message was well-received, he and Beau would go away for a quick weekend "honeymoon." At least, that's what the public would consider it.

If not, he would have to have another meeting with his public relations team. Reevaluate and come up with a new plan.

It would be better and easier if tonight went well. Of course, that meant then being completely alone with Beau on a honeymoon. Which was…well, his feelings on it were complicated. Best not to consider it just yet.

"Good night, Mother," Lyon said, giving his mother a kiss on the cheek, then leading Beau away. They would film their message in the library, and then it would be put online and broadcast as soon as his staff got everything edited to perfection.

As they took the stairs, Beau spoke. "I do not think your mother likes me," she said, in low tones only he could hear.

He frowned, looking down at her. Her expression was not…angry or hurt, exactly. More considering. "What gives you that idea?"

She shook her head and smiled up at him. "I'm sure I just need to get to know her."

"She has been wanting me to get married and solidify my place as leader for quite some time. I'm sure she's quite happy with the situation."

"Wanting you married doesn't mean she likes *me*. Especially if she liked Zia."

Lyon paused as they reached the top of the stairs. He looked at the woman who'd handled the entire evening with aplomb. She looked beautiful. The dark blue of the dress and glittering jewels she wore, along with the tiara, made her look just as a princess should. Elegant and sophisticated.

"You charmed an entire room of people this evening, Beau. Not just people. *Politicians.* Who want me to fail. You charmed them all the same. And you're about to charm most of the country, no doubt. I am very impressed."

The look of concern in her expression slowly changed. Her mouth curved, and a pretty pink appeared on her cheeks. She blushed quite a bit really. Did her cheeks heat with the color? He was tempted to touch, just to find out.

But they had appointments to keep, and it was best if he resisted his urges as much as possible. Control, always. "Mr. Filini, Alice—the head of my public relations team—and the videographer are waiting for us in the library."

She nodded and let him lead her to that room. Mr. Filini bowed. "Your Highnesses. We are ready for you whenever you are. We will have you seated here," Mr. Filini said, gesturing toward two grand chairs that had been placed in front of the fireplace. A fire crackled there, offering a warm glow to the room.

It would come across homey, traditional and steeped in *ancient* history—not the more modern history of a revolving door of his grandmother's brothers' families.

"Here are copies of the announcement we already went through, sir," Alice said, handing a folder to both Lyon and Beau. "Take your time looking it over, and alert Aldo when you are ready to film. He will get the lighting and whatnot ready while you do so."

"You don't have to memorize the remarks," Lyon told Beau as they opened their folders. "This is more of a guide, and my team will edit the video as needed. You'll simply follow my lead."

Beau looked over the paper, clearly concentrating while Aldo moved around them turning on lights, moving them this way and that, conferring with Alice as they looked at the screen. It no longer *felt* cozy, but Lyon knew they would ensure it still looked it on-screen.

"This is very well written," Beau said after a bit.

"I did the bulk of the work, though Alice smooths out my rough edges and we discuss anything that might be problematic. She wanted to be sure you had equal speaking time, so the audience gets the clear impression that this is a partnership. Of you and me. Of Divio and Lille."

Beau nodded. "Yes, that certainly comes across."

"Is there a problem?"

"No. Not at all. I'm just…" She shook her head. "It's strange to talk of Lille as its heir. I still don't feel like it, even though my father made it a reality." Her eyebrows drew together, as if she was thinking through some great problem. "They left without saying goodbye."

She hadn't mentioned her parents' quick departure, and he didn't think she really cared for her parents. Certainly not the way he cared for his mother or had for his grandmother. "Does that bother you?"

"I didn't think it did. It doesn't, exactly." She blew out a breath then fixed him with a smile he could tell was fake. "It doesn't matter. I'm ready when you are."

He wanted to poke more into that little flicker of vulnerability, but it didn't matter. They had pressing things to deal with. How she felt about her parents was really immaterial to him and his life. So he pushed away the desire to get to know her better, and focused on what was required of him.

He indicated to Aldo and Alice that they were ready, and then they began. Alice had them run through the message a few times, assuring both Lyon and Beau she would be able to effortlessly edit the best amalgamation of takes.

But it didn't matter how many times they ran through it, Beau was flawless. When Alice was satisfied, and Aldo was packing up, Lyon turned to his new bride.

"You were perfect. That was practically word for word."

Her smile bloomed. "I told you I have an excellent memory. And I am not prone to exaggeration about my positive attributes, I assure you."

"Perhaps you should exaggerate," he said, and it made her laugh. A low, throaty sound that had his thoughts traveling…elsewhere. Until Alice approached.

"That was perfect. We'll get to work right away and have it posted before the night is over. It will run on the local news program first thing in the morning."

"*Grazie*, Alice."

She curtseyed and then exited the library, leaving Lyon and Beau alone in the room. Cozy and firelit yet again, without a trace of video equipment. He found the strangest sensation of wanting to stay right here. Cozy and warm.

But it was getting late, and he would need to be up early in order to deal with the news response. He pushed himself to his feet, then held out a hand and helped Beau to hers.

Which had them standing close, toe-to-toe, really. She was short enough she had to tip her head back to meet his gaze.

He should have transferred her hand to his arm. He should have turned and led her to the door.

He counted the flecks of gold in her eyes instead. He let this strange, alluring sensation fill his lungs instead. No, he'd never allowed his reckless urges to win, but this was the first time he felt truly tested. They were alone in his favorite room in the castle, and the firelight made the skin of her shoulders gleam like gold treasure.

He wanted to know what they would feel like under his palms. What more than a brush of lips would feel like. He wanted, and he always denied wants this potent. It could lead nowhere good.

But she didn't move. She watched him with those direct, changeable eyes. She kept her hand in his. If he wasn't imagining it, she even leaned closer. Her breath was definitely coming quicker.

He should have handled this differently. He knew that, even as his mouth touched hers. They needed to approach this with *some* detachment. *Some* rules. Even if a physical relationship ended up being enjoyable, it needed to have boundaries.

Not stolen kisses in a dark library with only the fire in the hearth crackling. While there were much worse ways he could impinge his reputation, he didn't want to be like *any* of the crown princes who'd come before.

Beau melted into him though, before he could pull away. Slowly. Centimeter by centimeter. Small and soft in his arms. He tried to think of the necessary boundaries, but instead the only thing he seemed to be able to do was taste her. Sharp and sweet and addicting, so that for too many moments he took and took and took without regard to anything else.

Because she felt like a secret, this woman in his arms. One he needed to get to the bottom of. A mystery to be solved.

There was something dark and thrilling underneath everything she held on the surface. It pulled at him, spoke to him, whispered desires he couldn't indulge.

Couldn't.

When he pulled back, she blinked her eyes open. Cloudy and seemingly all green in this dim lighting. Her cheeks were pink, and her lips wet. Her breathing coming in short pants.

Something dark and dangerous swirled within him. A want he was very careful to keep deep within where it wouldn't get him into trouble.

She is your wife.

But this was the library. Definitely not the place for *any-thing* that gripped him. And everything that gripped him was…thorny. Complicated. Not as in control as he needed it to be. He had experienced lust before, identified it and set it aside.

Easily.

This did not feel in the least bit *easy*.

He cleared his throat, so that his voice would sound firm and in control. "I'm afraid your hair looks a bit tousled. And your…lipstick. There's a mirror over here if you want to fix up."

She didn't say anything for ticking moments. Just regarded him with those *eyes* he couldn't seem to read. "Perhaps it would be good for the staff to see me with mussed hair and lipstick. If the goal is to seem like a newlywed couple, that is."

He found himself nodding. She was right. It was smart.

But nothing about the situation he found himself in felt *smart*. Nothing about what was rattling around inside of him was in his control. There was no denying he was attracted to her, that he wanted her.

So instead of *denying it*, he needed to take control of it. It couldn't creep up on him. It couldn't take over so that he forgot everything he was, everything he needed to do. He would never be like the men who'd come before.

Step by step, he'd told her last night. And that was how he'd control this surprising desire.

Step by controlled step.

CHAPTER SIX

BEAU DID NOT know how to parse what had happened in the library. He had kissed her. For no...discernible reason. Except maybe...he'd wanted to?

She had to admit, she hadn't allowed herself to dream about the possibility her arranged husband might actually find her...attractive. The greatest hope she'd allowed herself had been that they could have a partnership built on mutual respect.

It felt downright dangerous to think of anything else, but he'd *kissed* her.

And now he led her down the hall to their bedchamber. *Theirs*. Because once again, they would share a bed tonight. She thought the second night would feel less nerve-racking, but that kiss changed everything.

Everything.

It *hadn't* been a brush of lips. It had been a *kiss*. She had spent a lifetime loving to read a scene about knee-weakening kisses without ever really believing that was a *real* thing, physiologically. But she'd had to lean into him just to stay upright. She hadn't been able to *breathe*.

Kiss? No. Devour? Maybe. Maybe she finally understood that as a descriptor for a kiss. Because...

Wow.

He opened the door to their rooms and gestured her inside. So much of this was like last night. An unwieldy dress she'd need help with. Nerves dancing, but not the kind that created *fear* or panic. No, there was something far more like anticipation wriggling around with nerves.

She felt full of pent-up energy. Like she simply wanted to...*run* or yell or something. So she kept walking, through the sitting room and into the bedchamber. She walked all the way to the large window that looked out over a dark night. The moon hovered at the edge of one of the peaks in the distance, partially shrouded by all that mountain.

She tried to find some sense of calm, some sense of *self* in the celestial scene outside. So they had kissed. So it had been unplanned, and wonderful. So they would have to do a lot more to produce heirs. This was what she'd agreed to. She needed to stop being so silly about it. Romanticizing it. When she'd promised him she didn't have romantic notions.

Because this wasn't romance. It was simply a physical reaction to one another. Besides, chemistry and attraction were good. It would make the whole thing less awkward. And it didn't mean she thought she'd fall in love or get swept off her feet. She was too practical, understood herself too well, had too much to hide to believe in any of that.

So, this was *good*.

Why did it feel so damn scary?

"If all goes well, we will travel to the vacation chalet for the weekend. A honeymoon, in the press. It's up there," he said, coming closer with every word until he was standing next to her and he pointed to the mountains in the distance.

"Is it as beautiful as here?"

"More."

"Then I hope all goes well." She tried to offer him a happy smile, but when she looked up he was gazing at her intently.

"As do I."

Then he didn't say anything. Just stood there. Close and intense. A huge wall of…of…*man*. And for some reason her dress just felt too heavy, too cumbersome, too much. Or maybe it was all of this just too much.

She wasn't sure how to broach the topic, considering what had just occurred in the library, considering the way he was looking at her, but even as off-kilter as she was, she was still *herself*. To the point, no matter the consequences. "I'll need help with my dress again."

His gaze slowly tracked down, from her face and then millimeter by millimeter down her dress, before taking a slow perusal back up to her eyes.

Slowly, his gaze on her, he undid the knot of his tie.

She had no idea why that made her breath catch in her throat, stay there. Particularly when he didn't remove it. Just left it there loose.

"Would you like to have me help you here or in the changing room?"

"My—my clothes are in the closet, so…" She gestured helplessly toward the door, but Lyon didn't move. And neither did she.

"Perhaps we should move on to step three."

For a moment, she didn't understand what he was saying. Then all at once it dawned on her, the memory of last night and him assuring her there would be *steps* to ease them into what they had to do. "Three?" She had to swallow at her suddenly dry throat. "What was two?"

His mouth curved, slowly. *Sensuously.* So that something seemed to curve inside of her in response. A deep, warm *yearning*.

"Step one was simply a brush of mouths. Simple. Something even friends could have shared. Step two was the taste of you."

Taste of you. God.

"Wh-what would step three be?"

He didn't respond right away, but he didn't give the impression that he was somehow thinking it over. No. He knew. He was just...drawing out the moment.

When he finally spoke, each word was carefully delivered in a low, controlled voice. But his eyes... There was something that reminded her of that moment in the chapel. Where despite all his control, all his rigid certainty, she'd seen the flash of something wild.

"I want to see you."

She could feign some ignorance there, but she knew what he meant. Naked. He wanted to see her naked.

Wanted to. She supposed if anything, *that* was the hardest part to reconcile. That these things—the kiss, the *steps* were things he *wanted.* When she'd assumed everything would be...very awkward business. A chore. A responsibility.

This was better. It had to be. Besides, didn't she want the same? "Do I get to see you?"

He lifted a shoulder. "If you wish."

"Well, it only seems fair," she managed to say, not sounding *too* strangled.

The smile on his face was an unfair advantage. The way he carefully pulled the tie from his collar and placed it across the back of the big, luxurious chair in the corner. Then he turned back to her, considering.

Her breath had completely backed up in her lungs, and it felt as though her face was on fire, while a tension coiled deep inside of her. A heat that centered between her legs. And still it wasn't the anxiety or panic she was used to when faced with an uncomfortable or scary situation.

Lyon moved his finger in a circle, encouraging her to turn around so he could once again deal with the buttons on the back of her dress.

She had to swallow through too many sensations coursing through her before she could manage to get her feet to take the order to move. To turn.

His fingers brushed lightly down the back of her neck. "You make a beautiful princess, Beaugonia. *Beau.*"

She had never been complimented on her looks. She had, in fact, very rarely been complimented. Only Zia ever seemed to see her positive attributes. Beau had thought she was sort of above it. She needed no one else's approval or assurances.

She knew what and who she was. She was almost always certain in her decisions. But that compliment felt...wonderful. She didn't want to depend on anyone else's opinion of her. Didn't want to be some sad version of her mother, twisting herself just to make everything easy. Just to be *approved of.*

But him thinking she was beautiful, or at least saying it, sent a new wave of satisfaction through her.

"I'm certainly glad you think so," she managed to return, without jumping at the contact of his hand on her neck, then back, then at the top button. She could feel his breath dance across her skin. It seemed an interminable stretch of minutes as the dress gently pulled and then began to sag.

She didn't hold it up this time. Even though the idea of baring herself to him made her shake, she kept her hands firmly at her side. Even as the dress slid down, though it stopped at her hips. She could feel him tug it down over.

So the only things she was wearing were underwear and a pair of stockings. Her dress in a heap at her feet. She focused on breathing evenly, just like she tried to do when she felt a panic attack creeping up. Careful, numbered inhales. Slow, controlled exhales.

It was just bodies. Just...inevitabilities. Better to get it over with, wasn't that always her motto?

"Step out," Lyon said. She couldn't quite ascertain what

his voice sounded like. Tense, maybe. Still, she followed instructions.

She didn't turn to face him though. She couldn't quite bring herself to.

"Turn around, Beau."

She wanted to make some quip about him needing to say *please* or something about not liking being ordered around. But in this strange, not-herself-at-all moment, she found being obedient was *exactly* what she wanted. It felt like a safety blanket. Something she couldn't do wrong. So she turned.

He muttered something in Italian, but she was pretty sure it was a *good* something, based on the intent glint in his eyes. The way it hit her like its own force, a flame. Her skin felt tight, and she wanted to shake but she wouldn't let herself. She held his gaze. She stood tall and proud.

Even as the air felt cool on her skin. Even as she felt hot from the inside out. Even as she felt the need to clench her legs together just to ease some of the wild tension stitching itself tightly within her.

How did she protect herself from this? From all these physical responses. Chemistry. Attraction. Desire. What-ever word, it didn't really matter. She had to find some way to survive it.

"I think it's your turn," she managed to say. Because this wasn't just her. It was both of them. Stuck in this strange place the world and their own stubbornness had landed them in.

She should enjoy it. Whatever pieces of it she could.

He inclined his head then undid his cuff links, set them in his meticulous way on a little dish on the end table. Then he unbuttoned his shirt in quick efficient moves. He shrugged out of the shirt, laid it across the tie on the chair. The entire time, his gaze never left her body. Like he was drinking in every detail, memorizing it, and everywhere his gaze landed she felt branded. Like every inch of her skin was made specifically for him to see.

To touch.

But he didn't touch. He stayed just out of reach as he un-buttoned and unzipped his pants. So that they stood there, in little to nothing, simply watching each other.

Strangers.

Husband and wife.

She had certainly never been in a room before with a man in his underwear. While she stood there, naked from the waist up. And if she'd dreamed of a scenario like this, she would have included some touching. Kissing. A *bed* maybe, instead of all this standing. Staring. *Breathing* like they were running marathons.

But there was something exhilarating about it. The an-ticipation. The wait. The soaking it all in.

"The tiara is an excellent touch," he finally said, break-ing that silence that had been building like some kind of crescendo in a symphony.

She lifted a hand. She'd completely forgotten it was still pinned to her hair.

"Leave it," he ordered sharply when she moved to pull out a pin.

He had never spoken to her like that before—with a hint of some…*edge*. It heated through her bloodstream like a shot of alcohol. If he didn't touch her… "Lyon."

But something changed. He stepped back. That intense look shuttered. "I think that should be enough for tonight, *tesoruccia*."

She could only stare at him. Enough? But she was…she was *throbbing*. She was *naked*, mostly. And he was near enough. He hadn't even touched her.

"Go get dressed for sleep. Step four will come soon enough."

Step four? What if she wanted *step four* now? What if she wanted to be touched?

But he'd turned his back on her, and all those soaring feelings, all those hopes, deflated. She knew she hadn't done anything wrong. He'd liked what he'd seen initially, so what would have changed? Nothing to do with her. Whatever it was came from him, internally.

And even though her new hopes might include an interesting and enjoyable physical relationship with Lyon while trying to produce heirs, she certainly wasn't foolish enough to think there would be some...emotional one.

So she went and got dressed for bed. Just as he'd told her to do. And if she felt a bit like crying, she doubted it would be the last time.

Lyon did not allow himself mistakes. If one crept on him, he immediately corrected it.

Which was why he'd ended things where he'd ended them. To prove he could. To correct the mistake of thinking he could somehow wield this thing inside of him in a productive way.

If he spent another uncomfortable, sleepless night in bed with his wife, this was punishment for allowing himself to step too close to that edge. Where he focused more on *want* than right.

And, oh, how he'd *wanted*. She was beautiful. Soft and golden. Like some kind of angel. Celestially made just for him. For him to want. For him to have.

But no. That was not his lot in life. His one and only job was to protect Divio. To stabilize it. To *fix* it. The men who'd come before him had hurt Divio over and over again—financially, in worldly reputation and most importantly in breaking the trust between the monarchy and the citizens.

The princes who'd come before had put their own selfish desires first and their citizens last. His grandmother had always made sure he understood that, and that it was his role to be their opposite. To *earn* and *keep* their trust. To pay the debt her family had carved deep.

So he had ended things without touching Beau, though it had felt a bit like cutting off his own limbs in the moment. But he'd done it. *He* was in control. Not desire, no matter how big and hot and uncontrollable the flame inside had seemed, *he* had stopped it.

He was not like his cousins, his uncles, his great-uncles, letting his wants rule the day and ruining the reputation and good standing of the monarchy. He was everything his grandmother and mother had built him to be. A crown prince. The last hope of his family and country.

When he finally took Beau to bed, he would be in control, not desperate. There would be no sordid stories, no pictures, no *whispers*.

He had a certain amount of privacy and freedom at the royal chalet. Particularly if he did not bring any staff. He would work out any…control issues there. When they returned to the castle, he would know how to handle his alluring bride. In all the ways his grandmother's oldest brother never had. *He* had scandalized a country with sordid stories about the wild life he'd led with his wife, the princess.

It had been the beginning of a long line of men who'd behaved worse and more selfishly with each pass of the baton.

Beau tossed and turned next to him, sometimes asleep, sometimes not. He dared not think about what she might be feeling, wanting. It didn't matter. He lay there and watched the gap in the curtains, until dark became light and he could feasibly get up and prepare for the day ahead.

He showered, dressed, then made his way down to his office where he called on a variety of staff members to determine the next steps. Alice assured him the video was well received, which allowed him to make arrangements for a weekend trip to the chalet.

Once he was satisfied everything would run well without him, he began to gather the things he'd want to bring with him in case of emergency. Including the romance novel Beau had picked out yesterday morning.

Which was when his mother walked in. Unannounced.

He didn't bother to chastise her for it. "I am on my way out, Mother. Did you need anything from me before Beau and I leave for the chalet?"

"That is what I came to speak to you about. I'm not sure jetting off on a honeymoon is best."

"I am hardly jetting off, Mother. We are simply going to the chalet. I'm even going to drive." He slid his laptop into his bag next to Beau's book. "A short, cozy honeymoon. It is what the people expect of a happily married couple."

"Are you sure you want time away when people could be conjuring up all sorts of stories about *her*?"

Lyon stopped what he was doing and looked up at his mother. Her expression was uncharacteristically pinched, and there was no missing the disdainful way she had said *her*.

He considered what Beau had said last night. That his mother did not like her. She had not been wrong. And what a good quality for a princess, to know when she wasn't liked, and not react much to it.

But he didn't know what to do with his mother. They had almost always got on. Their goals had always been aligned. Grandmother had passed that goal down to them. It had always been a family tie, and it had always been held with accord.

Perhaps if he thought hard on it, there'd been times as a boy he had felt…chained to his grandmother and mother's vision for him, but he'd been but a child. He could hardly remember those times. Didn't like to. Wouldn't have if his mother wasn't standing here concerned with Beau and *stories*.

When if there was any real concern, his staff would have informed *him*, not his mother.

"If someone finds something that I did not, then I suppose we will deal with it as we can. But I find that eventuality nearly impossible as I was very thorough in investigating the Rendalls."

"The Rendalls. Not her specifically."

"Mother."

"I don't trust her."

While he often listened to his mother's opinions of people, he found he could not take this one on board. She was good at understanding motivations, particularly of the political set. She knew how to handle threats, but Beau was not a threat. She was…

Well, she wasn't a threat.

"You do not need to, Mother. But you need to trust me. And treat your crown princess with respect."

Mother's expression went cool. "Very well, *Your Highness*." Then she swept out of the room.

Lyon sighed. He did not have time to smooth over things with his mother. Besides, she was the one acting out of turn.

She was just worked up about change, no doubt. Just because it was a necessary change they'd both agreed on likely didn't mean it was easy to realize she was no longer needed as his partner. Beau would take that role.

Beau. Likely still asleep. Cheeks flushed from the warmth of the bed, hair tousled from tossing and turning. She'd worn rather unattractive pajamas to bed last night, but that hadn't erased the memory of her standing before him in nothing but—

He shoved the last of his things in his bag. Forcefully. Before marching out of his office. He simply wouldn't think of it. He'd pretend it had been a dream he'd had. Even if she tried to bring it up, he would refuse.

He let that certainty take him all the way upstairs and into his rooms. He expected to find her still in bed, but she was dressed, seated on a chair in the sitting room. She was reading a book, a cup of coffee in one hand.

She looked up. Briefly. "Good morning," she offered pleasantly.

"Good morning," he returned. Then he waited. But whatever he was waiting for did not materialize. She went right back to her book and sipping her coffee. She was dressed perfectly in another pair of dark, loose slacks that looked like silk, and a more formfitting sweater. Today the color of ripe berries.

Which reminded him of…

"Our video has been well received," he said, stiffly and suddenly even to his own ears. "It even got picked up by a few European news affiliates. People are enamored with the story. So, we will head off this morning. I have much to do, and I don't like to be too far away for long, but we will take the weekend as a honeymoon of sorts."

After a moment, she set the book aside—his family biography that he'd given her, he realized—then she looked up at him. Her hazel eyes were a storm of things he couldn't name. She sipped from her cup, then nodded. "Do I need to pack?"

"My staff will take care of everything you'll need."

"Naturally." She got to her feet. "Are we leaving now?"

"In about fifteen minutes."

She nodded. "If you don't mind, I'd like to grab a few books from the library."

"Of course." But he found himself rooted to the spot, blocking her exit from the room. "I have requested next to no staff for this trip. There will be some security, but we will have the chalet to ourselves. Complete privacy."

Her gaze didn't falter, but she tilted her head to one side. Studying him. "For step four?"

He still wasn't sure whether he was delighted by her directness, or if he disliked it entirely. He never quite expected it from her because she was timid in so many other ways. So it continually surprised him, when he was no fan of surprises.

Yet he always found himself smiling anyway.

"For as many steps as you'd like, *tesoruccia*."

"What does that mean? *Tesoruccia*. I keep meaning to look it up."

He wasn't sure why he hesitated. He wasn't *embarrassed* or he wouldn't call her that. "Treasure," he offered.

She laughed.

"Is that funny?"

"The idea that I'm some kind of prize? Yes. Never in my life has anyone…" She trailed off and shook her head. For all her attempts at elegant dismissiveness, a shell of sorts as if nothing got to her, any time she spoke of her family some little hint of vulnerability snuck through.

And reached inside of him like a barb, stuck there, until he did something to smooth it away.

"The truth of the matter is, whatever it is that Zia has done that you do not wish to divulge, it is clear she wasn't going to marry me. The fact you stepped into her place is of great value to me, Beau."

She blinked at that, something soft and sweet in her expression. "I think the only person in my entire life who's ever felt that way is Zia."

"I suppose it is a good thing you ended up married to me then."

Her smile was small, shy. It made warmth bloom in his chest like it was some great feat to make that happen.

So he moved out of the way. So she could go get her books. And he could…figure out what the hell he was feeling.

CHAPTER SEVEN

BEAU WAS SURPRISED when Lyon led her to a heavy-duty Jeep vehicle, and then *he* got into the driver's side himself. She stood there for a moment, simply staring. Until he looked over at her and raised a brow.

"Do princes not drive in Lille?"

"My father said it was beneath us."

Lyon shook his head. "Your father does not improve no matter what more I know about him."

"No, I cannot imagine he ever will."

"Well, we shall get you some lessons when it's appropriate. As for today, I will drive us up to the chalet. We still have some security measures in place, so no worries there. Come now. Let us be off."

With halting steps, Beau made her way to the passenger side where one of Lyon's attendants waited with the door open. He helped her up and in, then closed the door. Once she was buckled in, Lyon started the engine and began to drive.

Drive. "I don't think I've ever been in the front seat of a car before," Beau said. It was a strange feeling, and stranger still realizing just how odd her life was that she was almost twenty-five and had never ridden in the front of a car.

"It is a day of firsts then," Lyon said. He seemed relaxed behind the wheel, driving this industrial-sized monster.

Beau felt tense. She was determined *not* to be, and thought she'd been handling herself quite well. She had let him be her guide. He had not mentioned last night, so she hadn't. He had mentioned the complete privacy at the chalet, so she had brought up *steps* to indicate she understood what was still expected of her. Even if she didn't understand him or his actions.

She had let his staff pack for her, and she'd only grabbed a few books hoping to have some reading time.

She was being the exact thing she'd promised him she'd be. Easy. Respectable. Flexible.

But she found she really, *really* didn't like riding in the front seat as the roads narrowed and began to twist—up and around the mountains that had been so pretty from a distance, and now looked more and more menacing.

"As I said, we will have almost no staff," Lyon said casually, like he wasn't navigating a giant hunk of metal around roads certainly not meant for something of its size. "I typically like to use a trip to the chalet as a kind of…reset. A reminder I can and will do things on my own when it serves. Do you know how to cook?"

Beau hung onto every word, because it helped her not think about hurtling off the side of the mountain. "In theory."

"How does one know how to cook in theory?"

"I've read a lot about it, but I wasn't allowed in the kitchens. I should definitely like to try to put what I've learned into practice though." She frowned at his large, capable hands on the wheel. "I have less interest in driving."

"Why?"

"Don't you feel…out of control?"

"On the contrary. I feel very in control. I am the one driving the vehicle."

He certainly looked and sounded it. "But the weather,

other people, traffic laws and etiquette." She felt a little band of anxiety around her lungs at just the thought.

He spared her a quick glance, with a bemused expression. "Perhaps we will stick to cooking."

She nodded emphatically. "I think that is good." When silence settled again, and looming mountains threatened to cause her to venture into the kind of panic she could not let Lyon see, she scrambled to talk. About anything.

"While I don't have many day-to-day skills, I'm happy to learn them. I pick things up very easily." She kept her eyes on his face instead of the world around them. "I'm very good at math. Exceptional with computers. You wouldn't believe the things I got around my father's IT team's pathetic excuse for internet security."

His mouth curved. "You are a constant surprise, Beau."

"I have heard that before. It's never a compliment."

"It wasn't an insult."

"But it wasn't a compliment."

He didn't argue with her, but the bemused expression didn't leave his face. Perhaps he hadn't *meant* it as an insult, even if it wasn't a compliment. That would still be a novelty in her life.

"It will be a few hours. The drive is quite beautiful though. Especially as we get up into the higher elevations where there's more consistent snow." He glanced over at her and must have read something in her expression.

"You could always nap if you'd like."

"Yes. I think I'll try that." She immediately closed her eyes. She knew she wouldn't sleep, but surely it was better than watching. And if she closed her eyes, she could picture him as he'd been last night. Shirtless. Tall and broad and... strong. Not bulky, but there was something about the way he held himself, something about the shape of him that left no doubt that he could…do all sorts of interesting things with those muscles.

Which left her mind skipping ahead to tonight. And then drifting back to last night. Why had he stopped? Without even *touching* her. Not one kiss while they'd both been nearly naked. It didn't make any sense.

Should she ask him about it? Demand to know what he was thinking? Would that make him angry? Should she just keep her mouth shut and do whatever he told her to do?

This was really not the line of thinking that would help with her anxiety. Particularly since she had some concerns about this trip. Not the privacy because of *steps*, or even that he might pull back from her once again, but because in a smaller place, with less people, it would be harder to hide if she had a panic attack. There was no rhyme or reason for why one hit, though they had gotten less frequent the past few years as she'd learned, thanks to reading books and even medical studies on the topic, coping mechanisms and different ways to keep her mind busy when it wanted to spiral out into anxiety.

She still often had attacks when she faced off with her father, as she had just a few days ago when they'd been visiting Zia at Cristhian's house. She was counting on that meaning another unexplained one didn't pop up for another few weeks at least.

But if she kept thinking about it, worrying about it, no doubt she'd work herself up. So she needed to focus on something else besides this *chalet*. And while she'd like to consider and perhaps discuss what had happened last night, and what would happen tonight, she wasn't sure that was the best *driving* conversation.

Or you're a coward.

That too.

So, she decided the next best thing was to deal with other

eventualities. The important ones they'd already agreed upon. She wasn't going to *sleep*, so she might as well prod.

"I was reading your family biography, but it doesn't mention much about your father."

"He was not from Divio, and the book is focused on the royal lines of Divio."

She supposed that made sense, but the two short lines about his entire life had made her feel almost sorry for the man. "Do you remember him?"

Lyon didn't even pause. "No."

As she'd expected. She'd done the math and Lyon's father had died when he'd only been two. His grandfather had died before he'd been born. But he did have a slew of uncles and great-uncles and older cousins. All who'd filtered through the role of crown prince in quick succession.

She knew this was the reason he held himself to high standards. So he would not ruin his time as prince. But what she did not know was if anyone had been a *father* to him. Because certainly no one had been a *father* to her.

"Since your grandfather was also passed by the time you were born, did any of your uncles or anyone fulfill some kind of father figure role?"

His eyebrows drew together and he spared her a look—which she didn't appreciate considering the narrow road. "Is there a point to this odd line of questioning, Beau?"

"I'm thinking about children." Because that was her end goal. Those heirs Lyon needed. Lives she wanted to guide. "You see, I did not have very good examples of parents. Mother or father, but I feel like the bad example is an example in a way. A blueprint of what not to do. But you have nothing."

"What a kind way of putting it," he said dryly.

She winced. "I apologize. I only meant…"

"That I have no example of what a father is meant to

be, one way or another." This time his tone was not dry, it was simply flat.

"Well…" She knew that wasn't a kind way of putting any of it, but it *was* true. How else could she put it?

"I had my grandmother and my mother. They were both incredibly strong role models for a young man and impressed upon me the importance of my role. They knew, long before I did, that Divio would eventually come to me."

"How could they know that? So many came before you."

"My grandmother's brothers were fools at best. Their children worse, and so on. Every single male heir from then on either died young, got into far too much trouble before they ascended the throne, or caused so much uproar they had to abdicate to the next. My grandmother always knew it would be me or complete revolution."

What a strange responsibility to put on your grandson. Even if she'd had little faith in the male heirs, it still seemed a stretch to prepare Lyon from *childhood* to potentially take over. But she supposed that was what made him good at his role. What he'd learned. That responsibility that had been pressed upon him.

One that made the word *revolution* sound so bitter on his tongue. "You're afraid of that, aren't you? That's why you're so concerned about…optics and stability." What would he think of a wife who became a shaking, crying mess out of nowhere? Not a comforting thought as they climbed higher and higher still.

"Afraid is not the word I would use," he said carefully, navigating a steep curve as if it were nothing.

She was almost entertained in spite of herself by how clearly he didn't like the idea he might be *afraid*.

"It is a concern," he continued. "But I am well-equipped to handle parliament."

She had no doubt he was. He seemed endlessly capable of handling everything.

Even you?

Well, he certainly made her wonder. It wasn't just the aura he had of…leadership. That passed-down royal thing that had skipped her entirely, that he could walk into a room and everyone would look to him to handle whatever problems arose.

But it was the kindness that she was struggling with. Because if he was kind, would he be cruel to her if he knew about her panic attacks? She wanted to believe he would, because that would mean protecting herself.

But kindness meant a little sliver of her mind sometimes thought *what if.*

"Particularly the parliamentary members who enthusiastically cheered on my family members' worst impulses," he continued, his expression growing dark. "They will not do the same with me."

"Why would they do that? Isn't that counterproductive? Don't they want a stable monarch?"

"You would be surprised what men would do for power," he said grimly. "Their goals were not the good of Divio. Their goals were the good of their own pockets and reach. Sometimes that meant a leader too dependent on the drink to do their job, or too busy chasing women to notice that money is not going where it should. It rarely means a leader who is in control."

"What about you?"

"What about me?"

"What do you want if not power? Being crown prince certainly gives you said power. Being a leader in control is just…power."

"Yes, but it is also a responsibility. I will not squander it as my family has before me. I care about my country. I will wield my power only insofar as it serves our citizens. That is my one and always goal."

Beau considered this, and wondered if it was a speech her father would get behind. It certainly *sounded* like him, but only the superficial words. Country first. Responsibility to country. Damn anything that gets in the way—like a frivolous wife and two rebellious children.

But she was not sure her father had ever considered his role a *responsibility* so much as a right. *His* birthright. What he was *owed*. It was power, and it was his.

In the end, it didn't matter how much Lyon sounded like Father or didn't. She'd said *I do*. She'd made this bed, and she had to lie in it whether Lyon was a monster or not. So far, he was…interesting. Confusing. But not a monster.

"Did it occur to no one to change the law, allowing female heirs to take the role?" Beau suggested, making the mistake of looking outside once more then, shaken by all that *sky* when they were driving on the *ground*, immediately looked down at her lap.

"A resolution has never been brought forward. But I will propose one."

"You will?"

"Once the timing is right. I want stability, and the kingdom to trust me. To trust what the monarchy offers. But not at the cost of moving on with the times. Divio must be a part of the modern world. But one thing at a time. First, we give them that which they have done without for so many years. A respectable, secure leader."

She nodded along with that. It made sense, and underscored the point that Lyon had *plans*. An entire blueprint for the rest of his life. Which now included hers. If she disappointed him, he no doubt had a plan for that too. She would have asked him about that, but the car came to a stop.

Beau gingerly peered out the windshield. She saw very

little aside from blue sky and intimidating mountain. Definitely not a chalet. "Why are we stopping? I thought you said the drive was hours? Is something wrong?"

"You are safe, Beau," Lyon said, reaching over and giving her hand a squeeze. "I want to show you something."

Then he did the strangest thing and got out of the car. It appeared they were on the side of the road, not parked in the middle of it, but still this felt decidedly *unsafe*. But her passenger side door opened and he held out a hand to her. "Come."

She wanted to shake her head. She considered refusing. But there was something about Lyon's directives that did not get her back up like just about everyone else in her life trying to tell her what to do. Maybe it was a confidence born of self-assuredness—rather than Father's bluster, Mother's desperation, or Zia's determination to protect Beau at all costs—even when she hadn't needed it.

Self-assuredness was one thing Beau, ironically enough considering her experience with social anxieties and panic attacks, understood quite well.

So, she took Lyon's hand and let him help her out of the car. He wound an arm around her waist as the side of the road here was slippery. But she realized it wasn't the side of the road, it was an entire parking area. And Lyon led her to a little iron gate.

Beyond it was sky and cloud and mountain. Below them, a smattering of little villages. Puffs of smoke. Bits of green and brown and white. A beautiful landscape. It was so idyllic it seemed like a painting. Not quite real, and yet there it all was spread out before her very own eyes.

Her stomach nearly dropped out, but even with that disorienting vertigo feeling, her heart…it leapt with joy. "Lyon."

"Beautiful, no?"

"I…" She had no words. Particularly when he stood behind her but kept his arm around her waist. Holding her there against him, like a warm, protective wall.

"There is more beauty to be had once the drive is done. I promise, the discomfort is worth the outcome."

She managed to tear her gaze from the villages below to look over her shoulder and up at him. He'd done this to help her. She didn't know what to do with that. How to feel about it. She couldn't say no one had ever helped her. Zia had.

But this was different. He wasn't *protecting* her. He was simply offering her a kindness. Which made her eyes water and her heart soften. Probably ill-advisedly.

But she smiled all the same. "Then I suppose we should finish the drive."

Beau's anxieties had not melted away when she'd seen the pretty overlook as Lyon had hoped, but she made the rest of the drive with a brave face. He supposed that was why he'd stopped. Courage in the face of discomfort deserved a reward, and it would hardly be the last time she was thrust into a situation that made her uncomfortable.

Oftentimes, a kindness was the best and only reward for such responsibilities. At least, he'd always felt so.

Being the ruling couple of the monarchy of Divio would be full of challenges over the next few years. If she faced them all with such determination, they would end up in a very good place.

When they pulled into the gates of the chalet estate, and he slowed the car, she finally looked out the vehicle windows. She made a soft sound of appreciation.

He was enjoying her reaction. Aside from her fear of the mountainous drive, she seemed delighted with just about everything. He pulled to a stop and got out of the car, then went over to her side. The skeleton staff they kept at the chalet would have unpacked all their things by now, stocked the fridge and whatnot, and left.

So they would be truly alone.

"I've never seen anything so beautiful," she said cheerfully as they walked toward the chalet, arm in arm.

"Are you just saying that because you're happy to be out of the car?"

She laughed. "No," she said. "Though that helps."

"I have been to Lille. It is hardly an eyesore."

"Lille *is* beautiful. But it is about all I've ever seen. There's something about seeing a new kind of beauty. It's exciting."

"I do not understand why you were so sheltered, Beau. All because of a childhood anxiety."

She stiffened a little but kept walking. Spoke easily enough. "I would think you'd understand perfectly. My father felt he could not risk being seen as weak, and a daughter who did not behave as she should, a daughter who was shy or terrified is certainly a weakness."

He frowned at her description of what he should understand. He paused in front of the door, looked down at her. "I do not need to be seen as *strong*, Beau. That is not the same as stable. As…dependable."

She studied him, her eyes going dark, the gold and green barely visible even out here in all this sunlight. Everything about her was suddenly very serious.

"Could your country depend on a princess who cried if the crowd was too big? Who shook like a leaf if required to speak to a group of people she did not know and feel comfortable with?"

Of course that would be…a problem. A challenge to be overcome, certainly. But it was also irrelevant. "But that isn't you any longer. I know, because I saw you at that dinner last night. You were wonderful."

"Yes, I can handle a crowd these days," she said, her gaze sliding away from his. She gestured at the door. "Aren't you going to show me the chalet?"

He didn't care for the change in topic. This seemed more important, but why would it be? She clearly didn't suffer those old anxieties. She dealt with the wedding, his staff, the dinner and video all with aplomb. Even her nerves over the car ride she had handled very well.

He knew the difference between being riddled with anxiety and being able to handle it.

So this was all...moot. He opened the front door to the chalet and gestured her inside. It was a huge, open airy space, with almost all rooms pouring into each other on the lower level. There were ample windows to see all that natural beauty from, fireplaces in every room and plenty of cozy furniture and warm throw blankets for the cold nights.

She moved forward toward the row of windows in the living room that offered a spectacular view of the mountains. She all but pressed her nose to the glass. "My God. I didn't think anything else could be more beautiful than that overlook, but you're right. This is even better."

There were no villages below. Only mountains and valleys, alpine lakes glittering like jewels in the sun. A stunning and breathtaking view. He'd always loved it. Always loved viewing it in privacy. He could not come out here as much as he liked now that he was crown prince. There was too much pressing work at the palace, but every time he came he felt...renewed.

But he'd never shared that with anyone. Always liked this as a *private* oasis. Where he could sort through whatever needed sorting in his mind. But he supposed privacy wasn't something he had anymore. A wife. Children eventually. He would bring them all here and...

Something about the reality of Beau made all those plans

he'd had…not change, exactly. Just flesh out. His children would be people, like Beau was a person. They would have their own wills and whims and irrational fears with some unknown combination of genes from him and Beau.

Beau with her hazel eyes and shy smile. Except it wasn't shy right now. She turned to look at him and she was beaming. Beautiful. But he stayed where he was, by the entrance and out of reach, because he did not trust any of the unwieldy storms clattering around inside of him. The desire, not just to put his mouth on her. To see every inch of her. To touch, to take, *finally* take. That he could deal with. Understandable and all that.

It was the desire to hold her just as he had at the overlook. And feel a strange peace he'd never known, never expected to exist. There was something about the way she *beamed* at him that twined a dark *lust* with some kind of incomprehensible soft desire.

And he didn't trust emotions that twisted. That couldn't be worked out. He needed to set it aside until it could be carefully picked apart and put into a careful compartment of the appropriate reaction.

"We should eat something," he said. Inanely.

Some of the joy on her face faded. He didn't know why. And it didn't matter, he told himself. He led her into the kitchen. He heard himself talk. About the sandwiches the staff would have left. About how tomorrow morning they would need to fend for themselves. About everything and anything that kept him from thinking about her.

"Tomorrow, we'll go on a hike." Bundled up. Physical exertion. Not alone in the same cabin.

"Sounds lovely."

Silence settled around them again. An awkward, uncomfortable silence. Which was new for them. Everything up to now had been fairly easy. All the moments following him on the edge of making a mistake had included a step back. A reset.

But there was nowhere to go here. Which made this feel like a mistake. They should have stayed at the palace.

He had brought her here to get this over with. To have her away from prying eyes and whispers. To not have to worry about...himself.

But he was worried. He forced himself to eat. Ignored the heavy, oppressive silence. When they were both done, he cleared the table. Beau trailed after him. "I also know how to wash dishes. In theory."

He smiled in spite of all these ugly things roiling around inside of him. She was such an interesting woman.

"Let's put that theory to work." He showed her the dishwasher. He instructed her to rinse dishes, then hand them to him so he could place them inside and he instructed her how to put them in properly so that she could handle this chore if she so chose.

But it put them close. Hip to hip as they worked. He could not pretend she wasn't there. That she smelled like something faintly floral. Just the hint of something he'd need to lean closer to identify.

When she handed him the last dish, he placed it inside and closed the door. He turned to suggest they take an hour or so to read before having some dessert, but no words came out as they stood face-to-face. Close.

And all too well he could picture all that pale skin underneath her clothes. The way color rode high on her cheeks, and her eyes darkened with interest when he'd had very little on himself.

She raised her gaze to meet his. He should lay out how the rest of the night would go. He should set out rules. *Then* they could go to the bedroom. *Then* he could control himself well enough to get this over with in an appropriate, heir-making way.

But she leaned in. With a slight hesitation, she slid her hands up his chest. Locked her arms around his neck.

Why did she fit so well against him? Why did it unravel and dissolve every tenet of discipline that had always come easily to him?

Then she rose to her toes and pressed her mouth to his. Initiating a soft, sweet kiss.

It should be sweet. It should be easy. But it lit a fire inside of him that was none of those things. Because he had never had soft and sweet inside of him. He was made by his blood, and the blood was tainted. A line of royal men who'd never resisted an impulse in their lives.

Grandmother had tried to convince him that he could be stronger, better, but he knew.

What he wanted, what he desired, was just as bad as what had felled the men who'd come before. The only difference between them and him was *control*.

Which had never once been threatened like this. When it *shouldn't* be called into question at all.

Whether she was his wife or not, she was innocent and sheltered. That should be enough to keep his desires on their usual simple leash. Instead he wanted to rip every scrap of clothing off of her, take her roughly, right here against the countertop.

Even as he told himself he *wouldn't*, he drove the kiss deeper.

Hotter.

Rougher.

Until she was pressed up against the island. Until his hands were tangled in her hair once more. He could lift her up onto the countertop and have her. Right here. Right now. This terrible pressure would be gone. The mistake made and done instead of hovering just out of reach. It would be relief. It would be a mistake, but he would fix it.

He could fix it.

Or it would open an insatiable desire he could never stop. Or it would get too dark, too wild, and he would be doomed just like every man in his royal bloodline before him.

Maybe it was in that blood—his uncles and cousins had often been brought to ruin by their unquenchable thirsts—but he would not succumb. He could not allow it.

He pulled away. Set her gently back. To prove that he could. To prove that he would. Tonight, he would touch her. But…in their bedroom. Appropriately. Carefully. Not with this wild thing whispering dark, lurid suggestions in the *kitchen*.

Except she frowned up at him, her dark eyebrows drawn together as she studied him. As if she could see right through him. "Why do you hold yourself back from me when we both know where this eventually must end up? When it seems…you enjoy it at least a little?"

No, there were times her directness didn't entertain him at all. Because he knew the answer, but he could hardly give it to her.

"I suggested steps for a reason, Beau," he said, trying to sound gentle if scolding. He was afraid his voice just sounded…rough. A clue to everything clawing at him.

"What reason?" she demanded.

She was seriously testing his temper. But he maintained his calm demeanor. Because he was in control. "You are innocent. Sheltered, you said that yourself. Jumping into things… It would be careless. Reckless. Sometimes if proper steps are not taken, miscommunications happen. People believe in feelings that aren't…accurate or suitable."

This did not seem to assuage her. Her eyes snapped with temper. She crossed her arms over her chest. "You think if we have sex I'll just…miraculously fall in love with you on the spot? I'll be so bowled over by the experience, I'll just turn into some mindless ninny desperate for love?"

"No, but…"

"But! But!" Her mouth dropped open in outrage. Her cheeks flushed with temper. And it did not help this roaring thing inside of him. It poked at his own temper. It stirred darker wants than he allowed.

"I do not wish to fight with you," he said. Through gritted teeth.

"Then don't be an idiot," she shot back. Then she blinked, as if she realized what she'd just said. Her expression was torn, clearly.

But she didn't apologize for her little explosion, no matter how contrite she looked. When she *should* apologize.

He told himself that's why he didn't let it go, when he should. When *he* was the one who'd said he didn't want to fight.

"Would you prefer I take you in a maddened rush? Right here? On the kitchen counter where we make our *food*?"

She lifted her chin. "Over this strange back-and-forth? Over you…getting me all worked up and then stepping away all icy and weird? Yes, I'd prefer mad rush over that."

Walk away.

The voice of reason was still there. But it was faint.

And he didn't want to listen. He'd show her, instead. Frighten her. Make her *stop*. She would want to stop once he showed her, and then…then…he could.

So he gave in to the roaring thing inside of him. The wants, desires, the dark, twisting need. He fisted his hand in her hair, holding tight so she couldn't move. So she was at his mercy. His for the taking.

Then he crashed his mouth to hers and *took*. It was rough, demanding. The scrape of teeth, his fist in her hair. He gave her no quarter, offered no gentleness. He only took and took and took until those alarm bells he was usually so good at listening to rang in his head.

He wrenched his mouth away, but he couldn't seem to pull his hands from her hair. He couldn't seem to put distance between himself and the soft warmth of her body pressed up against his.

"There are parts of myself I keep leashed for a reason, *tesoruccia*."

Her gaze was steady, her eyes seemed to glow gold. "You are not a dog, Lyon."

But he felt like one, even as her palm slid over his cheek. Like someone trying to tame the snarling, wild beast that roared within.

"You would be surprised," he said, each word a scrape against the thinnest wall of control he maintained. "The things I want. The things I like. Not suitable for the prince I am, but there all the same."

He managed to unclench his hands, detangle them from her hair. He meant to step back. Surely she'd learned her lesson now.

But she reached out, fisted her own hands in his shirt, and held him close.

CHAPTER EIGHT

BEAU HAD NOT meant to call him an idiot. She had not meant to fight with him. That was not the way a dutiful princess acted.

But if this was the punishment, perhaps she'd fight with him all the time. If the way he kissed her was unsuitable but made her feel alive—for perhaps the first time *ever*—then maybe she wanted all that unsuitable punishment.

She looked at him, hands fisted in his shirt so he did not walk away, and saw something in his eyes she didn't understand, but wanted to. Something in his expression she wanted to soothe. But not with sweet words or gentle touches. She wanted this wild thing he offered.

Because she'd never had wild. She'd never been able to follow an impulse. She had lived in shadows and corners and locked rooms.

Now she had…freedom, and she wanted the recklessness that came with it.

She pulled him closer, so that he had to bend down, then she put her mouth to his ear. "Show me."

He made a sound, something she could only describe as a growl. An electric thrill went through her bloodstream at it. At him reaching out once more. With one hard yank, he pulled her pants over her hips, let them fall to the ground.

Then he reached out and simply *ripped* the underwear from her body.

Her breath came out in a gasp. A wild thrill swept through her. This, *this* was that wildness she'd seen in him. A hint of it. *Leashed* as he said. And maybe she should be afraid of that being *un*leashed. Certainly she should be.

Instead, she was intrigued.

Instead, she wanted to see where it all led.

Then he cupped her. His big, rough hand on the most sensitive, vulnerable part of her. With no warning, no preamble, his finger slid deep inside.

She wasn't sure of the sound she made, some kind of keening whimper, while he hissed out a breath that seemed to explode inside of her, like a match to friction. He stroked her, slow but seeming to unerringly find just the spot to turn everything into flame.

"Little Beaugonia, so ripe and sweet." He was touching her, doing miraculous things that made pleasure wave through her, build into something tense and needy. "You don't know what you're getting yourself into. But you want it, don't you?"

She couldn't form words. Her blood seemed to run hot in her veins, her breasts heavy and sensitive. She wanted to fidget, but he didn't let her. She wanted whatever her body was building itself up to, but he didn't let her.

He pulled away. Not the way he had before though. No, instead of that detached, cold look in his eyes, they were alight with fire. His mouth a sensuous curve, full of dark amusement.

He pulled the sweater off of her, then his hands were on her waist and he lifted her, set her on the counter island.

The wild pirate she'd always known was lurking under all those chains. And now he was hers. He would be *hers*.

He jerked her bra down, not off. So her breasts were

bared, but not free. He brushed a thumb across her nipple, eliciting another gasp from her, the pleasure shocking because how could there be more? His expression went wicked, and he brushed his thumb, back and forth. Until she was squirming. Until she felt…mindless, desperate. She wanted his hands back on her. She wanted *him* inside of her because it felt like that would only ever be the cure to all this need.

"Lyon," she said breathlessly. Needing…needing…

"Yes, I like the way you say my name. Like you're begging. I'd like to hear you beg, Beaugonia. Beg and beg and beg."

Beg. She did not beg. She did *not*…and yet. All those old determinations she'd always believed of herself seemed so weak in the face of how close she was to some unknown pleasure, some great, big feeling *just* out of reach. The kind of thing she couldn't have brought herself.

It could only come from him.

"Lyon, please."

His laugh was dark, cutting. *Perfect*, because it rumbled through her like its own touch. Then his big hands slid up her thighs, then pulled her legs apart. So she was completely bared to him. On the kitchen counter. He pulled her to the edge, his expression dark and feral.

"My banquet. My feast. Do you taste as sweet as you look?" They were shocking words. Everything about this was *shocking*, and yet… She liked it. The wild rush of it. How she knew she should feel some kind of shame, but she only wanted more.

Then she had it, when he dipped his head between her legs. His big hands holding her thighs wide. His dark head at the most sensitive part of her. The chaotic thrall of sensation whirling through her as he tasted her, devoured her like a feast. She could scarcely catch her breath.

And then it all simply…imploded in on itself. She cried out, pulsing through a climax so all-encompassing it seemed like the world went dark, like every inch of her exploded in pleasure and joy and then simply collapsed.

But he caught her. Still sitting on the counter, she leaned her forehead to his shoulder, struggling to breathe. But not like a panic attack. This didn't grip her like fear.

She was smiling. She wanted to *laugh*.

She wanted more.

"Have you had enough, Beau?" he murmured.

"No. No. Lyon, please… We have to…" She looked up, met his gaze. Every inch of him seemed tense, like he was holding back. She didn't want that.

She wanted all of him. She reached out, undid the buttons of his shirt, pushed the fabric off his shoulders, their eyes holding contact the entire time. She let her hands move over him, study him, learn him. And the whole time, she watched his eyes. His wild pirate eyes grew more fierce, his jaw more tense, the fingers on her waist dug deeper.

She trailed her fingers down his chest, the hard cut of his muscles, the trail of dark hair. Then her fingers found the button of his pants. The zipper. She pushed the fabric of his pants and boxers down as far as she could sitting there on the counter.

She didn't allow herself nerves. Like cooking, like loading a dishwasher, she knew how to do this *in theory*. She'd read about it plenty. She only needed to put it into practice. So she reached out and touched him. Closed her hand over the hard, hot length of him.

She groaned in time with him. She didn't know why it should be a thrill to her, but something about holding him in her hand felt like pleasure spearing through her. And that was what she wanted.

Everything.

"Make me yours, Lyon."

She watched whatever thread of control he'd held on to simply snap.

"Here," he demanded, as if she'd argue.

She wouldn't argue with anything if he made her feel that wild, dizzying climax again. If he was inside of her. If finally, *finally* this all made sense. Who cared *where* as long as it happened.

"It is likely to hurt," he muttered.

She wanted to throw her head back and laugh. She knew that was true, but it felt like nothing could ever hurt her again. Not with all this going on inside of her. A weakness and a strength. A joy and something so beautiful it almost made her want to cry. Likely to hurt? Did it matter?

"Only at first," she assured him.

His gaze held hers, as they breathed in tangled tandem. Even as he entered her, slow, too much inch by breathtaking inch. There was something, not pain exactly, but an expanding. Pressure, too much, too much, and yet not enough. Nothing was enough with him.

She wasn't sure she breathed, but she watched him and he watched her. Until they were one. Until whatever discomfort felt secondary to everything else thrashing against her like a storm.

And then he moved, opening up a new world. A new *universe* that was only the two of them together, and that was a wonderful, beautiful, exhilarating thing. Where nothing else mattered, except the way they fit together, moved together, made each other feel.

Both out of body and so deeply within their bodies it was as if there was nothing else. Not palaces or countries or mountains surrounding them. Just the delicious friction two bodies could create.

Until she was crumbling apart by some great seismic event

that threatened to rearrange everything she'd built each forward step on. Because what could possibly come after this?

He kissed down her neck, her chest, then his mouth fused to her breast, until that amazing, stomach-flipping climb started all over again. Up, up, up as his grip on her hips tightened. As that tension coiled again, tightened, burst.

This time, with him. He roared out a release, thrust deep inside.

They leaned into each other, ragged breaths, sweaty bodies. Throbbing with all the pleasure that still hummed between them. Beau sighed into his neck, mouth curved into a smile.

She had bemoaned her fate for much of her life, but it no longer felt quite so stifling if it had brought her to this moment.

There was a ringing in his head, an echoing roar in his ears. She was pliant and warm in his arms. Precious and wonderful.

And he had…behaved a clumsy fool. He had handled this all consumed with such selfish desires and needs, with no thought to his *responsibility*. He didn't even have the words for an apology.

He pulled his pants into place. Looked at her. Rosy and flushed, naked on the kitchen counter. Beautiful and wonderful and this was everything he had not wanted. Everything he should have resisted.

But that was not her fault, though it was tempting to think that considering he'd never been driven to be so reckless before. Still, the fault lay with him. Only weak men blamed others for their own mistakes.

Gingerly, he picked her up off the counter and then carried her through the chalet into his bedroom. He laid her on the bed. He needed to leave her. He needed to…to…

He sank onto the edge of the bed. Sat there, head in his hands. What had he done? What had become of him? How did he fix this mistake?

He heard her move, and then she was behind him, palms on his shoulders. "What's wrong?"

"That was not how it should have gone, Beaugonia."

"Why not?"

How could she even ask that as if she had no idea? He looked at her over his shoulder. "Rough and frenzied in the kitchen? This is not appropriate. This is not what a man in control of himself does." He looked back down at his hands. "It was wrong to treat you like that. Wrong to lose…" He didn't even know what other words there were.

All he knew was he looked at his own hands and saw every man in the royal line who had squandered the responsibility of the crown. For power. For a woman. For fun. All to follow their selfish desires to ruination.

He hadn't ruined anything yet, but this felt like the first step down a slippery slope.

Her palm trailed down his spine. "Lyon. I liked the way you treated me. I liked it, and you did too. If we both enjoyed ourselves, why should you feel badly about it?"

He supposed she had enjoyed it. She wasn't experienced enough to pretend, and even if she was, there was no denying she'd been a willing and animated participant. And still he felt like he'd defiled everything he was supposed to keep respectable and stable.

"I must be in control at all times. I am not like my cousins. My uncles." He could not allow himself to be. Perhaps most of them had made their disgraces with women who were not their wives, over money that was not theirs, but anything that could be leaked to the public could be used against him. His grandmother's brother's wild exploits with his wife might not make waves today, but it had at the time.

And no doubt, the man had known better, known it would. But he had cared more about his own wants than what he owed. Which is what Lyon had just done.

It had to end right here. "I will not be like them." Maybe if she understood that, they could move beyond this…misstep.

But she pressed her mouth to his back. In comfort. Like she understood. Like everything she was and offered could be enough.

"This isn't about countries," she said gently. "Citizens and responsibilities. It's simply what we do in the dark. We're married. And… And it's a requirement. How else are we going to have an heir? I mean, I can lay on my back and think of England if it really makes you feel better, but I like what we did tonight better. Well, I assume I do anyway."

He wanted to *laugh*, and he couldn't for the life of him determine why. This wasn't the least bit funny. "Beau." She didn't understand. He could not let feelings and his own wants outweigh responsibility.

Too many before him had.

There had to be a time and place for things. Not kitchens and whenever the need struck. There needed to be lines uncrossed, boxes things were kept firmly in. Anything that even whispered at personal wants had to be done with control and privacy.

But when he turned to face her, she was the most beautiful, glorious thing he'd ever encountered. She was his *wife*, and they *did* need heirs.

But he would have to find some way to put a wall up around all this…dangerous desire. She would need to get pregnant soon. He'd heard from his mother pregnancy was an uncomfortable, painful experience. Beau wouldn't want him then, wouldn't tempt him then. And then there'd be a child.

It could stand between them and…this.

"Our things should all be unpacked. Perhaps you would like some pajamas," he suggested.

She flopped back onto the mattress and spread her arms wide as she looked up at the ceiling. Perfectly, beautifully naked. So that he found himself stirring again already.

"I think I should like to sleep perfectly naked," she said with a smug smile.

"Beaugonia."

She lifted her head, gave him an arch look. "What?"

It seemed imperative then. That she understand. Above all else. No matter what happened. No matter what he felt or didn't. No matter what he resisted, or how he failed. There was one truth to his entire life he could not let go of.

"My country will always come first. My responsibilities. My control. It is my birthright. The promise I made to my grandmother before she died. Nothing can change that."

She studied him with those eyes that would haunt him until the day he died. Like she simply knew everything, and that was why every color danced there. "I didn't ask you to change, Lyon. I didn't ask you to put me above anything. I didn't ask you for anything."

There was something about the haughty way she said that, the little lick of temper in her voice that allowed him to…relax.

He had failed at keeping his boundaries built with her. This was a mistake, but not fatal. It was here, alone, not at the palace with witnesses. It was early in their marriage, and as she'd said…no countries or responsibilities were expressly harmed.

They had two more days of privacy here. He wanted to return to the palace with every possibility she was pregnant so that he could build back his careful walls of decorum. So…this could be okay. His mistake was not fatal and wouldn't be.

He would get her pregnant. *For* Divio and his family legacy. He could relax, at least for another day or two.

"That isn't precisely true, Beaugonia. You did ask. In fact, I seem to recall you begging."

Her cheeks flushed a beautiful shade of pink, but then she reached across the bed and grabbed a pillow. Then she *threw* it at him.

And the laughter that she brought out in him at the worst moments bubbled free. In spite of himself, she made everything feel like…it would be all right. She was a smart woman. She would understand. She would follow suit.

And all would be well.

CHAPTER NINE

BEAU WOKE UP in a cold sweat. Her breath coming in pants. The world dark around her. A strange bed. A warm man. Her mind whirled with something just out of reach.

But she knew one thing.

It had been years since she'd woken up in the middle of a panic attack. And this was the worst possible moment for this to happen to her again.

She struggled to gulp down a breath, but Lyon didn't stir beside her. So there was still a chance. There was still a chance he didn't wake up and find out.

Would it be so bad?

She eased off the bed, struggling to breathe, struggling to feel her legs well enough to walk. The room was dark, but her vision felt even more off than just that.

Would it be so bad? For Lyon to wake up and see her greatest weakness? Something that was decidedly *not* stable or respectable?

Yes, it would be *so* bad.

She tried to move through the room quietly, relief fighting with everything rioting inside of her. Because Lyon didn't stir, and she managed to make her way to the bathroom without making any loud noises.

With shaking arms and increasing panic, tears already

streaming down her face, she managed to close the door without slamming it.

Then she simply collapsed onto the ground. Shaking and gasping. Cursing *everything* that made her the way she was.

Maybe it was lucky. It had gripped her at a time when she'd been able to slip away and hide. Lyon would not have to know. If it could always be this way, then she would be fine.

She tried to let that thought calm her, but once it started there was usually no going back. The attack had to run its course. But she was lying naked on the bathroom floor and that was ridiculous.

She didn't trust herself to stand with as shaky as she was, but she could crawl across the floor to the closet. She left the lights off and tried. Her limbs shook and she didn't want to make any noise so it was slow going and more pushing herself across the floor than anything else.

Pathetic. Stupid. Crazy.

But those were her father's words, not hers. She understood that panic was simply…what it was. A misfire in her brain. She couldn't control it, and it certainly didn't make her any of the things her father called her.

But something about the night with Lyon, sleeping in his bed, made her feel more a failure than she usually did after a panic attack. Because there was no one to prove wrong. No one to spite.

There was only a man she had to hide this…defect from. And not just to protect Zia anymore, but because…she liked him. This life they were creating. It was the happiest she'd ever been. And maybe that was a low bar, but it was a low bar she was determined to keep reaching.

She made it into the closet. There were clothes of hers in here somewhere. She couldn't trust herself to stand to reach the light, so she just reached out around the walls and tried to find a shelf or drawer or something.

Stop shaking. Stop crying. Breathe, breathe, breathe.

She counted breaths. She ignored the tears. Her hand finally blindly landed on something that felt like fabric. Once she managed to get it over her head, she realized it was not hers. It was too big and baggy, but it seemed like a sweatshirt and that would work, even if it was Lyon's.

She brought her knees to her chest and sat there, as her body shook against her will. But with time, her breathing became easier. The tears stopped. The shaking wouldn't go away for some time, but it would lessen. It usually went quicker when Zia sat with her and talked to her as though it weren't happening. Or even her last one, when Cristhian had sat with her and told her the story of when he'd first met Zia.

Even now, the memory warmed her. Whether Zia knew it or not, Cristhian was desperately in love, and Beau had known in that moment that everything she had done was correct. Allowing Zia the freedom of a life with Cristhian and their children free of the palace rules meant they could build a life of joy. For themselves and each other and their impending twins.

Beau was finally able to breathe deeply for the first time. Whatever caused this panic was not from a place of reason, but she was still *reasonable*. And reminding herself how well her choices and gambles had turned out…helped. At least mentally.

Zia would be happy. And this…*thing* between Beau and Lyon… Lust. Chemistry. But also at least a surface enjoyment of each other. It was better than anything she'd had back home. Maybe she had to hide her panic attacks from Lyon and Divio for the rest of her life, but that was better than being treated like some kind of abomination.

The thought of Lyon finding out and making some proclamation about...stability. It made her want to throw up.

So she wouldn't think on that too deeply. It simply wouldn't happen.

Her shakes were better, her breathing normal. She could return to bed and Lyon would never know.

She crept back into the room. It was still dark, and she heard nothing but steady, even breathing. She let out a slow breath herself to steady her steps, and then moved as quietly as possible to the bed. She eased back in.

Lyon shifted, rolled over. "Is everything all right?" he murmured, clearly still half-asleep.

"Of course. I just got cold." And even though she'd gotten dressed, she still felt iced straight through. But her voice sounded calm, so there was that. "I suppose sleeping naked isn't for alpine chalets."

Then he did something that made tears spring to her eyes. He reached over, pulled her into the heat of his body, tucking the blankets around them. Warmth encased her.

Was this what love felt like?

Don't be an idiot, Beaugonia.

Love—real love, not whatever had twisted inside of her mother to make her bow and scrape to Father—was built on trust. And as much as she *liked* Lyon, liked the way he made her feel inside and outside of the bedroom, she would always be keeping a part of herself hidden, because she couldn't trust him with it.

That could never be love.

Which felt like a very heavy, depressing weight in her chest. And while she rarely had panic attacks back to back, she didn't like the way this made her feel. The way tension was creeping back into her. Her thoughts whirling in a loop.

No, she didn't want that. And the only thing she could think of that would stop it was *him*.

"Lyon?"

"Mm?" He was drifting off into sleep, but she needed… something. And never in her life had she had the opportunity to reach out and take it. She turned in the circle of his warm, strong arms and pressed herself against him.

"Touch me."

She felt the shift from half-asleep to immediately alert, and it soothed something inside of her. This effect they had on each other. The way this want felt wild and free and all-encompassing so nothing else mattered.

She fitted her mouth to his. Relief sliding through her along with the post–panic attack exhaustion when he kissed her back. Everything would be okay. Everything would still be better than she'd had.

He pulled her closer, his hand sliding over her back, the curve of her hip. Till he found bare leg, because she only wore his sweatshirt.

Desire slowly sparkled to life as his fingers brushed her leg, up and under the shirt, until his hand rested at her hip, his mouth taking a sweet tour of hers.

But she couldn't do sweet. Not now when she was so vulnerable.

"Don't be gentle," she said against his mouth. She wanted that wild storm of what they'd had earlier.

His grip tightened, then released. She knew he resisted it, though she didn't understand why he thought this had anything to do with how he led Divio. But she couldn't concern herself with his resistance.

"Please. What we had in the kitchen, *that* is what I need." Beyond thought. Beyond reason. Beyond his precious control.

"This cannot be who we are, Beaugonia."

"Just tonight then. Just tonight. Please, Lyon."

And he gave her just that. She knew it didn't solve anything, didn't change anything. This couldn't be who they were, and he could never fully know who she was. Divio was his guiding star and always would be.

But for tonight, she got everything she wanted.

The next morning, Lyon woke up later than he could ever remember waking. But he did not allow himself to think of last night and why that might be. That was over. A new day had dawned, and it was now time to make all the right decisions.

Beau still slept, the covers heaped around her. She looked peaceful if more unkempt than he might have expected. But he could not allow himself to think of the reasons her hair was tousled, her shoulders bare.

A new day. A new page.

They would eat their breakfast, go on their hike. Maybe spend a late afternoon cozied up to the fire with their books before making, eating and cleaning up dinner together. Then, and only then, would they retire to the bedroom. New desires clearly under his control, and then satiated. So there was every possibility a pregnancy came sooner rather than later.

Which he wouldn't think about now.

He went into the kitchen and decided to put together a breakfast and some snacks for the hike. It was rare he got the opportunity to just *be* in his kitchen. Any kitchen. He liked the process of it. Putting things together, having some-thing come out on the other side that even if it didn't look perfect, might taste well enough, and would certainly do the job of nourishing either way.

When he was nearly done with all his preparations, he heard her approach. He steeled himself for a day where *he* was in control of himself. He turned, pleasant smile pasted on his face.

She was dressed in a good base layer for a hike. She had brushed her hair, but she still looked oddly sleepy. He had slept like a rock, except when she'd woken him.

But he wasn't thinking of that. "Good morning."

"Morning," she offered around a yawn. "Is that breakfast? I'm starving."

"Yes. Have a seat."

She approached the table then sat down as he put a plate in front of her. "I will bring a pack for our hike. Water, snacks, but a good protein-rich breakfast is the best way to keep your strength up if we are to make it the full distance."

"Of course," she replied pleasantly. She did not look at him. She did not bring up last night. She wolfed down her breakfast.

She wasn't making things awkward or uncomfortable, and yet he did not fully feel like himself. His entire life had been in service of one thing—becoming the kind of man and leader who would step into his station once the knock of fate came to the door. He had never considered anything else.

And now he was considering this strange woman who was only supposed to be a business associate at best.

He forced himself to eat his breakfast even though he tasted nothing. Then, once they were both done and the meal cleaned up, they put on layers for hiking in the cold snow. Beau said nothing about last night, and seemed eager to get started, so they set out.

The day was sunny and bright and beautiful. The trail was not marked. It was one of his own making.

She followed along, and he had to slow his pace because she wanted to stop and look at everything. Every rock, every overlook. She poked at ice and made snowballs.

He was surprised to find himself not the least bit frustrated with her constant stops. It was pleasurable to watch her get such enjoyment out of the most simple things.

"Do you always inspect every little thing when you hike?" he asked when she threw one of her little snowball creations and it landed a little too close to him. He turned and gave her an arched eyebrow to get her to laugh.

She didn't. She didn't even meet his gaze. "I haven't been hiking much. My outdoor time usually consisted of finding a hidden away reading spot in the gardens at home."

Lyon frowned. He'd known she'd been hidden away after a fashion with Zia being the heir and her not, but he hadn't considered how much that might extend to *everything*. He'd simply thought it meant events and whatnot. Not actual... life.

"You were *always* kept in the castle?"

She paused, then focused very steadily on a new small sphere of snow in her palm. She took her time responding, as if considering what to say. "It was my father's belief that if I did not show myself in many places, that no one would ask about me. That as long as Zia sparkled, and it seemed as though I did not exist, no one would connect those childhood...tantrums, as he called them...with the monarchy. So, I spent most of my time in the castle." Then, she hurled her little snowball over the edge of the trail. It landed with no sound at all, everything hushed in the snow.

Something in her expression seemed disappointed, and he did not want to see that, feel it twist inside of him like his own disappointment. So he kept walking. "You seem well-equipped to deal with the world for someone kept so isolated."

"Reading opens worlds, even when you don't have any."

He supposed that was true, but he'd never had to put it into practice quite so starkly. And it made him want to... do something for her. He didn't know what. Whatever he offered her had to fit in with the mold he'd created for the perfect princess. The perfect wife of Divio.

But there were little things, he supposed. "Speaking of, I have begun to read one of your romance novels."

"Have you?"

"Yes. And while the writing is quite skilled and the characters interesting enough, it seems to me the whole thing could be solved twenty pages in if they just sat down and had a mature conversation."

"Perhaps, but how often are we as mature as we'd like to be? How often do humans go through great lengths to avoid difficult conversations? How interesting would it be if every fictional character acted perfectly reasonably and maturely—especially considering we as a species rarely do."

It felt pointed, even though when he turned to face her again she wasn't looking at him. So he kept walking on, until they reached the destination of this trail he'd made. A perfect opening to look out over the chalet below and everything they'd just climbed. The beautiful, ancient mountains all around them. And the perfect weather for everything to sparkle with seeming magic.

Her face broke out into one of those beautiful smiles, just pure, simplistic joy at a beautiful landscape. Her eyes were almost perfectly green up here in all this sky and white, her cheeks and nose flushed.

"How often do you make it up here?" She was looking at the chalet, so he assumed she meant this place in general, not the hike.

"Not often. It's hard to get away. Especially with how things are with parliament. They'll take any excuse to paint me the same as my uncles and cousins."

"That must be a difficult legacy to live down."

He frowned a little. "Duties aren't meant to be *easy*." When he'd been young, and still childish enough to complain about what his grandmother expected of him, he'd always been lectured on his privilege. On the special space he held and how he owed it to the men he'd never met to reclaim their legacy. "My *existence* is a payment of a debt, and so I will pay it."

Beau looked at him, her forehead furrowed, her expression one of confusion. "Why should your existence be a payment of a *debt*?"

"My grandmother would have been an excellent ruler, but she was not allowed. I believe my mother would have been as well, should it have been expected of her."

But the look of confusion never left her face. "So? What has that got to do with you?"

"I am finally the male heir Divio deserved. It should have been my grandmother. So I pay the debt lost."

Still, she looked at him as though he were speaking in Italian instead of English. "None of you can control what sex you were born as. That…makes no sense. It was just… The way things happened. Like Zia being good with crowds when we were young. It's just…the way we are."

Lyon resisted the urge to rub at his chest where an odd tension banded. "I am not explaining it well then. I simply meant that I always knew this would be my responsibility, and that I would meet all challenges."

"That doesn't make the challenges less difficult, Lyon. A duty can still be…a weight. A struggle. Even if you do it with a glad heart."

No one had ever put it that way. It was strangely…satisfying for someone to acknowledge nothing he did was *easy*. That it was *work* to be everything his grandmother had wanted him to be.

She would have given him that assurance, he believed, if she'd lived long enough to see him crowned. Then he finally would have garnered her approval. He was sure of it.

"I suppose," he agreed, wanting to get away from this uncomfortable topic. The way his short breathing wasn't from hiking, but from that weight in his chest.

"Well, I quite like it up here," Beau said brightly, as if she sensed his need to move on. "Hopefully once we convince parliament of your stability, we can come up here more often."

He could not account for how much he liked the way she said *we*, as though they were a team. A partnership. He had not thought of it quite like that. She was an…aid to something. A tool. He had never expected to *share* responsibility with anyone. The responsibility was his.

You are the only hope of Divio, Lyon. All rests on you.

Him and him alone. But now he had a wife. A partner and no doubt Beau could handle her own weight, and that was…amazing, really.

"You will have to make that drive you hated more often to come up here." He even managed to smile as he teased her.

She wrinkled her nose. "That *is* a great shame."

"You have no fear of any of these ledges," he pointed out, as she got closer than he liked to the edge of an overlook. The view was beautiful, but the results of one wrong move catastrophic.

"I trust my own two feet. I do not trust big burly machines to navigate narrow roads."

He smiled in spite of himself, she was such a funny little thing. "Do you have any other peculiar fears?"

"I don't consider it peculiar at all," she replied, all haughty offense.

It was wrong, surely, how much that tone, that *look* affected him. How immediately it sent a thrill to his sex. A desire that threatened to obscure all those rules he'd set for himself this morning.

He turned on a heel. "We best head back." And he set a quick pace. Perhaps unfairly so. She kept up, but when they returned to the chalet with the afternoon sun beating down on them despite the cold air, she was huffing and puffing. Cheeks and nose red. Eyes watering.

But she didn't seem the least bit put out as he opened the door and gestured her inside.

"I know we have to leave tomorrow, but perhaps we could do a shorter hike before we do in the morning," she said, shrugging out of her first layer of coats. "What a wonderful way to start the day."

He did the same. "If we get up early enough."

"Then I suppose you shouldn't keep me up all night." She smiled at him, a glint of mischief in her eyes that lent themselves toward brown now. But there were hints of green and gold. Hints of other worlds entirely.

Especially when she moved closer, reached out and helped him with his first layer of jackets. Not that he needed her help. But he took it all the same. Particularly when she lifted on her toes and fitted her mouth to his.

Her nose was cold, her mouth was hot. She wrapped herself around him like a vine. Surely it was some kind of spell she put over him, because he did not set her back. He kissed her. Sucked under by the taste of her, the *thrill* of her.

She met every nip with one of her own. She arched against him. Moaned against him. Until there was only the beat of desire. Only the need for *more*.

But there were so many layers between them, and the attempt to start getting through them was enough of a reality check to bring him back to himself. To his control.

They would not do this here. There had to be *lines*. Of respectability. Of correct action.

He wrenched himself away from her. Managed to untangle her arms and put some small but necessary space of air between them. It felt like more of a triumph than he should allow himself to feel. He had still kissed her here. Maybe there was no staff, but there were windows. Maybe there was no public here, but he had to be better. Tomorrow they would be in a crowded castle, and he could perhaps excuse some inappropriate kisses with a *newlywed* phase, but he didn't want to give anyone a reason to look at him and think he couldn't control himself.

To look at him and know how little handle he had on his desires for his wife. Because where would that lead? Thanks to the princes that came before, everyone would wonder.

Beau stood there, panting. Looking at him with a hazy desire mixed heavily with confusion. He wanted his hands on her more than his next breath, but he would not give in. He would not be weak.

Divio was his touchstone. Not *her*. Not *this*.

Then she kneeled before him.

CHAPTER TEN

BEAU THOUGHT HE might stop her, but he only looked down at her with arrested desire. Nerves battled in her chest, but she wanted… She wanted.

For the first time in her life she was getting things she wanted. So she would take until it was all gone. Was she pushing too hard? Maybe. But she had never been good at stepping back when she should.

Why start now?

She reached out and put her palms on his thighs, watching his reaction to her every move. His nostrils flared, his jaw clenched, and those dark, dreamy eyes flashed.

"I also understand *this* in theory," she said, her heart hammering against her chest. Not nerves. Just want. "But I'd like to know in practice." Because even if he'd ended the kiss, even if he was worried about *respectability*, she could see the thick, hard line of his erection against his pants.

He wanted her. She wanted him. And she couldn't understand why he didn't want to indulge. She just had to get through to him, that nothing they did together felt wrong. *Was* wrong. She would take that shame away from him. Bit by bit.

Because it sounded like everyone held him to too high standards. She wouldn't do the same. She wouldn't heap unfair responsibility on him. Not when they were alone.

Not when they were newly married and had every reason and right to explore this explosive desire between them.

So she pulled his pants down, freeing the hard, heavy length of him. She used one hand against his thigh for balance, then used the other to touch. Explore. Grasp and stroke.

She leaned forward, her eyes on his. And then she used her mouth. Slow, steady. Watching his face. His gaze hard and hot on where she tasted him. Tension wound through his body, and into his clenched fists. Each gentle glide of her tongue made it harder for him to catch a breath, and it spurred her own.

She was throbbing everywhere. No longer cold at all. Just heat. Just need. And a pulsing, skittering feeling of power, when she'd never had any power before. When every act she'd ever engaged in had been hidden.

But this wasn't. Her need for him. His for her. It was theirs and it was everything. Surely he'd see that. Surely—

With no warning, he jerked her back, and then up to her feet. She did not know if he was angry. She did not know what this was, as he held her there, his eyes a series of dark storms. She wanted to find a way to calm them, to ease them.

"Lyon."

"Go into the bedroom," he said, his voice a rough growl that sent a shower of sparks over her body. "Then and only then, you will remove every last article of clothing."

Relief nearly made her sag, but she swallowed and mustered her strength to do as he said as he released her. Turn. Walk away from him and into the bedroom. A tremor went through her hands as she began to get the rest of her clothes off, but it was not panic shakes.

It was *all* anticipation.

She carefully divested herself of the rest of her clothes.

She heard him enter behind her, but before she could turn, he spoke in low, authoritative tones. The kind that made her feel alight with incandescent pleasure.

She could not be wrong if he was telling her what to do.

"Put your hands on the edge of the bed, and then bend over."

She hesitated though, not because she did not want to, but because...

"Now."

There was something about the order, the dominating way he was speaking to her that made every lick of pleasure in her body leap higher, twist deeper. She wanted to do everything he demanded.

So she did. Clutched the edge of the bed and bent over. She didn't know what he would do. Time seemed to stretch out, hazy and lost to anticipation. She tried to hold her breath, but still he did not *do* anything. So she was forced to let out a shuddering exhale.

She was about to look over her shoulder, to see where he was. How far away. Just what was keeping him from *touching* her, but before she could finish the move, he spoke.

"Keep your eyes ahead, Beaugonia."

She swallowed. Her full name in that deep scrape of a voice made a tremor run through her, then center in reverberations at her core. Her entire body was like a throb, and the dark presence of him lurking behind her like a portent only made the waiting more and more impossible.

"Lyon." She wanted to beg. If he didn't touch her soon, she might simply shake apart. She needed an anchor. She needed him. She needed a focal point for all this sensation to go.

"I did not tell you to speak, *tesoruccia*. You would do well to keep that dangerous mouth of yours shut."

But then she felt his hand. His palm slid up her leg, over

the curve of her backside, and then his fingers curled at her hip. He stood behind her, so close she could feel the heat emanating off of him.

His free hand slid up her spine, to her shoulder. And then finally, finally, she felt the blunt edge of him enter her, a slow, perfect glide. His grip on her hip, her shoulder. Being filled while her fingers clasped her bedsheets.

Finally, everything had a point, a reason. Lyon moving inside of her, so there was only this. Them. The beautiful passion they created when they came together. A joy that had her falling over that first wonderful edge with a little gasp of pleasure on a particularly slow, deep stroke, her forehead pressed against the mattress.

Then his hand moved. From her shoulder to her neck, to her hair. His fingers tangled, fisted, until he pulled, so her chin had to come up off the bed. Sparks of something just at the edge of pain twisting even deeper into the pleasure of it all. Until she was falling apart, shuddering into a million pieces all over again. And still he did not stop. He only increased the pace, the madness of it all. Wilder. More out of control. She was only sensation. Only moans and fevered words of *begging*. For more, for him, for all he was and had.

He let out a wild, savage growl on one last, thunderous thrust, collapsing on top of her, his hands still tangled in her hair.

She struggled to find her breath, to find center and the real world again. She wanted to laugh. She had never believed in fairy tales for *her*, happy endings for *her*, but she was beginning to believe in one.

Finally.

She was his downfall. Everything he'd built himself into being. A strong prince with impeccable morals and control.

She'd stripped them away so easily he now realized he

was no better than anyone who'd come before. Because he kept making the same mistake. And it got worse every time. Maybe they'd made it to the bedroom this time, but not before he'd let her kneel before him and take him in her mouth at the *doorway*.

Not before he'd spoken to her in ways he never let himself speak to anyone. Not before he'd taken her rough and harsh with that unquenchable need roaring through him like a disease.

He knew how this ended. It spiraled out. Got wilder and wilder until it became a *whisper*. And then a *story*. Maybe it wasn't as bad as stealing palace funds or wreaking havoc with an affair, but it wasn't *good*.

So, fix it.

He carefully withdrew from her, pushing himself away from the bed. For a moment he just stood there, and she didn't move either. Still gripping the edge of the bed, in this deplorable state he'd put her in.

All for an *orgasm*.

She finally sighed heavily, then pushed herself into a standing position. She shoved her hair out of the way and then had the gall to smile at him. She held out a hand. "Let's lay in bed for a while."

He turned away from her hand, gathered his clothes and put them on. Then he turned to face her. She'd arranged herself on the bed, sheet drawn up. Her expression unreadable.

"Do I have to suffer through another lecture?"

It enraged him, this…haughty disdain for all that he was. But he did not explode. He iced it all out. "You clearly did not understand the first one."

Her eyebrows drew together, and she leaned forward. "Lyon, I do not understand this. You are making the strangest problem out of a quite enjoyable thing. A thing we kind of have to do if you want all those heirs."

"When we return to the castle, we must behave with respectability," he returned, locking all of those dangerous wants and needs away. He was only the crown. Only a leader. Not a man, not really.

Hadn't he always been reminded of that when something he wanted did not align with what his grandmother had envisioned for the crown?

You are the crown.

And he would be. "We must, at all times, put forward a royal face. Decorum in every step. No outward displays of affection. No hint that anything means more to us than our roles as crown prince and princess."

"So, I can't do what we did out there in public. Got it." She didn't roll her eyes, but somehow gave the impression of it anyway.

"You do not understand the precarious position we are in, though I've explained it to you. You do not understand how rumors and whispers turn into demands. These hedonistic desires will not rule me. I cannot let them control me. I need you to understand that. Because if you cannot…" He trailed off, no threat coming to his mind.

Because she was beautiful and naked in his bed and looking at him with some unreadable expression. Or maybe he didn't want to read it.

But he would find an appropriate punishment. He would have control, and he would not allow her to keep…undermining it.

"So, we must be polite in our own bed?" she asked, each word delivered carefully and devoid of emotion. As though she were asking a real question, not trying to make some *point*. "Just in case someone is listening in?"

"We must behave in any potentially public space with respectability, Beaugonia. Perhaps it will be a moot point.

Perhaps you are pregnant even now and we will not have to worry ourselves with these…mistakes."

She blinked at that, then looked down at her stomach as if it hadn't occurred to her.

"Would that make you happy?" she asked quietly.

"Of course. That is the entire point of all this. Enough heirs to ensure stability for centuries to come."

She nodded, though she did not meet his gaze. "Of course," she agreed. *Agreed.*

So he didn't know why her agreement felt sour.

"I apologize then," she said at last. "I will endeavor to be as hands-off and respectable as you." She smiled thinly at him. "Despite the fact two married people enjoying sex should hardly be some proof that you're as foolish as your uncles and cousins."

Proving she refused to understand. "When you give in to your own selfish wants and desires, you begin a downward spiral. Until you'll excuse anything. All for the sake of a little fleeting pleasure."

"I see." But he could tell from her tone that she didn't see at all.

"I hope this is a lesson you can learn, Beaugonia. Because if you can't…" He hated the words before they were even out of his mouth. Felt them twist like regret deep in his gut. But he had to say them. Drastic desires called for drastic measures. "…we may have to have an arrangement more like you had back in Lille."

"Are you threatening to lock me in a room, Lyon?" she returned, all haughty fire that threatened to stir up that which should be satiated. Damn her.

"I am simply telling you that you will obey my wishes, or you will not have access to me at all," he said through gritted teeth.

"And if I'm not pregnant? If there are, in fact, no heirs yet in the making? What then?"

"I suppose there are more scientific ways to go about the impregnation process. We do not actually have to have sex for you to conceive."

Her mouth fell open. "You cannot be serious."

"It isn't ideal, but if it becomes necessary, we will do it. I will always, *always* do what is necessary. I suggest you accept that before we return to the palace."

And because he did not trust himself to say more without this…devolving into all those wants and desires he had to shove aside, he turned on a heel and left.

CHAPTER ELEVEN

BEAU HAD HALF expected him to order her out of the chalet. Back to the palace and his precious controllable life. But she lay in bed for at least an hour, and he never returned with more ridiculous orders or arguments.

Or an apology.

She'd finally gotten dressed, accepting that he wasn't coming. And it was her own fault. She had believed that no matter what happened, this new life would be better than her old one.

But it was just going to turn into the old one, wasn't it? He'd threatened to lock her away. An old threat. One she should be fully familiar with.

But she hadn't expected it from him, and that made her want to cry. But she'd be damned if she gave him the satisfaction.

She sat in the chair by the window and figured she was already miserable so she might as well call her sister.

"What have you done?" was how Zia answered the phone.

"What needed to be done, of course," Beau returned, trying to sound flippant. "But you may lecture me if you wish." Maybe that would take her mind off of Lyon's threats, and how awfully familiar they were.

There was a beat of silence. "I never lecture."

Beau smiled in spite of herself. "All is well, Zia. I promise. I even…" She looked at the closed door. She couldn't tell Zia everything. So, she stretched the truth. "Lyon's been very kind." Minus a threat or two. "I'm not unhappy. Nor will I be." She wouldn't let herself be. "Everything is well. How is it with you?"

"I am not happy with you."

"Of course not."

Zia grunted in irritation. Then caught Beau up on the past few days. A slight pregnancy scare, but she was healthy if on bed rest now. Cristhian, who had been insisting on marriage, walking that back so that it was up to Zia. She complained about that bitterly, but Beau could read what was really under all that bitterness.

Hurt and fear.

Beau sighed, thinking of what Lyon had said on their hike. About being a payment to a debt. It made Beau very much not like his grandmother, which was ridiculous since she was dead and Lyon was clearly devoted to her memory.

But it also made her realize that his outburst, his threats had come from *somewhere*. And if she didn't quite understand from where, maybe it was the same as Zia.

Hurt and fear.

Could she excuse that his hurt and fear meant if she didn't bend and scrape to what he wanted, she would be locked and hidden away once more? Artificially inseminated into having his heirs, all so he avoided this supposed slippery slope of desire.

Why don't you tell him all about your panic attacks then? That'll really get him going.

But the thought made her sad rather than mad. Because she did not *agree* with him about anything he'd said, but she was beginning to understand it all the same. He believed he had to be…perfect, she supposed. Better than his uncles and cousins.

A responsibility put there by someone he cared about. Not just himself.

"How am I supposed to know what the right choice is?" Zia demanded, pulling Beau out of her thoughts.

But Beau didn't know. Even if she did, Zia had to work it out on her own.

Beau listened and made the appropriate comforting noises. Maybe this was how she needed to deal with Lyon too. Maybe there was no pushing. Maybe he had to come to his own conclusions. Maybe he had to realize on his own that threats were...cruel.

But was that fair, she wondered after hanging up with Zia. He wasn't like her father. There was something noble about what Lyon was trying to do. It wasn't about *his* position, it was about what he felt he owed to his grandmother's memory and his country.

She sat with that for a moment, an uncomfortable worry creeping in. That she was excusing his bad behavior because...because she cared for him.

She rubbed at her chest that suddenly felt too tight. He *wasn't* like Father. That was a fact, not her being blinded by...whatever it was she felt. Not love, no. It was too soon for that. There was still so much they didn't know about each other, and she'd never trust him with her secret.

But there was the chemistry. That was undeniable. And she enjoyed his company. But why she *liked* him *was* the sense of being...noble or responsible or something. An inherent sense of right and wrong. It made him a good man.

These were facts. Not things she'd convinced herself of because she had feelings for him. And facts were what she should focus on. She reached into her bag and pulled out the boring, dry biography of Lyon's royal line.

Maybe the answers to his...rigidity were in these pages. She skimmed the first few chapters. All ancient bloodlines and wars for "freedom" and "ways of life" which were really only ever about one group having power over another. The history of the world forever.

Eventually she reached his great-grandfather. It seemed he'd been an excellent leader. Loved by all, as his wife had been. His life had been cut rather short by a sudden heart attack, and then the instability had begun.

The next crown prince, his grandmother's eldest brother, it didn't appear had done anything all that wrong. There had been rumors and stories about the prince and princess, and some lurid pictures printed, apparently, but nothing illegal or particularly wrong. He'd died young though. Another heart attack.

The next crown prince, another brother, had held the position for only a year before he'd been forced to abdicate to his brother after it was brought to light he'd been using palace funds to pay off illegal gambling debts.

The next prince had held the position for almost three years—before the grumblings of the female palace staff had become so great they couldn't seem to hire anyone to work at the palace. It didn't take a detective to figure out why.

He'd abdicated, claiming health issues. It went on from there. Sons. Brothers. Each story a little more salacious than the last so that she had to consult the internet to fill in the blanks as the book glossed over the more despicable acts.

A series of prostitutes given free rein and then stealing historical artifacts from the palace. Affairs that ended in public feuds. An inappropriate relationship with an underage woman that would have ended in actual jail time if the prince hadn't "suffered a heart attack."

There were all sorts of internet conspiracy stories about his death.

Yes, Lyon had quite the history of men who couldn't handle themselves or their power stretching out behind him. She didn't understand why the misdeeds of his family would hang around his neck like a noose, but she could see that they did, and why that might have him lash out in all that fear and hurt.

She closed the book and put it away, considering. If he truly believed giving in to anything he desired was a slippery slope to destruction, then perhaps she should not be angry with him.

Or are you turning into your mother?

She scowled at that thought. She was hardly going to twist herself into a pretzel for him, but she had promised him she would be the wife *he* needed. For Zia's future, she had promised to be a picture-perfect princess.

If that meant ignoring chemistry and enjoyment and keeping her distance from her husband who made her feel *alive*, well. That was the deal she'd made, wasn't it?

She blew out a breath, her stomach's growling only growing louder. Loud enough she could no longer ignore it. She finally got up and left the room. Perhaps he'd abandoned her here.

But the minute she left the bedroom she smelled food. She followed the scent to the kitchen. Where he stood over the stove, working on something.

Quite the sight. A handsome prince cooking a meal in his beautiful chalet kitchen. She had no mad left, and it filled her with a certain amount of anxiety. Shouldn't she still be mad? He had threatened to essentially lock her away. She should be furious.

But she found none of her ire watching him cook. Thinking of what he'd said about debts and payments. Bloodlines and respectability.

"It is almost ready," he said without looking at her.

She sighed and settled into a seat at the table. He served

them dinner, making no eye contact whatsoever. It was a hearty-looking stew, and warm rolls glistening with butter.

"You've utilized your afternoon wonderfully," she offered, hoping to ease some of the tension choking the air.

He only made a vague agreeing sound before taking a seat at the table.

Beau was half-tempted to say something shocking, just to get a reaction out of him. But that wasn't being a good princess, was it?

So she said nothing. They ate without speaking to one another at all.

It kind of made her want to cry. But she was going to prove to him that she could give him what he wanted. She was going to try, anyway. So, she did everything he did. She helped him clean up the dinner without saying a word. When he retired to their rooms to take a shower, she retired to their rooms and read in the chair until he emerged. Then she silently went into the shower herself. She put on her coziest, baggiest pajamas and returned to the room.

He was already in bed. All the lights off, save one.

The small one by her side of the bed. It was an oddly thoughtful gesture that had tears springing to her eyes. And a horrible thought infiltrating.

She wanted him to care for her. In little ways and small ways. And she worried that it would come at great cost to herself, that want.

So maybe she understood him and his worries after all. She didn't want to be her mother. She'd never once thought she could be.

Until she'd started to develop these soft, caring feelings for him, and sometimes considered putting his own needs before her own. Would that only get worse? Until she too was bowing and scraping to make him happy at the cost of everyone else?

Terrible, *terrible* thought. One that made her cold straight through. But in that cold, she felt even worse for having argued with him earlier.

They really weren't all that different, were they? And his concern about falling into the traps of his family wasn't so outlandish, was it?

But she didn't know how to broach the topic with him. She didn't know how to apologize or make this right. And still, she couldn't stand the silence any longer.

She slid into bed, searching for the right words. "Are we going to awkwardly toss and turn all night or can we discuss the elephant in the room?" Definitely not the right words.

"There is no elephant," he replied gruffly.

She snorted. Hardly. "I accept that you find our…chemistry…appalling."

"I didn't use that word."

"Horrifying?" she asked, because she didn't know how to have a conversation that wasn't her poking at someone. She didn't know how to just be…open and vulnerable.

"It isn't the chemistry itself, Beau. It is how it makes me behave."

She supposed if there was anything she respected about this entirely frustrating and nonsensical thing it was that he blamed himself. Not her. Usually she was the easy target for blame in an argument.

Which didn't help with all this…*softness* in her heart when it came to him. But instead of continuing to think about her mother, she shifted her focus to what she'd learned about relationships. She knew things only in *theory*, but that was something, she supposed.

Mature adults had mature conversations. Just like the ones Lyon bemoaned had been missing from the book he was reading.

"I read about your uncles and your cousins. What the book glossed over, I looked up on the internet."

There was nothing but silence from his side of the bed. She could take that as a sign to stop talking, but she didn't want to return to the palace like this. Or worse, have to fake smiles and conversation for the staff, and then retreat to stony silences when they were alone.

"It helped me understand better, I think. It is quite a lot of bad behavior from one prince to another, and it makes your place all that more…challenging. To prove you are not like them."

It was not in her nature to apologize. She generally thought she was correct in everything she did. But this wasn't actually about being right or wrong. It was about a promise she'd made, and something he felt strongly about.

It was about, like him, the need to do the right thing. It wasn't about caring for him so much she needed to smooth this rift over. It was simply the right thing to do.

"I apologize, Lyon. I…may not agree with everything you've said today, but I understand where it's coming from now."

Lyon did not move. He continued to stare blindly at the darkness in the room. Apologies were a dime a dozen, his grandmother had always made sure he understood *that*.

But the way Beau said hers made him want to…believe her.

"I made a promise to you when we arranged this," she continued. "I would be what you needed. I promised to give you heirs and be a steady, respectable presence for your country. I'll admit, I don't understand why there needs to be such a hard line on decorum when people are meant to believe we're…in love, but I don't need to understand to respect that this is how *you* feel."

He finally rolled over to face her. She was sitting up in the bed, knees drawn to her chest. She was mostly a shadow, but he could tell her hair was free around her shoulders.

There was a humming need to reach out and touch, but he did not indulge himself. If he gave in tonight, not only was he a complete failure to himself, but he would be failing her.

She was apologizing. Saying she understood. He could hardly be the reason that didn't matter.

"My grandmother used to say apologies are pointless. Pretty words meant for the recipient to ignore what can't be fixed," he said, pushing himself into a sitting position like she was.

"That's a rather dire view of apologies. Particularly ones honestly given. Besides, I don't wish you to ignore anything. I'm only…reassuring you that I have not forgotten the promises I made. I can't promise to be perfect, that has *never* been in my nature. But I promise to try."

For a moment, he couldn't find any words. Couldn't understand this. He'd expected icy silences and perhaps another fight before they returned to the palace. He'd expected to have to make good with his threat and keep her as much out of view and away from him as possible.

But she undercut it all. With an *apology*. One that sounded so sincere, he did not know how to ignore it. One that felt like a bridge, past the struggles they were currently facing and toward a mature relationship of mutual understanding.

"No one has ever apologized to me in a way that felt genuine. I have always agreed with my grandmother's estimation. Until this. I accept your apology, Beau. Thank you for understanding."

She inched a little closer. Hesitantly. Until her shoulder pressed to his. He didn't want to push her away. This was a *gesture,* to go with her apology. To bring them back to accord. So he carefully placed his arm around her shoulders. Not pulling her in, but not pushing her away either.

There was a danger here. In the warmth of their bodies comingling, in the sweet, floral scent of her. But there was also a strange, sweet comfort. If they worked through this so early in their marriage, that was an excellent precedent to set for the future.

She leaned her head against his shoulder. "I do not wish to return to the palace at odds."

"Neither do I." He wanted to kiss her then. He wanted the sweet comfort of her body next to his. Under his. "I apologize as well. I should not have resorted to threats. Fights have no place here."

She didn't say anything to that, just sat next to him. He could have stayed right in this moment forever, but even this unknown gentleness felt like the kind of thinking that pulled a man down and under. Perhaps more so than straight desire. Desire was fleeting.

But caring about her... What kind of slippery slope would that be? So he very lightly brushed his mouth against her temple.

"Good night, Beau," he said, then moved over to his side of the bed.

"Good night, Lyon," she returned, moving over to hers. Just as it should be. Just as it would be.

CHAPTER TWELVE

BEAU HAD SLEPT well enough. She'd woken up the following morning in the middle of the bed, and like happened so often, Lyon was already up and gone. She lay there for a moment, not sure what to do with this strange tide of grief inside of her.

What was there to grieve? They had made amends. They would return to the castle today on the same page. Respectable, stable royals who respected one another, but didn't so much as have one lustful thought.

On a groan, she rolled out of bed and got dressed. When she shuffled out to the kitchen he was already dressed for the day and had made and cleaned up breakfast. Only a covered plate remained on the table, no doubt for her.

Because he was full of small gestures that no one had ever really given her, and she did not know how to reconcile this with a man who'd threaten to lock her away—when he didn't even know her full secret.

But he greeted her with a smile and "good morning." When she sat down to eat, he told her about some bird he'd watched fly around outside the window and surprised her with the idea that it was a good omen.

"You have never once struck me as the superstitious sort."

"Well, I only accept good superstitious."

It made her laugh. And she tried to hold on to that humor, that story as they drove back to the palace. The drive down was not quite as anxiety-inducing as the drive up, but she still didn't enjoy it.

They returned to the castle, a flurry of staff, a sit-down meal with Lyon's mother. Two days away without staff should not have had time to feel like normal, but suddenly all these people and space felt *overwhelming*.

But she knew her role. She smiled through dinner, ignored the countess's backhanded commentary about their *vacation*. She set out to be exactly the princess she had promised Lyon she would be.

Back then, she'd been doing it for Zia. Funny how it felt...different now. Like she was doing it for *him*.

When they retired to their rooms for bed, all the tension she'd felt from the night before seeped back into the silences between them. He wasn't angry, and she wasn't angry, but there was this gulf of not knowing how to be between them.

She wanted to reach out to him. Even if just for a hug. It could be something platonic. Just the feeling they...they...

But he took a gentle sidestep. "I think we should...wait."

"Wait?"

"It is possible you are already pregnant. We should wait to see if that is so."

Every time he said *pregnant*, she had a strange pang deep in her chest. The idea of already growing a child filled her with...a twist of so many different emotions. There was a deep yearning she really hadn't known was there until Zia had become pregnant. Then she'd started corresponding with Lyon about taking Zia's place and he'd made it clear he needed heirs.

She'd started to think of what it meant to be a mother. To care for someone else and show them love in the way her parents never had. She wanted that.

The idea of *love* was also causing strange pangs these days, because when she looked at Lyon, even not wanting to *wait* to see if it was so, she wanted to give him what he wanted. She wanted to find a way to make him happy.

So she hoped she was pregnant. For him just as much as for herself. But she'd also read enough books to know that not everyone got pregnant right away. Though Zia had with Cristhian, so maybe...

But what if she wasn't? They still needed heirs.

And he stood there, distance between them, hands behind his back. Stiff and uncomfortable but set in this decision he'd made. All on his own.

"And if I'm not?"

"Then we will develop a schedule."

"A schedule?"

His mouth firmed, but he didn't get angry. He stayed perfectly calm. If a little sarcastic. "Do I need to explain what a schedule is?"

"No." She looked away, feeling small. Angry she'd let something twist inside of her so that she allowed someone to make her feel small. She had promised herself she'd left that behind when she'd escaped her father's grip.

And now she wasn't just *allowing* it to happen, she was... wanting to find some way to take that stiffness away that would make him *happy*. That would bring back the *ease* they'd had around each other.

Not just the sex, but the comradery. The feeling there wasn't some invisible box around the both of them.

"There are times when a woman is more...susceptible to getting pregnant, are there not?" Lyon said, when she couldn't come up with any words. "We will develop a schedule based on the best possible time."

She found herself nodding along even though the idea

sounded…terrible. A *schedule*. For sex? When they *enjoyed* sex with one another?

She had promised him she understood. She had promised to be the princess he needed. If that meant waiting and schedules… Did it really matter or change anything? It was better than being locked away.

So days passed, and Beau settled into a schedule as crown princess of Divio. She settled into a life. She dined with Lyon, and sometimes the countess. She got to know all the different staff members, started developing projects with her own assistant. She talked to Zia almost every day, even video calling into Zia and Cristhian's wedding.

She had watched over her phone as Cristhian and Zia had made vows to one another, far away in Cristhian's place close to Germany. She had seen the love shine between them even on a small phone screen and had been overjoyed her sister had found it.

Overjoyed they had both found their freedoms. Because this *was* better than the life she'd had in Lille. And if every day she spent more time convincing herself of that…well, it *was* better.

Even if every night she slid into bed with her husband, and he kept his back to her. Even if he never so much as held her hand in public. He was always courteous and kind. He made sure the books she wanted were ordered, the meals she liked served. They talked about books. He read things she suggested and vice versa.

They had developed a friendship. It was better than her wildest dreams of what her life might look like when she'd been locked in her room, the threat of an *institution* hanging over her head.

It was *better*.

For two weeks she convinced herself of that, and then

one afternoon when it became clear that she wasn't pregnant, she finally realized the truth.

She was miserable.

"Your Highness?"

Lyon looked from the window to Mr. Filini, who had been talking to him about the upcoming parliamentary dinner. Lyon wasn't sure when his thoughts had strayed. What information he'd missed because he'd been *brooding* about Beau.

It was becoming frustratingly common. He couldn't focus. He couldn't stay in his present moment. Every day he became...more and more uncomfortable.

It wasn't even just the wanting her. Which he still did. With a fire that never truly seemed to go away. But he controlled it. Resisted it. He could almost convince himself he'd conquered it.

But he was worried about Beau, and he didn't even understand why. Everything was just as it should be. Just as they'd agreed.

They'd been back at the castle for nearly two weeks now. It should feel like normal.

But no matter how he tried to ignore it, he missed the way they'd been at the chalet. Even in turmoil that had at least been...real. It hadn't felt like playacting.

But playacting was better than failing everything he'd set out to do. So there was that. Now he just needed to figure out how to resist thoughts of her, what she might doing, what was going on in that fascinating brain of hers when he needed to be focused on the task of ruling a kingdom.

"A list of what you still need to sign off on will be in your email within the hour, sir," Mr. Filini said.

"Thank you," Lyon said. Maybe he hadn't been focusing well, but nothing had slipped through the cracks yet.

Everything was going on just as it should. Parliamentary business addressed. The public response to Beau was increasingly positive.

Everything was going just as it should.

And damn it, he couldn't relax.

Perhaps he should talk to Beau. Point-blank ask her what was wrong. Would she stop taking up so much of his brain space if he did? He could fix whatever problem was vexing her, and then it wouldn't feel like his tie and all those old anxieties were choking him by the end of every day.

Unless it was…the lack of intimacy that troubled her. But she'd said she understood that. She'd *apologized* for not initially understanding.

They needed to have a conversation. There was no getting around it. Hadn't he complained of her books avoiding them? Well, he was not a coward. He would ask. She would tell him. He would fix it.

The end.

He strode up to their rooms. She was not in the sitting room or the bedroom, but before he could call out for her, she stepped out of the bathroom.

When she saw him, she smiled, but he could tell she had been crying. He was almost certain of it. Her eyes were red and puffy. He'd never seen her in such a state. His entire being simply…bottomed out.

He strode forward, some horrible feeling gripping him. Like if she wasn't okay, nothing would be. "Is everything all right?"

"Yes, all in all." She tried to keep the smile, but it faltered. "I am… I am not pregnant. Not a tragedy, of course. Just…"

"Ah." It was the most insipid thing to say, but he had no words for this. He wanted to hug her close and take that pain she was trying to hide away, but he couldn't allow himself that.

It *wasn't* a tragedy, she was right, but she clearly was saddened by it, and he wanted to fix it. But there was no… fixing. Not in the moment.

He should be disappointed as well. But for a soaring, blinding moment all he could think was that he would be able to touch her again. He would have the opportunity to stop this deep, rending pain at keeping his distance and have her in his arms. It would be his royal duty once more.

He had been hoping for an heir, or so he told himself. But in this moment he realized what he'd really wanted was the excuse to touch her again.

Because deep down he was selfish. He was a product of the men who'd come before. Driven by only his own wants.

"I have read up on the subject," she continued, moving slightly away from him. "And it's quite commonplace for it to take up to a year even if both parties are perfectly healthy. Particularly for the first child." She peered out the window as if something of great interest existed out there beyond the mountains that always lurked in the distance.

"Yes, that makes sense." Why did he sound so damn stiff?

"In happy news, Zia has had her twins." Her smile was genuine, maybe, but it trembled at the edges. "I should like to plan my visit."

She had told him of Zia's marriage to Cristhian Sterling a few days ago, and that Zia was expecting to have her children any day, and that Beau would need to visit and meet her niece and nephew.

"Of course. I'm afraid we'll need to make it through the parliamentary dinner before you can go, though."

She nodded. "That's all right. I'm sure Zia would like a few days to settle in with her new family."

"We shall visit together," he said, wanting to offer some

kind of…something. He didn't have the words, but maybe an action would get across what he was feeling.

"You could get away from Divio?" she asked. Almost like she didn't believe him. But at the same time, he saw something in her expression he hadn't seen in a while. A kind of openness. Maybe even…hope.

"I may not be able to do it right away, but I'll find a few days. It will be a good look for us. Proof that there are no hard feelings."

Something in her expression shuttered. That blank that was seeping into his bones like worry and fear. An old anxiety that had him loosening his tie in spite of himself.

"Are there no hard feelings?" she asked at length, not meeting his gaze.

He blinked. He had not thought of Zia in ages. Why would he think of her when there was Beau? She occupied nearly all of his thoughts whether he wanted her to or not. "None."

Beau let out a great sigh, her gaze back on the window, making her eyes fairly glow green. Her voice was rough when she spoke. "She would have made you a better wife."

He heard the anguish in that, saw it in her slumped shoulders. He did not understand where any of this had come from, but he could hardly…stand it. He moved over to her, and carefully, lightly touched her chin, nudging it gently up so she would have to look at him.

"You are the best wife I could ask for." Which was just the most basic truth. She tested him, yes, but in all other ways she was better than he could have imagined. She handled the staff perfectly. She didn't wither under his mother's ridiculous commentary. She understood him, and it was… different than everyone else.

His mother understood him, but she depended on him. To uphold the name, the kingdom, her bloodline. Beau understood him to…support him. She had acknowledged his place could be difficult. She…

Didn't she understand that? Apparently not because her eyebrows drew together and she studied him with eyes still shiny from her earlier tears.

He hoped they were her earlier tears.

Then she looked away, pulling her chin away from his touch. "Would it look unseemly if I missed dinner tonight?"

Lyon had no idea how to fix this. Except to give her whatever she wanted that he was able. This was one of those things.

"No, of course not. There are no events scheduled. I'll make sure a meal is brought up."

She nodded.

More of that oppressive silence he didn't know what to do with, so he made a move to leave. Not sure why that felt so dissatisfactory.

"Lyon?"

He stopped, turning back to face her, even if she wasn't looking at him.

"Do I make you happy?"

Happy was not what he felt. Happy seemed simple, and nothing about what she did to him, what was rioting through him was *happy*. But it was…good. Positive. She was a positive in his life. So he nodded. "Yes, Beau. Very happy."

Her mouth curved then. He could hardly call it a smile, but it was better than bleak and blank and all the ways it had felt like she was withering before his eyes.

"All right then," she said with a nod. "If you'll have Mr. Filini forward me a copy of the etiquette document guests receive for the parliamentary dinner, I'll go over it with my dinner."

"You have the one for the crown princess."

"Yes, but I'd like to understand what's expected of the

guests as well. What they see, so I can make sure I can put them at ease in whatever ways I can."

"You don't have to do all that."

"I'd like to," she said firmly.

"All right. Well. It will be done then."

"Excellent."

Then they stared at each other. She said nothing. He didn't have the first clue what to say. So...he left.

CHAPTER THIRTEEN

BEAU COULD NOT pretend she was happy. Misery seemed to seep into every corner of her life. Every moment felt like more of a chore than it should. She tried to maintain a positive outlook on everything, but the only thing that made her even feel remotely happy and alive was video calling with Zia and the twins and reading the most outrageous books she could find. Dragons and alternate universes. Time travel and postapocalyptic worlds that allowed her to forget all about her very boring world.

A world where she felt increasingly in love with her husband, and increasingly miserable for it. Even though she'd only had one panic attack since the one at the chalet, and she'd hidden it easily, she couldn't even be happy about that. She was living in a world where she did everything she swore she'd never do.

Bend and twist and hide in an effort to make a man happy.

All because he'd said she was the best wife he could ask for. All because he'd said she made him happy. Day in and day out, no matter how many nights she spent chastising herself, she twisted herself into a more miserable pretzel because making him happy felt like…like…

Oh, she didn't know, so after she finished up her usual morning call with Zia, she picked up a book about a young woman who went through a portal to a land full of dragons, fairies and evil. It was far better than wondering if her husband was ever going to touch her again for those heirs he claimed to need.

The countess chose this moment to sweep into the library, the usual disapproval in every line of her face. Beau wanted to groan aloud.

"Well," she sniffed. "It must be nice to *relax* when the entire palace is readying itself for tomorrow's dinner."

Beau smiled as she always did. Not out of politeness, but because when she didn't bristle it only seemed to make the countess more angry.

Well, at least she hadn't *completely* lost herself.

"What a welcome interruption then," Beau said brightly. "I was under the impression I had prepared in every way possible, but is there something you think I've missed?"

The countess sniffed. "*I* would be ensuring that I knew everything I was supposed to know, backward and forward. Not reading…filth."

"Ah, well, I'm afraid I *do* know everything backward and forward. So filth it is."

The countess scoffed, which scraped against Beau's last nerve. She hated for her intelligence to be insulted. She hated the way the countess was always harping on her to do things differently. No wonder Lyon was obsessed with control and doing the right thing.

The woman who'd raised him was *equally* obsessed, if not more so. Then if she added in stories of his grandmother, well, she understood why they were all such…external perfectionists and internal messes.

"Quiz me then," Beau said, barely resisting tossing her book down like a gauntlet thrown.

"I beg your pardon?"

"If you do not think I have the knowledge to handle this

event, quiz me." She kept the fake smile firmly in place. "I would love to show you just how prepared I am."

"That is no way to talk to me, young lady."

Beau happened to think she was being very calm, but there was no point arguing with someone who wanted her to be at fault. "I apologize. I only meant that I'd be happy to prove to you that I am quite ready so you needn't worry so."

The countess made a haughty sound and then turned to leave. Or so Beau thought. After a few steps, she whirled back around.

"Who is Giorgio Amato?" she demanded.

"The MP from Cana. His wife is Amelie. She is from France. They have two children. Girls. Would you like their names?"

The Countess got *very* pinched-looking. "And who will be seated at the secondary table?"

"The parliamentary aides, and their guests. Twelve of each. I can recite names, if you'd like."

"That won't be necessary."

"Excellent." Then, to try to smooth things over, which was so foreign to her and yet necessary in this role as a *visible, respectable* princess, she continued. "I understand it must be…concerning to worry that I am not up to the challenge of taking on your role of hostess that you've held for the past year of Lyon's reign. Everyone has told me you were excellent at the job and made certain I knew I had incredibly big shoes to fill."

It was a bit of an exaggeration—another thing she wouldn't have done for herself. But for Lyon? She was an utter fool.

"You see, Countess, I have an excellent memory. It usually only takes reading something for it to be lodged here." Beau pointed to her temple. "Along with reading dossiers on every guest invited to the dinner, I have also read a book on Divio history, parliamentary etiquette, and the guide sent to guests. Is there anything else I should read?" Bend, bend, bend.

Just like her mother.

"Perhaps you should have asked me for help prior to the day before," the countess said.

Agree. Agree.

But her temper was snapping, and it felt *good*. Felt wonderful to feel something other a numb detachment from everything around her. "I'll ask Lyon for help if I need it." Then because that was *rude,* she tacked on a "thank you."

"He has a kingdom to run. Don't you think you've been distracting enough?"

Beau laughed. "Distracting?" Her husband barely looked at her, did everything he could to keep his physical distance. And sure, she'd leaned into that over the past few days, because she couldn't *bear* the thought of talking about schedules or when she had the best chance of getting pregnant.

But Beau doubted very much, no matter how happy Lyon claimed she made him, that she was any kind of *distraction*. Because he didn't want that, so she hadn't been that.

"He hasn't been the same since you came back from that little honeymoon," the countess continued. "The fault of that lays directly in your lap."

Her lap? If only the fault of anything was hers, then maybe she could fix it. "Did it ever occur to you that the fault might be yours?" Beau countered. In the back of her mind she knew she was making a mistake. Lyon would be displeased.

And she just didn't *care* anymore. She wanted to break something. If it was them, so be it. "That it was you who put unreasonable expectations upon him? That you demanded he be so perfect that he's terrified of any misstep?" Beau did slam the book down then. She got to her feet and looked the shocked countess right in the eyes. "Or not you. Your mother, perhaps."

"How dare you speak of my mother."

"I have heard so much about her. In these bright, glowing terms, and yet all I see is a woman desperate for control, with no worry of how all that control might hurt and twist a little boy."

The countess reared back like she'd been slapped, and Beau knew she would pay for this. In so many ways this very moment would backfire on her, but she couldn't stop herself.

After all these weeks of shutting all her emotions away, she wanted to feel *everything*.

"I happen to think that perhaps *distraction* would be the best damn thing for a man who thinks the entire country's fate rests on every single step he takes."

Anger was power, but it was also emotion. And she felt it take over. The way her legs started to feel a little numb. Her vision started tunneling and for a terrifying moment she couldn't catch her breath.

She would not have a panic attack here in front of the countess. So she acted quickly. She walked right past her mother-in-law, ignoring the woman's sputtering protests. She didn't *run* to her rooms, but she hurried. Up the stairs. Trying to keep count in her head. Trying to breathe.

She reached the hallway to their rooms and nearly sobbed when Lyon stepped out of the door and into the hallway.

Not yet. Not yet. Not yet.

He said something, but she didn't hear it. She walked past him, not making any eye contact.

"Beau. What is the matter?"

She could hear him follow her, but she did not look back, she did not stop walking. But she forced herself to speak, as clearly as she could manage.

"I h-had a p-public fight with your mother. She said I've d-distracted you, so I told her I thought she had p-put unreasonable expectations on you and that is why you are s-so afraid of making a mistake that n-nothing else matters." The tears were starting, a sob threatening to escape, so she moved into the bedroom, and slammed the door behind her.

She locked the door as she sank to the floor, as the shakes took over. It felt like that moment back at Cristhian's house weeks ago, after listening to her father berate her for all her failures.

Because he had been right.

The only thing she could do was fail.

Lyon stared at the slammed door for countless seconds trying to make sense of what had just happened. He had never seen Beau even remotely that worked up. She'd been stuttering. Struggling to breathe. It almost reminded him of…

Then he heard footsteps and turned to see his mother charging into his sitting room where he stood. But it wouldn't do to talk here. If there'd already been a public fight, everything needed to be nipped in the bud *now*.

He stopped her then took her by the arm and led her across the hall into a little-used office.

He closed the door behind him, then surveyed his mother. Her color was high, her eyes were flashing with anger. For a moment, he was reminded of his grandmother. A woman who he'd idolized.

I told her I thought she had put unreasonable expectations on you and that is why you are so afraid of making a mistake that nothing else matters.

Unreasonable wasn't fair. They'd placed expectations upon him because no one else could be trusted. No one else had been able to handle it. They had given him strength and belief in himself by thinking he could.

For a strange moment, he remembered that moment at the chalet. When Beau had apologized to him. A real apology. The kind his grandmother had claimed didn't exist. It had been the first time he'd ever considered the woman he'd idolized might be wrong.

But even before that, Beau hadn't understood him being a payment for a debt. No matter how he'd explained it, she hadn't been able to absorb it.

Because she simply didn't understand. Not because it was wrong... Right?

Any more it seemed like a cascade of wrong was happening all around him.

"What has happened?" he asked. He had to focus on the task at hand. The public fight his mother and wife had just engaged in, and how he would...fix it.

"Your wife just made a scene, Lyon. First, she tried to show me up. Then she made wild accusations. And *then* she stormed away. This is why she was the hidden Rendall. She is a spoiled—"

"You will not speak of Beau in such a way to me," he said firmly.

"Did you *hear* me?" his mother all but screeched.

Lyon took his time responding to her. A wall of calm to his mother's upset. "You two had a little spat. Unfortunate."

Mother's eyes were wild, but she didn't yell anymore. She sucked in a careful breath. Venom throbbed in every word she spoke, but she spoke calmly and quietly. Mother and Grandmother had always done that so well. Tied up all their fury into cold, calm, *sharp* ice.

"In public, Lyon. Where any staff member could see. That she is *not* what you or this country needs."

He realized then his mistake—because the mistakes were always his. He was the one who would save everyone. From the moment he could remember, he'd known he was the payment of a debt. So all missteps were his. All messes his to clean up.

And he was failing. Over and over again.

He had assumed his mother would realize over time Beau was the perfect wife for him.

He should have made it more clear. So this fight was his fault. And he had to fix it. First, by showing his mother how ridiculous she was being. "Would you have me divorce her?" he asked blandly.

"Of course not. What a scandal! The *opposite* of the stability you *assured* me you could handle."

Lyon studied her then. Had he assured his mother of that? He couldn't remember anything but his grandmother and mother *insisting* that he handle it. Capable or not. It had always been up to *him*.

Now she was claiming he'd…taken that on himself?

"Then what would you have me do? What is it you think you are accomplishing with this attack on her? She is the princess. She is my wife. A wife you encouraged me to have. I cannot divorce her. So why are *you* adding to this scene?"

The outrage was written all over his mother's face, but it soon morphed into a sharp look that, again, reminded him of his grandmother. He braced himself for the attack, the takedown.

Because it always came after that look. From either woman.

"Perhaps this could be handled if you didn't have such a soft spot for her," Mother said in a viciously quiet voice. "*You* will make a mistake."

Yes, of course. *Him.*

He loosened his tie, that familiar choking feeling that was getting a little too common again. It seemed every day, no matter how careful he was, no matter all the precautions he took, those old anxious habits were creeping back in.

"You mustn't," his mother whispered at him. She leaned close, even though they were alone in this room with the door closed. She put her hand over his that was loosening his tie. "Have you been taking your medication?" She tried to tighten his tie for him, but he stepped back.

"Yes, Mother." A careful secret, of course, but the anxiety medication was the only way he'd gotten through his teenage years. Things had eased in his early twenties. After his grandmother's death…

Had he really never put it together before? He wanted to laugh. He'd told himself grief had eased the anxiety. One feeling taking over the other, but in retrospect that was ridiculous.

His anxiety had eased because one of the sources of it had been gone.

He shook his head. That was a terrible thought. A terrible way to feel about the woman who'd given him so much. Besides, this was all…the past. He needed to deal with the present. The parliamentary dinner was tomorrow, and everyone needed to be in accord. Everyone needed to be ready so they could continue to prove they were a strong, stable unit.

"What is it that bothers you about her?" Lyon asked. "Her as a person, or the soft spot you claim I have for her?"

"Claim? I have *eyes*. You are my son. I *know* you. The point of a wife was a partnership. An arrangement. Not… love."

Yes, that was true. That had been the point. And he'd never questioned it. Until something that felt far too close to *love* had taken hold. And he was afraid of soft spots, of desire, of losing his focus.

Of love.

Because he had been made to be afraid of all these things. But he also knew, that for all the ways he didn't remember his father, his mother had never once talked about him like a…pawn. He had not been an arrangement.

"You loved my father."

Mother blinked up at him, then turned away. "We must deal with the problem at hand. Not ancient history."

"Mother. You loved him."

As if sensing he wouldn't give up the topic, she sighed. "Yes." She turned away, refusing to look him in the eye. "What does that have to do with anything? I was not in charge, and never would be."

"Why would it be so terrible for me to love Beaugonia? Simply because I'm in charge?"

She turned back to face him, and he saw all the ways she looked like her own mother. The dark eyes, the way her mouth nearly disappeared when she was angry. "You are the ruler. You must love your country above all else. How else will you rise above the legacy the men in this family leave?"

Years ago, when he'd been quite young, he'd had the nerve to ask his grandmother why that responsibility had to fall to *him*. Why he was the only one.

She had slapped him across the face. He had cried. Which had earned him a night in his room without dinner. He hadn't thought of that in years. He'd blocked it out of his mind.

Lyon didn't care for old, ugly memories. He preferred to think of her as a strong leader. The woman who'd shaped him. But if she'd shaped Lyon… "Did she never give you a choice either?"

"What are you talking about?"

"What pressure did she put on you?"

"Who?"

"Your mother."

"Your grandmother…" Mother's brow furrowed and she shook her head. "This is ridiculous. Your wife created a scene and now you want to discuss your grandmother with me?"

"Yes. Because it all goes back to her, doesn't it? Why

we're here. Worried about…scenes. Afraid of love and soft spots. Things that normal people think are *good*."

"That poor woman watched her family destroy every tradition, every positive relationship, every bit of honor her father and grandfather had built. And instead of letting it destroy her, she focused on us. How we could save it. It could never be me, Lyon. That's hardly her fault or some pressure she put upon me. But she taught me just the same, for when I would give her a son."

A payment to a debt. He'd always accepted that as a perfectly acceptable thing to put on a child. But there was something about soft spots, and the possibility of love. The idea of making his own child with Beaugonia, and the way she'd looked at him when he'd tried to explain. It all added up into a sick feeling in his stomach.

His child would never be a payment to anything. They would be a *person*. An heir, yes, but a *child* first.

"Give *her* a son?" he asked his mother gently.

She whirled away, frustration and temper in every harsh move. "You sound so much like your father right now. And he was *wrong* about her. He *died*, and she and you remained."

"Wrong about her? I thought Grandmother approved of him?"

"*She* did. Because he was a good man from a good family. Upstanding and honest. Your father found your grandmother…difficult. But he simply didn't understand. He wasn't royal."

This was the first Lyon had ever heard of it. The first he'd ever asked. Because…his grandmother had discouraged any talk of those already gone. Or so she said, though she spoke of her own father plenty. "Did you think he didn't understand. Or did Grandmother think that?"

Mother looked up at him like he'd just stabbed her clean through. "Why are we talking about this, Lyon?"

He didn't know. Only that it was crystallizing things for him. Things he'd been trying to push away ever since the chalet. All the ways Beau had, without meaning to, flipped the truths he'd believed from his grandmother on their head.

And he looked at his mother now and saw himself. She had believed his grandmother's hard, cold truths. But someone had loved her, and she had loved someone. Father had been her soft spot, and then he'd died. Too soon, too young.

"Losing him must have been very hard."

"People die," she said, but he heard the grief in her voice all the same.

"Yes, that was Grandmother's line, wasn't it?"

Mother straightened, lifted her chin. "She was right. Everyone must deal with death. There is no point in grieving, in letting it mark you."

"I don't think all emotions have to have a point, Mother. They're just there." Anxiety. Grief.

Love.

Such a false equivalency they'd passed down. That one love might blot out another. That responsibility to his wife would mean disaster for his country.

But wasn't that the false equivalency he'd employed back at the chalet? Desire would lead to forgoing all…sense, responsibility.

"Have you ever wondered, Madre?" he said gently. "If Grandmother put an unreasonable weight upon our shoulders?"

"She only wanted what was best for Divio. And you should as well. Letting that wife of yours *poison* you is beneath you."

But he saw something desperate in his mother's eyes.

Like he had gotten at least a little through to her, even if she wouldn't admit it.

"I do want what's best for Divio. And I will fight for it. But why does that mean I cannot care for my own wife?"

"She's poisoned you."

"Or she's set me free." He wasn't certain he believed that, but it felt good to say. It felt *true* to say. "Now, I would appreciate it if you would have lunch with Beau. I will go talk to her, and then you two will sit down and have a civil conversation. A *public* civil conversation to undo this."

Mother scoffed. "She will not agree. Or she will not be civil. You cannot get through to that girl. She is...*unhinged*."

"She is not. She's incredibly reasonable. But she's also... incredibly herself. Without fear. Nevertheless, she will have lunch with you, she will be civil, because I'll have asked her to. You see, Mother... Perhaps I have a soft spot for her, but she has a soft spot for me as well. Grandmother treated us like little soldiers. There were no soft spots. I thought that was the only way to be."

"It got you here, didn't it?"

"No, happenstance did. Maybe the other family's genetic predispositions to giving in to excess as well, I can't deny that. Perhaps Grandmother taught me in ways her brothers, nephews and so on had never been taught. Perhaps it will even allow me to rule Divio with all that tradition and stability she so worshipped. But it didn't *get me* here."

"She loved you."

Lyon thought about that. And then he thought about Beau. How she listened to him. Tried to understand him. The comfort she offered. The heartfelt apology. Those things were closer to love than cold demands, hard rules and harsh punishments.

"No. I'm not sure she really loved either of us. She loved the idea of what her progeny might do to one-up her brothers. Love is…helping one another, apologizing when you're wrong. Love is soft spots, Mother."

"You must run a country, Lyon."

"Yes. I've been doing an excellent job of it the past year, if I do say so myself. It was good, to start off just me. But now I have added a wife, and some adjustments could be made. If I am going to start a family, adjustments *will* be made." He would not raise his children with the weight of the entire country on their shoulders.

Respect for their role, yes. An appreciation for hard work, ideally. But he would not lay down the burden of centuries. Not on them. Not on his wife.

And not even on himself. Not anymore.

CHAPTER FOURTEEN

LYON RETURNED TO their rooms. The door to the bedroom was still closed, and when he went to try and open it, he found it locked.

He knocked. "Beau?" he called through the door. "You must unlock the door for me. We need to talk." He would confess everything. Love and soft spots and what he hoped for the future. He would tell her the realizations she'd brought out.

And together, they would build some sort of future where his fear of failure did not rule him. Where he could make *her* as happy as she'd made him.

But she didn't respond in any way. And the door did not unlock. He jiggled the knob once more. "Beau?" He set his ear to the door. It wasn't like she could have disappeared. She had to be in there somewhere. Perhaps she'd gone into the bathroom and couldn't hear.

He had a key to this door somewhere, but he didn't want to have to call Mr. Filini to track it down as then there'd be speculation as to why his wife had locked him out of their bedroom. Or should that matter? Should he—

Then he heard it. Not her responding, but the faint sounds of…gasping? Like she was struggling to breathe. She must be having some kind of…medical event.

Terror speared through him, and he shook the door in renewed earnest. "Beau? Answer me."

He didn't hear her say anything, but as he was rearing back to fling himself against the door, the knob moved. Then the door creaked open the tiniest crack.

He rushed forward into the room, heart pounding and worry and fear clawing through him. The light was dim— the curtains drawn. He looked around in a panic, and didn't see her at first, but he heard her. A terrible, gasping noise. Coming from...

She was on the floor. Tears were pouring out of her eyes, and every breath sounded labored and terrible. She shook like she might simply shake apart.

For only a second he was rendered completely frozen with terror. "I'll get the doctor," he managed to say. He wanted to run to her, but she needed help he couldn't give.

She shook her head violently. She opened her mouth but no sound came out. Then he strode forward, gathered her in his arms. "I will *take* you to the doctor," he said firmly.

"It's n-not an ill—illness," she managed to say, though her voice was weak and her entire being shook in his arms.

"Then what—?" But the fact she could speak now had eased something inside of him enough to recognize certain things. If it wasn't medical, that meant it was something else. And the only something else that he knew could have physical symptoms like that was anxiety.

"You've had a panic attack," he murmured in surprise. It was hard to believe Beau panicked about *anything*.

She didn't respond, but she leaned into him and he held on. He settled them both onto the bed, her in his lap as he rocked her gently and murmured reassuring words that she was all right. She would be all right.

It took time. First, she began to breathe easier. Then the tears stopped and she allowed him to brush the wet off her face. The shakes remained, but they lessened in severity.

When he thought she was calm enough to talk, he ran a hand over her hair and held her close.

"Is this because of the fight with my mother? I've handled it, *tesoruccia*." He pressed a kiss to her temple. Something inside of him that had been tied tight these weeks eased.

This was right. Not that she would be in such a state, but that they would be close. That he would hold her and she would lean against him. That they would have soft spots for one another. That they would *talk*.

Not hide from everything they were. And poor Beaugonia had gotten herself into such a frenzy she'd had a panic attack. Which was probably his own fault. He'd put too many responsibilities on *her* shoulders.

Well, no more.

"We must talk, Beau. We must... This has not been working, has it? I am to blame. We will sort it all out. Don't worry any more, *amore mio*. Everything will be fine."

But she shook her head, even as she sagged against him. "It will never be fine."

"Beaugonia..."

"These attacks are never because of one thing," she said, sounding utterly exhausted. "I admit, this one stemmed from my argument with your mother, but that's hardly the reason I have panic attacks."

Anything that eased began to tighten up again. Those words... *These*...attack*s*...as if a panic attack was a common occurrence for her. Not because of something he'd done. Not because of a pressure that was too much.

He looked down at her tousled hair. He tried to make sense of this. She'd mentioned her childhood social anxiety, and he'd understood. His anxiety had not been related to crowds. It had been more...generalized. But he'd never had a full-blown panic attack. Or at least, nothing that looked like this. Still, he could see how if it had been left unchecked, he might have.

But she had claimed that…she had grown out of her anxiety. That it no longer defined her, though her parents had continued to define her by it. He had assumed that perhaps, like him, she had gotten help. Because she *had* been fine in all social situations. She had been perfect at their wedding dinner, on the video. She handled the staff well, and her position.

Maybe she had gotten help but because they hadn't communicated, such help had fallen by the wayside. Maybe this was just… He didn't know. He was misunderstanding something, surely. "Do you take anything?"

"Take anything?" she repeated, like she didn't understand the question.

"Medication? For anxiety or panic disorders?"

"I…" She shook her head. "No. My father was insistent I never be treated. I did research on my own, but I was too…worried about what might happen if he caught me with medication or speaking to a therapist even via video. It was a blight against our name, in his eyes."

"Your father…" And then a few facts started to fall into place. The fact this was not…new, or out of place. Her father and research and the resigned way she spoke of all this, like she knew exactly how this went.

She didn't have medication because it was not allowed.

Because *this* was commonplace. And had been.

And she had never told him.

"How often do you have these attacks?" he asked, still searching for some way to understand this that did not cause this terrible rending inside of him.

She stiffened against him, then began to ease away. He would have held on to her, but his limbs felt numb.

"I'm feeling much better. Do you mind if I take a bath?

And then a nap? I'm quite tired." She didn't get to her feet, but she edged away so there was space between them on the end of the bed.

He could only stare at her. Avoiding the question. A simple question. What should be *simple*. Unless she'd been lying to him. "Beau."

She sighed heavily. "Yes, I have panic attacks. They are sporadic. Uncontrollable. Sometimes there is a cause, sometimes there is not. You needn't worry about it."

He made a noise. He wasn't sure what kind of noise, but no words would encompass his reaction to *You needn't worry about it*. He *was* worried. She'd *terrified* him.

She'd *lied* to him. To his face. Over and over again for all these weeks.

"I *can* hide it," she said firmly. "I have been hiding it. And still, you're the only one who knows beyond my family. It's all right. No one else has to know. You needn't…" She trailed off, but she didn't look at him.

He was still sitting on the bed, trying to work through this turn of events. "What is it you think I'll do?"

A long looming silence settled in between them. She didn't answer, kept her gaze on the opposite wall, and he found himself relieved.

He didn't want to know what horrible thing she thought of him, it turned out.

All this time, and she'd been lying to him. Hiding this from him. And then it dawned on him. Not just this lie, but… "This is why your father did not want you to be his heir."

For a moment she did not respond. He heard her swallow. "Yes."

This was the secret his mother had been worried she'd been keeping. It was hardly the end of any worlds. If she'd kept it a secret this long in her life, they could continue to

do so. It wasn't the panic attacks themselves, he of all people understood that one could not always control the things
the brain did.

But she had *lied* to him. She did not trust him with this
information even now. When he'd been ready to…

Change *everything* for her. Admit soft spots and *love*,
and this was how little she thought of him. He knew she
hadn't been happy, but he thought she felt at least some of
what he did.

Surely there was just something he wasn't understanding. He needed more information. "How many have you
had since coming here?"

She looked over at him miserably. "Does it matter?"

That she had had them? Hid them? Lied to him? And still
he thought details would somehow…help ease this yawn-
ing ache inside of him growing deeper and more painful
by the moment. "How many?"

She looked down at her lap. "Three."

Three. They had been married only three weeks. She
had hidden *three* panic attacks from him. Well, two. But
she would have hidden this from him if he hadn't… "When
were they?"

"I'm very tired and—"

"When were they, Beaugonia?"

She lifted her chin. There was something, a hint of *life*
in her eyes, but it was shrouded in a misery that settled in
him like a stab to the gut.

"If you must know, though it matters not at all. The first
night at the chalet. Last week in the library. Today, after
arguing with your mother."

The chalet. "How… But we were in such close quarters
at the chalet. How?"

"I know how to hide it. I told you. It was the middle of
the night. I got out of bed without waking you."

And then she'd come back. Lied to him about being cold. And then… Lyon got to his feet. He wanted to rip the collar off his neck, the pressure squeezing just there. He stalked away from her, then turned back.

"So once a week. Once a week you've had these…attacks. And hidden it from me?"

"Yes." She didn't sound the least bit repentant. She just sat there on the bed, staring at her lap.

"Why would you have kept this from me?"

Her head whipped up. "Are you joking? A weakness like this? When you're obsessed with being seen as stable and respectable? Why would I ever admit this to you?"

"Obsessed." It felt like an indictment. One he could hardly defend himself from. It was true.

Except he hardly viewed a panic attack as some *weakness*. The fact she thought he would…

"Can you please leave me be now? I'd like to rest. Alone."

Alone. When he'd thought… It was all too much. He needed to sort through the…layers of it all. So perhaps alone would be best. She could rest and he could think.

But he didn't want anything hanging over her head, worrying her unnecessarily. "You do not need to attend the parliamentary dinner if you do not wish." He would make her excuses. Find a way to make certain she didn't have to deal with it. "I'll leave the decision up to you."

She looked at him then, her hazel eyes reflecting a hurt he did not understand. She didn't say anything.

So he gave her what she wanted. Time to rest. *Alone*.

Beau didn't rest. Because she felt the wreckage of everything like a sharp weight against her lungs.

He would never look at her the same. He would hide her away.

You do not need to attend the parliamentary dinner if you do not wish.

He did not need to be any clearer. He was embarrassed by her now. She'd ruined everything. All the years of refusing to believe what her parents thought of her, but now...

Maybe they were right. She was weak. And Lyon needed strength, stability, respectability. That could never be her.

What is it you think I'll do?

He'd sounded so horrified. So affronted.

Lock me away. Hate me.

She wouldn't stand for it. Not again. Maybe she loved him. Maybe it broke her heart into a million pieces, but she would not be locked away. And if she told herself it was *that*, and not that the worst thing she could imagine was having to live with him knowing he viewed her as what she was: *less*, then maybe she could get through this.

Because there were always options. She could fall apart. She could let this break her into all the pieces she stitched together after each and every panic attack. Or she could refuse to be ended no matter how much her heart hurt.

She hadn't been herself for weeks now. So maybe this was an opportunity. To get back to the person she'd been before she'd been stupid enough to soften her heart to someone who expected perfection.

That Beau had been strong, determined, sure of herself. Maybe there'd been a decided lack of joy, a loneliness, particularly after Zia had run away and she'd been left alone with her parents, but she hadn't felt destroyed.

Nothing was worse than this feeling. It would choke her until there was nothing left. She had to...get out.

She grabbed her phone, called Zia. "Zia. I know you're busy, and the babies must come first, but..."

"Beau, what is it?"

"I need help. I need...to run away." It was the only answer. She wouldn't be locked away. She wouldn't be hidden. She wouldn't keep living this...strange, gray version of turning into her mother.

She wouldn't stay and make Lyon unhappy. He would be angry about that, because it didn't look good from the outside, but she was tired of the damn outside. He could make up a lie. The version of her that was his wife could be a story people told, just like the story of her as a princess had always been.

She existed. She wasn't seen. Only instead of hiding in his castle, she would be free. She would be *free*.

Zia had run away and all had worked out, so this would too.

"What's happened? Did he hurt you? I'll kill him. Well, no, I'll send Cristhian to kill him. That's far scarier."

She wanted to be warmed by the viciousness in Zia's voice, but she didn't feel the least bit bloodthirsty. She wasn't *angry* at Lyon. She was just...devastated. "No, no. It isn't that."

"Then what is it?"

"Lyon...discovered my panic attacks."

There was a beat of silence. "Did you think you could hide it forever?" Zia asked gently.

The truth was, Beau had thought exactly that. Or maybe held on to the hope she was in control of some facet of her life and that she would be able to.

All up in smoke now.

"No, I suppose not, but... I can't be what Lyon needs me to be now. He knows I'm defective, and he'll hide me away."

"Did he call you that?" Zia demanded. "I *am* going to kill him. With my bare hands."

Beau thought back. No, he hadn't said anything like her father would have, but she'd seen it in his face. In the way he'd pulled back. He saw her differently now. Maybe there was enough kindness in him not to say it to her face, but she was broken now in his eyes.

She would not make him happy now that he knew this. She could not be the partner he needed, expected. "Not in so many words, no. He has a kindness to him. This isn't about…cruelty. I just can't be someone's dirty little secret again, hidden away. I won't be."

Again, Zia was silent for a few seconds. "All right. Then we'll get you out. All you have to do is get out of the palace. Find somewhere to hide. No need to call. Cristhian will find you. It's what he does."

"But the babies…"

"I am hardly alone, Beau. I have help. Cristhian will find you. And we'll have you back here before the day is out. Here and safe. I promise. Just get out of the palace."

Beau looked around the room that had begun to feel like hers. The life that held both misery and joy. Complicated feelings she'd never expected. A life she wanted… and couldn't have.

At least that was familiar.

Then she hung up the phone.

And planned her escape.

CHAPTER FIFTEEN

LYON HAD A staff member tell his mother there'd be no lunch. Then he had meetings to attend. He brooded, the whole afternoon, trying to determine what the hell to do with all this.

And he approved all the last-minute changes and hiccups on the parliamentary dinner. He dealt with problems, questions. He was distracted, *yes*, but he was not incapable of doing what needed to be done because of it.

Because, it turned out, the women who'd raised him were wrong. He could do both. Love and grieve and hurt and make good choices for his country. It turned *out*, that when he gave himself a chance to do everything without the fear of taking a wrong step, he did what he'd always done.

The right damn thing. Soft spots or no.

Perhaps a time would come when that would not be the case, but even if he held himself to some impossible standard of isolation—upsets would still come along. Natural disasters or worldly problems challenging all Divio was. Loss or illness or who knew what else when it came to his family, to himself.

He could do the right thing—avoid scandal, meet his responsibilities—but he could not control the world around him by doing such things.

It was a strange, out-of-body moment, all in all. To be

both distracted and capable of dealing with—or delegating—everything that needed to be done. To watch as nothing crumbled around him simply because his role wasn't the only thing he took into account.

To consider that maybe, just maybe, there could be a life where he balanced both. Not the expectations his grandmother had set for him, but meeting the needs of his citizens. While at the same time meeting the needs of his family, without letting selfish desires ruin everything. Without worrying that…every private decision would ruin his public persona.

Beau was his family. His wife. He hated the idea that she suffered so. It tore him up inside and made him want to go talk to her and beg forgiveness. He would protect her and defend her from *anyone* who dared say a negative word about her.

But she had *lied*. She had kept this from him from the very beginning. She had been in the wrong as well. Whether it was his fault or not that she hadn't trusted him with this, had hidden it from him, she had not given him the opportunity to be right or wrong.

They both needed to find a way to do that. Give each other chances, instead of being too afraid and making everything worse. Making everything get to the point of falling apart.

Maybe balance wasn't so much about everyone being one hundred percent happy or everything getting his full attention. No, it was finding what needed him the most in the moment and responding to it.

Because his grandmother's will to one-up her brother had no bearing anymore. Both were dead and gone. He was here. Beau was here.

Right now, everything was set for the dinner tomorrow, he'd responded to every pressing item on his agenda. So what needed him was Beau, and working through what had happened today.

If he owed her an apology, which he did, he should offer it. And if she did not offer one of her own, then he would deal with that in the moment. They would talk through it. Have those conversations that had been sorely missing in her book until the very end.

But when those conversations had come—the couple in the book had worked things out. So that is what he would do. Make it all work out.

He left his office and went in search of her. It was late, but she wasn't in their suite of rooms or in bed, so he went to the library next. And when she wasn't there, he began to…worry. He searched everywhere he could think of, and then finally he had to page her assistant.

The woman was wide-eyed and nervy when she came into his office. She had clearly been asleep. Her curtsey was awkward at best. "I'm sorry, Your Highness, it seems no one has seen her since this morning."

"This *morning*." Lyon's body felt as though it emptied fully out, then inch by inch filled back with rage.

All the ways she'd pushed him. All the ways she'd claimed to want him. All the ways she had understood him, and she hadn't given him the damn opportunity to understand *her*.

She had run away.

Where—but Lyon immediately knew where she would have gone. The only place she would run away to. She talked to her sister almost every day. The only thing she ever spoke of with any positivity was Zia and her babies.

"Find out the residence of Zia Rendall…or whatever her name is now. And ready a plane. Once you have the address, I will leave at once."

"I… I don't know…"

He growled, couldn't help himself. Luckily Mr. Filini entered, unfortunately his mother did as well. Someone must have woken her up and told her Beau was missing. Oh, well. It didn't matter. All that mattered was getting to Beau.

"Mr. Filini—"

"I heard, Your Highness. We'll be on it at once." He gestured to Beau's assistant and they both left.

Lyon thought briefly of packing, but what did he need? Nothing. He would bring her back here and they would have their reckoning. She did not get to just *run away* and have that be that.

"Lyon, you can't miss the dinner," Mother said.

He looked at his mother. For a moment there was a pang. She was right. He should stay. Focus on responsibilities first and *then* deal with Beau. He couldn't possibly risk the potential he might not get back in time. What would people say?

It was knee-jerk. Everything he'd been taught. *What would people say?* They would compare him to all the negative that had come before.

But if he gave it space. If he let himself consider it for what it was, not the debt he had to pay, it became ridiculous.

Responsibility to host some frivolous, meaningless dinner? That had nothing to do with the actual rules of law or running of the kingdom. That wasn't in service to the citizens but was simply meant to feed a bunch of pompous members of parliament, so they decided to *like* him? And maybe, just *maybe*, not compare him to the reckless men who'd preceded him?

To hell with that.

"If I am not back in time, I trust you can handle it."

She sputtered, but he didn't bother to listen to any responses she managed.

He was going to find his wife.

* * *

Cristhian had indeed found her. That was what he did, after all. And in no time at all Beau had been on a plane, flying back to his estate with him. He didn't offer her any words, didn't try to get her to talk. He simply ushered her where she needed to go. He was a good man. Worthy of Zia and their beautiful twins.

Who Beau would finally get to hold.

When she arrived at Cristhian and Zia's that afternoon, she was greeted by her sister, who had one baby in the crook of her arm, and the other arm open and ready for Beau.

Beau was not much of a crier. She had always chalked it up to crying so much when she had panic attacks. It took away any need to release her emotions that way when she wasn't panicking.

But when she stepped into Zia's outstretched arm, and Zia hugged her close, the tears filled her eyes. She blinked them away before she pulled back and looked at the tiny bundle in Zia's arms.

"This is Harrison," Zia said, her voice rough. A mewling cry, followed by a much angrier one, sounded from deeper in the house. "And there is your namesake announcing her displeasure, as she is quite adept at doing. Come." Zia led her into the house and a cozy little living room with all sorts of baby paraphernalia strewn about, including two little bassinets in the corner.

Beau followed Zia to one and looked down at an angry little bundle. Her face was red and scrunched up.

"And this is Begonia. Our little Bee," Zia said, the love and joy in every word even as the girl screamed in a tiny but loud cry. "Go on," Zia said, nudging Beau with her hip. "Pick her up."

But Beau felt completely ill-equipped to deal with any of this. Or any of her life right now. It was all too big and unwieldy. She swallowed the emotion clogging her throat, or tried. "I don't know how."

"Allow me." Cristhian scooped the baby up, and the girl immediately began to quiet.

Something about a very large man holding a very small bundle made Beau want to weep. But she held it together and Zia moved her over to the couch, and then Cristhian sat next to Beau. Beau tried to hold her arms like Zia was and Cristhian transferred baby Bee into Beau's arms. Zia sat next to her, cradling Harrison.

It was just so amazing and beautiful. That her sister had brought these two precious lives into the world. Beau gazed down at the little girl in her lap. "Aren't they the most perfect things in the entire universe?"

"Mostly. I don't *quite* have those feelings when they're screaming their heads off at two in the morning, but ninety-nine percent of the time they are the most perfect things in the entire universe." Zia stroked her son's cheek.

After a few minutes of silence, Zia sighed. "What's happened, Beau?"

Beau couldn't tear her gaze away from Bee. She couldn't really find the words either. "I don't know. It was so good at first, and then…"

"Good?" Zia pressed. "You…got along with Lyon?"

Beau nodded. "I wasn't lying to you during all those calls. I…" *Love him.* "He was very kind. He has the most beautiful library, and he likes to read. He even read a book I liked to get to know me. It was actually… I was very happy for a bit. Maybe if I'd been pregnant, it would have gone differently."

Which was not a productive thought. She'd just be sitting in his castle being miserable. Not allowed to go to things like parliamentary dinners. Even though she'd proven she could handle it. A baby wouldn't have changed anything, except she would have had someone to hold in her isolation.

"So you two... You..." Zia cleared her throat. "There was...a *chance* you were...pregnant?"

Beau looked up at her sister, then realized Zia had clearly not considered that just because the marriage had been arranged to save Zia, that there might not be the making of heirs involved.

"We had sex, Zia. We *are* married."

Cristhian made a dismayed sort of noise and stood. "Perhaps I will go...do *anything* else."

Zia rolled her eyes and waved him off. "We can handle the babies. Go do something manly."

He smiled at Zia, the kind of smile that spoke of many things. Affection, amusement, intimacy. Zia watched her husband leave, the love so evident in her eyes that Beau had to look away. But she could only look at the child in her lap and feel a terrible, terrible yearning.

"I wanted to be pregnant," she heard herself say, without really meaning to.

"Oh, Beau." Zia's free arm came around Beau's shoulders.

She shook her head. It was the wrong thing to say. She blinked back the tears. "Best this way."

"Tell me what happened. All of it. Beginning to end, and then we will figure out what to do."

Beau didn't really want to rehash it yet, but she might as well. She didn't know where to start, really. At the wedding? The chalet? Even though she spoke to Zia almost every day, she had mostly kept her sister in the dark about the Lyon Beau had come to know. She hadn't known how to talk about falling in love with the man she'd married to save Zia. She hadn't known how to talk about sex, because it hadn't felt right to talk about Lyon's reaction to things.

And maybe she didn't want Zia flying into protective mode when Zia had been carrying so much on her plate. So Beau had been vague about everything.

Now? She told her sister everything. From Lyon's "steps" to the chalet to the horrible fight with the countess. To Lyon discovering her. In the midst of a panic attack.

"This dinner has been everyone's focus for weeks," Beau said. She'd managed to hold back tears, but it was getting harder. "Talked about how important it is for the guests to see a united monarchy. To be fed and wooed and complimented as if that will wash away the poor deeds of the past princes. And maybe it would. Men in power are so very simple. But the moment Lyon saw me... The moment he realized what was happening... He saw what's wrong with me and then because of that he said I didn't have to go."

"He sounds like Father," Zia said with disgust.

Beau so wished she could agree. "But he's not. Not in the least." Maybe that's why she felt bruised straight through. Maybe that's why running away didn't feel right or righteous, just depressing.

She didn't want to punish Lyon, didn't want to hurt him. Which added to the depression. "If anything, I've fallen into being our mother."

"Impossible," Zia said, but it was knee-jerk, she didn't *know*.

"I pretzeled myself to make him happy. I... I made myself *miserable* to make him happy."

"That's not quite the same as Mother, Beau," Zia said gently.

Beau stared at Zia in utter shock. "How can you even try to claim that?"

"Mother...isn't miserable. I'm not saying she's happy, but she's not...trying to make Father *happy*."

"She certainly wasn't attempting to make us or herself happy."

"No. I think she's afraid of Father. Of what he'll do. How he'll react. She never stood up for us, not because she *loved* him more than us—though I admittedly thought that for a time. But… I'm in love now. Both with my husband, and I have these children whom I love. Mother is all…fear. All that talk of bending and not breaking. She just wants things to be easy and smooth. Love is neither of those things. For good or for ill. It takes…work, compromise. It means losing pieces of your heart to be out of your own control. It's why it was so easy for her to just…let us be married and then wash her hands of us. It's easier that way, than to maintain a relationship."

Beau frowned a little at that. She hadn't expected love to be easy. No book had ever claimed it would be such. So maybe it's why it never occurred to her that her mother's motivation was the path of least resistance, not some passionate love that only extended to her husband and not her children.

"There is a certain give-and-take to love." Zia looked at her children. "Perhaps it helps that I had them, growing inside of me, long before I considered *love*. If I'd only felt my love for Cristhian, perhaps it would have terrified me to turn into Mother too. But them? Oh, Beau. I'd give them anything. I'd give up anything to make them safe and healthy and happy. And that extends to my husband. So, I can't believe it's…wrong to want to make someone happy. There's something right about that. Something *loving* about that."

"So you think I should go back and be miserable and hide away and—"

Zia put her free hand on Beau's shoulder. "Not at all. I said give *and* take. Not you giving and him taking. If he thinks because of one little panic attack you're somehow not worthy of going to dinner, he can sod off forever. That's on *him*. Not you. And it's nothing at all to do with love."

Beau didn't understand why that didn't make her feel any better, but she pushed it all aside and focused on her sister. Her niece and nephew. On simple, easy love.

But was it *simple* when she'd sacrificed herself for Zia? When Zia had sacrificed herself for Beau for years? Or was that give? And take. Hard decisions to make someone else happy. A willingness to survive the miserable, if someone else could be okay.

But Beau didn't want her life to be what it had always been, so how could she go back to Lyon? Since there was no easy answer to that, she ignored it. She had a nice afternoon with her sister. A reaffirming evening watching Cristhian and Zia act as a team. The love they shared with each other and their children was clear.

Beau couldn't go back to a life that didn't look like that, so she'd done the right thing.

Of course, she didn't know what to do about the future. Lyon would hardly grant a divorce. But, she couldn't go back. Maybe it was her turn to disappear. Zia had gone to a little polar island for a while when she'd first discovered her pregnancy, maybe Beau could follow suit.

She would be alone, but wasn't that better than hiding half of herself to please someone? Or being hidden away in a castle that wasn't hers? Better to isolate herself than be isolated by others. She had always thought so, and she tended to be right.

Late into the evening, really early morning at this point, she helped Zia with the twins' middle-of-the-night feeding. They sat together on the couch under a very dim light, Beau feeding Harrison with a bottle while Zia held Bee to her. Even in her fog of misery, this felt so nice. To be an adult with her sister. To sit here in a life that did not involve their parents or threats or *kingdoms*. Just late nights and quiet rooms and sweet babies.

Cristhian came in. He was dressed in dark sweats and a T-shirt, his hair sleep-rumpled.

Zia looked up at him with some surprise. "Beau helped me. You should have kept sleeping."

But Cristhian was giving Beau an odd look, before he turned to his wife. "Zia? Can I talk to you for a second?" He nodded toward the hallway.

A secret. Beau frowned. Zia raised an eyebrow.

"I'm in the middle of something, darling," she replied dryly, pointing to the child latched to her.

"Yes. I know. It's only…"

Beau shared a look with Zia, because never any time had she ever seen Cristhian seem even remotely uncertain as he did now.

And then she heard a shout from somewhere deeper in the house. Both Beau and Zia straightened with alarm.

"Is something wrong?" Zia asked.

Cristhian cleared his throat. "Well. It seems the prince has arrived."

"Who's the prince…?" Beau began to ask, but then it dawned on her. She recognized that shout, though she had never heard Lyon shout in such a way. Her eyes widened. What was he doing here? "Oh."

Oh.

Zia reached over, clutched her arm. "You don't have to see him if you don't want to. Cristhian will send him away."

"We have tried." Cristhian cleared his throat. "He is quite…insistent."

"So insist him right back," Zia said fiercely, as she transferred Bee to her shoulder and rubbed the baby's back until a small burp sounded. "With your fist," she added darkly, a very strange tableau.

But not as strange as Lyon being here. *Here.*

"I'm trying to avoid an international incident," Cristhian replied, his voice equally as dry as Zia's had been earlier.

"Well, I'm not." Zia got to her feet as if she was about to go instigate such incident. But before anyone could do anything, Lyon stormed right into the room.

His hair was wild, his tie loose and one of the top buttons of his shirt unbuttoned.

For ticking moments, Beau could only stare at him. He was as unkempt as she'd ever seen him. He was angry, certainly, and in *front* of people. And still her heart leapt.

What an idiot she was. What a stupid thing love was. She clutched Harrison close and steeled herself for whatever he was going to say.

Because she wouldn't go back and shrink herself. No matter what she'd done, no matter what she'd promised. She would be free.

And he could go to hell.

CHAPTER SIXTEEN

LYON WAS RUNNING on little sleep and too much anger. He had thought he would calm down by the time he arrived at Cristhian Sterling's estate from simple exhaustion if nothing else, but every minute of knowing Beau had run away, without *talking* to him, poked his temper higher.

When Cristhian's staff and then Cristhian himself had tried to bar Lyon from Beau, it had been the last straw. Whatever last dredges of propriety and concern for his image had gone up in smoke.

I will see my wife.

And he had been prepared to fight whoever might try to stop him. But once Cristhian had left, it had only taken moving past the sleepy man trying to tell him that he wasn't welcome.

Who gave a damn about *welcome*?

He had heard quiet voices and followed them down a hallway. He had charged into the room but came to a halting stop. He saw Beau right away. She sat on a cozy-looking couch, dressed in fuzzy pajamas. Her hair was pulled back. But it wasn't the gorgeous, perfect sight of her that stopped him dead.

She was holding the smallest infant he'd ever seen. For a moment the sight took him so off guard, he had no words. He could only *stare*.

After a few moments like that, she stood. "You cannot simply barge into people's houses this late at night," she said to him, haughty and royal. She moved over to Cristhian and handed the baby off.

Then she turned to him, chin up, eyes flashing.

"And yet here I am," he returned, wanting her and wanting to *shake* her in equal measure. He pointed a finger at her. "And *you* are going to listen to me."

"You'll be careful where you point that finger," Zia said, stepping in between his finger and Beau.

He surveyed the sister he'd been meant to marry. She had once even worn his ring. It felt like a different lifetime ago, all that. Like he'd been a different person then. He supposed he had been.

And now she stood here, holding her own child, with her husband watching with wary eyes, and a child in his own arms.

"Ah, my former fiancée." Lyon gave a short, sarcastic bow. "So good to see you again now that we are in-laws."

Her eyes narrowed. "For now."

Over his dead body.

But he didn't care about Zia. He cared about his *wife*. Who stood in this dim room with anger and hurt flashing in her eyes, and no *shame*. When she *should* feel shame because she had *run away*.

"Perhaps we should give them their privacy," Cristhian murmured to his wife.

But Zia was staring at Lyon with daggers in her eyes. "Over my dead body."

"I don't care who stays or goes," Lyon muttered, moving around Zia so that Beau was in front of him instead. Nothing mattered except this woman. So he stopped engaging with the two other people in the room, and focused on why he was here.

On what needed to be said.

"You should not have run away, Beaugonia." He supposed there were better ways to say that, better ways to start this. He supposed any of the speeches he'd practiced on the flight here might have gone over better.

But it was all he could think. He loved this woman, had somehow realized all the ridiculous things holding him back on account of his childhood because of her, and she had *run*.

"You should return to Divio at once," she replied. "You are making a scene and it is nearly morning. If you are not careful, you will miss your dinner."

"To hell with the dinner!" He shouted it. Really shouted it. He could not remember the last time he'd actually allowed himself to *shout*.

It felt too damn good. *Slippery slope*. And maybe it was. To allow himself to feel. To allow himself to run with emotion and make a mistake because of it. Maybe he was ruining everything.

But if he ruined it and she came back to him, it would all be worth it.

She blinked at him. Finally, *finally* completely taken aback. It lit something inside of him. One of those dangerous fires he wasn't supposed to indulge.

But what did it matter here? It was only him and her.

And her sister and brother-in-law, and two infants, but they weren't even royalty any longer. And the babies couldn't speak. So.

"I do not know why you are so angry, Lyon. But I am not going back. We… We are ill-suited. I know that will be a problem for you, but so would be staying. I'm sure we can reach some sort of private agreement to maintain a public image. But I can't—"

He couldn't let her say another word. "You don't know why I'm angry?" He had not thought he could be more incandescent with rage, and that she would be so…outrageously ridiculous. "I am angry at you lying to me. I am angry that you hid something so important from me. And I made a gesture out of *kindness* to allow you not to attend the dinner that I *wanted* you at, as my wife. As my partner. As…everything you are, and you *ran*. Without so much as a word."

"Kindness?" she all but shrieked. "A kindness? To want me not to attend your precious dinner because I'm such an embarrassment?"

"Embarrassment?" He yelled it right back. To hell with decorum and anything else. He was so angry he didn't even notice the two people holding babies quietly leave the room. "Who said anything of the kind? I *love* you. I would do anything for you. And instead of giving me the decency of a discussion, you *ran*."

"I will not be hidden away. Not again. I will not be your dirty secret. You will not drag me back to—" And then it was as if what he'd said caught up with her. She stopped short. Her breath came out in a loud, sharp gust. "What did you say?"

She looked so beautiful. So shocked by words he thought obvious. He thought it had been…a neon sign on his very face. That soft spot. That distraction his mother had accused him of.

And she seemed utterly and thoroughly shocked as if it had not occurred to her.

Because, clearly, it hadn't. A mix of his own failures, and perhaps some of her own.

But that also gave him hope now, instead of fury. Something to hold on to that might…lead them to where they needed to be.

He moved to her, and when she didn't back away, just stood there still staring at him as if he'd grown another head, he took her hands in his. He looked her in the eye. And he said the words this time—not yelling, not accusing, but with everything he felt inside of him.

"I love you, Beaugonia. My entire life I have been a tool. A payment to a debt. No one has ever cared what I might like or want. Not until *you*. You read what I asked you to. You enjoyed the chalet even though you hated the drive. You were honest with me—I *thought* you were honest with me. And then I discovered you had been hiding this…" He didn't have the word for it.

"Failure? Blight? Weakness?"

He stared at her. At the anger on her face. She didn't believe those things. Surely… Surely, she didn't believe those things. His self-possessed princess. And then it dawned on him.

When she had looked at him as though she didn't understand a word he was saying back at the chalet, he had been talking about his grandmother's words. The things she had passed down to him, whether he'd really considered the truth of them or not.

So these words were not *Beau's*. They were not even his. They had come before. They were her baggage. They were, no doubt, her father's words. And she didn't even realize it.

But they had likely been the words her father had used when he'd kept her hidden away, and it hadn't been all that long ago when he had threatened the very same. Maybe for different reasons, but that was the problem. They both had a lot of reasons they did not fully understand, they had not fully dealt with.

But now they would.

Beau was certain she was shaking, but Lyon's hands still held hers. He was looking at her like she'd suddenly started speaking in tongues.

"I have never once used those words to describe you, Beau," he said, very calmly. Very carefully. "I understand now why you thought I might, but I do not care about panic attacks. I have been on anxiety medication since I was fifteen. The state of your brain chemistry is not what dismayed me. It was that you lied and *hid* yourself from me."

She thought she had been floored when he claimed to love her, but this… He said it as if it was fine. As if…all his talk about stability and respectability had nothing to do with… He said he'd been on anxiety medication as if it was *nothing*.

"You've been on *what*?"

"I would not call what I had panic attacks, but the consistent cycle of catastrophic thinking was interfering with my studies. My mother…" He frowned a little as if he was realizing something. "Looking back, I think she was afraid if she did not do something, my grandmother would be… very unhappy with me. So she found me a therapist. I was prescribed medication. It has helped, infinitely."

"Helped," she echoed. Stupidly. But… It had never occurred to her in a million years that he might have anxieties. Real ones, not just his obsessive worry about respectability. An actual condition that needed some kind of interference. "I need to sit."

And he didn't let her go. He just led her to the couch and sat next to her when she all but collapsed into the seat.

"Beau, I do not think your panic attacks are any of those words you said. Those are *your* words. Not mine."

But as she sat there with the reality of all this…new information, she knew that wasn't exactly true. Not her own words. Not really. "I never cared about my panic attacks. Not in that…way. I can't help it, so I wasn't about to beat myself up about it."

"But your father did it for you."

She looked up into his eyes. Even before she'd loved him, she had always thought they were more alike than different, but this was... How could it be true that he understood so well? That they were *this much* alike?

I love you.

He had said that. Plainly and simply. In the midst of a very loud scene. Where he had yelled and not cared who heard.

"You really love me?" she asked on a whisper. "Even with..."

"I am here, *tesoruccia.* I told Mother to handle the dinner. I do not intend to make it back in time. I intend to make everything right. So that we can build a life together. One of balance and stability...but not...sacrificing ourselves on the altar of our images. Our people should know that *we* are people. Love. Soft spots. Anxieties."

It sounded too good to be true. And yet...

She thought of what Zia had said. About give-and-take. She had given, and she had taken—when he'd offered comfort, when he'd been kind. But only rarely had they *discussed what* they were doing, and so perhaps they hadn't had a chance to understand one another. Their gives and takes were careful, shrouded, because they had both been burned by people who should have loved them, but had only taken instead.

So much of him she understood—what had shaped him, why he felt the way he did even if she didn't agree, but she could admit now that she was perhaps not the best judge of understanding him when it came to *her.*

Because she had her own baggage clouding her judgment. But he was helping her see past that. Love had done that.

And when his baggage had clouded his judgment, he had used his words. He had told her about his legacy. About what he felt he had to do to pay that debt he thought he owed. Maybe he'd been wrong, but he'd never run away. He had been honest.

She had not been.

"I am sorry."

"You are?"

"I…jumped to conclusions. Based on my own issues. I was so…unhappy. But you said I made you happy and I wanted to. I wanted to do anything I could to make you happy. Because I love you, Lyon. Your kindness. That desire within you to do what is right. But I cannot be that thing you need. I cannot pretend as well as I wanted to. I don't wish to…sleep in the same bed every night so far apart. I don't think I am capable of being the robot you wanted. I—"

He squeezed her hands together. "It was wrong. Or at least, misguided. But we are learning. We will forge a new path. It will be…a challenge. We have the country's baggage stacked against us, but if we have learned to carry our own, if we help each other unpack our own, perhaps we can do the same as royals."

It sounded like a dream, but also…possible. And she wondered why it hadn't occurred to her. Why her own response to everything was all or nothing. Misery or run away. "I suppose we both need to work on our compromising."

His mouth curved, and she started to allow herself to hope…to really hope.

"I am quite sure my mother will come around eventually, but it will take time. Parliament might not care for it or me, but the citizens of Divio will. I believe they will. I cannot be perfect for them, or for you, though I will still try. But what I know I can be is there. I can find balance. If you'll share a life with me, Beau. I think we can accomplish anything."

Anything.

It was such a big promise, such a hopeful future. It made her realize how small her dreams had always been. Because she had never dreamed of a love that might not be concerned with her panic. She had not allowed herself to dream of… *anything* except the bare minimum.

"When I was a very little girl, the only thing I ever dreamed about was my own little place. Hidden away from my father. Just me and Zia. Lots of animals, but never people. I never truly believed anyone but Zia could see me for who I was."

He touched her cheek. *"Tesoruccia…"*

"You made an effort. To know me, to love me. You call me a treasure, and I have never felt like one until you. I'm sorry I didn't know how to make an effort back, to…believe you'd see something lovable. But I will learn. I promise to learn how to stay instead of run, to reach out instead of hide."

"Come home with me. Be my wife. My princess. Let us figure it all out, always together."

She pulled her hands from his, but only so she could wrap them around his neck. And he held on, even as her tears spilled over. He whispered endearments, words of love, rubbed her back. He gave her so much she'd never had, because though Zia had tried to be there for her, so much of their relationship was Zia acting as barrier between Father and her, not actually being able to *comfort*.

And it was scary, really, to believe that she might have something so beautiful, so wonderful, when she had spent so much of her life being told she wasn't good enough for it. When she hadn't realized how deep those scars went.

Until someone new had tried to love her. And it hadn't always been right or good. Because they were both flawed, in their own ways. But there was nothing inherently *wrong* with that. Not if you tried, not if you talked, not if you loved.

"You must only promise to never run away again," he murmured against her hair.

She nodded, still holding on to him. "I do. I promise. To work everything out, no matter how ridiculous either of us are being. I will not run away again, but you must promise the same."

He pulled away slightly, frowning down at her. "I never ran away."

"You did. You pulled away from me, hid yourself away from me. Perhaps it is not exactly the same, but it felt the same. Like a limb had been lost."

He nodded slowly. "Yes, exactly that. Then I promise, *amore mio*. With all that I am. I love you, Beau. I will always find a way to come back to that."

Beautiful words, but they were beautiful because he meant them. She could see it in his eyes, and because she knew him.

Lyon Traverso did not make promises he did not keep.

And this promise would last them a lifetime.

EPILOGUE

NINE CHILDREN WERE currently rolling in the snow outside the chalet high in the mountains of Divio. Muffled shrieks and laughter made their way into the kitchen where Beau stood hip to hip with her sister making a stew that would feed both their families tonight as they watched the goings-on from the large window.

It was moments like these, perfect, beautiful, crystallized togetherness—with the kids just far enough away not to be demanding all her attention—that Beau could feel completely full up with love and joy and relief that this was the life she got to lead.

Cristhian and Lyon were outside, dutifully pulling the younger children in sleds, aiding in the construction of snowmen, and breaking up fights that looked as if they'd turn physical in equal measure.

Five of the children outside were Zia's, and she would introduce a sixth in the coming months. Beau thought of her own pregnancy. Still new enough only Lyon knew so far, but they'd had a doctor's appointment before they'd herded the children up to the chalet for the holiday. All was well, and Beau wanted to tell her sister.

But for a moment, she just watched her husband and her children. Her brother-in-law and her nieces and nephews. And allowed herself to be filled with gratitude.

Things had not always been smooth sailing, even after she'd gone back to Divio with Lyon. They had endured some growing pains as a newly married couple, and balance had been a slow, laborious process for them both to get comfortable with. There had been some difficulty getting pregnant with their first child. But then Lucia had come into the world, perfect and vibrant—with Beau's hazel eyes and Lyon's serious mouth.

She hadn't fixed everything, but the first grandchild Lyon had given his mother had certainly eased some of the bitterness between Beau and the countess.

With more children came more struggles, but more love. More hope. More joy. As a family, they had grown and evolved and *loved*. As a country, Divio had learned it could lean on Lyon as a leader. Also not smooth sailing. As Lyon had attempted to open up his country to more modern ways of thinking, allowing their eldest to be their heir despite being a girl, opening avenues of discussion about the importance of mental health, there had been stiff opposition. Much mudslinging. But Lyon had remained firm and fair, and the excellent leader he was. And he had been right, if they worked together, they could accomplish anything.

Since more citizens than not wanted these changes, parliament was hard-pressed to completely ignore the will of the people.

So Beau and Lyon had remained the crown prince and princess, popular with many. Particularly as their family grew.

"Do you ever sit back and pat yourself on the back?" Zia asked her. They had finished the stew preparations, but still stood watching their families play.

"For what? Still having my hearing?"

Zia laughed. But she turned to Beau. "This all began with you. You helped me escape the castle for my weekend of freedom before I was supposed to settle down and marry Lyon. If you hadn't done that, I never would have met Cristhian."

"But if it wasn't for you running away, I never would have met or married Lyon."

"Technically, that was Father's doing."

"And Father is the one who hired Cristhian to find you. I guess we should be patting him on the back."

They shared and a look and then laughed.

"Never," Zia said firmly.

"Then I suppose we shall have to pat ourselves on the back for being brave enough to search for much better than he wanted for us."

"I like that," Zia said with a nod of her head. She looked outside once more, then gave Beau a sideways look. She leaned in close. "Are you pregnant?"

Beau scowled. "You never let me tell you!"

Zia shrieked and clapped her hands together, engulfing Beau in a hug. "Oh, they'll be so close together." Though age hadn't really mattered when it came to the Traverso and Sterling cousins. The pack were as close as siblings, begging to see more of each other all the time so that Zia and Cristhian had agreed to spend a good deal of their time in Divio these past few years.

Still, it was nice. To be in the same place, to share their experiences. No longer protectors or martyrs to each other. Just sisters. Living a wonderful life.

Zia pulled back, studied Beau's face. "My brood is still going to outnumber yours."

Which made Beau grin. Because that wasn't true at all. "Try again. I'm having twins this time. We'll be tied."

Zia laughed, then squeezed her tight again.

They had loved and protected each other first, and now

they got to share in the love they'd learned how to share with their husbands, their children.

And when a pile of snow-covered children came rushing in, demanding warmth and food, followed by two snow-covered truly *good* men, Beau knew that all the romance books she'd always and still loved to read were right.

Love was everything.

* * * * *

Did Princess Bride Swap
leave you wanting more?

*Then you're bound to love
the first installment in
the Rebel Princesses duet*
His Hidden Royal Heirs
*And why not dive into these other
Lorraine Hall stories?*

A Son Hidden from the Sicilian
The Forbidden Princess He Craves
Playing the Sicilian's Game of Revenge
A Diamond for His Defiant Cinderella
Italian's Stolen Wife

Available now!

COMING SOON!

We really hope you enjoyed reading this book. If you're looking for more romance be sure to head to the shops when new books are available on

Thursday 21st November

To see which titles are coming soon, please visit

millsandboon.co.uk/nextmonth

MILLS & BOON

MILLS & BOON®

Coming next month

RESISTING THE BOSSY BILLIONAIRE
Michelle Smart

She stepped through the door. 'I am your employee. I have a contract that affords me rights.'

The door almost closed in his face. Almost as put-out at her failure to hold it open for him as he was by this bolshy attitude which, even by Victoria's standards, went beyond minor insubordination, Marcello decided it was time to remind her who the actual boss was and of her obligations to him.

'You cannot say you were not warned of what the job entailed when you agree to take it,' he said when he caught up with her in the living room. She was already at the door that would take her through to the reception room. 'It is why you are given such a handsome salary and generous perks.'

Instead of going through the door, she came to a stop and turned back round, folding her arms across her breasts. 'Quite honestly, Marcello, the way I'm feeling right now, I'd give the whole lot up for one lie-in. One lousy lie-in. That's all I wanted but you couldn't even afford me that, could you? I tell you what, stuff your handsome salary and generous perks – I quit.'

Continue reading
RESISTING THE BOSSY BILLIONAIRE
Michelle Smart

Available next month
millsandboon.co.uk

LET'S TALK

Romance

For exclusive extracts, competitions
and special offers, find us online:

f MillsandBoon

X @MillsandBoon

○ @MillsandBoonUK

♪ @MillsandBoonUK

Get in touch on 01413 063 232

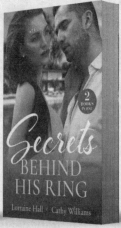